KAKISTOCRACY OF THE TECHNOCRATS

NATALIE TRIUMPHS

HOUSE OF INDIGO

DISCLAIMER

Fiction Disclaimer: This book is fiction. All similarities between the characters, organizations and events in this book and real persons, organizations and events is purely coincidental.

DEDICATION

I am dedicating this book to the memory of the late Supreme Court Justice William O. Douglas, who would be shocked by the attacks on freedom and human rights that have taken place in our country since his death. William O. Douglas was a strong advocate for the Bill of Rights and more, finding a penumbra of additional rights emanating from the Bill of Rights. Had Douglas or Justices like him been on the U.S. Supreme Court, today, Julian Assange would be free and lockdowns and medical mandates would have quickly been declared Unconstitutional.

Valiant took several turns. I noticed we were on Wisconsin Avenue heading towards Observatory Circle and Embassy Row. A tank pulled in behind us. "Now, we've got two vehicles tailing us?" I asked, rhetorically.

"At least, nobody's shooting, yet," Valiant said, echoing my earlier optimism. "Scratch that."

Fire bombs were launched out of the tank and we were the targets.

"We're going to die," Jerry said, matter-of-factly.

CHAPTER 1

"Is the President ready?" Lee asked as the President entered the press room, accompanied by Jerry, the Press Secretary, for the press conference.

"Yes, complete with the explanation of the attack. Will he be defending another attack he doesn't know about tomorrow?"

"This one was top secret. Only the President and his trusted advisors knew," Lee said coldly, as if I should know that.

You mean only his trusted advisors minus the President knew, I thought.

"His tie is wrong," Lee said.

"Can he even tie a tie?" I responded.

Lee glared at me. I needed to watch my mouth or I'd get fired before I finished my job.

"Sorry," I said. "The press has picked up on it three times. They are being told he is setting a new trend."

The President moved to the podium, tripping over a---well there was nothing to trip over. He just tripped.

"As you now know, we have bombed Sri Lanka. The native people there posed a national threat to our culture and heritage."

"Totally in character," I told Lee. For a President who had a history of pushing racist legislation and making racist comments while pretending to support minorities, he always got a pass on the subject from the press.

"Um, um. Sri Lanka is the most biggest threat in the Mediterranean Sea."

"You mean the Indian Ocean," a voice came from the room of reporters.

"Yes. The Indian Sea," the President continued. "That's what I said."

Another glare from Lee.

I shrugged. "You want to explain a sudden increase in his IQ? Without the gaffs, it wouldn't be him."

"Now, I'm taking a question from Albert," the President said, looking at a card.

Two reporters stood up. One spoke, quickly. "Is the report true that you are mandating glyphosate be put into all the children's lunches?"

"Shit," Lee said. "Wrong Albert."

"Thank you for that question Albert. Yes," the President said, looking down at a card. "The threat posed by Sri Lanka has damaged the psyche of the American public."

"That wasn't my question," Albert corrected.

"Bret, I believe you have the next question."

"You do believe that we will be successful in Sri Lanka?"

"There are no guarantees. Swift action to correct the problem, the issue, you know, was taken care of with the dropping of the thing that has now saved the country."

Saved the country by exterminating those objecting to the theft of its resources.

"Back on track," Lee said, breathing a sigh of relief. "Karissa, after the press conference I need to have a word with you. In the new music room."

"Yes, sir." This couldn't be good. I thought over what he might take issue with. The invited press would all cover for any gaffs. They always did. I looked at Albert. He had been here before and his news service, CBA, had always portrayed the President in the best light.

The President's final question was about his relationship with the First Lady.

"My sister, I meant my wife, is the love of my life."

"I think the President was very much himself," I told Lee.

"It's not for you to think, just do as I say."

"Sorry. I'll make sure there are no more goof-ups in the future," I said, with my fingers crossed, hoping to find a way to stop the President's next attack plans that he probably didn't know about.

As the President left the stage, Jerry escorted him to the Oval office, from which I accompanied the President to the elevator where I was greeted by Valiant, the tech guru, on my way to the sub-basement. Valiant was almost as young as me, but a genius that my bosses couldn't pass up. He was the one person on my team I could always rely on.

"Lee has summoned me to a meeting. Can you take over from here?"

"Sure. Is he upset about the Albert mix-up?"

"Probably. Don't worry about it."

When the elevator arrived at the proper sub-basement, Valiant said, "Don't take any knives in the back, I think I can find you a knife-proof vest."

I smiled as the door closed.

I went to the Music Room and waited for Lee, who would probably read me, well hopefully not, the music. Lee always liked to live out idioms and I knew this meeting location couldn't be good. There were other music rooms in the White House, but this one was especially reserved for people creating jingles in support of the President and his party.

I sensed that I should be nervous as Lee entered the room, but how bad could it be? Lee's smile told me very bad. Here was a guy who took pleasure in pain and war.

"It was perfect," I stated, hoping he'd agree. "Except the detail in the Mediterranean situation and the reporter mix-up."

"The latter part's handled. The press was told that he was ignoring stray questions posed by the Russians. Albert works for one of the top news networks and it's a U.S. Corporation. They won't publish the goof-up. You know that."

"You wanted to speak to me."

"Karissa James." He never called me by both names. Even worse than I expected. Lee lifted the lid of the piano and pulled out a file. It had a blue horizontal stripe at the top and the number 1-5992. He handed me my application that I had filed when I came to work at the White House.

"Yes."

"Nice work, but something is off," he said, fingering the file.

"Yes?"

"Eve Gordon. Now that fits better." I froze as he read from another paper in the file. Lee had found me out. My cousin's friend, whom he had called Charlie, had arranged for any identifying details to be switched on my transcripts, birth certificate and Social Security records. I had never met Charlie. I didn't even know if that was his real name. Had Lee gotten to him?

"My name is James."

"Mother. Elisa James Gordon. I remember her. She was an intern here. According to this record, her name was changed to Gordon one day before you were born. Interesting." He smiled broadly. "And yet, you didn't list the alternate name on your application. Very naughty."

I bit my lip. "That's because I don't have an alternate name. My name was never Gordon. You must have me confused with my cousin Eve. She passed away. You can verify my identity with my brother."

"You mean your cousin."

"Brother."

"You are smooth. Your explanation just doesn't fly. Why wouldn't your mother suddenly want you to have the name she had gone by for years? Oh, yes. She came to me after an incident. Then she resigned in lieu of being fired. Your mother Elisa got married right before your delivery."

"My aunt."

"She came to me about nineteen years ago."

"And?"

"You were born about nine months later."

"I have a father, David James and I am not eighteen."

"You do have a father. But not Mr. James. I had a DNA test run on you."

"Well, if the incident you spoke of were connected, it would be a bigger scandal than my aunt's change of name. Maybe my cousin should have had a better funeral if what you say is true." I almost bit my lip. He hadn't gone there yet.

"You are a good actress."

"You have the wrong girl. My medical records will back me up."

"You are the spitting image of your mother. I knew I had seen you somewhere when you were hired. The resemblance is unmistakable." He pulled out a photograph that looked almost identical to me. "When she was your age."

"Apparently, you feel Eve's father is pretty important,"

"We both know the identity of your father."

"So, if you are telling the truth, why wouldn't I want to claim my heritage?"

"A little planned blackmail? Revenge?"

"I don't have to be subjected to this. I am doing my job." Probably a dumb statement but it's all that came to me at that moment.

"An interesting dilemma. I have here an interesting report on another matter directly involving you. I suggest you resign before I present it to the police."

"I've committed no crimes. Are you planning a false arrest?"

He handed me a paper, signed by Juan Martinez, one of the janitors, stating that he had seen me take a Ming vase from the White House and that I had told him I had been responsible for other losses as well.

"Thieves get booted off and discredited. You'll be in prison before you can say 'Daddy.' And your friends and family can't help you because I can nail them as part of a cover-up. I want your resignation on my desk immediately."

"I could go straight to the press room and tell them what I know."

"And who would believe you?" He was right. If I told the truth about what was happening in the White House, nobody would believe me. Well, my family would but I wasn't going to put them in danger.

"I expect this on my desk in the next hour." He handed me a pre-typed resignation, took the folder and walked from the room. I didn't know what to do. My plan was going down the drain. I had let down my mother and the rest of my family and put them all in danger. They wouldn't hold it against me. In fact, my mom hadn't wanted me to put myself in any danger. I had volunteered over her objections. Of course, I hadn't stolen anything. Was there a way to salvage things? Even if I tried to get this fixed, anyone who helped me could be in danger if I were exposed.

I moved from the Music Room, unable to stop tears from coming out of my eyes. I went upstairs. There was one person I could trust. Maybe he could think of something. But should he get involved? He could be on the chopping block too. I walked unfocused toward the Deputy Chief of Staff's office, not noticing when I bumped into Juan.

"I'm sorry," I said and then realized he was the one who had lied about the thefts. "I, never mind."

"I'm sorry," he replied. He looked sincere. "I need this job for my family."

"I get it," I said. It hurt, but everyone was under threat here.

I continued on towards Paris's office.

I passed Sandy and Jennifer, a couple of interns, who were gushing about some guy they thought was extremely hot. "Valiant," I heard Jennifer say.

Valiant was cute with his dark hair and blue-green eyes and he was always more than eager to accomplish everything I asked of him, but he was a boring techie who was simply doing his job. When he found out I had lied and been fired, that would probably be the end of any respect he had for me. With his technical skills, he definitely had a bright future falling in line behind whoever took my place.

As I arrived at Paris's office, he was rushing to the door to leave. "No time to talk."

"What?" I asked.

"Your boss. Sit tight."

I guessed Lee had already made everything known.

"Wait," I said. "Did he?"

"He's dead."

"How?"

"Murdered."

CHAPTER 2

I stood there stunned for a minute as Paris rushed off. Terror went through me. I tried to collect my thoughts. *I was probably the last one to see Lee, to confront him. There were cameras through most of the areas where we walked, though none in the room where we talked. The file! It would give me a motive. At least, the cameras will clear me—unless he were poisoned or killed in a way that the cameras couldn't detect. We had been alone.* Guilt ran through me. *How dare I worry about myself when Lee had been killed! No matter, how awful he was, he didn't deserve to die.*

"Are you alright?" It was Paris's secretary Janet.

"Shocked. Paris said my boss was murdered. Let's hope they catch the person."

"The cameras are down. The Secret Service is on its way to his office."

"Who could turn off the cameras?"

"Your department and of course, security."

With the cameras down, the file would make me the number one suspect.

"Do they know who did it?"

"I don't know. Paris ran off to check the situation."

"How was he killed?"

"Shot in the head. But this is not for release."

I stared at her.

"Of course, you know that. Nothing involving your department is for release."

At least, I don't own a gun. Hopefully someone got a glimpse of the person. What's wrong with me? My boss has been murdered and I keep thinking about myself.

I moved quickly through the halls to Lee's office.

"Karissa, we can't let anyone else in," Trey of the Secret Service detail told me. He was standing outside the door.

"She's his top assistant," Paris said, coming out of Lee's office.

Some suits that I assumed were FBI pushed through the door. They weren't Secret Service.

"You came quickly," I heard Jerry say to the agents. He was inside the office.

I had seen the lead FBI guy in the White House before, but I didn't know him. I thought I had heard someone call him Ted. "We were checking out a matter across from the White House when the call came through."

I started following them through the door.

"Halt. You can't come in," Ted said, turning and blocking my passage with his hand.

"As Paris pointed out, she's his assistant," Jerry told him. "She might be able to shed some light on who might have had a motive—"

"You should both wait across the hall," Ted responded. "What's the press secretary doing here?"

"I," Jerry started to say.

"He found the body," Trey answered for Jerry.

"I'd like Karissa in here to see if anything is out of place," Paris said.

Jerry moved out past me. He put his hand on my arm. "I'm sorry."

"Thank you."

"I'm calling it," a voice from the other side of the suits said. I recognized the voice. It was Frank, the in-house doctor.

"Where is Gene?" Ted asked.

"Out of the country. So I'm in charge," Paris said.

"Not during an investigation."

"There is national security documentation in this room. Above your clearance."

At that moment, I was able to look past the suits in the room to the body on the floor. Lee was lying face up. Blood was all around the body, seemingly coming from his forehead. In his right hand was the file. It was recognizable. It had the blue line at the top and my vision was good enough to see the number 1-5992. How could I get the file without incriminating myself?

As I stood, trying to figure out what to do, an FBI photographer and a couple of other individuals, looking like part of a forensics team, pushed their way in, followed by a couple of EMTs with a gurney. The room was getting crowded. Frank shook his head and the EMTs respectfully stayed silent.

"Agreement 1527 and 18 USC, section 3056 puts the Secret Service in charge of the investigation," Trey said. "We'll forward the report."

"I can get an order."

"If you want to play it that way, go and get one."

"I assume you won't block our personnel, in the interim," Ted practically growled at Trey.

"As long as you do not disrupt official security."

A photographer took a series of pictures and then another examiner started checking out the body.

"What if there's a chance to save him?" I asked. "CPR?"

"He's cold," Ted said.

"You didn't even feel him. It couldn't have been that long," I said. "There was just a press conference and he was there."

"I'm sorry. I checked him," Frank said. "From the location and damage, the shot would have been instantly fatal. It went clean through a critical part of his brain. Lee is gone."

As the EMTs loaded Lee onto a gurney. Ted, now gloved, was reaching down for the file.

"That's our latest confidential project," I said.

"I'll have to take that," Paris said.

"It's part of the investigation."

Paris, Jerry, Ted and Trey were all reaching for it and started arguing. "You don't have gloves," Ted said to Paris.

"That file is above your clearance. A bag," Paris told a tech and received two gallon plastic bags. He put his right hand in one and picked up the file and turned towards Ted as he started to put it inside the other. Apparently neither realized there were loose papers in it. The papers slid out and fell on the floor. *I'm dead,* I thought.

Paris quickly reached down and picked them up. "Like I said, above your clearance. This is today's national security briefing," he said, quickly stuffing them in the folder.

Was he covering? The fallen papers looked different than the ones I saw in the Music Room, but it was the same file. Maybe the papers Lee showed me were below the security briefing.

Paris turned to me. "You should follow the ambulance to the hospital." He turned to the EMTs. "We want a rush autopsy. Have forensics there collect any evidence on the body."

There was something cold about this all. Nobody in the White House—except maybe Paris and Jerry—seemed to care that one of our own had died. It was all procedure. Lee hadn't gone out of his way to make friends but there was something sad about this.

It took me a few minutes to get to my car and through White House security. The ambulance had already left, but I knew where they would be taking Lee.

At the hospital, Felicity Fowl joined me. She was a Special Assistant to the President, but many of us thought of her as a cleaner, who made sure everything looked apropos. Felicity could have been a fashion model or maybe a movie star with her flaming red hair, her thin figure and her bubbly personality. "I saw the press conference. Good work—except for the glitch. Jerry likes to use first names and we'll have to make sure the President is given first and last in the future."

"Lee is gone," I said, still in shock, partially from his death and partially from what would come out when they saw the file.

"Are you prepared to take over?"

"Take over?"

"You are familiar with the Department, and we don't have time to vet someone else we can trust. We can't have leaks."

"I always took orders from Lee as to what the programmers needed to code."

"He took orders from DS Central and some other special people. You'll just be one step up. More duties, but you should be able to handle it."

I knew about DS Central. It was a group of military contractors, Big Pharma contractors and Wall Street execs. They didn't know how we made things work, but they knew they could give orders that would be provided to the President to follow.

The medical examiner Dr. Newport came out. "Cardiac arrest. Did anyone do CPR?"

"Cardiac arrest? That's not possible," I said.

"It's not just possible. It's how he died. Did someone do CPR?"

"The in-house physician was there."

"At least it wasn't the Surgeon General."

"Don't put down the President's Cabinet," Felicity advised him.

"He was shot," I said.

"There is no evidence of that."

"I'll show you."

"You can't," he started to say. But it was no use as I, followed by Felicity, pushed my way into the hospital morgue.

"Where is he?"

A medical tech pointed to a body with a sheet over the face and left the room with the medical examiner.

I pulled back the sheet. "This isn't him."

"Of course. People look different after they are dead," Felicity said. "I recognize him."

There was no way I was wrong on this. People couldn't change that much after death. "What corpse grows a mustache?"

"Here, we should put this on him in case he's contagious," Felicity said, putting a blue surgical mask on the corpse's face. I knew those didn't stop anything and often were heavily bacterialized.

"The forehead. He had blood all over his face and it looked like it had come from his forehead."

"Oh. They probably cleaned him up," she said going to a tray, picking up a vial of blood and pouring it onto his face. "Now, doesn't that look more like him?"

His face could not be seen. "I don't think we're supposed to do that."

"He probably hit his head when he fell dead."

"That wasn't—" I stopped. This was going to be the official report, I realized. Heart attack and then hit his head. I saw Felicity taking a couple of pictures of the person I knew was not Lee.

Felicity had a call. "Jerry, this is not for public release yet, but Lee Carpenter died of a heart attack." She paused. "No. When he fell he hit his head and people mistook the blood for a bullet wound. We must stop those conspiracy theorist rumors."

This was wrong. It let me off the hook and so I should be okay with it but it felt so wrong. Nobody ever questioned Felicity though. So I kept my mouth shut.

CHAPTER 3

"You need to go home," Paris told me. "This has been a tough day."

"You don't know the half of it," I said. "Can we talk somewhere?"

"I can't. I'm doing damage control."

"Was it just the intelligence briefing in that file?"

"I can't provide information on that with the investigation open."

"Anything about any personnel?"

He looked a little taken back. "Nothing specifically? Why?"

"Did anyone hear the shot or see someone?"

"Heart attack," he said, looking way up, as if he also found it incredulous. "I'll meet you at Pedro's after work tonight. Now, go home."

"Haven't you heard? I have new duties."

"You are taking on Lee's duties in your department. The second in command of Hushpuppies is moving up as well. I'm sure he'd like Lee's position, but you've got it."

"Did you have anything to do with that?"

"Not directly, but Felicity feels that my sister would be the loyal choice."

"The President?"

"There's been a tragic death at the White House. He's out of action for the rest of the day. In mourning. Jerry is doing a press conference. Apparently Lee's family had a history of heart problems and he hadn't gotten checked over in years." He looked upward, again.

I couldn't leave without talking to the staff. I went down to sub-basement C, a level that didn't exist as far as the public was concerned.

The President was sitting in a chair, staring straight ahead.

"Valiant, you heard about Lee?"

"We all did. Are you alright, Karissa?"

"I'm still shaken. They've promoted me to interface with the—well you know."

"I do. If you need any extra assistance, I'm here, any time." Valiant was always very supportive towards me. He was one of the few people who made my position worthwhile.

"Apparently, they don't need the President tonight. But I'm sure there will be instructions for tomorrow."

He pulled me aside and spoke quietly. "I know you didn't like the Sri Lanka situation. I didn't either."

I looked around, hoping we weren't being monitored.

"It's safe here. We run scans every half hour."

"People died. Children."

"If we hadn't followed orders, they would have gotten someone else."

"That's what the death camp administrators told themselves."

He looked down. I knew he felt as trapped as I did.

"It won't always be like this," he murmured. "They did it, like the Bay of Pigs and the President was supposed to just take credit. We had no more foreknowledge than he did."

I looked to the President who hadn't moved. "Do you think Lill knows?"

"If he mattered to her. Separate bedrooms. They only get together for planned appearances, and she rushes off as soon as they get out of public view."

"No wonder his dementia got bad."

"Or maybe it's from all the deaths he has caused or all the little girls he's sniffed. Maybe they had aluminum in their hair."

"We shouldn't talk here. I know it's safe, but."

He looked over at the President. "He's not going to talk. He's not bugged and I turned him off for the night."

CHAPTER 4

When I got to Rosped, a quiet little restaurant in Baltimore, I was really antsy. Pedro's was a bar in D.C., but we never met there and I knew it was just code.

I went to a table in a corner where I could watch the front entrance. Paris arrived just after I did. "Hello sis," he said.

"Lee knew."

"Knew what?"

"That I'm Eve."

"Well he's not talking now."

"That was what was in that file. He was going to accuse me of stealing stuff if I didn't resign."

"The file had his copy of the intelligence briefing, which he should have filed away or destroyed. It also had a list of names of top staffers with numbers next to each."

"Nothing about me?"

"No."

"Then whoever shot him must have taken the information. Now I don't know who to fear."

"Before the cardiac arrest report came through, I asked around. Nobody heard any shots. The killer must have used a silencer. Nobody noticed anyone going in or out of Lee's office, but nobody was looking. I don't know if you noticed, but Lee wasn't too popular—except with the contractors."

"And Felicity. She just covered up the whole thing."

"I don't agree with Felicity's actions, but it was a wise move for political reasons. If the public found out about your sub-division of Lee's department or about Hushpuppies, there would be—"

"Apathy," I interrupted. "Like following Snowden's leaks and Vault Seven. The mainstream media would have hidden or explained away anything we wanted gone, and anyone questioning the official narrative would have been called a conspiracy theorist."

"But the Indies would have picked it up and run with it."

"So what do we do now?"

"Go back to work and stick to the plan."

"People died in Sri Lanka. If we had exposed everything before that happened." I paused. Guilt was overwhelming me.

"They would have covered it up, and we'd both be in no position to stop any further wars."

"How long will Gene be out of the country?"

"Just until tomorrow."

"And in the meantime?"

"We keep busy and keep the public in the dark. You do know that everything is just for show. In the real scheme of things, you are more important than I am."

"Anyone can take orders and feed them to the techs who do the programming. And demented? Couldn't they add a little more brain power?"

"Someone might notice the difference. Especially the First Lady."

"She really doesn't know?"

"Probably suspects, but it's of no concern to her."

I shook my head. "If the public only knew."

"Even if we brought live TV feed into your sub-department, they'd claim it was all special effects, fiction."

"Juan, the janitor, signed a statement that I was stealing from the White House."

"That wouldn't have held."

"But Lee would have used the accusation to discredit me."

"I would have called him out."

"You would have been completely undermined if you had tried to help me. At least one of us needs to be there."

"Lee's gone now."

I shook my head, again, and repeated myself. "If the public only knew. There's Juan and there's whoever took Lee's records on me. They can undermine me at any time."

"You are taking over his office. You can search for the file."

"If it's there. He was holding the same file folder. Someone switched the contents. And there's more. Lee ran my DNA and it was a match. I had always hoped that there was someone other than *him*." I shook my head, ashamed of myself. "Here, I'm concerned about me. Your sister is in my grave and nobody outside of the family mourned her death."

"There will be time to mourn in the future."

"Ouch. It's Jerry and Marissa Tracy," I said, watching them walk in the door.

"There's nothing odd about me having dinner with my sister. Our Press Secretary, on the other hand, has come to this out of the way place in Baltimore to meet with a reporter who is not all that friendly to the Administration. I wonder what he is telling her."

"He found Lee's body. Maybe he has the original contents of the file and is outing me or our whole operation," I said. I thought about the next day's possible headline, maybe declaring me a fraud and the killer.

Paris shrugged. "Maybe he just didn't want Monica to see him two-timing her."

"I can't imagine he'd be two-timing Monica. Especially not with a mouthy reporter."

"Maybe she's into racquetball. That's how he keeps in shape."

"He plays racquetball?"

"I see him on the courts."

"I don't think Marissa is the racquetball type," I said.

"Well, maybe it's those Italian looks."

"He's Italian?"

"One-quarter Italian, one-quarter Persian and half Anglo-American."

"I didn't think you were typing people like that."

"I'm not. We had a survey for all the new hires at the White House. We had to list at least one minority background to get hired. Gene had me go through the profiles of the possibilities for Press Secretary."

"What are we?"

"Same as Lizzy. Actually better. We're descended from Sitting Bull."

"She lied."

"So did I."

When I got home, I turned on the news. It wasn't because I believed anything on the news. Most of the Mainstream Media's, or rather MSM's, information was actually written for them by the intelligence agencies and Wall Street. Most of the popular MSM reporters were former or current government agents, something that was handy when the government wanted to push narratives or suppress information. There was barely any mention in the news of Lee's death. Lee was considered a lower-level employee of almost no importance. If only they knew.

The FBI and Secret Service had both seen the body and the gunshot wound. But, like the other fictional pieces of news, only the false claim of a cardiac arrest was presented.

I relaxed in a warm bath. I had often dreamed of having a father, but when I learned who and what he was, I hated him. He had raped my mother and then told her she was nothing, worthless. That had destroyed her. Just prior to my birth, she had had a quick marriage to a friend, who proceeded to ignore me after I was born. So she divorced him. At least, he didn't fight her for custody. Though a single mom, she had done her best to make me feel loved and wanted. Mom worked overtime to give me every opportunity to excel. Her family helped out some. Still, I could tell she was always sad, never really trusting men again and yet wanting so much to have a relationship with a good man. The sad news was there didn't seem to be many good men who wanted a woman with a child. The men who wanted a child often seemed to have nefarious purposes. Mom had to move a few times to avoid the usual trafficking activities for which Child Protective Services was known.

My mom homeschooled me, and I did some college classes concurrently with my high school. I had been accepted into a couple of universities for the next year when the switch happened. I had a lot of faking to do. My cousin Karissa was a little older than I was and a little taller. We both had golden blonde hair and hazel eyes, though mine had more green. Karissa had graduated from high school at sixteen and was close to receiving a college diploma in political science when she died. Fortunately, she was camera shy and the only pictures that needed to be altered when I took her place were the online high school yearbook pictures. I finished her courses online and arranged for the degree to be sent to me.

When my cousin Paris recommended me or, rather, her for the position, he embellished dramatically regarding my skills. Gene Hemmings, the Chief of Staff, had been desperate to put someone trustworthy in my position. Lee had fired the first tech team working for him in my sub-department and was displeased that Gene had selected his new top assistant, me, a non-techie, to be in charge of the tech team for the Technical Creations sub-department, which didn't exist. Supposedly we just did general research, assisting Lee, unlike Hushpuppies, his other sub-department which had a team that was completely off the records. For his first hire for the new team as lead technical engineer, Lee had discovered Valiant, who was considered a genius and could program circles around anyone else he had ever seen. Valiant had worked briefly with the old team before they were fired. For rest of the new team, Lee had hired away the top experts from Einstein Industries, a private contractor the Administration had used for certain top secret projects. They had proved trustworthy in keeping secrets and he felt they were an asset. After losing its top elite group of engineers, Einstein Industries went under.

Lee had thought he could groom Valiant to be a yes man and to monitor the other workers, including me after I was hired, keeping us all in line. But unlike Lee, Valiant seemed to have a conscience. He thought for himself and quickly discovered the work wasn't altruistic, something I knew before I was hired. I always suspected that the friendship between the two of us was the reason Valiant hadn't quit and taken the team with him when he discovered the extent of what was expected of him.

After my bath, I went into the living room. Pictures of the decimation of Sri Lanka were on all the stations. Reporters were talking about the glory of the bombing. I turned from station to station, noticing that the reporters from the various networks seemed to be following the same script, word for word. That was very common.

I wished I had my mom nearby. She had left the country. My idea. I felt a little freer and less worried about her safety with her far away. Paris had arranged for her to get a passport and an immunity card. His sister had an immunity card too or, rather, I had one now (hers), though I had originally gotten mine from a doctor who was opposed to the vax and covered for all the patients who didn't want one. Given the example of what happened to Karissa, the remainder of the family wasn't about to get any jabs. Paris had the connections to make sure nobody else in the family would have to suffer his sister's fate.

On the news, Raquel Madcow was going on and on about what a terror threat Sri Lanka was. No mention of the recent discovery of blue diamond mines on the island nation. I turned it off and started to head to bed. A sound came from the door to my apartment.

I moved towards my outer door, picking up a poker from the fireplace. I slowly opened it. Nobody was there. Instead, there was an envelope. Inside were the missing contents of Lee's file. Someone else knew and probably had copies.

CHAPTER 5

I looked through the contents. He really did have the DNA test. Behind the papers was a note: *"I didn't make copies. A gift from a friend."*

The note was reassuring, but without knowing who the friend was, how was I to know if I could trust him or her? The person who retrieved it could be lying. Even worse, he could be the killer. Lee could still have the information on a computer file or have made copies himself.

I lit the logs in the fireplace. I wasn't into gas fires. When I had the fire going, I threw the whole thing inside.

The next morning when I got to work, Gene was back. I was surprised when he called me into his office. I guess I should have expected it now that I was taking over Lee's work for my department.

"Lee didn't have much family. We're going to hold a private memorial for him later this morning. His son will be there. We are hoping you can attend," Gene said.

"Our Department does not exist."

"Still, you and Lee are White House employees and you worked more closely with him. Maybe you could pull someone you consider to be discreet out of your non-existent sub-department to join you at the memorial."

"I will be there and I'll make sure one of the assistants is there as well." I figured it was the least I could do, and being a no show would make me look guiltier when the truth came out.

"About Lee." *Did I dare say it?* "Have his children seen the body?"

"His son is flying in this morning."

"I was at the hospital. The body didn't look right."

"Nobody does after they've passed. We sent the body to a specialist to prepare it for the memorial."

I wondered what the reaction of Lee's children would be to his death. I knew he had been accused of abusing his wife and the kids had refused contact with him after they were emancipated at 16. His son was now an entrepreneur, working in Rio.

"His daughter?"

"She is otherwise occupied."

Even if the son hadn't been with his dad in recent times, he would be able to tell the difference between his dad and the guy I saw at the hospital morgue.

"The President didn't have any meeting scheduled for today. Has that changed?" I asked.

"He will be attending the memorial today. He should say something nice about Lee. You'll make that happen, won't you?"

"Yes, sir."

"Tomorrow, he'll be meeting with the North Korean Ambassador. This will be an important meeting. Not too many Congressional leaders want to meet with the President these days, but foreign leaders still expect his cooperation."

"Do the members of Congress suspect anything?"

"I think the people in Washington see him as a shepherd. They realize his experts are creating the policy in the various areas. Goldman Sachs outright picked Obama's Cabinet."

"Very perceptive of them. Is Lee's other sub-department under control?"

"Under control."

I had wondered if I would become privy to what Hushpuppies's function was, but Gene didn't elaborate. Theoretically, Hushpuppies was now under my direction and I'd have to acquaint myself with their duties.

On the way out of Gene's office, I ran into Jerry in the hall. "So we meet again."

He gave me a funny look.

"I was referring to last night."

"I didn't see you come in here last night."

"Not here."

He continued to look rather odd. "I was working late last night in the office."

"Of course. My mistake."

He apparently didn't want anyone to notice he had been out with Marissa. He had a girlfriend. Maybe it was pleasure, not business, that took him to Baltimore.

I went by the Secret Service office. Trey was inside with another agent named Chuck. "May we speak privately?" I asked him.

He looked at Chuck.

"I'll go," Chuck told him.

"Yesterday must have been a shock for you," Trey said after Chuck left.

"That's an understatement. Trey, you saw the body. You were there when I arrived."

He nodded.

"Remember the blood on Lee's head?"

I saw his eyes start to glaze over. He responded almost robotically, "Apparently, he hit his head on his desk when he fell."

"Did you see blood on the desk where he impacted?"

"No. Bleeding often doesn't start the moment of impact."

"Everyone said he was shot. The FBI was there preparing for a murder case."

He nodded. "They have to investigate all deaths in the White

House. Even natural causes. That protects the staff from any questions later on. 1527 is just a formality."

"Don't you think it was odd that the cameras weren't working yesterday?"

"An electrical malfunction."

"But the malfunction didn't affect anything but the cameras? And isn't someone normally watching the cameras?"

"Cameras were down. There was nothing to watch."

From the glazed look in his eyes and the robotic tone of his voice, I knew I wasn't going to get anywhere but into trouble if I kept inquiring.

"Well, thank you for answering my questions. The shock just kind of threw me."

"You don't expect anyone that young to drop dead from a heart attack. Only 40. I'm 41."

"I hope you're healthy."

"I try to stay fit. Is there anything further I can do for you?"

"No. That's it."

Down in the tech lab, Valiant came over to me. "Reporting for duty, boss lady."

I laughed. "Call me that again and I'll punch you."

"Threatening a subordinate. Worth big bucks in workers comp bennies."

"Dream on."

"So, what is the schedule for today?"

"A memorial for Lee. But we're to pretend that we are just routine co-workers."

He nodded. "Got you."

"Will the President be attending?"

"Yes, and we have to come up with some nice things for him to say about Lee."

"'He wasn't an asshole one hundred percent of the time. There are some people in New Jersey who don't hate him. Of course, they didn't know him.'"

"His son will be there."

"Ah, we can focus on making the son feel good."

"Good. Can you come up with something that won't get us all fired?"

"In other words, all lies."

"That's about it. I need to go through his files in case there is something else we need to handle right now."

"You'll need the password to his computer."

I looked at Valiant, hoping he would have a suggestion where to find it. As the lead tech and Lee's protégé, he was the only one who had direct access to Lee's computer.

"Rumpelstiltskin."

"You're kidding. With all we've got going on here, he used Rumpelstiltskin?"

"He figured nobody would be looking for something that simple."

"That's almost as bad as John Podesta's password. You remember?"

We said in unison, "Password."

"I bet Rumpelstiltskin was his hero," I said.

"Rumpelstiltskin was too nice for him."

Jack, one of the other techs walked in. I hoped he hadn't heard that. "Do you have any tasks for me today?"

"You'll be working on the remote server. We'll be accompanying the President to a memorial and we don't want any glitches, like at yesterday's press conference," I said.

"You're pre-programming him, aren't you?" he asked Valiant.

"Of course. After all, we want the son to feel the President cares. And the remote receiver will just be a backup. So Jack, you can just keep an eye on him in case he collapses or starts sparking."

"That isn't likely to happen?" I asked.

"Of course not," Valiant said. I knew he was teasing me, but we couldn't afford any such disasters.

I went to the Public Policy and Technical Research Coordinator and Liaison Office, which I was probably totally unqualified to run. It was an odd title as Lee had virtually no contact with the public. It was more acceptable than a name that accurately reflected our work. Policy, yes, but public, no. I was officially Lee's primary assistant. The team members were listed on the payroll as office help, but without them, I would have been lost—even in my prior position.

As I entered the office, I stood there in almost disbelief. File contents were strewn all over.

CHAPTER 6

"Duane, what are you doing?" I asked.

"I've moved up."

"This is now my office. Felicity's and Gene's orders. You've completely ransacked it."

"I need files for the work my sub-department is doing."

"I will make sure you get anything that is coming to you."

"Don't you think you are in a little over your head?"

"Felicity doesn't seem to think so." Thinking about what Felicity had done to Lee, it felt odd using Felicity as a reference.

"I'm going to speak to Gene. I think he'll see we need someone more experienced in this position. You just watch."

"That may be, but for now, the office is mine."

"But not any part of it related to my sub-department."

"I'll make sure all your files are sent down to you."

After he left, empty-handed, as far as I could tell, I started putting the files into a pile. He was searching for something he, apparently, had not found. I went to the computer. Rumpelstiltskin worked.

The first thing I searched was my name, well, both my name and my cousin's. Nothing came up. I looked for my real and fake job assignment. I was listed as C1. I searched for C1 and the computer only referenced my duties as performing protocols for briefings etc. Nothing specific about me personally or factual regarding the President showed up. Lee was doing weekly reviews on my work and, to my surprise, I actually got high scores. There was a lot of positive praise for my work that I didn't even know he felt. But nothing about what we discussed yesterday. I looked up my initials in caps, and nothing connected to me showed up in the search.

I searched for Juan Martinez. Nothing came up. I tried his initials in caps. It took me to a file called "Happy Days." Under JM, several things came up. JM had a flagged immigration status. There was a video. I turned to it. Juan was picking up what looked like a Ming vase and putting it into a trash bag that he carried off. No wonder he was scared into signing the statement against me. There were other initials there too. I could make guesses but I didn't have a lot of time before Duane would be back and demanding computer access. I pulled out a flash drive and copied the Happy Days file. It was a large one apparently containing a number of videos and photographs. Then I deleted it.

I called down to Valiant "How is the work going?"

"Quite well."

"Could you come up here for a moment?" I went back to looking through the physical files that I had put into a pile. It looked as if they were mostly financial records. Big bucks from donors inside the defense and pharmaceutical industries. I pulled out, not my regular cell, but an inactive one, and started taking pictures of the financial sheets. Maybe these would come in handy later. When I had looked through the computer, I had seen some financial information there as well. I didn't know if it matched.

When Valiant arrived, I explained the problem. "Duane is going to push for access to everything and I'm concerned about losing our files, both physical and computerized. I need to make sure we have a copy of the computer files. I'd like to find a way to preserve the physical files as well."

"How long do you think we have?"

A call came through from Gene. "Could you come to my office?"

"Yes, sir. Right away."

The call ended and I looked at the time. "I have to go to Gene's office. After that, we have Lee's memorial in the White House Chapel. Meet me there with the President."

"Sure."

With that, I went to Gene's office. Duane was there. All that information at my fingertips and I might lose it. My worst fears were confirmed. "I'm going to let Hushpuppies download and erase their files from Lee's computer. They'll leave the files not tied to Duane's sub-department. You'll still have charge of the office and you'll be interfacing with the representatives." I knew he didn't mean House Representatives.

"Yes, sir. But our information is confidential. Hushpuppies is not supposed to have access to it. That's why the sub-departments were separated."

"An interesting dilemma. I'm going to temporarily upgrade Duane's clearance to allow him to see the titles such that he can download anything connected to his sub-department. The code designation for your department is KP, isn't it, Duane?"

I had seen that before and wondered why Hushpuppies had the designation KP.

"Yes."

"You are to do a search for KP and only download the files that appear under that designation."

"If you can trust him," I muttered under my breath.

"How about Karissa's security clearance?" Duane asked. "Is she qualified?"

"She didn't need an upgrade for the position," Gene said, firmly.

Thank you to whoever created Karissa's top secret clearance, I thought. I had never known who Paris had gotten to change the pictures and fingerprints on our records and it was just as well.

From there, I went to the memorial. Paris had saved a couple of seats next to him for myself and Valiant. Across the aisle, I could see Lee's son, fretting. The casket was open. *How did they arrange this so fast?* Normally three days was considered standard. I guess, when there is a will to get over something fast without an investigation, there is a way.

I got up and walked over to the casket. It looked just like Lee. No evidence of a gunshot hole in the head. I knew for movies they could have make-up artists change the shape of people's faces and make them look older or younger. But getting rid of a gunshot wound and making it look like nothing had happened was remarkable. Then it occurred to me. The shot had gone through him. There should be evidence in the room somewhere unless it had been cleaned. Felicity would have taken care of that. I needed to check for anything she might have left behind. Never for a moment, did I doubt what I had been told and seen before the trip to the hospital.

"Disgusting, isn't he?" It was the son, Pan.

"His death?"

"No. The fact that he looks so peaceful."

"I gather you didn't like him."

"I celebrated last night. I'm just here for appearances."

"I heard he was terrible to you, your mother and your sister."

"That's an understatement. I could have killed him for what he did to my mother. Fortunately, I have an alibi. A heart attack. I always thought that some Good Samaritan would someday impale him. A peaceful end was not what he deserved."

"I'm sorry for what you experienced."

"You worked with him?"

"For him."

"Your job just improved."

I didn't quite know how to react. My job had definitely been upgraded in the last twenty-four hours.

"It's been a pleasure meeting you," I said, starting to go back to my seat.

"Would you like to get together for drinks afterwards?"

"I would, but I have to work."

"After work, then."

"Sure."

It would give me a chance to question him but I doubted he'd have any information on what had been going on with his father in recent years. There was a slightly inquisitive look in Valiant's eyes as I sat between him and Paris.

The benediction was as expected. We were told that God would protect Lee in the palm of his hands.

Pan started choking, loudly. "I'm sorry. I'm just so moved," he said loud enough for the audience to hear him. From where I was sitting, I could see him rolling his eyes.

The President got up to speak. "Lee was a great worker, kind, fair-minded."

Now, I felt like choking.

Pan started laughing. "I'm just remembering the good times with my dad playing baseball with my mother's head. Lots of—"

The President continued, cutting Pan off. "I remember Lee used to speak about his family often. His beloved daughter and his son of whom he was so proud. He told me about the baseball games he attended with Pan and the soccer games. They used to take walks together and fly kites."

"He was good at wrapping the kite string around my mom's neck and pulling. Brought him great joy."

"A loving father, a loving husband."

"This funeral will go down in memory," Valiant whispered to me.

"When Pan first got his license, he was so proud."

"That he almost ran over me with his car to let me know how dangerous cars could be."

I looked at Paris, who was biting his lips to suppress a laugh.

"Jack should be intervening," I whispered to Valiant.

"He's probably too busy laughing," Valiant whispered back.

"He can do that in the unemployment line."

Valiant pulled out his phone and texted Jack.

"I'm sure those who knew Lenny would like to share a comment about his life."

"Who's Lenny?" someone behind me asked.

"I came to the wrong memorial," Pan said. "Where's the one for my dad?"

"Lenny was a special name he wanted his special friends, like me, to call him."

"Nice recovery for Jack—even if nobody, here, will buy it," I whispered.

After the President finished, Paris got up and spoke about how Lee was always timely with his work and never missed a deadline. Gene spoke of how Lee had raised the morale of the White House staff. He looked at me, giving me the sense that I better fall in line.

Felicity was next. There were tears on her cheeks. I wondered if she had dabbed them there. There certainly weren't any when Lee died.

"Lee and I were very close, as close as a brother and sister. We would often stay and talk for hours after work."

"When did she ever stay here after working hours?" I whispered to Paris.

"I was one of those special friends he asked to call him Lenny," she continued, apparently covering for the President's gaff. "If something was bothering him, I was always the first person he would come to because he knew I was always willing to listen. My life won't be the same without him and I will need all of your support to get through this horrible loss."

"Great acting," Valiant whispered to me.

Paris touched my arm, encouraging me to go up. "Be diplomatic," he whispered.

"Lee was a one of a kind boss. I never met anyone quite like him. I believe my feelings about him were shared by everyone who worked with him. I am so moved by this memorial that it's hard to speak about what his loss means to me." I feigned wiping a non-existent tear from my eye and went to sit down.

When I got back to my office the computer was gone. Duane came rushing in the door. "You deserve nothing!"

"When am I getting the files back?"

"You're not." He didn't say anything else. He just stormed out.

CHAPTER 7

At least I had a copy of the Happy Days file. I decided to look at it later. Security checked electronics going in and out of the building. Someone high up in the White House didn't trust the staff. I took a small metal face powder case, my mother had given me long ago, out of my purse, lifted the metal powder holder contained inside and put the flash drive underneath. I didn't use powder, but sometimes used the bottom to hold small note paper. I closed it and put it into my purse to take home, hoping to not get caught taking it out.

I looked through the paper files. *Why were so many industries giving us so much money?* In addition to the pharmaceutical and defense industries, some of these were the top polluters and pesticide companies in America. I took a number of pictures with my cell phone.

Valiant came up to my office. "Any reprimands over the memorial?"

"Not yet. The press was there. I haven't seen the spin yet. We couldn't have anticipated Pan's reaction, could we have?"

"Lee wasn't bragging about the abuse. It was HR's responsibility to check his background, but they might have considered it a plus, given who we are working for. If anyone gets the blame, it's HR."

"Still," I couldn't help smiling.

Valiant smiled back, visibly trying to hold back a laugh. Then he looked more serious. "I wouldn't worry about Duane or the computer." He put his hand to his lips and pulled a device out of his pocket. It was a bug detector and it was reading off the charts. I figured Duane's people must have wired the office when they took the computer.

"Gene said he had elevated his clearance and so I guess it will be alright," I said.

I escorted Valiant into the hall. "Do you think they have video on the office?"

"I'll have Jack come up. He can do a full check and remove the bugs. The lab is safe."

"Let's have some fun."

We went back into the office. "I am glad that Lee didn't fire Duane," I said.

"He died before he could. Lee kept railing on him. He talked as if he had something that could bring Duane down."

"I like Duane in spite of the confrontation over the computer."

"Lee got really angry when you stood up to him on Duane's behalf the other day. He accused you of having a crush on Duane."

"I was just standing up for him because it was the right thing to do."

"Do you think Lee really had some evidence that could destroy Duane?"

"I hope not. Well, nobody will ever know now. Unless he gave someone else a copy of whatever. It might be in the files Duane took."

"Felicity?"

"I guess we'll find out. I don't think she likes Duane. So if she knows, Duane could already be in trouble."

———

Down in the lab, we spoke further. I said, "I wonder if Duane is freaking out. Of course, if it was Felicity or the Secret Service who bugged the office, Duane could be under investigation by now."

"Never know what they could find in his background."

I realized I was being a little too friendly with a subordinate. But that was my style. I couldn't get into being obnoxious and cold, no matter what my position. Of course, I had been told that being too familiar would result in employees failing to respect me and ignoring my orders. "I may have to change my management style in my new position. Be a little more formal with the team. Don't take it personally if I do."

"You? That wouldn't fit you."

Jack came into the room. "I have the President undergoing a daily check on his operating system. The memorial was hilarious. I mean sad." He laughed. "It got a million views already on *YouTube* before it was removed. But they were portraying the President in a positive light, trying to speak well of the dead, even when the guy didn't deserve it. Now the media is just showing excerpts and the original is gone, but there are undoubtedly thousands of downloads."

"Our government is closing down the alternative platforms. But more keep springing up all the time," Valiant said. "Could you believe Felicity?"

Jack put his hand on his hip and started moving around in a show-off feminine way. "I am so wonderful and everyone's best friend."

"Do you even know Felicity?" I asked Jack.

"I ran into her one day in the coffee shop. She spent a few minutes telling me how wonderful she was and why she was too important to take up any more of her time talking to me."

I smiled. I knew not to put down upper management with the lab techs but Jack's reading was on point.

"Maybe we can get the Surgeon General to name a new disease after her," Valiant said.

"And I'm sure that Big Pharma will already have the vaccine ready when the Felicity disease is discovered."

"Get your Felicity vax here. Do you really want to kill Grandma?"

"Guys, we need to be respectful."

"Of course," Valiant said, smiling. "Felicity is a goddess."

Brandon, another lab technician, came into the outer lab room. "The check is complete. The President is functional."

"Thank you."

"Jack, we need a discreet spying device sweep and removal in Lee's office," Valiant said.

"Someone bugged Lee's office?"

"My detector says 'yes,'" Valiant told him.

"I'll get my equipment and take care of it right away," Jack said.

"Discreetly," I advised. "I don't want them to know we knew they had it bugged. Make it look like it just malfunctioned."

I followed Jack, Brandon and Valiant into the inner lab to speak with the other workers. "I want to thank you all for your service. I realize I've been a bit overwhelmed today, but I want you to know I appreciate each of you. My office upstairs is always open to you."

"May we ask for a raise?" Brandon joked.

"You know what it takes to get a raise here. I'll try to put in the paperwork. I'll call it an employee good performance bonus. No guarantees. It's over my head."

"I like this new boss," Brandon said.

"I still haven't gotten my mean legs yet. Working on it."

I gave them a stern look.

"Doesn't fit," Valiant said.

* * *

On my way to Paris's office to chat about events, Duane bumped into me in the hall. "Sorry," he said. He seemed to be distracted. Maybe he was nervous about what he might have heard. "Say, I'm sorry I was so abrupt earlier."

"I should have been more supportive of your situation. I just worry about losing information my sub-department needs for operations," I responded.

"Now, you know how I feel."

"Huh?"

"The disc was empty. Wiped. The operating system didn't even work. I thought you might have erased everything."

It took me a moment to come to terms with what he was saying. "Wiped? How could that have happened?"

"Maybe it was Lee's last revenge before going into cardiac arrest."

I knew it wasn't wiped before the memorial as I had looked at it and copied a section, but I didn't want to mention that to Duane.

As I got to Paris's office, I noticed the TV on in Janet's reception area. She had her hands to her mouth. From that and the expression on Paris's face. I knew something was up.

"What?" I asked.

"You remember that reporter who is always trying to get the dirt on the White House? Marissa Tracy."

"The one we saw with Jerry, but he said he was working and not there," I whispered. Janet was so busy watching the TV I doubted she was listening to us.

He didn't respond.

"What?" I asked again.

"Dead."

CHAPTER 8

"Like Lee?" I asked.

"No. This is officially being declared murder," Paris responded.

"It happened today?"

Paris ushered me into his office for a private discussion and then closed the door.

"They found the body today. She was killed last night. There could be repercussions against us if we report what we saw last night. Loyalty. Silence is the key to working in this White House."

"This may seem odd, but I believe Jerry. I don't know if he was actually here, but he seems to really believe he was here, working late, last night."

"Maybe he was suppressing what happened or covering for himself."

"There were other people in the restaurant. It may not matter what we do or do not say."

"It's a pretty discreet place. I don't think the restaurant staff would officially say anything that would implicate the White House staff."

"Unless the restaurant manager, or anyone else who noticed them, voted for the other guy."

"If the FBI or police question us, we tell the truth. Otherwise, we keep it to ourselves."

"Wise. I don't want to wind up on a witness list."

"Exactly."

———

I met Pan in the Dead President's Bar. The location was his suggestion. Tasteless name but if a band and movie can pick that name, why not a bar?

"So what made you stoop so low as to work for my dad?"

"I was hired by Gene, the Chief of Staff. I didn't know your dad until I was working for him. How is your mom? It sounds like she had a rough time."

"Very rough. If I had stayed around him, I probably would have killed him. Guess I didn't have to."

"What did they tell you when they called?"

"At first, they said he had been shot, and then they called back and said that that was a mistake and it had been a cardiac arrest."

"I didn't see any bullet holes at the memorial. He looked just like himself."

"Except for the scar."

"Scar?"

"He had a scar just under his right ear. It wasn't that noticeable unless you were forced to look at him for years."

"And it wasn't there today?"

"No."

"I understand the person who makes up the bodies for the funerals tries to make them look good. Maybe he covered it over."

"I felt it. It wasn't there."

"I don't know what to tell you. Are you doubting it was him?"

"You think I'm crazy."

"No. But that's nothing you can say publicly without proof. The press says what the government tells it to say and discredits anyone questioning government narratives."

"I saw that in the memorial coverage. Do you know something?"

"I don't know what I know. Did anyone have a reason to kill your father?"

"Everyone."

I had heard that before.

"You think the first call was correct?" he asked.

"I'm not a doctor. I'm as in the dark as you are." I didn't dare say outright what I knew.

"I heard you were at the hospital morgue."

"That's right. The doctor there said it was a cardiac arrest."

"Do you believe that?"

"Let's say I'm skeptical. I question everything. Did your father have any heart problems?"

"Not to my knowledge and none run in the family."

"Have you spoken to the FBI?"

"No. I didn't want to sound crazy."

"You sound pretty sane to me. But you may be right about the FBI. What about your sister?"

"She had Dad removed from her FAFSA due to domestic violence and tried to have him charged. She and mom wanted nothing to do with Dad."

"I can understand that."

"It didn't affect his top secret clearance."

"It never does. I think the government seeks out abusers, but I didn't say that."

From there I went home. I was making myself dinner when there was a knock at the door. It was Jerry.

"Hi. This is a surprise."

He was nervous. "I got a call. Someone claimed they saw me with Marissa last night."

I didn't say anything.

"I swear I was in the office until almost midnight."

"Security should have the records," I said.

"That's just it. The security records, including any videos, are missing from last night."

"First the cameras went down and then security?"

"Everything was up when I checked out, but today it was gone."

"So there was a record of you checking in yesterday, but not checking out. That could be an alibi."

"Except that I checked in this morning and that is in the records. I know your tech team is skilled and supposedly your department doesn't exist."

"Research Liaison."

"I'm not totally unobservant. I know Lee had high power tech teams working on some pretty top secret matters that were above my clearance."

"If that were true, I couldn't discuss it."

"But your team might be able to figure out what is going on."

"If Paris can okay it, maybe one of the research assistants can help check out how the system malfunctioned."

"You do believe me? I was not with Marissa."

"The last couple of days have been crazy. Right now, I don't know what to believe." I looked at his face. The concern and the appearance of honesty struck me. Maybe I was gullible. "I don't believe you would harm anyone."

"Thank you."

"Have the authorities contacted you about this?"

"No."

"Well, maybe they have a lead on a real suspect. There could be footage of someone else with Marissa right before she was killed."

He started breathing more easily. "Have you had dinner?"

"Not yet. Aren't you having it with Monica?"

"Not anymore. I told Monica I was too busy tonight. I shouldn't have lied, but I didn't want her to see me like this."

"Do you like spaghetti?"

"One of my favorite dishes."

"Sit down and relax. We'll call this a work session."

"If it's not too much trouble."

"A secret about me. I hate doing dinner for one. You're doing me a favor."

Instead of sitting down, he came into the kitchen and helped with the sauce. "I'm a pretty good cook, myself. If I lose my job, I have a backup," he remarked.

As we were sitting in the living room, eating, I inquired further. "When was the last time you spoke with Marissa?"

"Yesterday, after the press conference, she came by my office to tell me she had a lead to a crazy story and she wanted to know if it had any basis in reality."

"Did she say what it was about?"

"She said it would send seismic waves through the government if it was true."

"What would?"

"She didn't say."

"Then, she meets with someone who looks like you and dies while the cameras and security that could have proven your whereabouts are down."

"You think the caller wasn't a prank. He actually saw her with someone?"

"I saw her with someone. I was in Baltimore having dinner with my brother and Marissa walked in with someone I could have sworn was you."

"Paris saw them too?"

"Yeh."

"So why do you believe me? If I saw me with Marissa, I wouldn't believe me."

"Let's just say, I've seen odder things. Also, you are one of the nicer people in the West Wing."

"Thank you."

"What if this crazy story was true and someone wanted to suppress it?" I wondered if Marissa was on to what was happening in my sub-department or in Hushpuppies.

"Like her source?"

"Or someone who would be brought down if her story were true. I wonder if there is a way to find out what she is working on. Is there someone she might have confided in?"

He looked thoughtful. "Seth Moore."

"He works at the *Washington Checker* with her, doesn't he?"

"Rumor has it, they were close."

"Let's go."

"Where?"

"To see Moore."

"You aren't going to tell him," he started to say as I interrupted.

"I never saw you and you have an alibi."

"You've got a friend for life."

We drove over to the address we had for Moore. He had an apartment in Frederick, Maryland. It was a nice place. There was no answer at Moore's door.

I knocked on the manager's door. I had Jerry stay out of sight. He was a public figure and didn't need more people seeing him connected to this matter.

"What do you want?' The manager was standing in the doorway and clearly not inviting me in. Maybe that was just as well.

"I was looking for Seth and he doesn't seem to be in."

"That's because he's not."

"Do you know where he might be?"

"Who is asking?"

"I'm on a special assignment and I need to speak with him."

"Another reporter. The last one who visited him here is dead."

"I'll watch my back."

He seemed to simmer down a little. "He's at his cabin in the Western Maryland Mountains about two hours away. Why didn't you call him before you came here?"

"I tried, but the line was busy. He and I will both be in trouble with our boss if I don't confer with him on this story. Two hours sounds like a long drive. He gave me the address once before. But I misplaced it."

"So you work with him?"

I hesitated, wondering if my lies would catch up with me.

"Is this story about the dead girl?"

"I'd love to share it with you, but I'm not allowed to share it with anyone before tomorrow."

"You seem like a nice girl. OK. My name is Storns."

"Karry."

He let me in and I followed him to a desk in his living room. He searched a drawer for and found a paper with an address on it, pulled out a notebook, tore out a page, copied the address and handed it to me. "Do you like sports?"

"Of course." Seemed like the right answer.

"Drop by some night. I have a premium sports channel."

"Maybe I'll do that. Thank you."

"Would you like to stay for a drink?"

"Very tempting, but if I don't get over to Western Maryland quickly, it could be curtains for both me and Seth. Looking forward to seeing that premium sports channel some night." Of course, I had no intention of returning.

It was going to be after one in the morning before we got to Seth's mountain home. As curious as I was about this Earth shattering story, I knew Jerry was even more curious. We had a robotic President, but it seemed a waste of resources for someone to come up with a robotic Jerry, just to frame the Press Secretary. Maybe it had just been someone who looked like Jerry. I had read that everyone has a double or two.

"You aren't going to use your mapping program are you?" I asked Jerry.

"I was."

"I wouldn't even bring my cell."

"Do you know a good place to drop it off?"

I stopped by the side of the road. "See that tree? Dig a little hole beside it and bury it. We'll come back for it."

"Clandestine. You aren't really CIA, are you?"

"No. Just aware."

"What about yours?"

"Burner. My other cell is at home. I do have a recorder with me." I thought for a minute. "Did you have your cell with you at the White House?"

"I did."

"Then your location could be traced."

"It was out of power, and I didn't realize it until I got home."

"That may not have mattered."

"Unless someone mucked with the towers."

"I don't think we need to go there just yet. Hopefully Seth has some answers."

When we got to the cabin, Jerry threw out a concern. "What if Seth killed Marissa? We could be next."

"You can wait out here," I said.

"And let you handle this by yourself. I hope I'm a better gentleman than that. Besides, I wouldn't want to face your brother after something happened to you."

"I'm sure someone at the White House would thank you."

He followed me to the door.

I rang the bell and knocked. No answer. The door was unlocked. I opened it and called Seth's name. No answer. I walked in.

"I don't," Jerry started to say. I held up my hand to encourage him to stay outside, but he disregarded, coming in behind me.

The place looked ransacked. I didn't have to get any further to guess what had happened. As I looked towards the open kitchen door, I saw shoes and legs stretched out horizontally on the floor. I rushed in. Seth was lying there cold, dead.

CHAPTER 9

Seth appeared to have been dead for some time. He was cold and rigid. Most of his coloration was pale, except for the part against the floor that was visible, which looked flushed. "The smell," Jerry said. "Poor man. He must have been here for some time."

My guess was he'd been gone at least a day or two. I grabbed a napkin and picked up a prescription bottle for Darvocet. The lid was separated and on the floor. I looked for signs that the pills had simply fallen out, but there were no pills on the floor.

"There might be fingerprints on this if he didn't take it himself," I said.

"Do you think someone who killed him would leave his prints on the bottle?" Jerry asked me.

I pulled out my burner phone and called 911 and then the White House Secret Service.

As we waited in my car, I asked Jerry, "You knew him. Did he seem either the type to commit suicide or accidentally overdose?"

"No. He seemed like a solid guy."

"This might be a validation of what Marissa told you after the press conference. You need to tell them what she said when she saw you. We'll just skip the part about the dinner you weren't at."

He nodded.

The first to respond was the Secret Service, arriving by helicopter. Trey was accompanied by a fellow agent named John Carrow.

"Trey, good to see you."

"You say he had some information about something that might affect us?" he asked me.

"Maybe. We don't know what. His contact who informed Jerry after the press conference is also dead."

"Marissa Tracy?"

"That's why we came here. To see if Seth knew what she was working on," I said. "Seth's place was ransacked when we arrived. The door was unlocked. Maybe you can find something the killer missed."

"You don't think it was a suicide?"

"Why would he ransack his own place if he was going to kill himself?" I asked.

"She's got a point," Jerry chimed in.

As Jerry spoke, we heard the police and an ambulance show up, an hour after I had called them.

"We'll need you out of the way," an officer said.

"Trey Martin, Secret Service. We're taking over the investigation. You can get the body to the morgue once we're through."

"This is our jurisdiction."

"This is part of an ongoing federal investigation."

"Then, where is the FBI?"

"There might be some classified information."

The two argued for some time. Finally the local officer received a call and backed off.

"Will you need us further?" I asked Trey. "We've got work, bright and early tomorrow morning."

"We all do. You can go."

"Thank you."

"Well whatever they were onto, maybe the Secret Service can figure it out," I told Jerry as we left the area.

Morning came too fast. I couldn't come in late on my second day in the new position.

"Did you hear? Another reporter died. Seth Moore. Suicide," Valiant said excitedly as he came into my office. "They think he killed Marissa Tracy and then went to the mountains and offed himself. He even wrote a note."

"I didn't know they had labeled it a murder-suicide." I also hadn't seen the note. But I didn't search the place.

He shook his head. "I've read Moore's posts and he didn't seem like the type."

I didn't respond.

"The office is clean today. No bugs."

"Thank you. I want you and the other techs to know that I appreciate all you do."

"New boss better than the old one."

"Let's not go there."

A minute later, Paris burst into my office.

"I was just leaving," Valiant excused himself.

"What were you doing at a suicide scene? You could have blown everything."

"I didn't, though. That wasn't Jerry we saw the other night."

"Sure looked like him."

"So does our friend downstairs; I mean, look like someone familiar."

"You don't think,"

"No. I don't know what to think, but I'm certain it wasn't Jerry."

"Murder-suicide?"

"I don't believe that either."

"Marissa came to Jerry after the press conference. Trey told me. Apparently she said she had a story that would shake up Washington. Trey wanted to know if I had any idea what it could be."

"Do you think it has anything to do with our department? First Lee. Then Marissa. Then Seth."

"We have too much security, and our records wouldn't reveal anything."

"Except for the major funds coming in from the defense and pharmaceutical industries."

I went to the file cabinet and pulled out some files and handed them to him. "Duane says the computer is wiped. But there are these records."

He looked at them and handed them back. "Do you think someone got a copy?"

"They'd have a hard time getting it through security, wouldn't they?"

Felicity popped into the office as I was putting the records back into the filing cabinet. "You heard about those pesky reporters, didn't you?"

"They're dead," Paris said.

"Yes. Dead with all their theories and ideas. A day to celebrate."

"I don't celebrate peoples' deaths. Excuse me." Paris left.

"I am sorry about how the memorial went," I said. "We should have had better research on Pan."

"It, actually, is putting the President in a positive light, trying to say kind things about an employee who is being savaged by a disgruntled family member at his own memorial."

"Good. We'll try to do better advance research in the future."

"I understand that the President is meeting with the North Korean Ambassador this afternoon."

"Yes. The techs have programmed him with all the latest information on the situation with North Korea and we have a remote person standing by in case there are any surprises. Gene will be there as well to usher the President away if there is an emergency."

"You look tired. Lee's death seems to have hit you hard."

"I've lost a lot of sleep."

"Why don't you go home and get some rest."

"I'll take a nap on the couch here if I need to. I'll be fine."

"You should listen to Mama." She left.

As if she was my mama or even old enough to be my mama.

A little mouse scurried across the floor. I didn't care for mice but was too tired to worry about it. "So do you think it was a murder-suicide?" I asked the mouse. Getting no response, I said, "I don't either."

As I got up and sat at my desk, the chairman of the President's party walked in the door. "I trust you will be as cooperative as Lee," was her first remark to me.

"You are Stacey Duncekins, correct? We try to accommodate the wishes of the constituents, but I'm in research."

"And this Department has, shall we say, the ear of the President. It's his job to do as we say."

"Are you saying the President takes orders from you?"

"Let's say, we have the same interests and he knows where his next election comes from."

"I am certain he will take your ideas into consideration."

She handed me a printout. "These are our demands for his upcoming meeting with the North Korean Ambassador."

I looked at the sheet. "You actually expect him to say this?"

"Naturally." With that, Stacey Duncekins turned and left, not even shaking my hand.

I guess we are considered subservient underlings.

I picked up the phone. "Gene, we have a problem."

After I delivered a copy of the items to Gene and was told to make it happen, I returned to my office. Paris was there. "So what did you think of Stacey? I saw her marching through the hall to your office."

"What a bitch."

"I wasn't going to say it, but yes."

That gave me a smile. It didn't last long. Into my office, without knocking, strode a man in his mid-thirties in a suit that looked like it cost maybe ten thousand dollars.

"Alfred, good to see you," Paris said.

"How's your golf game?"

"We can check it out when you're available."

"Maybe next week."

"It's a date," Paris told Alfred. "Karissa, this is Alfred Lebon, the President of Dynozap Corporation, a division of Ebonyliquid."

"Karissa. Definitely an aesthetic improvement over your predecessor."

"Pleased to meet you, sir."

"Here is our list of demands for the meeting with the North Korean Ambassador." He handed me his own sheet.

"Well, this will go nicely with the demands the DNC made."

"Good. I have to run."

"Have a good afternoon."

"I will now. Oh, here." He handed me an envelope. I looked. Money, lots of it, was inside.

"I can't take this," I said.

"What?"

"This one's on the house," Paris told him.

"Pretty and smart. I look forward to our future ventures. Nice doing business with you," Lebon said, putting the money back into his coat pocket and leaving.

"Was Lee taking illegal funds?"

"Is anything we are doing here legal?"

"You're not?"

"No. I don't want to be on the list if the ship goes Titanic."

"Do you know where the nearest bomb shelter is? Because after today's meeting, we're going to need one."

"One nuclear bomb can ruin our whole day."

"Ha! Ha! This is what Lee did up here?"

"And then he gave you the instructions and your team fed them into the President."

"Well, I better get down there and see if there is a diplomatic way to program this."

"If anyone can, you can."

"Don't count on it."

Down in the lab, Jack reacted as he and Valiant were looking over the lists, "Holly shit. No. That doesn't describe it. Omnipotent shit."

"Is there a way to lighten this up while not getting us fired?"

"A threat of war? Would you like some coffee with the nukes we're about to drop on your country? Maybe some sugar with it?"

"Stacey is demanding that half the government in his country be Black to avoid military confrontation?" Valiant noted, shaking his head.

"Don't forget that the President is supposed to call him a racist," I said. "You have two hours to figure out how to put this together so as to not end all life on the planet."

"The planet will be a lot more peaceful without life on it," Jack remarked.

"Agreed," Valiant said, tapping knuckles with Jack. He turned to me. "What will you be doing?"

"I think I'm going to have about four Singapore Slings for lunch. Just so I don't feel the bombs going off," I said.

"Oh, you won't feel them. One minute you'll be there and the next you'll be vaporized."

"Will you be at the conference?" Jack asked.

"I'm just a researcher. Gene will be there."

"Think of the bright side," Jack said. "Today, it's a little too much on the warm side. Tomorrow, it will be nuclear winter."

"We're going to be monitoring from down here, won't we?" Valiant asked me.

"And make sure you have an over-ride control on the programming."

Upstairs, I saw Felicity, flitting through the hallway. "Karissa, I'm hearing good things about you."

"Me?"

"Lebon spoke highly of your first meeting."

"He's certainly is one of a kind."

"Oh, they're all like that."

"All? Will more be coming in this morning?"

"Probably not prior to the meeting."

"I better get going to prepare for the rest when they arrive."

On the way to my office, I stopped at the West Wing kitchen and made myself a one-fifty-one piña colada for lunch.

"New job getting to you?" It was Jerry.

"You could say that. What's your job like on the craziest of your days?"

"You should make that a double."

"Jerry, do you think everything is on the up and up in this Administration? I mean like money and policy?" It was a question that I probably shouldn't be asking the staff, but Jerry might have some insight.

"This is Washington D.C."

"And?"

"That's my answer."

"Great. Then this may become my standard lunch."

"You ought to order some Hawaiian pizza to go with it. Some nutrition so you'll be standing at the end of the day."

"I'm not sure anyone will be standing at the end of the day."

I went back to my office and started looking at the financial information. I wondered how much of this was bribes and how much of it was payoffs for government contracts, both of which were illegal. Then there were the under-the-table payments and I suspected a lot of them were not catalogued. I wished I had the computer with the full information.

I looked at my watch. At one in the afternoon, I went down to the basement. "Is he ready?"

"In addition to Stacey's demands, he's programmed with Lebon's demands that Kim has to allow U.S. contractors to enter his country and take charge of all his military and police operations, and he has to turn over his cook's recipe for Orange Curlew, to name a couple minor details that any world leader would agree to in order avoid being nuked," Jack said.

"North Korea definitely has the bomb, doesn't it?"

"And Russia will join with North Korea in any war with the U.S."

I escorted the President to Gene's office. "Sir, I think the demands could be problematic."

"I'll be by his side. I'll rush him out of there if it gets too problematic."

I went back downstairs.

"You missed the start. He just finished calling the Ambassador a racist," Valiant said.

"Great beginning to a diplomatic conference."

The Ambassador seemed rather quiet during the demands. At one point, Gene supposedly got a call and said the President needed to go elsewhere. *Why couldn't he have done that before the list of demands?*

I rushed upstairs so I could escort the President. I saw the Ambassador step out of the Roosevelt Room. He had a stern look on his face. Suddenly he broke into a wide smile and started laughing, almost doubling over at the waist.

"Sir?"

"You're President is quite a joker. I'll have to bring him to North Korea for comedy night. Everyone will get a real kick out of him."

"I'm glad you were amused."

"It was hysterical. It was worth the long trip. I can't wait to tell Kim what a charmer he is."

I went inside the Roosevelt room. "The Ambassador thought the President was joking."

"And he made all the demands, as requested," Gene replied.

"But what happens when the Ambassador finds out he wasn't joking?"

"Do you think the military would actually nuke North Korea? We'd have open revolt."

I shook my head. The military hadn't stood down in Afghanistan, Iraq, Syria, Libya, and a host of other nations. Maybe it would be different with nukes.

I escorted the President down to the basement. "Good work team. Turns out we're not going to war."

"The military might not follow through, but what about Dynozap?" Valiant asked.

I pulled Valiant aside. "Do you think I could put a recording device in my office that I can accidently turn on discreetly?"

"I think that can be arranged."

"I wish I had had one there today. The rep from Dynozap tried to bribe me."

"If you expose the contractors' operations, it could bring down the whole Administration."

"I didn't take the bribe."

"Smart."

"Also, do you think you can do some background research on Marissa Tracy and Seth Moore and keep it confidential?"

He looked a little perplexed.

"They were looking into something?"

"Wait, it wasn't a murder-suicide?"

"I didn't say that. I just was wondering if one of her crazy theories might show up in the press. I want to know about it first. I understand you are good at checking the dark web."

"The government's infiltrated it and closed down any dissent."

"They must have posted something online somewhere."

I started up to my office. I glanced at the elevator on the way. I didn't plan to get that lazy—except when escorting the President. He had been known to trip. I decided to go for the secret stairs.

I was in my office for about five minutes when Jerry entered. "I wanted to thank you for last night."

"Do you know of anyone else Seth or Marissa might have spoken to?"

"Reporters are in competition for the top stories. They don't normally share leads."

"But she may have provided her ideas to her editor. Who is the editor of the Washington Checker?"

"Greg Jones."

"Let's go."

———

Jones had an estate in Bryn Mawr. It was a bit of a distance by car. It was one of the wealthiest areas of Pennsylvania.

"I guess their type of news pays off bigtime," I said.

The maid answered the door to what looked like a mansion.

———

"The President's Press Secretary and a White House researcher. We're in the presence of royalty," Jones told the maid as she escorted us in.

Jones addressed Jerry. "You here to give us a lead?"

"We're hoping you'd give us one," I said.

"That's a change."

"Do you believe Seth Moore murdered Marissa Tracy and then killed himself?" I asked.

"That's what the police and the FBI think. They've closed the case."

"Doesn't it seem odd that they closed the case this fast?"

"I thought so. What's your connection?"

"Monday, after the press conference, Marissa told me she had a lead on a story, something important. I thought it was a fishing expedition and brushed her off," Jerry told him.

"You didn't go to dinner with her the other night?"

"Why do you ask that?" I inquired.

"She said he was hoping to speak with you over dinner," he said to Jerry.

"No. I had to work late that night. It may have been some kind of setup."

"We want to know what she was working on," I said.

"So you can suppress the story?"

"So we can investigate. If the story is tied to two deaths, there might be something to it."

"This is another first. The White House trying not to suppress information."

"I'll make you a deal," Jerry told him. "If you help us locate information on the story, if there is something approved to tell, I'll give you an exclusive."

We accompanied Jones into his home office. "Since 2020, I've been doing much of my work from here. It's easier than taking the train to D.C. Too many protocols. The other day, Marissa sent me a video message about a story she was working on. I dismissed it as ridiculous. Here." His computer was already on. He went into his email. "That's impossible. I never erase messages." He went into his trash. "It's gone." He did a search. "All my messages from Marissa for the last week are gone."

"What about from Seth? Could it have been his story?"

He searched under Seth's name. "Seth's emails for the last month are gone."

"If they wiped Seth's emails, maybe it was his story," I said to Jones. "Does he have any family?"

"He has an estranged daughter and wife, but I don't think he's seen them in years."

"Who was his emergency contact? Maybe we can tactfully speak with that person."

He searched for personnel records. "Missing. Both of theirs."

"Do you remember anything about Marissa's message?"

"North something."

"North what?" I urged.

"This is ridiculous. It has to be in there somewhere?" Jones looked flustered. "This is my desktop."

He went back to his computer. A loud spark could be heard and then the lights went out.

Jerry used his cellphone spotlight to allow us to see. Jones was on the floor, gasping.

CHAPTER 10

I pulled out my phone and called 911. "Please send an ambulance quick."

There had been a power surge and Greg Jones was injured. The White House was also involved, given that Jerry and I were in the room when it happened. I called Trey.

"Again?"

"He's still alive. We called 911."

I hung up. Jones was awake and trying to speak. Jerry was kneeling on the floor beside Jones. I dropped to my knees as well.

"Take it easy. An ambulance is on the way," I told Jones.

He started muttering something. He spoke again and then went unconscious. All I could make out was "North."

Jerry listened to Jones's chest and then started trying to do CPR. This was serious. He continued until the EMTs arrived.

I heard a bell and a knock. Seconds later, the maid followed the EMTs into the room. "Oh no!" she screamed.

The EMTs took over the CPR. They had brought their own power generator and spotlight. We stood around as they worked for half an hour, at which time they called it.

"The surge. What caused it?" I asked.

"Power overload maybe. It took out the whole block," the lead EMT responded.

"He's got a surge protector on his computer and yet it sparked."

"It must have malfunctioned."

The maid was crying. I went over to her and put my arm around her. "I'm so sorry. He seemed like a really nice man."

"He was the best. He gave bonuses to all his employees and invited us to a resort every six months."

"Did anyone else have access to his computer?"

"No. There was a technician here yesterday."

"Technician? From where?"

"It was a security expert the office contracted with. He was cleaning and securing all the WC computers."

"Did he have a card?"

"Maybe in the desk."

The EMTs were carrying Jones out and the maid followed. One of them carried out the spotlight and generator. I went back into the room, followed by Jerry and then over to the desk. Using Jerry's cellphone spotlight, I checked the desk. The main drawer was locked but I detected a key underneath when I felt around. The key opened it. There didn't seem to be anything important, but there was a card. "Blackmoriuntur Technology and Secure Services."

I pulled it out and handed it to Jerry, who put it into his pocket. I closed the drawer. The maid came back. "I think you should be going."

"I'm sorry. I was feeling a little woozy," I lied.

Jerry took my arm and escorted me out.

I turned back to the maid.

"Will you be OK?" I asked her.

"What do you think? I'll go to my sister's for the rest of the night."

***

Before going back, I had Jerry put his phone in the trunk. Inside the car, he asked. "Do you think they were listening to us on that?"

"I don't believe in coincidences. Just as he was trying to find our information, he was shocked. The tech could have bugged his home office. You said your phone was down the other night. Do you think someone tampered with it?"

"You don't believe it was a neighborhood surge?"

"I think it came straight from his computer. I wish we could examine his hard drive. If we only knew North what?"

"Grail. He said 'Northgrail.' It was the last thing he said."

"What's that?"

"I've no idea."

"Well, we need to find out. I wonder if it's something like Operation Northwoods," I said.

"You mean where the military was going to set up Cuba for blowing up planes that were supposed to be carrying American students over Cuba."

"There were many parts to Operation Northwoods. Lots of potential false flags, but Kennedy turned them down."

"A man of integrity. No wonder they killed him."

"So you don't buy the official miracle bullet theory either."

"Seventy percent of America doesn't believe the miracle bullet theory."

I dropped Jerry off at his car and drove home. When I got there, the door was unlocked. Someone was inside.

CHAPTER 11

I backed away and got the manager to accompany me into the apartment. To my surprise, the manager had a gun.

Inside, I breathed a sigh of relief.

"Is this how you greet your brother?"

"Paris, you freaked me out. Next time, let me know when you are going to break into my place."

"So, it's alright?" the manager asked, putting his gun back into his belt.

"It's fine. Thank you for accompanying me."

As I closed the door, Paris said, "I hope he has a license for that gun."

I flopped down in a chair.

"Have you had dinner yet?" Paris asked.

"No. I haven't even thought about it."

Paris took me to a busy sports bar outside the city limits, where he ordered two plates of spaghetti with mushrooms. A busy place with lots of noise seemed the best way to go.

"I guess you've had a busy few days."

"Trey called you?"

"Part of his job."

"Have you ever heard of something called Northgrail?"

"I've heard the term, but I don't recall from where."

"Marissa's boss died trying to tell me that word."

"I'd watch out to whom I mentioned it."

"Could someone disguise themselves as another person?"

"Signature Soldiers."

"What?"

"It's a special program out of the Pentagon. The person who helped me switch those records was tied to the Signature Reduction Soldier program."

"They disguise themselves?"

"They have *Mission Impossible* type disguises, complete with thin coverings for their hands that change their fingerprints."

"Why?"

"Spying. Mostly on the American people. The government is not supposed to be spying on Americans, though it does, and so they try not to get caught. They enter businesses under fake names. They are often covered in electronics and can eavesdrop on calls and conversations as they walk down a street outside of residences."

"Should we be talking about it?"

"It's a known program. It was exposed sometime back."

"Is there more to their activities?"

"They have a team of people who fake background information so that they can easily switch identities and have all the medical, employment, residential and school records lined up to support their new identities."

"Could this be what Marissa was planning to expose?"

"It's no longer secret. There have even been articles on the subject, and indie journalists have done videos on the subject."

"The person who messed with Jones's computer was from a company called Blackmoriuntur Technology and Secure Services."

"Any name that starts with Black is suspect. Nothing to do with race, but with—"

"I know. Like Blackwater and Blackrock."

"I think you should let this one go."

"People are dying, including my boss. When I discovered someone was in my place tonight, I thought I could be next."

"Whoever is doing this is deadly and has access to the White House."

"In books, the killer is generally the friend the main character trusts the most."

"Who would that be for you?"

"Aside from you, Valiant."

"It's not good to get so chummy with your subordinates. That could backfire on you."

"I was just a coordinator, working under Lee, until two days ago."

"Wasn't Valiant Lee's protégé? He may be eager to move up. Keep an eye on him."

"Do you trust your contact in the Signature Soldiers? Lee had a copy of my records, even my DNA. Somebody got them for him."

"It could have been a tech from your department or from Hush-puppies."

"What does Hushpuppies do?'

"That's top secret. I do have to respect some protocols."

"How about you? Do you think this is all coincidence?"

"Somebody murdered Lee and got into his office without anyone knowing who he was. He was able to take down the cameras. If it was someone from the Signature Soldiers, he could have disguised himself as Jerry later that night and then killed Marissa."

"Then, you do believe Jerry."

"I'm starting to. There are stranger things going on. Bribery. Robotic Presidents. Murders that are turned into heart attacks. If we simply told someone about it, who would believe us?"

"Who knows about the President?"

"You, me, Gene, and the people in your department."

'How about Secret Service?"

Paris looked thoughtful. "Maybe."

"And Felicity."

"I'm not certain."

"She knows."

The waitress came to our table and we started in on our spaghetti.

"I'm thinking that some of those papers in Lee's office might be records of bribes he's received."

"He's dead. They'd just show a former employee was on the take. We need something more, something believable that wouldn't make us look insane."

"Like four murders?"

"We need to avoid being five and six."

I looked around. I didn't think we could be heard amongst the other chatter. We were speaking in hushed tones and nobody was that close to us. We had left our cell phones at my place. Still, I changed the subject. "This spaghetti is delicious. I hope it's glyphosate free."

"The President has stepped up his program to put glyphosate on every table."

"That's why I cook organic. I wish more restaurants did."

When I got home, I started looking at the copy I had made of the Happy Days file. A lot of illegal and scandalous things were going on. I opened a file, designated JC. "Heroin. Bribes, Breeches." *That couldn't be my Jack. His last name was Whitegale.*

I looked at the attached video. It showed Secret Service Agent John Carrow receiving a package from a man I didn't recognize. Carrow opened it up to check the contents, which appeared to be baggies of white powder. He nodded and handed the man what looked like a White House ID. Some heroin dealer had access to the White House.

"VR." *That could be my Valiant.* "Hacking." I clicked on a video. Lee was monitoring someone's computer. The screen showed every word typed. Lee must have had some kind of keylogger on the person's computer. It showed the typing of a login that I recognized as Valiant's login name. From watching it, I could also see his password. I wondered if it was still active. Suddenly, there were some interesting strokes and I saw Gene's login and apparently his password appear. The computer screen itself must also have been monitored or the keylogger just had access to what was showing on Valiant's screen. Next, the video showed the computer going through several alternate locations and then hacking into the NSA website and monitoring a meeting. If the video was as it appeared, Valiant had actually used the NSA computers to spy on their activities. I watched the meeting. It was about pandemics and other events that were being orchestrated. The NSA director was telling someone that all they needed to do to get results was to create another national emergency, such as another pandemic, attack, war, or climate fear and people would be oblivious to the final loss of freedom. The NSA director pointed out that nobody had even noticed the concentration camps set up during the prior pandemic or the mass graves in which they buried detainees, pretending they were killed by the pandemic.

My mind started racing. Valiant had impressive skills. But this would also give him a reason to kill Lee if he knew Lee had hacked his computer or installed a keylogger. Valiant could have received prison time for hacking into the NSA. But hacking wasn't the kind of earth-shaking scandal that Marissa and Seth would have exposed. Instead, they would have made a deal for a copy of the video of the meeting and kept their source anonymous. The heroin and the fake security badge wouldn't have been that major either.

The files were not alphabetical. I wondered if there was a different reason for the order. I looked towards the bottom in case they were in level of seriousness or seniority. The robotic President wasn't there. Of course not. The scandals and dementia were known when he was elected and the robotics were part of Lee's department. Lee wouldn't have exposed himself. GH. *Gene Hemmings?* I opened the file. "Murder, prison break, fraud."

If murder was part of his M.O., what difference would four more make?

I started to open an attached video file. There was a knock at my door. I had to put the flash drive somewhere. I shoved it into a flower vase and went to open the door. I really needed to start looking through the viewer in case the killer paid me a visit. Despite my concerns about finding someone had entered my apartment earlier, part of me just couldn't get into the fear of visitors who knocked. That was probably dumb, given that there had already been four murders or so I believed.

It was Jerry. He looked rather solemn.

"Jerry, what's wrong?"

"Monica."

"Your girlfriend?"

"She read a report that I was with you last night. When she confronted me, I admitted that I was with you the last two nights, but I assured her it was work-related."

"It was, sort of."

"She didn't believe me. I've never lied to her and she still didn't believe me."

"I'm sorry. Would you like me to speak with her?"

"I don't think it would do any good."

"I'll follow you over to her place in my car. That way, we won't go there together."

"I'll wait outside while you go in. So she'll know we arrived separately," Jerry said. "On second thought, this is ridiculous. I shouldn't have to prove that I'm not having a relationship with you."

"Nobody would ever accuse you of that. I've seen Monica. Any guy who would cheat on her would be crazy."

"Don't downgrade yourself. But we've been going together for years. I'd think she'd know me by now."

"Of course. Sometimes, girls just need extra reassurance."

"This isn't an imposition?"

"No. I'd do it for anyone I wasn't involved with. I mean, there's my reputation too. I'd never steal another girl's guy."

"I've heard of this chick loyalty thing, but most of the women I know are always undercutting each other."

"You mean like Felicity Fowl?"

"I wasn't going to mention her, but she's tried to put the make on me more than once, right before she cozied up to Monica and pretended to be her best friend."

"I thought Lee was Felicity's best friend."

That gave us both a laugh.

"She only likes Monica because her dad is Senator Maxwell."

"I'd say that was cynical, but I'm pretty sure that, for Felicity, that was a major motivator. How is it going with the daughter of the enemy? I mean Senator Maxwell is the lead Republican trying to stop the President's policies."

"We have an agreement not to talk politics."

"Does it work?"

"For me it does. Monica tries to move me over to her side of the aisle. I'm sure she'd appreciate me telling her about work activities, but I keep my mouth shut."

"While you learn what the enemy is up to."

"It's mostly propaganda stuff."

"Of course."

"But do you get the impression that there is no difference between the two parties?"

"Welcome to the twenty-first century. Old master same as the new master. Only this time the new master is a little more demented, which may or may not be superior."

"I'll say." He laughed. "Until the other night, I really hadn't spoken to you outside of brief greetings at work. If Monica wouldn't misunderstand, I wish we could chat more."

"Girlfriends always misunderstand. It's part of the nature of relationships. Boyfriends, usually likewise."

I followed Jerry over to Monica's D.C. condo. He parked on the street as I drove up to the security gate.

"Are you expected miss?"

"No. I'm here to see—" I was going to say "Monica Maxwell in 329," but I was interrupted by the sight of her rushing out the gate, past my car to another car to be picked up. Looking back I had a clear view. They were apparently preoccupied or they might not have recognized my car. Coming out of the driver's side to help her in the passenger door was John Carrow, the Secret Service agent with a history of providing fake credentials.

CHAPTER 12

This time, Carrow was with the daughter of the "enemy." But it was more than a ride. Carrow got back into the driver's seat and leaned over, giving her a quick kiss and then took off. If he had been smart, he'd have had his windows tinted darker.

"You're visiting who?" the security guard asked me.

"You know, I just realized I have the wrong address. Thank you for your time."

He had me go forward and turn around to leave. I drove down the street in the direction Carrow's car had gone and pulled up in front of Jerry's car. I got out and went back to speak with him. He was staring straight ahead.

"She's not home."

"I saw."

"I'm sorry. It could be anything."

"He had his arm around her and was driving one-handed. That was after the kiss."

"That's not easy to misunderstand. Maybe he's a distant relative."

"Seriously?"

"I didn't believe my suggestion either."

"Care to go to Skippers for a few drinks?"

"You might need a ride home after that. How about my place? I have some Cherry Kijafa there. If worse comes to worse, I can drive you home."

"Is that a Danish wine?"

"Borderline liquor. And delicious."

"Have anything stronger?"

"I have an unopened bottle of one-fifty-one for piña coladas and daiquiris."

"Perfect."

"I was so stupid. I've been thinking about all the times she regularly waited in security for me. I thought it was sweet. It didn't seem odd at that time, but John usually waited with her. I figured it was because her father was a dark-side VIP and she didn't want to call attention to our relationship." He made a fist and brought it to his head as if he felt like hitting himself.

"Something you should know is that girls who cheat are not the norm, and it has nothing to do with the guy. They're just built that way."

"But not most girls?"

"Loyalty is too often one of our downfalls."

"I haven't seen you with anyone."

"Loyalty is definitely one of my downfalls. I don't have time for a relationship. But when I do, I want the perfect guy, just so my loyalty is not misplaced."

"How will you know for sure?"

"That's the dilemma. How does anyone know?"

"I should have known. Monica was always flirting with other guys. I just thought it was casual friendliness, but now that I reflect on it. Boy was I stupid. And tonight, she made it about me and you. John probably told her about seeing us at the cabin. He knew we were there to check on a story."

"Tomorrow, just smile at him when you enter, like he's the one who got the albatross around his neck now."

"Good advice."

A thought entered my mind. If John was giving White House passes to the "enemy" as I now suspected, how much did others (including the opposing party) know about secret operations at the White House? John had never been down to my department and I didn't think he knew about it. Trey had escorted the President through the White House frequently but not to the computer lab.

It didn't even take two drinks for Jerry to fall asleep on my couch. I put a blanket over him. I figured I'd get him up in time to go home and shower for the new day.

Thursday morning, I woke up bright and early. I went into the living room. Jerry was gone. A note on the couch said, "Thank you. I owe you." He really was a good guy. I hoped he would find someone who deserved him more than Monica.

Before going to my office, there was something I had to handle. I went to see Gene. "I got an anonymous note that someone had been giving out bogus White House Security passes. Maybe you could check into it."

"Do you have the note?"

"I went back to look for it and it was gone. It was anonymous. Maybe, someone here knew about it and wanted to bring it to my attention."

"I see."

"If it's not true, no harm is done by checking into it. We have had some breaches. Cameras down on Monday as well as security data missing."

"Better safe than sorry."

"Right."

I went to the lab. "Valiant, could you check to see if there is a keylogger on any of these computers?"

"Keylogger?"

"Also, recheck for any bugs."

"We just did a check ten minutes ago."

"How about the computers?"

"What has you so worried about security?"

"We're working on top secret stuff here. The whole White House may be beefing up its security."

"A threat?"

"I didn't say that."

"You seem different. Is it all those deaths? They're making me a little jumpy too."

"Would you like to go out for lunch?"

"Really?" He sounded enthusiastic.

Darn, that may have come across as an inappropriate invitation to an employee. "It's not personal. Your work is top quality and I thought lunch might be a way of saying 'thank you.'"

Valiant looked a little fallen. "Sure. Lunch would be great. New boss is definitely better than the old boss."

Next, I went to Paris's office. "Paris, you had a hand in interviewing Valiant for his job, didn't you?"

"He was Lee's hire. Valiant was a kid genius. Lee said he wanted someone who could work miracles and Valiant certainly has. The President looks and speaks just like himself."

"So Lee found him?"

"No. Gene did. Gene taught a class at a university where Valiant was driving the Administration crazy with his skills."

"Do you think he's a hacker?"

"Rumor had it, he had hacked the NYU system but instead of a reprimand, he was offered a special scholarship that covered room, board and all school expenses."

"Reward for misconduct?"

"Good way to keep misfits in line."

"And you hired him? Lee didn't have the final say."

"Valiant was never charged with the hacking."

"Do you trust him?"

"You can answer that better than I can. Is there anything I should know regarding his work at the White House?"

"Nothing concerning his work here. He is very cooperative and supportive."

"He hasn't come onto you, has he?"

"No. Nothing like that."

"This morning may be tough on you."

"Tough?"

"The President is supposed to go to a school to supervise the vaccination program for the Bermuda variant."

"That doesn't exist." I almost bit my tongue. I hoped our conversation wasn't being monitored.

"You can't say that. It's on the record that the White House staff has been fully vaccinated for it."

"All the staff?"

"That's what the employee records say."

I wondered if it was Paris's Signature Soldier friend who faked that or someone at the White House who wanted everyone to survive long enough to put forth the agenda.

"Felicity will be giving the shots."

"Does she have a medical degree?" I asked.

"She took health science in grammar school. You are technically a researcher and so you don't need to be there."

"Someone from our department should at least observe—in case something goes wrong."

"My thoughts too."

"How many kids have died from being injected with this latest vaccine?"

"CDC VAERS has been officially closed down. It used to report about one percent of the adverse events. The news and social media won't cover the deaths. The FBI and NSA have made sure of that. Anyone talking about deaths is classified as a Russian terrorist." Paris didn't seem concerned about being monitored. Maybe the truth was acceptable within the Administration as long as it wasn't shared with anyone outside.

"I know the White House has some figures on the deaths."

He paused. "It's high. Between us, mostly the only babies being born healthy in the last three years have been children of those who got nothing or the substitute, mostly actors and politicians."

"Those who got the saline."

"Currently, when someone else has a healthy baby, Homeland Security generally pays a visit to see if they are a dissident or faked their status."

"And then, CPS uses that as an excuse to confiscate the kids." I didn't need an answer on that.

———

I went back to the lab. "Valiant, the President will be overseeing child injections this morning."

"You don't look happy."

"The parents no longer have a choice if they don't want their kids confiscated, and the children are a little young to understand the risks."

"Got it."

———

The event was in the cafeteria of Oliver North Elementary School. The President was going to start with a speech on the stage and then Felicity was to give the shots, followed by hot fudge sundaes for all recipients. John came with us. I wondered if he was high from heroin. His eyes were a little dilated. He stood at the entrance, looking very distracted. *Monica has really stepped down,* I thought.

The students sat in assembly-style arrangement as the Principal introduced Felicity who introduced the President. The news crews were late. Odd. Felicity's phone started ringing. She pushed the button to reject the call. It happened again.

"That was from my parents," she whispered to me. "I better go outside to get it."

The President started to discuss the vaccine. "By getting this vaccine, you are being good public servants. After all, you are risking death and loss of the use of your arms and legs. That's a major service to protect your country. While you might lose your ability to speak or walk after getting the jab, we will make sure you get lots of ice cream and we will pay for the cost of a special day at Disneyland."

The news crews arrived as he was speaking and began setting up cameras. I noticed they seemed hesitant to record the speech. Still, photographers were getting lots of images. It occurred to me that the President's speech might be viewed as misinformation. What's funny was that this Administration was the most suppressive of documented information and vigilant in its prosecution of Indymedia journalists reporting verified facts. The mainstream media news crews were likely afraid of losing their jobs if they reported on the President's actual words as he continued.

"Playing ball and sports are nothing compared to the wonderful taste of ice cream. If you are not capable of feeding yourselves after the vaccine, we can arrange to have someone spoon it into your mouths. We'll provide you with college scholarships and orthopedic devices to operate your computers. If you are unable to speak, we have devices that can read your thoughts and put those down on your computers. So now, I'm certain that you great citizens are all eager to get these wonderful shots and serve humanity."

As Felicity re-entered the auditorium, the teachers and principal stood and applauded with teachers pulling up students alongside them and whispering encouragement to the kids. The applause continued for about five minutes, though the kids didn't appear to be smiling. Most were looking at the exits. I assumed none of the kids were related to any of the teachers or staff. The teachers and staff, who were cheering as if this was the greatest speech of their lifetimes, seemed to ignore the look of terror on the faces of the students.

The principal and one of the teachers came onto the stage. I noticed the video crews starting to record. "That was a great speech and we are so lucky to have you here to help encourage the children to fulfill their duty to society," the principal said. "This is Clara Farmer, our teacher of the year, who would like to say a few words."

"I really appreciated your speech. It showed the importance of sacrificing and surpassing fears for the good of all. I know I and the teachers will feel so much safer when all the children are fully vaxxed."

"It sounds like he outdid himself with his speech. Your department has been doing much better work since you took over," Felicity whispered to me.

"We do our best."

John escorted the President out of the cafeteria.

Felicity put syringes on a table and the kids were to line up next to it. She waved to me to assist the teachers and staff in lining up the students. My jabs were all faked. If a kid I helped inject died today, it would be on my conscience for life.

CHAPTER 13

Most of the students were looking at the main doors where other teachers and members of the school staff were standing. I heard the school nurse ask for a key to lock the doors. The principal handed her something and a boy snatched it out of her hand and put it in his mouth. The nurse and principal were pounding on the boy's back to try to get him to spit it out. I wondered if he had swallowed it.

"But I have to go to the bathroom," one of the students said.

"Me too!" others shouted.

"I'm going to pee in my pants."

"After the shot. Nobody is going to the bathroom until after this wonderful process," Clara said loudly.

At Felicity's urging, I worked to put the kids into a straight line. The news crews had started a live feed. I guessed they felt this was more in keeping with the agenda than the President's speech and they wanted to verify which kids were in school getting jabbed. The government and corporations were keeping track. I noticed the nurse and several teachers chasing the boy who had taken the key around the stage. He had jumped onto the curtains on the side and was swinging into several of his pursuers, knocking them down. They almost caught him, but he freed himself and rushed off.

I noticed the first few kids in line looked as if were trying to move out off to the side.

"Maybe you can calm them down," the principal said to me.

I went over to the front of the line. I kneeled down and whispered to the first girl, who appeared to be about seven. "Can you act? Like a play?"

She nodded.

"Have you ever seen an epileptic rolling on the floor in a fit?"

"My sister."

"Then the moment the needle is about to touch your arm, before it goes in, fall to the floor and pretend to be your sister. Stare straight ahead or roll your eyes up to where you can't see and let out a lot of saliva. Can you do it?"

"Can I get out of the shot?"

"I hope so."

I stood up. "Sorry. I was giving her a pep talk about how important the vaccine is."

"I can always count on you, Karissa," Felicity said cheerfully. "She is my top protégé," she told the principal.

"Good job," the principal said to me.

I watched as the girl approached Felicity. Felicity uncapped the needle and lifted the girl's arm. The girl went into her acting spree a little early. I looked at the news crews. I was hoping from their angle they didn't see that the needle didn't quite touch the arm. The girl was writhing on the floor. One of the teachers tried to calm her and she wildly bit the teacher. I had picked a future Academy Award winner.

"But I didn't insert it," Felicity said.

"Apparently, you gave her enough of a dose to be effective. Remember these side effects mean the shot is working."

"That's true. See," she turned to the reporters. "The shot is working. Isn't this beautiful?"

The girl was slobbering all over the floor.

The news crew was turning their cameras at that point to record the other children who were rushing for the doors, pushing the teachers to the side. The boy who had stolen the key was among the first ones out of the door. I wondered if one day, he'd lead the second American Revolution.

"Wait. You haven't received your shots!" Felicity called.

"Don't forget. The shot transmits. When she plays with the other students, they'll get the mRNA," I told Felicity. "You did a great job and now all the students will be immune."

Felicity moved in front of the cameras. "Thank you for being here. As you can see, our Administration has made the health of America's children top priority."

I walked over to the Principal. "Make sure they all get the ice cream."

"What about the shots?"

"I think they are all getting them by transmission from the first girl."

As we were leaving, I saw Felicity speak under her breath to the school nurse. "Make sure each and every student gets a shot, even if you have to tie them to chairs while they scream." After that, she turned towards me and smiled. She said more clearly, "We did good work." At that point, we exited the room and met up with John and the President, outside.

On the way back in the limo, Felicity said, "That principal needs to be fired."

"What?"

"The first girl had a history of epilepsy. The principal should have kept her back until the end of the line when the press had stopped recording."

"After what happened, a teacher told me the girl's sister was epileptic but she wasn't."

"She doesn't have a sister. Whoever told you that, must have been covering for their mistake in allowing her to go first."

"I doubt the press will show it. Their news license would be revoked if they did."

"Revocability of news licenses for misinformation was one of the best changes instituted by our Administration. Only the services with licenses issued by the President are considered news and other media outlets can be arrested for any unapproved stories."

"I think the government started going that way with the arrest of Assange."

"It was something that needed to be done. We've been trying to track down all the Indymedia misinformation sources, but they keep slipping by. One day, all those freaks will be in indefinite detention."

So the girl's reaction may have been real. She didn't need my prompt. The fear probably did it to her.

"I hope that call wasn't something serious?"

"My parents, but when I called back, there was a message about an emergency and to keep calling if I didn't get through. I never did get through."

Before going to lunch, I passed Valiant a note to leave his cell phone behind.

We went to a new organic restaurant called Darrel's. It was packed.

I had an avocado sandwich and Valiant had a plate of sautéed shrimp and mushrooms.

"Thanks for the speech, but Felicity ordered the nurse to vax all the kids after we left."

"Not today. After you left, the fire alarm system had a malfunction. The alarm might still be going off."

I laughed. "You are a treasure. Hacking into the fire alarm system."

"Are you calling me a hacker?"

"Have you ever done any more serious hacking?"

He leaned close. "Is the NSA serious?"

"NSA?"

"They're coming after Americans. I'm thinking of releasing the video, but they'll try to pull it quickly unless I also hack the broadcasting system."

"You're being pretty open."

"Why not? Lee had a keylogger on my computer. I guess he told you?"

I hadn't been as subtle as I thought.

"Is it gone now?"

"And not coming back."

"Good. I guess you didn't kill him."

"You thought I killed Lee?"

"It did occur to me."

"Thanks for the vote of confidence. My father was a conscientious objector and a minister."

"Ministers have been known to commit crimes."

"My father had scruples and they unfortunately rubbed off on me. I wanted to save the world, but the corruption is a bit too deep."

"You realize what I could do with your admission?"

"I've watched you at work. You don't like what's going on any better than I do. And if you do get me fired, at least, I've had a great lunch."

"Personally, I think your actions have been pretty heroic if they don't get us both fired. Wait. Were you the one who turned off the cameras and the security the day Lee died?"

"You still think I might have done that?"

"No."

"I suspect it was someone in the security office."

"John, maybe?"

"Carrow?"

"I have some information on him, but I can't reveal how I got it at this time. I also need to track down a story a reporter was looking into?"

"You mean Marissa Tracy or Seth Moore? You mentioned them in the lab the other day. They're dead and so is their boss. You think they knew about you-know-who?"

"I don't know. But someone doesn't want anyone knowing what they were working on. I'm willing to bet their computer files on the story have been erased as well."

"They could be backed up in the cloud. Depending on their email server, anything they sent out might be backed up."

"Is any of that accessible?"

"It's possible. Now, you've asked me a number of questions. May I ask you one?"

"Go ahead."

"Are you and Jerry dating?"

"Where did you hear that?"

"Rumor."

"Great. No. I don't take another woman's boyfriend. Not that Monica is that much of a girlfriend."

"I didn't think so. He seems a little dull."

"We're trying to find out what story Marissa was working on. What could bring down the Administration?"

"This Administration? Take a pick."

"That's the problem. We need to find out the what before it blows up in our faces."

"You're thinking whoever killed Lee probably killed Marissa, Seth and their boss? It fits."

"Do you think anyone in the Administration could have done it?"

"Everyone. Well not quite everyone."

"Lee was collecting information on people," I told him.

"If this were a mystery, I'm your trusted friend. At least, I'd like to think you trust me. The trusted friend would be the one most likely to be the killer."

"I was telling that to my brother. On the other hand, you may be the only one who can help me find out who did it. So I'm hoping you aren't some stock storybook character."

"I'm very unique."

I thought about the fact that Lee had evidence on me and someone else knew about that. Someone, possibly the killer, had removed the evidence from Lee's hands after he died and put it under my door. Did someone kill Lee while, at the same time trying to protect me? Killing is always bad—even if Lee was awful. Jerry was the one to find Lee. Maybe he saw the file when he found the body and took the evidence to protect me.

"One more question."

"Yes?"

"Felicity got a call from her parents and then couldn't reach them to call back."

"Maybe someone hacked into the phone system."

I decided not to inquire further about that.

The President was scheduled for a meeting with the Cabinet to take place the following morning. Gene had taken over for him at most of the Cabinet meetings. The Cabinet members actually preferred it that way. Apparently, they didn't have sympathy for a demented leader. There was a special appropriations bill up for a vote in Congress and the President didn't have an excuse for missing this one.

I met with Gene and Paris for instructions on details for preparing the President. With nobody in the Cabinet knowing the truth about the President, we had to be prepared for unexpected questions or comments. Gene planned to field the questions.

Afterward, I went to my office and sat down at my desk. Suddenly, all the lights went out. I went to the door. The hall lights were also out. Someone was rushing by. From the size, my guess was it was John. He pushed me out of the way and kept running. Someone was following him.

I backed into my office. The door opened. I backed up against the wall. "Karissa?" It was Jerry.

"I'm here," I said. It was too dark to see, but I could hear him step into the room and close the door.

"Are you okay?" he asked.

"Yes. Why are the lights off?"

"I don't know. I think there's a security breach."

"Don't we have backup lights and power?"

"Someone must have turned those off too."

I heard a sound from behind me. There was someone else in the room.

"This way." It was Valiant.

He pulled my arm and started to guide me somewhere. I reached for and pulled Jerry with us. Where was Valiant leading us? To a back corner? It was as if the room had expanded and even the texture of the floor was different. The wood floor had turned to some kind of tile. We must have gone through a door that wasn't there. I could feel Valiant move his other hand past me. It sounded as if a door closed. It wasn't loud, but I could hear something click, and I sensed a change in the air pressure right in front of me. Valiant guided me down a narrow staircase. Jerry clung onto me and followed. Down, down, down, we went. Some kind of door or panel opened up. I recognized this place, even in the dim glow of a power-failure backup light behind a computer across the room. We should have had stronger ones. It was the outer tech lab.

"How?"

"It was part of the architecture. There are secret passages to the Oval Office and most of the rooms where the President can find refuge. You know about the tunnels underneath the White House too, don't you?"

"I think everyone does," Jerry said.

"Whoever got to Lee wasn't seen," I said. "Could they have gotten in through that passage?"

"The cameras were down. It could have been anyone." Valiant said in an irritated tone. "It wasn't me!"

"Someone is making us all look guilty," Jerry said.

Valiant pulled a flashlight out of a drawer and turned it on. "Yeh. Someone is making us all look guilty." We looked at the floor. The President had been ripped to pieces and part of his face was missing.

CHAPTER 14

"Well, someone knows our secret," Valiant remarked.

"What? What is this? Some kind of mannequin or robot?" Jerry asked.

"Meet the President," I said.

Valiant pulled out his bug detector and quickly checked the room as I put a finger to my lips to encourage Jerry to stay quiet.

"Nothing detectable."

"Let's look in the cupboards and closets in case someone is still here," I suggested.

Valiant and I went through the various possible hiding locations, including under desks and behind cabinets.

Jerry reached for a chair and sat down. "I think I just entered *The Twilight Zone*."

"Any other secret passages out of here?" I asked Valiant.

"The door," he answered. "I locked it and deadbolted it before I got you." I went over to the door. It was unlocked.

"Someone has a key or a good lock pick," I said. "We're going to have to report this to Gene. Do you think the President can be repaired by morning?"

"I'll call in Brandon and Levitson. The exterior is going to take some work. We might have to order materials."

"I'm going to find Gene."

"Whoever did this could be out there somewhere," Valiant said.

The lights came on. Valiant picked up the lab phone and pressed a speed dial that I assumed was security. "Valiant Rimmel."

"Thank you."

"They don't know the cause of the power outage. It's back up and all is clear."

"You don't use your cell?"

"It's locked in a steel safe." Valiant turned to me. "Even your burner phone can be tracked."

I guess he had noticed me using my phone. I turned to the Press Secretary. "Jerry, you didn't see any of this."

"I don't believe what I'm seeing, anyway. This is a dream, right?"

"Right."

I escorted Jerry upstairs to his office. He laid down on a couch. "Is anything real?"

"Life here is all an illusion. You are actually enjoying a nice dinner at home."

"That's good. I could use something stiff to wash it down."

"I need to speak with Gene."

"Nothing is real."

"I think the couch is real. Just relax for now and remember, silence is, maybe not golden but, safer for our jobs." He put his hands over his eyes and slightly nodded.

The first issue was whether we had what we needed to repair the robot.

"What about the backup?" Gene asked.

"It's not programmed."

"Is it intact?"

"I didn't check. It's in the locked storage behind the inner lab. But someone knows enough to have destroyed the original."

"They destroyed the robot. So all further appearances are from the real President."

"As far as they are concerned?"

"Correct."

"Do you think they know about the backup?"

"Nobody was supposed to know about the primary robot outside of yourself, your team, Lee and a few others on the executive staff," he said.

"Do you think one of them did it?"

"Earlier today, Trey said he had found a security breach. Apparently, a number of unauthorized security passes have been given out. We were about to reset the system when the lights went down."

"Cameras?"

"They were out too."

I went down to the lab. Valiant had called Jack and Brandon back in. "Did you check on the backup?"

"It's intact."

"Can you program it by morning?"

"I can do anything. Why don't you go home and get some rest. What are you going to tell Jerry?"

"What can I tell him? To keep his mouth shut and conduct business as usual."

"You're not much of a grifter, are you?"

If only he knew. "I guess I've had any grifter scared out of me."

Jerry was sitting in his office. It seemed an improvement over the last time I had seen him. "Do you have your phone?"

"I think you've talked me out of carrying it."

"I'll follow you to make sure you get home okay."

"Tell me I have a wild imagination."

"And it's very vivid. Don't worry. Tomorrow everything will be back to normal."

On the way to Jerry's place, I tried to figure out how to explain things. The same answer kept coming back. If I lied to him tonight, he'd never trust me again. Somehow, I didn't want to lose an ally. Was he an ally?

"Would you like me to make dinner for you?" I asked when we arrived outside his place.

"Maybe you can explain a little over dinner."

My mind went to Valiant. He knew a back way into Lee's office. He could have killed him, switched the file and left. Today, Valiant could have ripped apart the President and unlocked the door before he came upstairs. Outside of my team, the people who knew about the President were above question. Except Gene had the words "murder, prison break and fraud" next to his initials. I needed to watch the video. I also needed to look at the other initials. Maybe even Jerry was on the list. Valiant could have been guilty, but if he was worried about the hack into the NSA, why did he so openly tell me? Maybe he knew I already knew and wanted it to seem like nothing.

As Jerry and I made salads for dinner at his condo, I asked, "What is your impression of Valiant?"

"I've seen him around. I don't know him well. He seems like an upfront guy."

"Did you find it odd that he knew about the secret passages?"

"He's a techie. Those guys know more trivia."

"I wouldn't consider secret passages in the White House to be trivia."

"There have been movies about the secret passages for years. I bet a lot of techies have researched the subject. Why? You don't trust him?"

"It's not that. I am just having a tough time knowing who to trust. I asked him to help us track down Marissa's story. I am hoping I did the right thing."

"How would he benefit from the murders?"

"That's the question. Who did benefit?"

"Maybe someone who didn't want the world to know the President is a robot? The Administration would be kicked out. Was he a robot during the election?"

"I wasn't there then."

"Is the real President alive?"

"Above my pay grade. So, you think the story might have been about the President?"

"Blackmoriuntur. I Googled it today."

"And?"

"There are dozens of businesses with similar names but none seemed relevant. All of the businesses that start with the name Black—"

"I know. We all heard about Abu Ghraib. Could the name be wrong?"

"I thought about that. So I called a friend of mine in the NSA."

"You have friends in low places?"

"He was my roommate in college."

"Have you heard of the Signature Reduction Soldiers?"

"Signature Soldiers?"

"Apparently, they have *Mission Impossible* quality masks and fake backgrounds, and they spy on Americans for the Pentagon."

"Now that's a scandal."

"It's already made the press and nobody cared. I just heard about it the other day."

"The person who impersonated me?"

"They infiltrate organizations."

"The White House?"

"Maybe, or maybe whoever orchestrated all this was simply high up." The disk flashed into my mind.

"After dinner, I want to show you something at my apartment."

"This isn't a come-on, is it?"

I gave him a look that said, "You've got to be kidding."

"Oh well. Just hoping."

"No, you weren't. I'm not a rebound girl. But it was flattering."

Jerry was waiting at my door when I arrived home. "And I thought I was a speed demon."

"I know a few shortcuts."

"I guess."

He followed me into my apartment and I went over to the vase. I pulled out the fake flowers and dumped the vase. Water came out, along with a very wet flash drive.

CHAPTER 15

"I never put water in this vase."

"You don't seem like the artificial flower type."

"That's why this has been a good hiding place in the past."

I blow-dried the drive in the hopes that it would be usable. I got errors when I went to look at it on my computer. I tried to just copy the files but it said they couldn't be read.

"What was on it?"

"Initials and things I assume Lee was holding over people or planned to."

"You got that from his computer?"

"And Duane said, when he looked at Lee's computer disc, it had been wiped."

"Maybe Duane was the one who erased it."

"But Duane didn't have access to my apartment."

I thought about who had been here. Jerry, Paris and the manager. Someone else could have gotten in I supposed.

"Did you look at any of the names?"

Something about this was giving me doubts about Jerry. "Just a couple of things that could be used to get people fired. It's the ones I didn't look at that I wanted to check out." A partial truth.

"We might be able to get a computer expert to repair it. Maybe Valiant?"

"Maybe. It's getting late. It's been a long week."

"Thank you for believing in me."

"Sure. You're an upright guy. One of a kind."

He started to reach out his hand and then gave me a friendly hug. I had missed those. Nobody hugged me anymore.

"Thanks," I said. "I needed that."

That night I had trouble sleeping. I kept going over the possibilities. Jerry. Valiant. Gene. John. Paris was in my apartment. So I'd have to include him. And was the real President alive? If not, the robot should not have been holding press conferences and Cabinet meetings. Even if the President had been replaced before the election, the real President's 411 would have been on the Affidavit that allowed him to run. I thought about my real father, the real reason I had chosen to work at the White House. I had no feelings but disgust for him and no pity. I had come to the White House for revenge and found that his dementia had mostly finished him. Paris had brought me in because of the death of his sister, a death he attributed to the Administration. She died after a college jab like the ones they wanted to give the younger kids today. What we pulled at the elementary school was only a temporary measure, but maybe the kids went home and convinced their parents not to send them back.

I remembered an old *Truthstream* video I had watched as a kid before the censorship got so bad. People had complained that someone unknown had broken into their homes and left signs of the break-in but took nothing relevant. A wall would be half painted or something would be moved when they returned home. Usually, this happened to women who were living alone and not likely to be believed. Could that have been the Signature Force or some other agency or was it just in the women's minds?

Friday morning, the President was as ready as possible. He seemed more vibrant than normal. In fact, he was bouncing through the hall on the way to the meeting. "We found a new medicine," Paris told people who came out of their offices to watch him pass. He and Gene would both be at the Cabinet meeting. "Valiant said there was a glitch in the program that they are trying to fix. Somehow it was altered to make him think he was a former athlete," I whispered to Paris. "They are going through the program, but it will take until later today to fix it."

"It beats falling all over his own feet."

"True."

"Maybe you can stick around to watch the meeting."

Gene looked worried as he watched the President enter the room. The President's tap dance on the meeting table was making everyone a little nervous.

"Does he also think he's Fred Astaire?" Paris whispered to me as we stood at the side of the room.

"At least, he's not imitating Baryshnikov," I whispered back.

"You know Fred and Ginger aren't performing tap dances these days. In fact, they're both dead. Maybe, they'll invite the President onto the late-night TV shows," Paris said.

"Nadia Comaneci?" Gene asked me as the President did a backflip.

"Must be old videos." Paris turned to the Cabinet members and then said more loudly, "There have been questions about his physical health from the radical Republicans. He wanted to prove his healthy physique and agility."

"I'm in as good of shape as when I won my gold medal for the high jump." With that, he jumped up and hung from the chandelier.

"No doubt about his physique, but he might want a different type of checkup," the Surgeon General said. "Maybe we should call in Frank."

"He's out on a call," Paris said quickly. Frank, the resident physician, wasn't one of the informed when it came to the President as amazing as that was.

"Good thing the Surgeon General has never practiced medicine," I whispered to Paris.

"I don't think he/she, whatever the pronoun is, even knows what a doctor is. I suspect the SG's experience came from medical interventions using dogs at Abu Ghraib."

Gene helped the President down as he broke into a chorus of Mandy. "I guess he thinks he is Barry Manilow too," Paris whispered to me.

"We only had one night to fix the situation," I quietly pointed out to Gene.

As the President literally leaped into a chorus of "I Write the Songs," a fire alarm went off.

"Everyone out. You have now seen a preview of the President's performance for the staff talent show," Gene said, ushering people out. "We want everyone on the staff to prepare to show the public how talented the entire Administration is."

"I can sing 'Like a Virgin,' the Vice President said on her way out.

"Wouldn't fit," Gene advised her.

"In my office," Gene told me.

"Keep your cool," Paris said. "I'll escort the President back."

"That's my specialty," I replied.

Paris took the President's arm to escort him back to the lab. The President pulled it away from Paris and proceeded to do pirouettes down the hall as staffers were rushing out of their offices for a glimpse. His dancing was met with applause. I could see Jerry holding back a laugh. Paris and I ran after the President and pulled him in the correct direction.

"I must go outside and give my speech."

"I can't wait to see his next performance," Paris muttered. Together we managed to get him into the elevator.

"Four score and seven years ago."

"He's learned history," I said, as the elevator closed on the three of us. I put in my key and the sub-basement floor numbers appeared.

"Our forefathers brought forth on this continent."

The door opened.

"A new nation conceived in liberty and dedicated." We opened the outer lab door.

Valiant and Jack quickly tried to squelch their laughs rather unsuccessfully.

"To the proposition that all men are created equal."

"Okay boys," Paris said.

"Now we are gathered on a great battlefield." He stopped midsentence as Valiant turned him off.

"I hope you all have a job at the end of the day," Paris said.

"The program was corrupted. So we improvised by feeding in the personalities of some of the older celebrities available on *YouTube*," Valiant explained.

"At least, they haven't been censored," I said.

"We probably will be after your meeting with Gene," Paris noted.

Up in Gene's office, I told the Chief of Staff, "You handled it well."

"That could have been a disaster."

"Sections of the program were corrupted and they improvised. They didn't expect him to have the talent of the people they programmed in to fill the gaps."

"He's supposed to be the President, not a Broadway star."

"They should have him fixed by Monday."

"See to it."

"The talent show was a great idea."

He glared at me.

"Yes, sir. I just meant that you saved the day. I'll get back to the lab and see that the repairs are expedited."

When I arrived back in the lab, I told the gang, "Okay, you can stop laughing now."

"We should have thrown in some Gypsy Rose Lee or maybe some Mae West."

"This could be our great last act, getting the President put under seventy-two hour observation to determine whether he's a danger to himself or others," I commented.

"Astaire, Lee and West aren't going to sue him for copyright violations," Valiant said.

"Manilow might," Brandon said.

"Guys," I said sternly and then broke into the laugh I couldn't hold back anymore. "That was priceless. It was the best thing that's happened all week. But he really needs to be fixed by Monday. Boring. Dull. Demented."

"Killjoy," Valiant said.

"Monday, he's going to be addressing Congress and the nation."

"You know that at today's meeting, he was supposed to get the Cabinet to mandate appropriations for post-birth abortion of unruly kids and young adults up to twenty-five," Valiant said. "It's a good thing my mother likes me."

"My mom might want to take advantage of that when I'm late for visits," Jack said.

I thought about my own dad. "I bet my dad wouldn't mind invoking it if I embarrass him."

"Your brother doesn't need to worry," Jack said. "Paris is over twenty-five."

"True."

"The call for those appropriations is supposed to be in his speech before Congress on Monday morning," Jack said. "Sure you want him fixed?"

I wished we could get the speech canceled or that Congress would vote against the appropriations.

I started to the door.

"Did you hear about the school you visited yesterday?"

"What?" I responded to Valiant.

"None of the children showed up for school today. They had a one hundred percent sickout."

"The Administration supports mandatory vaccines. That's too bad," I said, barely holding back a smile.

"Of course. Have you had yours?"

"I have an online record of mine."

"So do we all," Valiant said.

"Of course. We couldn't have gotten these positions without proof of the vax."

"They are planning a mandate to put all our medical records online all the way back to our mothers' elementary school records."

"All? Our mothers' school records are part of our medical history, now? Last I knew, school records were not medical records."

"If they want to nail us for hereditary rebelliousness, they are—according to the memo that was sent to all employees while you were at the meeting."

"Memo from whom?"

"Who else? Felicity. They don't want people working for the government with potentially inherited conditions that could show up while here."

"And is there more?"

"They'll be available for all businesses, insurers and creditors to see."

"Got to love this government," I said flatly, as I exited the lab.

"Baryshnikov?" Jerry asked, laughing as he closed the door to my office.

"Laugh all you want. You should have heard his Manilow."

"I think the person who got into the lab last night did us all a favor."

"Well, that's going to be over on Monday."

"Would you like to do lunch?"

"I've got to supervise the fix."

"Dinner?" I was having reservations about Jerry after seeing the water in the vase. But we were going to meet with his NSA friend later tonight. I didn't want to blow that.

"Sure."

"I'll pick you up at seven?"

"I'll be ready."

At 6:45 P.M., I was still fretting over the damaged flash drive. If I trusted Valiant more, I would have asked him to try to get the data off. I was still uneasy about the prior day. He had the opportunity to rip apart the President and the access to have killed Lee without being seen. Plus, he probably had the technical skills to hack into the cameras and lights.

When Jerry arrived, he had flowers: long-stemmed red roses. "I realize this is business, but I wanted to be a gentleman."

"They are beautiful. I'll put them in a different vase. I'm ready to break the one I threw the flash drive in."

"Valiant could probably help."

"Valiant's been great, but I don't know who to trust."

"Does that include me?"

"Unfortunately, yes. You and my brother were the only ones in my condo after I put the drive into the vase."

"That you know of."

"Good point."

"I swear. That drive could have helped."

"At least with them declaring Seth and Marissa a murder-suicide, you're off the hook."

"Except, neither of us believes it was a murder-suicide."

He took me to The Rusty Penguin for dinner. Needless to say, it doesn't serve Penguins, but it did have a well-stocked salad bar. We were given a seat overlooking the Potomac.

"How are you going to introduce me to your NSA friend?"

"He knows I work at the White House. I'll introduce you as a researcher."

"That fits my title."

"Unless you'd like to pretend to be my girlfriend. It might seem more casual if you did."

"And he might open up more. Sure. But just pretend."

"Got it."

"Jerry, about Monica, I don't think John is a good catch. He has White House access, but yesterday at the school, he looked a little drugged out."

"Then, they deserve each other."

"You aren't going to try to win her back?"

"I started thinking about the way she interacts with other guys. Even when I was there, she was flirting. She always had issues with this, that, or the other thing about me. I don't think she was ever into me."

"I'm sorry."

"I'm glad. It took the other night to wake me up. I wonder if I was dating her for the right reasons too."

"Meaning?"

"Her father was influential and she has connections. That wasn't why I told myself I was dating her, but maybe subconsciously, I had the wrong motivations."

"Her father could definitely help your career."

"I need to make it on my own."

It was nice being around a guy with integrity. I hoped it was real and that, when the truth came out, he turned out to be a good guy.

From dinner, we went to Club 21. We sat at the bar. He ordered me a piña colada and himself a black Russian.

"Better watch out. They'll call you a Russiabot."

"At least I'll have a drink to go with the label."

"They're detaining people these days. Remember what they did to those January 6 people and anyone who is known to oppose the President's policies."

I thought about what I had heard about the mass graves and the concentration camps and hoped that was fiction. There was a part of me that didn't want to believe that could be real. After what I'd seen since I'd been at the White House, I was ready to believe anything.

A man, who was dressed down a bit, sat on the stool next to Jerry. He ordered a scotch and soda. As the bartender left, he said, "You look like a light drinker."

"Have to drive my girlfriend home."

"Girlfriend or co-worker?"

"Both. I was thinking of ordering a Blackmoriuntur?"

"I'd stay away from anything with Black in the name."

Everyone was saying that. Images of the dogs at Abu Ghraib kept coming into my head when I would hear the comment.

"I was thinking that it would be a good technical drink."

The bartender sat down the man's drink and went to a customer at the end of the counter.

"Best advice. Stay away."

"Did you hear about Greg Jones? He had wanted to order a North-grail but had accidentally ordered a technical Blackmoriuntur. Gave him quite a shock."

"I bet."

"Why?"

"Those drinks are only for the people with money or power."

"Who would have ordered it?"

"Not a good place to go."

"Maybe you could go there. You look like you hit a lot of bars."

"I'll get back to you. Little lady, if you get bored with this guy, my name is Ray."

"Hi, Ray. I'm happy with Jerry."

"Suit yourself." With that, he got up.

"Is his name really Ray?" I asked.

"It is. I think he likes you."

"Would you like to get going?"

"Sure."

On the way to drop me off, Jerry asked, "Did you pick up on the drift of the conversation?"

"I think so. Black anything is dangerous, no racial implications. Only someone with money or power would have paid for the hit. He'll check into it and get back to you. Let's hope nobody else was listening."

"Ray generally carries a bug detector. He would have cut out if it had gone off."

"Why is he so secretive? You went to college together. It's normal for you to see each other for drinks, isn't it?"

"Maybe he figured I was being watched."

"Did you see anyone looking at us in the bar?"

"Nope, and we took several turns in the wrong directions to get there. If he had seen someone suspicious, he would have left quickly and given me a clue. He may know something about our situation. He didn't buy the girlfriend bit."

As Jerry stopped his car in front of my apartment, he asked if he could call on me the next night.

"If it's work-related. I'm not dating."

"Is it me?"

"I'm really not dating. Personal reasons."

"Your career?"

"No. Look, if you repeat this, I'll deny it."

"You didn't tell anyone about Monday night. I owe you."

"I haven't been vaxxed, and I don't want to get the mRNA via a relationship."

"That's great!"

"I didn't expect that."

"My brother is a doctor. He faked mine."

"Your brother?"

"Dr. Ben Stafford."

"Ben Stafford?"

"You know him?"

"He faked my Cousin Eve's vaccines before she died." Paris had introduced me. In truth, he had only faked mine and my mother's as Paris had simply gotten fake credentials for his immediate family.

"What did she die of?"

"An early heart attack."

"How old was she?"

"Seventeen."

"That's very young for a heart attack. More like what I would expect from the jab."

"She was forced into it for college. I mean, for college admission. Just one and—" Karissa had only had one. Even my online courses required the jab, but Dr. Stafford has actually faked multiple jabs for me.

"There is a long list of heart attacks following it."

"I know. If Monica had the vax, she could have transmitted it to you."

"Our relationship didn't go that far."

"Monica didn't seem like the 'Wait until marriage' kind of girl."

"That's why I wanted our relationship to be different from her other ones. Apparently, that wasn't enough for her."

"Like I said before, I'm not a rebound girl."

"You're definitely not a rebound girl."

He walked around to the passenger door and opened it.

"Would you like me to see you in, check out the apartment?"

"I'll be fine."

I went up to my apartment. Valiant was sitting in front of my door waiting for me.

"I didn't know you knew where I lived."

"I'm a hacker. I can find anyone."

"Have you hacked my email?"

"The employee address list."

At least, he was upfront.

"And what was important enough for you to give up your Friday night to sit and wait in front of my door?"

He held out a box and opened it. Inside was a computer hard drive. "Lee's. I switched it before Duane grabbed the computer. I couldn't find a way to get it out until tonight."

I opened my door. "Okay, come in." He followed me in.

Before closing the door, I heard, "Karissa." It was Jerry.

"Come in. This is not what it appears," I said.

"Oh, it appears that Valiant shanghaied you when you got home?"

"See any drinks in my hand?" Valiant responded. "And you? You're here because?"

"She could use some protection."

"You?" Valiant asked. "You aren't the hero type."

"And what type am I?"

"Boring. Dull."

"Techies are boring and dull by nature."

"Guys. Enough." I closed the door after both guys followed me in. "Have a seat."

"Don't you have to get back to the lab to fix the President?" Jerry asked Valiant. "I mean those pirouettes need some work."

"And don't you have to prepare for your next press conference so you can satisfy the public without telling them anything?"

"Valiant, Jerry, listen." That cut them off, but they glared at each other. "First, I'm not dating anyone and I don't need a competition between two co-workers to elevate my ego. Second, there have been four murders this week and we are the only ones who doubt the official narratives. Well, the only ones outside of the killer."

"Five."

"What?"

"If you include the President, five," Valiant explained.

"The President is a robot. You have to be a person to be murdered," Jerry said.

"Wonderful. Let's say four and a half," I jumped back in. "I'm suggesting we work together to find the answers."

"I don't," Jerry started to say.

"You admitted, yourself, that Valiant might be able to fix the flash drive. And he could help us track down that organization we're looking for."

"And what use is Jerry?" Valiant asked.

"He knows people. You two want to find some answers, don't you?"

"Of course," Jerry said.

"But," Valiant started to say.

"Three of us can get further than one or two. Now shake on it."

CHAPTER 16

Jerry held out his hand. Valiant hesitated and then reached out his.

"Now what about this flash drive?" Valiant asked.

"Have a seat," I said.

As Jerry and Valiant sat down on my couch, I went to my cupboard and took out a bottle of Vitamin Cs. I reached in, pulled out a plastic bag with a messed up flash drive inside and took it over to Valiant.

"This is?"

"A blackmail list, I gather. It was on Lee's computer."

"What happened to it?"

"Waterlogged."

"I'm not going to ask how."

"Good."

"So you think blackmail was the reason?"

"I doubt it. I think it may have had something to do with the story Marissa Tracy was investigating. Whoever killed Marissa, Seth and Greg, likely killed Lee. Valiant, you've been there longer than me. Did Lee have you do anything illegal?"

"Aside from having a robot replace a President and feeding an unconscionable agenda into it?"

"Did he have any connection with Marissa Tracy or Seth Moore?"

"Not that I know of."

"They'd come in for the press briefings and we'd make sure they left afterward. They weren't exactly on our side," Jerry said, rejoining the conversation.

"Valiant, did Lee ever mention anything called Blackmoriuntur?"

"Technology and Secure Services?"

Jerry sat upright and I moved closer and sat on a chair across from where Valiant was sitting. "Go on," I said.

"They had a technician go over the White House computers to install security."

"Did he or she go into the lab?"

"The lab doesn't exist. No contractor has that high of clearance."

"Who put the keylogger on your computer?"

"Maybe Lee?"

"He wasn't a techie."

"But a techie could have told him how. Do you think Blackmoriuntur is behind these murders?"

"They could be the hitmen. One of their techs worked on Greg's computer before it blew up and killed him. Or it could be a Signature Soldier."

"Or Blackmoriuntur Technologies could be part of the Signature Soldier force," Jerry speculated. "They need tech to have the ability to create fake backgrounds."

"We're dealing with the Signature Soldiers?" Valiant asked.

"You know about them too?" It looked as if everyone but me had known about them.

"Jason Bermas did a video on them years ago."

"You watch Jason Bermas?"

"He's not a conspiracy theorist," Valiant pointed out.

"I didn't say he was. I used to watch him."

"Who's Jason Bermas?" Jerry asked.

"He produced, *Loose Change*," I said.

"Loose what?"'

"A documentary about 9/11. He does a lot of videos, most of which have been censored by the new agenda. But that doesn't keep him down."

"Do you have any of the videos?"

"I have *Loose Change.*"

"I'd like to see that."

I went into my room and grabbed a copy that was tucked inside a book. "Bring it back when you're done. It's hard to get copies of this, these days."

"You must have been a baby when 9/11 took place," Jerry said.

"I wasn't born," I said. Neither was the real Karissa and so that was safe for me to say. "Jason didn't stop with *Loose Change.* He's exposed a great many government lies over the years."

"Alright, I'm going to trust you with this," I told Valiant while pointing to the flash drive. "You have a lot of work to do on the President this weekend. Let me know if you find anything suspicious."

"You have been a magnet for trouble," I said to Jerry. "Keep us informed and call us if you even suspect you might need help. Now, I'd like to get some rest."

The two got up and headed to the door. "Great seeing you tonight," Jerry said.

"It's great seeing you every workday," Valiant told me.

"What about the hard drive?" Valiant asked.

"Maybe you could check it out too." I had to be upfront. "Oh Valiant, there is information regarding a certain hack on a file on that flash drive. I think the list is in order of seriousness and that's towards the start where the least serious matters are."

He smiled. "You didn't look surprised at lunch."

"What hack?" Jerry asked.

"Into an ice cream parlor when I was a kid. I was hungry."

"Oh." I think Jerry believed him.

"What if it has information on someone like your brother?" Jerry asked me.

"We'll deal with that when we get to it," I said. "Paris couldn't harm a spider. He picks them up and puts them outside." That wasn't actually true, but I had to stand up for Paris.

The phone rang. It was Paris. My guests paused their exit while I took the phone.

"Gene is going to the lab to check on the President tomorrow. Make sure he's done," I told Valiant.

"Great."

"You need to get the President up to speed ASAP."

"I'll leave the disc and drive here until tomorrow, then."

"I won't put them in a vase."

"Vase?" Valiant asked.

"Never mind. What do you say we all meet back here at 6 P.M. tomorrow?"

"See you then," Jerry said.

"If the President passes inspection. No. He'll pass. See you at 6."

Two people knew my hiding places. I had to pick another. I went into my room and pulled out my bottom drawer and put the disc and flash drive under it, taping them to the bottom. A professional would find them but not some random burglar.

As I went to bed that night, I first pictured how and why Jerry might have been the murderer. Then Valiant. Then Paris. I dismissed those thoughts. I didn't believe it was any of those three. I wondered if they were thinking about me as the murderer. Somebody knew my real identity.

The next day, I went to grab a cup of hot chocolate from Rand's, a coffee shop across the street from a Deathbucks, a known GMO drink counter, so popular that there was one on most street corners. I was joined by Dippy Nowhit, the current Surgeon General and a very large person, who seemed to have trouble clearing the sides of the door while entering.

"So have you decided to have your operation yet?" she asked me. I had been told that "she" was her preferred pronoun.

"Nope. I like being a woman. Apparently, you do too."

"I haven't had the operation, but I've talked a great many children into having it. It allows them to have an open mind."

"I see."

"Wasn't the President wonderful yesterday? He's coming out. I wonder if he'll have the operation soon."

"I wouldn't count on it."

She looked a little fallen. Then she looked stern. "You're only a researcher. When you work with people in the real world, you'll understand the importance of the operation."

"Thanks for the advice. I heard you say you thought he needed a checkup."

"I don't recall that. He might need to check out the talent. I loved his speech about how we all needed to show the selves others don't see. I am so looking forward to the talent show."

"I thought the meeting was supposed to be about appropriations," I noted.

"We did that too. You must have missed that part. We appropriated post-birth abortions of babies up to twenty-five years of age. After all, it's for the good of the country. They could become violent and harm someone."

"But everyone cleared the room before they got into the discussion, didn't they?"

"You must have phased out. I think you should come in for a checkup. I'll do a good job with you."

"But you don't practice medicine."

"I'm better than any of those idiots who treat patients. And maybe after you see me, you'll be eager for that operation."

"I bet I will." *After some drugs and a lobotomy.*

I ordered a couple more cups of hot chocolate to go and took them over to Paris's condo. "Hi, sis. Good to see you."

"Is the place bugged?"

"I've had a blocker installed. I thought you knew that."

"I'm not going crazy, am I?"

"Not as far as I can tell. Maybe a little high from the sugar in these."

"Drink yours and maybe you'll get a little high too."

"What's going on?"

"There was no real Cabinet meeting yesterday was there?"

"It was more like being front row at a musical."

"I just ran into Dippy."

"She's big. I hope she didn't hurt you."

"More like confused me. She claims there was a meeting yesterday and they approved the appropriations for the post-birth abortions."

"It may be those sex hormones she's taking."

"I don't think it was drugs. She really believes it."

"Wishful thinking on her part."

"Didn't it bother you how easily the Secret Service accepted the lie about Lee's death?"

"Once the word came down, we all had to go along with it."

"So maybe it's just politics as usual. Can they go through with the appropriations without a real meeting on the subject?"

"Congress, not the President, is supposed to do appropriations, but nothing is as it should be. The President's backers have access to a lot of funds."

"And Big Pharma has his ear or, rather, bribes."

"The Cabinet meeting is simply a formality these days."

"So what are you going to do for the talent show?"

"Stage manager."

"Cheat."

"You aren't going to see me singing and dancing on stage."

"I've heard you sing. You aren't bad."

"It's a big gap between not bad and good. How about you?"

"Maybe I'll take my knitting needles and start knitting."

"I didn't know you could knit."

"I can't. So it will be a long number. That person who helped you with the records; can they find out if the Signature Soldiers have someone in the White House?"

"He's away on vacation. When I see him, again, I'll ask."

"If there is still a government. There have already been four and a half murders."

That afternoon, I went by a computer store and spoke to Felix. "I want a computer with no tracking."

"You want a computer that doesn't exist. The government requires backdoors into all computers and those backdoors have also been provided to private industry."

"So everyone knows what I type on my computer?"

"Pretty much."

Most government personnel were pretty clueless, so I assumed most didn't know. I wondered if Lee found a way to eliminate his back door. Otherwise, countless people could have that Happy Days list. "So what would it take to get one without the tracking?"

Felix smiled. "Come back here." I followed him into a backroom, where he introduced me to a man named Harvey. "This is where we do our special orders."

"I see. And how do you know you can trust me?"

"You didn't set off any radio wave trackers when you came in."

"Radio wave trackers?"

"The vaccines all have them. People can be identified by information bounced back by the magnetic nanoparticles, which emit and receive radio signals. Of course, the latest vaccines have more informative nanochips."

"And what can those do?"

"What can't they do? But you're clean."

"Everyone is required to have a vaccine."

"Some of them are defective. And there are the saline ones the special people get."

"I see."

"So either you are special, in which case Harvey and I need to eliminate you for knowing too much, or you have managed to avoid the vax."

I didn't respond.

"I say you're cool. And if you're not, my cousin Alfredo will handle you." With that, he smiled. He probably figured that the elites wouldn't be as worried about being tracked since they were in charge of the reset.

"Now, even in the basic Linux system, the government has found a way to track. So we have a more advanced version that also reads files from other systems and eliminates any tracking materials they contain."

"How much?"

"For you? Two thousand dollars."

"That sounds cheap."

"That's because you can be a go-between for us and other trustworthy interested people you may know. We'll even give you commissions."

"I'm not interested in commissions—just a computer. How do I know you aren't one of those putting trackers in while saying you aren't?"

"You don't. But if I'm lying, I'm sure you'll find out soon enough."

Later that day, I brought home a new system. Both Jerry and Valiant were at the door when I arrived. "Nice and timely." Both of them offered to take the box I was carrying. I handed it to Valiant.

"I haven't heard back from that friend yet. It might take him a few days," Jerry said as they followed me inside.

Valiant closed the door behind us. "The President was doing heroic couplets today, but Gene said it was a dramatic improvement that he could sell. If I can't get that eradicated by Monday, he'd have it announced that the President was starting a new educational program to get the kids to read Alexander Pope."

"Isn't *Paradise Lost* a bit too religious for the Administration? The White House prides itself on being anti-religious."

"Gene was distracted. He got a phone call. Something about Sri Lanka."

"The helpless country we bombed," I commented.

"I get the impression that the bombing didn't produce the results they wanted."

"What? Are the dead people contaminating the blue diamonds?"

"Is that why we bombed them?" Jerry asked. "The nukes probably made the diamonds worthless."

"Radioactive diamond dust for sale," I responded.

"Diamonds are used in millions of products but whatever is left of those will likely set off the radiation detectors for centuries," Valiant pointed out.

"I figured out what politics is about. They find the least qualified people in all industries and a puppet to promote their agenda."

"I think you're onto something," Jerry responded to me.

"Valiant, could you check out this system?" I looked at the box. "Supposedly it has no back doors in the chips or programs."

He put the computer down on the table and started going over it with this bug detector. "It has no detectable bugs." He moved around the condo with the detector as we watched. "Nothing. I have a program that closes the backdoors in the chips and makes it invisible on the web. But I'll check it out."

"How come that didn't pick up the keylogger?"

"It was a new type of keylogger embedded in the system. I had to go into the code to find it. Give me a couple of hours and I'll have the code checked out on this one."

"Do you think Lee's disc has spyware on it?"

"I'll run a check on the disc and the flash drive before we use them."

"The strangest thing happened when I spoke with Interior Secretary Ross," Jerry said.

"I didn't realize you had a meeting scheduled for today. I hope this didn't pull you away from anything," I responded.

"We play racquetball at the same court."

"I didn't realize that Press Secretaries had the energy for sports. Of course, racquetball is really mild," Valiant commented.

"And what do techies do? Twiddle toothpicks."

"Krav Maga."

"Israeli Defense Force self-defense. I didn't realize you were in tight with them," Jerry shot back.

"They just created the sport. The guy who teaches at my studio is Syrian."

"Well, if we need a bodyguard, you're it," I said. I turned to Jerry. "So what happened with Ross?"

"He said he was very impressed with how quickly the President pushed through the appropriations at the Cabinet meeting. It's going to be an expedited program."

"I got the same nonsense from the Surgeon General." They looked at me. "I saw her at a coffee shop this morning. I was at that meeting. There was no discussion of appropriations."

"Ross spoke rather matter-of-factly. He wasn't kidding."

"Dippy wasn't either. Something odd is going on." I thought back to Tuesday. "And after Lee was shot, even Trey seemed clear it was a cardiac arrest.'"

"Do they all belong to a liars' club?" Valiant asked.

"Maybe."

"The transcriptionist is working this evening to transcribe yesterday's meeting. She was complaining about it on her way in as I was leaving."

"She could just copy the Barry Manilow lyrics from the Internet," Valiant noted.

"Let's go."

"Not all at once," Jerry suggested.

"We'll drive our cars and take slightly different routes, ten minutes apart. Valiant, you are working on the President. I'm assisting with research for Monday if anyone else asks. I'm going to try to organize more of Lee's files, anyway. Jerry, is there something you need to pick up in the press room?"

"I have a press conference Monday morning before the President's speech. I can review my notes."

"Let's see what we can find out."

When I arrived, Gene was going down to the situation room with the three military chiefs. I asked him, "Would you like me to locate the President?"

"He's already been notified and asked me to handle this."

I went into Lara's office. "I remember what happened, but it doesn't match my notes," she said.

"What do your notes say?"

"'Shadows of a man. A face through a window' and things like that."

"But you remember differently?"

"I remember this magnificent speech about the welfare of the children and their mothers and the threat of unruly brats."

"Was there anything in your notes about tap dancing?"

"Yes."

"Backflips?"

She slumped in her chair. "You know, I wonder if what I remember was all in my mind. I'm starting to remember the tap dancing and flips. And a gold medal for a high jump."

"It's important to get this down, accurately. It will have a major impact on policy."

"You're right. I'm going to just follow my notes. I'm starting to remember it much more clearly. There was nothing about appropriations in my notes. Did he talk about them?"

"You're the best judge. You are always thorough at taking notes. Was it recorded?"

"This one wasn't."

"Then, the only source is your notes."

"I'm going to type them up and send them out."

As I left her office, Paris was rushing down the hall.

"You're here this evening?"

"Blue diamonds," he whispered. "We promised them to Israel and Saudi. We need a solution."

"Bomb Tahiti."

"Don't joke about it. They'll probably do that."

He headed off for the situation room. I went by my office and then down to the lab.

"Now he thinks he's Emily Dickenson," Valiant said.

"We've gotten him to stop the Heroic Couplets, at least," Brandon informed me, coming into the outer lab. "I felt like I was already burning in hell. We'll be continuing to work on him through the weekend."

The President walked from the inner lab into the outer lab room.

"How dreary-to-be-Somebody! How public-like a Frog." Valiant turned him off.

"How much of his personality was gone from the backup?"

"Clearly too much. Part of the problem is that this model had AI in it and it's re-interpreting everything we're feeding in in terms of its vast wealth of knowledge."

"Why does he have so much knowledge? The real President could barely speak English."

"The initial programming on this one was done before I came here. It has defenses against new programming that conflicts with its earlier programming."

"And they just put it in storage that way?"

"They were initially going to send him to China as a novelty butler for the Jade Spring Hill Palace. A reward for their lab work on that virus. Gene thought we needed a backup for the President and sent a robot resembling the VP. I understand they put it in a trash compactor when they couldn't stop its laugh."

"Wait. The Chinese know we have a fake President?"

"The original plans just called for him to be smart and to entertain. Who would ever program a Presidential robot to be demented?"

"We would."

"Right."

"When they sent the VP robot, Gene told the Chinese that they couldn't get the President to sit still long enough to copy his image."

"And they bought it?"

"Probably not. Nothing more I can do tonight. Maybe we can declare Monday to be Emily Dickenson Day."

We went upstairs. In the West Wing, we bumped into Jerry. "Jerry, it's such a surprise to see you here today," I said. "Valiant, do you know Jerry?"

"I've seen him in passing. Never had a chance to speak with him before."

I noticed that John was watching us closely.

"Hey, John, how's your romance going?" Jerry asked.

"I'm told I'm the best."

"You mean she actually got someone to do it with her?" I reacted. "Wow. I hope she's over her hepatitis."

He opened his mouth to speak but Jerry ushered me forward. I looked in on Lara. "I know I got it correct. Don't tell me to stop playing games. I'm not." She was alone but appeared to be speaking to someone who wasn't there. "I'm sticking by my notes." With that, she grabbed a letter opener and stabbed herself above the top of the inside of her right thigh. Blood started gushing out.

CHAPTER 17

"Oh my God!" I reacted, rushing over to her. I took off my jacket to use it to try to stop the bleeding. I didn't touch the opener as removing it or jiggling it could make the bleeding worse.

"I am forgiven," she said as she went fully unconscious.

Jerry and Valiant, apparently overhearing my shriek, rushed in. "She's dead," I murmured, almost in shock.

I called Frank, but he wasn't answering. Jerry listened for a heartbeat and started CPR.

"Won't that make the bleeding worse?" Valiant asked.

Jerry continued. Valiant took over the compressions while Jerry started breathing into Lara's mouth. I rushed out. I asked the Secret Serviceman on duty to call for a medical team fast.

One of the medics who arrived checked her over, looked at me and said, "She was stabbed in her femoral artery. She was probably dead before you started the CPR. Did you see who did it?"

"She did it to herself. I was outside the door when I heard her freak out. Then, she just stabbed herself."

"We'll have to get statements from each of you," John said as he looked in and then walked off.

"Certainly."

Gene came in. "Oh, no!"

"I think she was upset about your reaction to her transcript."

"That's ridiculous. I never saw her report."

"She was muttering about it right before she stabbed herself."

"With her letter opener?" Gene asked, observing the item sticking out through my jacket that was tied around her leg. "Is this her—no it's your jacket, Karissa."

"I tried to stop the bleeding."

"We all tried to help, sir," Jerry said.

"Did any of you touch the letter opener?"

I shook my head and noticed Jerry and Valiant doing the same.

"It will probably be declared a mental breakdown," Gene said.

I suspected a note about prior mental problems would soon appear in Lara's employee file. But she had always seemed sane to me until then.

The EMTs were preparing to lift her onto the gurney. "Do not touch the opener. We'll need fingerprints from forensics—just to prove it was suicide," Gene advised them.

"We know our job," one of the EMTs responded. They put a sheet over her and wheeled her out.

"She has a daughter. One of us should visit her," Gene said.

"I can do that," I said. "I always liked Lara."

Gene pulled out his phone and then scratched out an address on a piece of note paper.

"If you want, I'll go with you. Show her the Administration cares," Valiant said.

"Don't you have more work to do, Rimmel?" Gene asked him.

"Sir, I was just going to dinner. Jack and Brandon are working."

"Grab some food from the kitchen. We need to solve this problem."

"A new robot," He looked at Gene. "Without the security mechanisms against reprogramming might be the easiest solution."

"And how long would that take Jack and Brandon to put together?"

"About two weeks after they get all the necessary supplies. We might be able to fix the primary one about the same time..."

"The press conference is on Monday." He looked at Jerry. "We're talking about a research computer."

He turned back to Valiant. "The President needs the data ready by then. And Friday, he's flying to Mexico City to meet with the President there. He's got to have all the information on the past official relations with Mexico before he leaves." That should have been innocuous enough, such that Jerry wouldn't pick up on it if he didn't already know.

I could tell that Valiant wasn't happy with the assignments.

"It would look caring if a couple of us went to see the daughter," Jerry said. He looked at the blood splattered on our clothes. "If you give me your address, I'll pick you up in an hour. That will give us a chance to change into clean clothes." I knew he said that for Gene's benefit.

I wrote it down on the note paper and handed it to Jerry.

"You need to get a smartphone," Gene encouraged me.

"Let me know if you need anything, Gene. I hope that other problem has been handled."

He looked a little dismal. I had a feeling that money was on the line, given all the bribery that was going on in this Administration.

On the way out, I noticed Felicity's car. She was the Special Assistant to the President—even though she had almost no contact with the President. *She must be in the meeting about the blue diamonds*, I thought.

Lara's daughter Grace lived with her. Grace opened the door. "You're the President's press secretary," she said to Jerry.

"Yes, and this is Karissa, the head of special research."

"Mother had to go to work, today, to do a transcript." There was a nervousness in her voice.

"May we come in?" Jerry asked.

"Sure."

"My mom has spoken about you, Karissa. She said you are one of the nicest people at the White House. You talk to her as if she matters. Everyone else pretty much just barks orders at her. Well, she didn't say that about you, Jerry." I could hear the fear in her voice while she rambled on as if she sensed what was coming.

"I wish I had spoken to her more."

"Something's happened to her."

"She," I couldn't get out the words as I didn't believe them myself.

"She had a bit of a breakdown and stabbed herself with a letter opener," Jerry said.

"Is she in the hospital? Is she going to be alright?"

"I'm afraid not," Jerry said.

I found tears forming in my eyes. "I'm sorry, Grace. She was a great lady."

She stood there, not responding at first. "You said breakdown?"

"She was having some confusion about yesterday's Cabinet meeting and then she remembered what to report on and sent it out. She didn't think it was acceptable, but Gene said he never saw it and I wish I had realized what was going to happen in time to stop it."

"Confusion?"

"Her notes said one thing, but her memory said something else until she remembered her notes were correct."

"It's my fault." She looked almost in shock.

"You weren't there. It had nothing to do with you." I, myself, felt so guilty about encouraging Lara to report the truth. If I hadn't, maybe she'd be alive.

"No. She took the shots for me."

"What?" I asked.

"She didn't want me to get the vaccine, and so she got my vaccines and boosters on top of her own. This last time, she started acting weirdly as if she was hearing things in her head."

"That happened today, right before she—"

"And she was magnetic. And she started emitting radio waves. I couldn't watch TV with her around as it would go haywire when she was in the room."

"The TV would go out?"

"No. It was like it was boosted, and as if there was a voice going on in the background. The voice always sounded like my mother. Maybe I'm the one who's crazy and hearing things."

"But everything was normal when she wasn't in the room?"

"That's right. Please don't turn me in."

"We wouldn't do that. Did you notice anything else?"

"She had a lot of bleeding after she got the vax. But she was past menopause. Sometimes, she would start shaking. And then, at times, it was like she was talking to that voice in her head. Other times, it was like someone was talking to her and ordering her to follow instructions. I'm not an anti-vaxxer. I just didn't trust that one. Please don't make me get it."

"Relax," Jerry said.

"But don't tell anyone else," I said. "The Administration has mandated vaxxes for everyone. You've been through enough. You have your proof of vaccination. Don't tell anyone, otherwise."

'She's right. Don't invalidate it," Jerry said.

"Make sure you hang onto your proof of your jab," I said.

Jerry pulled out a card. "The next time they require you to get a booster, this is a good doctor whom you can trust. He won't do anything you don't want." He winked at her.

I think she picked up on his meaning.

"Thank you." That was when the loss seemed to really hit her and she burst into tears.

"Is there anything I can do? I'm sure you'll want to have a memorial service for your mother."

"My aunt lives in California. I'll see if she can fly in with my—" She was crying so hard, she couldn't finish. I held her for a minute and then she slumped down on her couch.

"If you need anything, here is my phone number." I gave her the number of my burner phone. "It's not on a list and I'd rather it didn't wind up on one."

"I understand."

"Would you like me to get you something to eat or drink?" Jerry asked.

She shook her head.

Before leaving, I hugged her, again. I whispered, "I think you're right about the vax, but it's not your fault. Your mother didn't want this to happen to you. That would have been far worse for a mother."

<hr>

On the way back in the car, I told Jerry, "I'm glad you and Valiant were there. With my jacket on her, they could have claimed I stabbed her. John wouldn't have supported me."

"We could all look like suspects in one or more of these—" He paused. "Events. I almost touched the letter opener, myself."

"When I saw Lara before, she was giving me the same story as Dippy and as Ross gave you. I got her to follow her notes. It's my fault."

"No. It's not. You didn't put the voices into her head."

"You think someone hypnotized them?" I asked.

"It's not that easy to hypnotize people."

"You don't buy Grace's vax theory, do you?"

"I know that the vaccines increase the odds of death and that some people are more magnetic after those nanoparticles are injected into them. A lot of experts have predicted that they will cause serious conditions leading to an early death if not outright kill the recipients."

"Maybe whatever was in them finally drove Lara crazy. It wouldn't take much to make Dippy crazy."

"I always thought Ross was solid," Jerry remarked.

"If we think too hard, our imagination will drive us crazy."

<hr>

Valiant was waiting for us when Jerry and I got back to my place. "I'm on a break. I think Gene expects me to sleep at the lab."

Inside, he went back to work on the computer. "Do you have any idea what Felicity's special assignment is?" Jerry asked.

"She is one of the people who oversees my Department. She, Gene, and Paris all know what we are doing. And now, you, Jerry. She has more duties, but I don't have clearance to know about them. I think her goal is to make sure the Administration follows whatever agenda someone has selected for it. Why do you ask?"

"She was there today."

"I saw her car too. Maybe she's invested in blue diamonds," Valiant said.

"She's a real piece of work," Jerry said.

"Do you think the vax could cause someone to hear voices and kill themselves?" I inquired of Valiant.

"Wouldn't be surprised."

"You've been vaxxed, haven't you?" Jerry asked him.

"I had to present proof in order to work at the White House."

"Cagey answer," Jerry said. "I'm an expert at those."

Valiant looked at me. "You two join the vax squad?"

"I didn't turn you in for what happened at the school."

"I'm a hacker. Take from that what you want."

"You're that good?"

"Remember where I've hacked into. The other day was a piece of cake."

"What about Brandon and Jack?"

"They aren't magnetic. I recommended them for the job."

"What about the old team that was there before you came?"

"They left."

"Do you have their information? Who they are?" I asked. Somehow, as the sub-department didn't exist, their personal profiles and information weren't on anything I had seen.

"I may have it on my old contact list. They weren't too personable. And they weren't that skilled. Hence the original programming disaster."

"You working tomorrow?"

"Probably."

"But not all day?"

"What are you getting at?"

"Well, we need some information with regard to the original team members. Maybe we can come up with an excuse to see them. Tell Gene, China complained about their special butler."

He ran through some programs on the computer. "The system should be OK now. Let's see that hard drive."

I retrieved it and gave it to Valiant. He inserted it in an external case and started reading the information after doing what looked like some kind of security bypass. "A lot of financial stuff on here."

"I wonder if it matches the paper records."

"It's not clear what the amounts were paid for, to, or from. Here's a file called credit. It lists some smaller amounts."

"Maybe, those are the personal bribes."

"So Dynozap actually offered you money to get the President to threaten North Korea?" Jerry asked.

"I wonder how he knew I would be influential when I had just walked in the door for my new position."

"Maybe the secondary title for your office is the bribe office," Jerry said.

"Maybe. At least, the military isn't ready to bomb North Korea."

"They've been depleting all the thinking people from the military. Vax requirements. I wouldn't count on the military acting in a sane way for long. This is odd."

"What?"

"This file is doubly encrypted."

"The Happy Days file just had initials. You couldn't be sure of whom the subjects were unless you watched the videos."

"He couldn't have video in our lab."

"Of the computer action via the internet link I think."

"That would have been easy with a key logger."

"What is this?" Jerry asked, apparently trying to make sense of our discussion.

"Not that important." I wasn't going to out Valiant.

"This will take me a little while to figure out," Valiant said.

"You say you copied the Happy Days file onto the flash drive and then erased it?"

"That's right. It's just blackmail information. I don't really want to get a bunch of people in trouble."

"What if one of them killed Lee?" Valiant asked.

"But they wouldn't have killed the reporters over what I saw on the list, I don't think."

I thought about the Chief of Staff. But I hadn't looked at the video. Those were just initials. It could be someone else.

"I've got to get back to the lab. We'll have to do more of this tomorrow." He detached the hard drive and handed it to me. I went to put it back in my hiding place. As I returned, Valiant informed me, "I've copied it onto the computer. To get into the file requires a special password: the name of a Massacre in 1920."

"Does he really expect you to sleep there?"

"Not sleep."

"Well, get some anyway."

"I'll do my best."

After he left, Jerry said, "I'll go too. Let you get some sleep tonight."

"Thank you for helping. It's not part of your job duties."

"Five people and a robot have died. I don't want to be next."

"Ditto. If the vaxxes are killing people, we may be the safest people on the staff."

"Except for the saline recipients."

The next day, Valiant managed to find the addresses of the old team by a method he didn't reveal. Valiant and I went to the first address on his list: Cenk Lugan. We had addresses for Cenk Lugan and Kyle Kinsky. We didn't yet have an address for Sam Seber, the third team member. An elderly woman answered the door.

"We're looking for Cenk. I used to work with him," Valiant said.

"You didn't know?"

"Know what?"

"My son died quite some time ago."

"That's terrible," Valiant said. "What happened?"

"Come in." She offered us some lemonade. "He always loved that job. A few months after the Inauguration, he was notified they would have to wrap up things as the White House would be terminating the project."

"It wasn't working. It did have promise."

"That's what he said. He was very unhappy about that."

"If it's not too upsetting, what happened to him?"

"When the project wrapped up, he and Sam were on their way to an event to celebrate the work they had done, and a truck rammed into their car. Cut both of them in half."

"I'm so sorry," I said.

"Did you work with Cenk too?"

"No. But I always heard such good things about him."

"I've been asked to document the work on the project. Some future projects can learn from what went wrong. Did Cenk keep any notes?" Valiant asked.

"I got rid of Cenk's things. Most people want to hang onto the belongings of their deceased loved ones, but for me, it was too painful."

"Do you know who got his notebooks?"

"I think those were thrown out. They weren't of any use to anyone and I was afraid they had confidential information."

"Maybe Sam's family will still have something."

"He lived alone and he didn't have any family. I doubt his landlord hung onto anything."

"I'm so sorry that we are bringing back memories," I said. "I've lost people I care about and it's awful."

"It is."

"Is that a picture of your son?"

"It's the one reminder I've kept."

"He was very nice looking."

"Mrs. Lugan, I hope I didn't cause you any suffering with my questions," Valiant said, as I went over to the photograph, slipped a small camera out of my pocket and took a picture. That wasn't Valiant's usual way of speaking and I sensed he was trying to distract her.

"It's actually nice to see a friend of his. It reminds me of how special he was."

"He was very special. It was such an honor to work with him and learn with him."

I came back to the chair on which I had been sitting.

"We've taken up enough of your time," Valiant said.

"Thank you so much," I said. "He was someone I really wanted to meet. But at least, I've learned what a wonderful person he was—from you and from Valiant."

In the car, Valiant said, "Well, two down. I remembered they didn't want the old team to know the project had continued and came up with that cover story. But I don't remember about the celebration. If there was one, I missed it."

At Kyle Kinsky's place, we spoke with his wife. "My husband committed suicide."

"What? Oh, that's terrible," I said. "Computer work can be very stressful." It may have been a dumb comment, but I was a bit flustered with all three dead. It seemed more than a coincidence.

"It wasn't that. There was something that was bothering him. Something he couldn't talk about."

"Well, he was a hero on our project," Valiant said. "Whenever someone couldn't get something done, he was always the one who came in with the answer."

"That's nice to hear."

"Did he leave any notes, records? We could use some of his inspiration on a current project."

"Whatever he did led to his death. I hope the project fails."

"It's not just that," I said, preparing myself to lie. "There is talk about a medal of honor, which I guess will be given to him, posthumously. It would help to have his notes or research so we can show what a genius he was. The project failed, anyway, as nothing could save it."

"I have a box of his things."

She went into a back room. "Good save," Valiant whispered to me.

"Let's hope there is something useful," I whispered back.

She came out with a shoebox. It had a set of keys with a flash drive attached, a cardholder with some business cards, a key card, an autographed baseball from some league and a rabbit's foot. I was looking at the rabbit's foot, feeling sorry for the rabbit, when Valiant almost went white, which was relatively noticeable on Valiant's olive complexion. I followed his gaze to Mrs. Kinsky and the gun in her hand.

CHAPTER 18

"Kyle always said someone might come here looking for his stuff and that it would be someone bad, who would try to kill me."

"You have us wrong," I said, moving away from Valiant as the gun followed me. "We're on his side. If someone wanted him or you dead, we want to know who. A lot of people have died in the last week and we think it may have something to do with," The gun went off as the baseball Valiant threw hit her hand knocking the barrel towards the floor. A second later, Valiant was on top of her, holding her down and the gun out to the side. He took the gun and tossed it partway across the room.

"We really are good guys, and I swear we won't hurt you. But someone is killing people, and if they find out you talked, they might kill you. So I'd forget we came here."

Valiant pulled Mrs. Kinsky up and took her to a chair. I kicked the gun under the couch. We left with the box.

"What was that all about?" I asked.

"She could have been one of those crazy vaxxed people or maybe Kyle found out something he shouldn't have known."

"We need a neutral place to take this stuff. Any suggestions?"

"My uncle has a place across the Potomac. He thought about selling it but decided to just hang onto it after the economic downturn for most potential buyers in 2020. He didn't want to deal with the rent moratoriums and figured he'd just wait as property will soon be the new cash."

"Where does he live now?"

"Texas."

"People there are a little smarter these days. That's something, I never would have said as a child."

"I'm going to take a round-about route there." As we passed by the Capitol Mall, Valiant said, "We've got a tail."

"What do we do?"

"Lose him."

Valiant was switching lanes. In the passenger side mirror, I could see our shadow making the same maneuvers.

Valiant cut around several corners and took us back towards Maryland, cutting onto Bladensburg Road. That's when shots rang out. The rear window shattered. Valiant cut onto Interstate 50 on the wrong side of the highway, dodging oncoming traffic, as another shot went through the missing back window, almost hitting Valiant's head and continuing through the front windshield.

CHAPTER 19

"Get down," Valiant insisted. He had almost been killed but was more worried about me.

"Hope, your insurance covers this."

"It's not my car."

"Hope, whoever owns it is covered?"

"I was renting it from a private person to buy. I've got a feeling I'm going to pay for the car."

We were approaching the bridge over the Anacostia River. "There's a plastic bag in the glove compartment. Take it out and put the box into it. Put your flip phone and mine into the bag as well and seal it."

"You're not going to—" I started to say as I followed his instructions. He remotely rolled down my window. "Maybe, you've been watching too many movies."

"These guys mean business."

As another shot was fired, he again urged, "Keep your head low." I noticed he was keeping his head down as well, just barely looking over the dash. At least, the headrests made us less visible from behind but one of the bullets had gone through his headrest.

"Perfect," he said. "A low-rider 1950 Chevy Fleetline." A car ahead had apparently seen us and spun around, facing away from us in the lane next to the edge of the bridge. It was one of those old 50s cars with a back that slanted all the way down to the bumper. We were coming up too fast on it. I braced for impact.

"You're crazy, you know," I said as calmly as I could while our car somehow mounted the back of the other car.

"I've been told that. Hold on very tight and unbuckle your seatbelt," he said as he spun the car off the top of the Fleetline and over the side of the bridge.

His maneuver sent me up, causing me to hit the roof. I braced myself with my arm. "Hold onto the bag," Valiant yelled as he pushed me out through the open window and followed me out. I was dazed as we hit the water and went down, but the cold brought back my swimming skills. A few seconds later, he was at my side guiding me up to the surface. I suddenly realized I had let go of the plastic bag. I wasn't sure if the contents would be secure enough for long in the cold temperature for us to retrieve them.

"The bag."

"I've got it."

He assisted me over to the side. I looked back at the bridge. I couldn't see anyone looking over it. I did hear sirens, though. He helped me along the shore to the Arboretum. He took some wet cash out of his wallet and we were let inside.

"Proof of vax?"

"Seriously?" He pulled out his White House card from his wallet. "Official business."

The clerk didn't take the time to read it but let us through. "Remember the six foot rule," she said as we walked inside. We must have been a silly sight, half soaked. We just walked on as if nothing was unusual.

"Why not a mile?" I muttered, facetiously, under my breath.

"It's a good thing you don't carry a purse," he said. "One more thing to grab in an emergency."

"I imagine everything in my wallet is soaked." I didn't want to pull it out of my pocket to see the disaster. "You know, there are cameras here."

"We're just two slightly wet people wandering around on an afternoon through the National Arboretum."

"What happens when they notify your friend that his car went off the bridge?"

"He's out of the country."

"Convenient."

"Very."

"You know they have facial recognition cameras all over D.C. They might recognize us from all the facial ID cameras on the highway."

He looked at me.

"Right. Hackers advantage."

"You didn't freak."

"I was too scared."

"Most girls would have been screaming."

"That's a sexist stereotype. How many girls have you done this with?"

"You're the first. What I meant is, you liked it."

"What? Ha!"

"You liked it. You can live your nice quiet life, but part of you craves adventure."

"I just like staying alive." I did feel rather exhilarated, but I wasn't going to tell him that.

He made a purchase in a gift shop and put the plastic bag with Kyle's paraphernalia into it.

On the way out of the park, Valiant told someone that our friends couldn't pick us up and bummed a ride from them to three blocks from my apartment. We walked the rest of the way.

As we arrived back at my place, laughing about how the day had gone, we found Jerry waiting outside my door.

"Maybe, I should just give you two guys a key."

"What happened to you two?"

"We just decided to go for a swim," Valiant said.

"After someone shot at us."

"Are you alright?" Jerry asked, seemingly very worried.

"Yeh. But somebody doesn't want us to find or know something about the former techs," I said as we went into my apartment. Jerry closed the door. Valiant pulled the plastic bag out of the Arboretum bag.

"How was the Arboretum?"

"A real adventure," I said.

"I'll remember that. When I take you there, I'll keep you dry."

"I think she's all Arboretumed out for a while," Valiant said. "I have to get back to the White House before Gene fires me."

"You'll need a ride," I said.

"I can give you one," Jerry offered.

"You sure, you'll be safe here alone? " Valiant asked.

"Here," Jerry said, pulling out a gun.

"Jerry?"

"After five and a half murders, I decided some protection would be a good idea. If anyone comes through that door before I get back—"

"Shoot first and then attend the manager's funeral," I quipped. "Good luck with the President."

"Blue diamonds?" Jerry asked.

"Sri Lanka was last week," Valiant said. "Another week, another war."

"Doesn't sound good," Jerry said.

"I guess I need to study Emily Dickenson so I can understand the President's speech," I noted.

"I understand from Jack, he's moved on to Charles Dickens," Valiant said.

"Bouncing around in literary history," I said. "Maybe they could have him teach British Lit."

"So all three of those past techies are dead?" Jerry asked.

"Apparently so. And the wife of one of them tried to shoot us," I replied.

"I guess the President isn't the only one who's demented. What do you think they knew?"

"Lara was just doing a transcript of a Cabinet meeting."

"Maybe, we should quit our jobs and go to the Bahamas to enjoy life," Jerry said.

"Former workers don't seem to have good longevity." I pulled out the computer and the disk. "What do you think 'Hemlock' is about?" I asked opening a file.

"Poison. That's all that comes up for me." Jerry said.

"It looks like a time displacement program. Is Duane's group into time travel?" I asked Valiant.

"I don't want to go there," Jerry said.

"I know. The thought that they could erase history, erase us, is a little freaky."

"It looks like they called it a failure. Look at the write-up. All they could do was some minor changes, like moving items, minor reality shifts. The major efforts were unsuccessful. So that couldn't be so serious," Valiant said.

"Unless the changes made everyone forget some major event," Jerry said.

"Rose pedals." I had gone on to a new file. "Holy."

"You know how Obama authorized the assassination of even American citizens over a decade ago?"

"Yeh. Look at this list. These are all people who suddenly died and not from government mandated injections: Gary Webb, Martin Burns, Michael Ruppert and Seth Rich are on the list."

"What was Lee doing with that?" Jerry asked.

"He also supervised Duane's Hushpuppies sub-department," Valliant pointed out.

"Maybe, he got fed up with the killing," I said.

"Lee?" Valiant asked.

"Maybe, a fight among criminals," I suggested.

Valiant looked at the time. "If I don't get back there, Gene may have my job."

"You kidding? You're the most essential person in the Department."

"No, I'm not," Valiant said. "Second most important."

Jerry shook his head and then added, "He's right about that."

After dropping him off, Jerry came back. "You wouldn't believe what I may have to explain away in tomorrow's press conference. My stock answer will be, 'The President will address this in his speech.'"

"We're working for a kakistocracy, a government run by the worst and least qualified people."

"For sure." He paused. "I think Valiant has more than a few screws loose."

"What? Why? He's always seemed more awake and aware than the vast majority of workers at the White House."

"There had to be a better way of evading that car than driving off a bridge."

"He tried. They were shooting at us. He even drove on the wrong side of the highway."

"That was crazy."

"We survived with the box."

"You don't have a problem with his actions?"

"No. Actually, it was kind of fun. I guess I'm an excitement freak."

"Five and a half murders aren't exciting enough for you?"

"Those are tragic. Sad. Excitement is like a roller coaster."

"Generally, roller coasters stay on the rails."

I didn't say anything.

"You're in the wrong part of government. The CIA is your calling."

"I hear that's more boring than it's hyped to be."

"Before we left, you were looking at some kind of hit list."

"There were official explanations for all those deaths on the list."

"Just like the ones here."

"Was Lee collecting it for investigation purposes or was he part of it?"

"What do you think?" Jerry asked.

"I was surprised about the bribes. I'm not making any guesses about Lee's other activities."

"The deaths we've seen were all explained too. Maybe if Lee had lived, they'd be on the list."

"You think Duane is behind this? Valiant is suspicious of him."

"Valiant is suspicious of me."

"No. He's not. He thinks you're a square."

"Is that what you think?"

"No. I think you're a really great guy."

"But not exciting."

"I didn't say that. This last week, there hasn't been a moment of boredom. I really enjoy your company. Until today, I thought Valiant would be boring outside of a computer lab and it was a pleasant surprise."

"That's the first time I've heard someone categorize almost drowning as pleasant."

"We've all got different aspects to our personalities. There are times when I'm a square. It wasn't until today that I realized how boring my life has been." An interesting feeling, given that I had a fake identity and was managing a robotic President. "I am more impressed with niceness and awakeness, like not getting vaxxed."

"It's not easy to find someone who hasn't been vaxxed. We need to stick together."

"Agreed." I looked back at the files. "There are a lot of lists, here, but it's hard to know what is what. When I saw the Happy Days file, I thought it was about blackmail. It's more widespread than that."

"Maybe Lee leaked the information and the recipients are being killed one by one."

"But what about the prior techs?"

"Maybe the key is to find out what happened to the real President. Argue it could help with the programming."

"Let's hope Valiant doesn't fully fix the President tonight. We can argue we need the real one to fix it."

"How about dinner?"

"What would you like?"

"To take you out somewhere."

"Sure."

"How about the Mumbai Club?"

"Sure."

I put the disk, flash drive and items from Kyle's home into a large purse and we took off. I hadn't eaten Indian food and it was a bit hotter than I expected, but it wasn't bad. As we were leaving and walking to Jerry's car, I felt a tug on my purse. Before I realized what was happening, it was gone. Jerry chased the teenage thief down the street. The teen ran into an alley and Jerry followed with me behind. Jerry managed to snag the purse as he grabbed the thief by the arm. "Who got you to steal this?"

"Nobody. I steal purses."

"That's a terrible way to earn a living," Jerry said.

Jerry handed it to me. As he did, someone stepped out of a doorway and hit Jerry over the head. The person was masked. The masked person, who was either afraid of COVID or wanted to hide his identity, pointed a gun at me. "I'll take that."

CHAPTER 20

"Be my guest," I said. "As long as you stop pointing that gun at me."

He moved the gun down a little and I handed him the purse.

"Take my advice. Be a good little girl and don't stick your nose where it doesn't belong."

The voice sounded familiar but I couldn't place it or whether I knew the person. It was heavily accented. The person left the alley, again, pointing the gun at us. "Don't follow."

I reached down and helped Jerry up.

"Did he get your purse?"

"It wasn't worth my life."

"Sorry."

"The purse is the least of my concerns. You should get checked for a possible concussion."

"My head is hard."

"Seriously. I got you into this latest bit. I don't want to worry about your head for the rest of my life."

"That's a pleasant thought. You worrying about me."

We walked back to the car. "Let's check under the back seat," I suggested.

He lifted it up. The disk, drive and other items were still there.

"I wonder how long it will take me to get a new passport and driver's license."

"I don't know about the license, but I'll ask Ross to expedite the passport tomorrow."

"I guess it helps to have friends in low places."

We arrived back at my apartment. When I unlocked the door, I noticed it was ransacked. "I could call the police, but I'm willing to bet he didn't leave any fingerprints."

"He might have planted something."

With that thought in mind, I decided to report both the robbery and burglary. D. C. had stopped making house calls for crimes against civilians, but they did take a report over the phone. "No sir, I don't know of anything missing from my apartment yet. But I haven't made a full search. I will," I said, taking down the officer's information and report number.

"Nice, how they have officers for jab and mask duty but not for burglaries and robberies," Jerry remarked.

"I can use the report number for getting a new passport."

"I'll give it to Ross when I see him tomorrow."

"You're not going to tell him we—"

He had picked up my habit of interrupting. "I'll tell him it was just dinner in exchange for research you had done for a press conference."

"That will work."

"I don't think you should be alone here tonight."

"I really don't need—"

"It's not a come-on. I'm worried about you. When he finds out the items aren't in your purse, he may come back here. Or do you just want to watch the door all night with the gun?"

"I don't feel safe leaving these things here during the day tomorrow."

"I know a safe place where we can leave them until after work."

Jerry took the living room couch, and I got a good night's sleep in the bedroom. Despite my protestation, I felt good about having someone to watch out for me. Still, I was worried about Jerry at the same time. He was a Press Secretary, not a super spy.

***

Monday morning, I went with Jerry to his brother's office on the way to his place. I waited in the car while, he changed for work and arranged for his brother to protect the computer, disks and other items.

"He put them in a safe. I told him they were for a novel I was writing."

***

In the lab, I asked Valiant what kind of shape the President was in.

"I'm a miracle worker, like Scotty."

"Could you be less of one? It might get us more answers."

He smiled. "His speech is in an hour. You never know if he'll have a relapse."

An hour later, I left the lab with the President. Trey, John and several other Secret Service Agents met us upstairs and accompanied the Presidential limousines with the President and the First Lady in the second car to the Capitol, where he was going to give a speech about our war policy.

First Lady Lill was looking prim and proper as she walked up to the President right before leaving. "We ready?"

"It's time," Gene said.

She lifted the President's arm and put his hand on her back as if he were assisting her, though it was looking as if she was guiding him. "You better not fall on me Moe," she said to him in a voice that was light enough that only those of us close could hear it. "At least your breath doesn't smell like it used to."

They moved out to the limos. Jerry, Gene and I were in the back limo. At the Capitol, the First Couple stepped outside the limo together. While Trey and Gene escorted the President, John escorted the First Lady.

It was a joint session. Gene escorted the President to the podium as everyone stood and applauded. The Vice President, wearing a red dress, and the Speaker of the House were sitting behind where the President stood. Jerry came and stood next to me at the back of the balcony.

"Nice press conference this morning. You didn't say anything," I commented.

"That's the sign of a good press conference. Say nothing and make it look like you cooperated fully."

"Ladies and gentlemen and others in Congress and the Cabinet, I am here to tell you that this is a state of war. Not only are we at war with invisible diseases, but we are at war with our friends or former friends."

"So much with him going demented again," I whispered.

"That sounds pretty demented to me, but not in the way you mean," he whispered back.

"As I always say, 'To be or not to be. That is the question,'" the President continued.

The Vice President coughed.

"We were at war with Sri Lanka last week and we won that war. Sri Lanka sounds like a peaceful place but 'What's in a name?' 'That which we call a rose by any other name would smell so sweet.' Sri Lanka 'Doff thy name.' We know your real name is terrorist."

"They never made war on anyone," I whispered to Jerry.

"But now, we have a new terrorist," the President said. "The Ides of March are upon us."

"It's July," Jerry whispered.

"Now, while some say, 'The quantity of mercy is not strained,' I say we have been too merciful. Mercy may fall as the gentle rain from heaven but we will not allow mercy to get in the way of our plan to drive the world to its knees."

"Oops. That doesn't sound good," Jerry said. I could see a little concern among some of the members of Congress as others stood and applauded.

"The wrong half of Congress is applauding," I noted.

"No. Now our half is standing and applauding with them. They all want war," Jerry whispered.

"We will not take any more assaults on our liberties. What is an American? 'If you prick us, do we not bleed? If you tickle us, do we not laugh? If you poison us, do we not die? And if you wrong us, shall we not revenge?'"

"He does remind me a bit of Shylock," Jerry whispered.

"We will not let our enemies destroy us without responding. And so to protect us from the next avenging country, we shall declare war on Kiribati."

"Kiribati?" I asked Jerry. "Do they have blue diamonds too?"

"White diamonds. I think he's planning a non-nuclear option for them." He looked at his smartphone, which he had apparently brought from the Capitol today. "Oh boy, two of the networks are saying the President has lost it."

"They don't like Shakespeare?" I asked.

"One journalist pointed out that Kiribati doesn't even have a national security force."

At that moment, the Capitol started shaking. "We will not let them bring us down. And who will bring me my horse? 'A horse! A horse!'" But the rest of his speech was inaudible as Senators and Congressmen started rushing for the door while the podium fell forward and the room shook like it was going to fall apart.

CHAPTER 21

The Secret Service rushed the President out. The shaking got worse. There was no easy way through the crowd scurrying from the balcony. I felt the rushing spectators pushing us towards the door through which we had entered and then towards the stairs. I saw people falling on the stairs and getting stepped on. I tried to reach down to help someone up but was pushed forward by an uncaring crowd. I would have fallen, myself, but for Jerry's grip on my arm.

"Maybe Kiribati has a better defense system than we knew about," I said to Jerry as several people almost knocked us down as they bolted by.

"Shouldn't we stand in a doorway?" Jerry asked, holding my hand.

"My number one goal is to not get trampled," I said as I continued to move with the crowd. "Standing in a doorway will get us flattened."

Behind us, I could hear loud noises as something was crashing down.

"This is supposed to be built to withstand an earthquake," Jerry said.

"Since when do we have earthquakes in D.C.? An earthquake is an act of God. So, maybe this is God's defense of Kiribati."

As the invited guests pushed, I heard screams as windows cracked and heavy items fell on the crowd. There was no moving in the direction of any screams as the wall-to-wall mob pushed and shoved to get out of the place. I kept wishing I could help those in danger.

"Now we see how brave, nice and orderly our leaders are during an emergency. We are surrounded by lobbyists and Congressional staffers who are killing each other."

"We should send them off to the next war," Jerry said, gripping me tightly so we didn't get separated.

Somehow, we managed to stay upright as we got outside. The Presidential limos had already left. "I guess we're walking," Jerry said.

I noticed breaks in the stone steps. "Careful," I warned him.

"This exciting enough for you?"

"This shouldn't be happening."

We managed to make it back to the White House. I looked around the West Wing as we entered. "Isn't it odd?"

"What?"

"All that damage in the Capitol and nothing, not even precarious glass vases have fallen here in the West Wing."

"I see that."

I went down into the basement.

"Any deaths or injuries?"

"They aren't saying."

"I know people got trampled. There was nothing I could do."

"You were in a house of vampires. You're lucky you weren't eaten," Valiant said.

"Good work with the speech, but he still managed to get out a declaration of war against Kiribati."

"At least, he didn't get to the mandatory euthanasia for under twenty-fives."

"Mandatory?"

"I intercepted a note this morning that the pharmaceutical company making the chemicals had demanded it. I was about to print up new birth certificates for everyone in the Department."

"Wonderful. Glad the country's in such good hands. But Kiribati," I lamented.

"I know. Gene demanded. I was hoping they'd declare the President incompetent before he got to that part. You should have seen the news reports, right before the earthquake."

He flipped through the news sites on the computer.

"Don't you have to pay to watch the approved news?"

"The White House is all paid up for the MSM. But for the public, the most economical options are the unauthorized and banned news services."

"As the government is finding excuses to execute anyone publishing the truth," I noted.

"He didn't make it through Richard the Third's speech," Brandon lamented as he came into the room. "That was the best part."

"Too bad he didn't trade off the country to someone sane for a horse," I said. "Wait. I meant good thing he didn't."

Valiant smiled.

After Brandon left the outer lab, I told Valiant, "Last night, someone stole my purse at gunpoint."

"Last night? Are you okay?"

"I'm fine. He got some personal items like my driver's license and passport and a copy of my vax passport, but it's uploaded online."

"So you have one."

"The proof? Yeh. Don't you?" I smiled and rolled my eyes up.

"Of course. Like I said, they checked when I came to work here." He winked at that. "How's Jerry?"

"Learning to live dangerously. If you two weren't haggling so much, I think you'd be great friends. You have a lot in common."

"With Mr. Boring?"

"He is not boring, just like you are so much more than a techie. Not that being a techie is bad."

"I gather it wasn't a random thief."

"Someone has me pegged, and the voice sounded familiar, like someone I had heard before, but not quite."

"I'm surprised the news stations dared say anything against the President," Jack said, coming into the room with Brandon.

"Their little act of rebellion didn't last long," Brandon chimed in. "The censors have closed down all the 'Russia-speak' criticizing him."

At that point, Gene brought the President down to the lab.

"Congress gave him a standing ovation," I pointed out.

"I saw that. He almost traded the country for—"

"He kept switching plays. He probably would have switched before the end of that sentence," I said.

"Still, I don't want any more close calls."

"At least, he wasn't singing and swinging from the chandeliers," I commented.

Gene didn't look consoled.

"I'll get the boys to continue working on him. Do you know where we can track down the old tech crew, the one that originally programmed him?"

Gene looked bothered by the question. I wondered if he knew about their demise. "I don't think they can help you. I'd forget that approach."

"If you feel it's not the way," I said. "I thought he made his point about Kiribati. Terrible country."

"You don't need to patronize me. We all know they aren't a threat."

"But the public is probably wondering if they caused the earthquake."

"Brilliant. I'll have Jerry work that into his next press conference."

I almost threw my hands up on my head. I wasn't expecting to have an influence on policy.

As Gene left, Valiant partially shut down the President and Brandon walked him into the back lab.

"It could have been worse. He could have decided to invade Virginia," I said.

"He already has. Have you seen all the military there? I'm not gung ho on Virginia, but all the military guns and tanks are starting to get to me," Valiant remarked.

"He wants to maintain the military vote," Jack remarked.

"Mandatory poisoning isn't the way to keep the troops happy," Valiant noted.

"True. And enough of them are having sudden deaths that he'll need the support of the ones still capable of handing their blank ballots over to a bundler before collapsing," I responded.

"Is he really going to go for re-election? He could cut the risk of exposure by turning things over to the VP now. She'd get nine years," Valiant noted.

"Particularly if she slept with all the male voters," Jack said.

"She'd lose the female vote," I said.

"She'd have to sleep with them too."

"Don't suggest it. Gene might put that into the plan," I commented.

Valiant turned on some of the mainstream propaganda as Jack left to work on the President in the back lab. From the approved news, we learned that most of D.C. had been damaged, partially or wholly by the earthquake. However, we were in the earthquake-free zone at the other end of Capitol Mall that just included the White House."

"What condition do you think your apartment is in?"

"Don't know. I was more worried about another location," I told him.

"I guess we'll find out after work."

After work, the first thing that happened was our discovery of a blockade on every street as Valiant gave me a ride. They were checking who was coming and going and their reason for being on the streets. "I hope Jerry doesn't have any trouble with where he is going," I said.

"We have to get out of D.C. The electricity is down, according to the news. Well, not in the White House. All the generators and backup generators at the hospitals are down."

"More mass deaths. COVID, right?"

"It'll be the unvaccinated who caused the quake. Just watch," Valiant said.

"Well, that will let Kiribati off the hook."

"The unvaccinated working with Kiribati."

We were stopped on the bridge, heading towards Alexandria. "We're going to dinner. D.C. is a mess. We'll be back later," Valiant told the armed National Guardsmen there.

"I don't think it will be fixed that soon," one of them said.

"The seat of government? It better be up quickly," Valiant played the indignant elitist.

As we went over the bridge, I said, "This is a much nicer car. I hope it stays dry."

"It is nice having a backup."

"Guess you'll have to be more careful robbing liquor stores."

He turned to me and smiled.

"Your sense of humor is not that different from Jerry's. Give him a chance," I said.

"I'll have to fix that. I don't want to sound ordinary, boring."

"Ha! You know that isn't what I meant."

"Well, I'm not gay. So don't try to match me up with him."

"And I assumed you were. I mean playing with dolls all day. And boy dolls at that."

"Want to go into the river again?"

Valiant took me to a dress shop. "It's best if you don't go back to your place tonight. This is on me."

"I can pay for my own stuff."

"Is Jerry bringing the computer?"

"If everything is where he dropped it off."

"The more laptops we have, the harder it is to trace."

"Planning some hacking?"

He gave me a look that said, "Yes."

"What about food?"

"I'm cooking tonight."

He and Jerry did have a lot in common.

Valiant's uncle's place was maybe about five thousand square feet and surrounded by trees.

"Nice and secluded," Valiant said.

"And if they come after us, our demise might go unnoticed," I commented. "Is there a security system?"

"The best. This is my backup home."

"Just like your backup car?"

"This one is not expendable."

The house was furnished with antique furniture. It was homey and yet expansive, like a country ranch house. It opened onto a small lake.

"Wait here," Valiant said. He went outside. He came back with an armload of avocadoes and a watermelon.

"Watermelons in Virginia?"

"Why not? We've had a warm spell. And my uncle has a greenhouse, which is high enough for the avocado trees. Blocks the chem trails and it can be heated during the winter. You do know for avocados, you need two."

"Right, a male and a female."

"Just like with people."

"You work for me. I'm not going there. The last thing I need is a complaint for sexual harassment."

"You serious? I'm the one who is interested in you. Hopefully, it's not just one-sided."

"How about we get to dinner?"

"I've noticed you like avocados on tortillas. I have some organic tortillas. All my uncle's fruit is organic."

"I love you-your garden," I said, enthusing over the organic food.

There was a knock at the door. It was Jerry.

"Oh, you would have to show up," Valiant said.

"I found a faster route here than the one you gave me. Your map would have taken me until midnight to arrive."

"Hi, Jerry," I said. "We were about to have dinner."

"I'm making it. I think I have a bottle of arsenic that will go great with your dinner," Valiant told Jerry.

"Thanks," Jerry said.

"We have frozen dinners, sandwich materials, avocados, and watermelon, among other things."

"I'll make my own," Jerry said.

"Suit yourself," Valiant replied. Valiant had Jerry take the equipment down to the basement and then showed him around the kitchen.

"Is there any estimate about injuries?"

"If you trust the news, a couple dozen people from the Capitol went to the hospital," Jerry said. "I didn't hear of any deaths."

"That's good. Not that people were injured but that nobody is known to have died."

"Not everyone is accounted for yet," Jerry said. "I spoke to Ross this morning and he put in the order for a replacement passport."

"I didn't know they could do that. I thought you had to apply all over again," Valiant said.

"He's cutting corners for the President's favorite researcher."

"How did I get to be the President's favorite?"

"Since I told Ross you were."

"I didn't see Ross during the speech."

"Ross said he had to take care of some business at his office in the Truman Building. He said he'd watch it remotely."

"I'm wondering if his memory of the speech will be like his memory of the Cabinet meeting."

"This one was televised and I bet a lot of viewers recorded it."

"Are we going to make July Shakespeare Month?" Valiant asked.

"I wouldn't be surprised. It was so good of the President to introduce literature into his speech," Jerry responded.

I laughed.

Valiant turned the news feed onto a large screen monitor.

"That's not a smart TV, is it?"

"You kidding? It's connected to a secured computer that is pretty much hack-proof. Of course, I could hack it."

It showed power lines down, buildings damaged. *"The most substantial damage was to the Truman Building. The firefighters are trying to dig out the rubble. Most of the people got out before the collapse."*

"Buildings don't just collapse."

"Unless they are hit with a bomb or have no steel beams," Valiant said. "The one that collapsed in Florida was built without steel beams."

The reporter interviewed Doris Claypool, the secretary to the Secretary of State. *"As soon as the shaking started, I got all the staff out."*

"Secretary of State Albert Ross sprained his ankle on the way out of the building. We are told he will be back on the job tomorrow," the reporter said.

"Well that's a relief," I said.

"I guess you may still get your replacement passport after all," Valiant said.

"He told me he was meeting with the DNC Chairwoman Stacey Duncekins in his office," Jerry said.

"She gave the orders for the North Korean reforms. Fifty percent Blacks in the Government, etcetera," I recalled.

"Fifty percent Blacks in North Korea? That's taking Critical Race Theory a bit far," Jerry said.

"Racist," Valiant joked.

Valiant turned off the news. He turned on some rock music to eat by.

"Green Day. Good taste," I said.

"I have an ear for the right oldies," he said. "Care to dance?"

"Sure." I got up, kicked off my shoes and started dancing around the living room. I noticed that Valiant knew some good moves.

"Hot chick," Valiant said as Jerry glared. "I mean supervisor."

"Me?"

"You could give President Astaire some competition."

Jerry got up and joined us. After Green Day, Valiant played some Eagles. Then we took the rest of our sandwiches downstairs, along with slices of watermelon.

We continued looking at the disc. "What is this?"

Valiant opened up a file called Operation Northwoods 7. "Wow," he said.

It started with a bunch of words. "Two shots, overdose, electric, dismantled, opener, quake, strangulation, drowning, explosion, crush, fall, microwave, collapse and fire." The rest of the file was mangled. There was a sub-file, marked D8 that was specially encrypted.

"This doesn't look like Lee's standard encryption," Valiant said. "I think he copied this file from somewhere. It looks like some of the files I saw when I broke into the Pentagon."

"You broke into the Pentagon?" Jerry asked.

"Hey, we have the best hacker in the world on our team. Celebrate," I told him.

"Could you go into my college records and make me valedictorian?"

"If you keep it up, you'll be at the bottom of your class," Valiant told him.

"You realize this follows the pattern we saw with the murders. But who was killed in the Earthquake?"

"Ross and his secretary got out," Jerry said. "Why was there so much damage to the Truman Building, compared with the rest of D.C.? It should have easily withstood an earthquake that didn't even shake the White House."

"The Capitol was shaking pretty badly," I said.

"That was mostly superficial," Jerry responded.

"Next is strangulation," I said.

"My mother told me never to go there," Valiant said.

"It all seems to be people connected to the President. It could be any of us," Jerry said.

"Lara killed herself in front of me. How could they plan that?"

"Her daughter said she was talking to voices in her head. What if they were real?" Jerry suggested.

"Maybe from her Bluetooth earpiece?" I questioned.

"Or maybe from one of the boosters," Valiant surmised.

"Valiant, we need to know now. Have you been vaxxed?" Jerry demanded.

"I'm just as vaxxed as the two of you. I know about your brother." That last comment shut Jerry up for a minute.

"You should have seen the speech Valiant wrote for the President to give at the school. I don't think any of the students will be returning back soon for the vax."

"They didn't go back today, according to what I saw on the school office memos," Valiant said.

"You hacked into the school?" Jerry asked.

"The staff got an email from the political director, saying the school should offer to forget the vax if the students returned."

"They'll probably call the White House for confirmation."

"There was a phone number for the political director in the email.

When they call it, they'll get a message to delay all further vaxxes as several bad batches are in circulation."

"I never thought I'd be grateful for an earthquake. The phones at the White House are down," Jerry said.

"There are cells," I pointed out.

"True. But those aren't official," Valiant replied.

"How did the phone service get damaged if there was no damage to the White House?" I asked.

"Must have been an outside cable or maybe a phone virus," Valiant suggested.

I thought about the list. "We're forewarned, but that doesn't mean we're prepared for what they plan to do to us."

"If it was the vax, no problem. We all have phony confirmation IDs. If they try to activate them, they'll be useless," Valiant said.

"The fact that we don't commit suicide or do something to get ourselves killed could also give away our status, and they'll simply try an alternate means," I pointed out.

"But it will be more difficult to finish the plan if we're supposed to be part of it," Valiant noted.

"They can always drug us," Jerry said. That caught our attention.

"Let's be careful what we eat or drink at work," I said.

"They ransacked your apartment. They could have gotten into the food there."

"Make sure we only drink from sealed bottles and eat unopened food," I suggested.

"Years ago, they came up with little pills that contained chips," Valiant said. "Do any of you take medicine?"

"Vitamins," I said. "I'll get a fresh batch at a store where I don't usually shop."

"I'll do the same with my vitamins," Jerry said.

"The killer dropped off some papers at my condo the night Lee was killed."

"How do you know?" Jerry asked.

"It was the contents of the file that he was holding when he died."

"So they've been monitoring you from the start?" Jerry asked.

"This one takes a different encryption key. If we knew whose file it was, we could figure it out," Valiant said, still looking at the encrypted file.

"Someone in the Pentagon authorized the hits?" I ventured.

"There's the shadow program and the signature program," Valiant responded.

"How about Blackmoriuntur or Northgrail?" I suggested.

"Those would be contractors. This might not be a Pentagon program at all. The Pentagon has been hiring outside contractors for some time," Valiant said.

"The killer needs access to the White House," Jerry pointed out.

"The head of Dynozap came into my office a week ago," A thought hit me. "The cards. We haven't looked at the cards from Kyle."

"We also haven't checked out his flash drive," Valiant said.

Valiant quickly made a copy of Kyle's flash drive as I started looking through the cardholder. "There's a Blackmoriuntur Technologies card in there, one for Stacey Duncekins and one for Dynozap."

Next, Valiant pulled the slim board of my flash drive out of the housing and put it into the housing for a blank flash drive. "Definitely waterlogged. It will take me a while, but I am going to copy this and then try to make the copy readable. I have a program that will repair data." He inserted the drive into the computer and made a direct copy, then opened a hidden panel in the wall and put the originals of the two flash drives into it.

"It will take a few hours to run through the program as bad as this looks. Let's go."

"Go?" I asked.

"We have a number of cards to go through right now. We can check out the people on them."

"There is safety in numbers," Jerry said.

"Going in threes will slow us down," Valiant noted. "But you're right. We don't want any of us winding up strangled." He looked at me.

"I can take care of myself. But I agree."

"Do you do Krav Maga too?" Jerry asked me.

"No. I couldn't fight my way out of a breadbox," I replied.

"I've got a gun and Valiant has the self-defense."

"Do you know how to use the gun?" I asked Jerry.

"Not really. I had to take a class to get the gun."

"Maybe you'll get lucky. Just don't point it in our direction," Valiant told him.

"Let's start with this one." He held up Stacey's card.

The car raced down several back highways on the way to Stacey's home in North Carolina, where she had moved after losing a number of elections in Georgia. "Did you win the Indy 500?" I asked Valiant.

"Just the modern equivalent of the Cannonball Run."

"Congrats," I said. "How does this car even go this fast?"

"My uncle's hobby was race car driving. For fun, he liked to put fast engines in cars that didn't look like they could go a quarter of that speed. Throws off the cops."

"Didn't he use actual race cars?"

"He took those to Texas with him."

"And I suppose he was the one who taught you to drive?"

"How did you know?"

"How about taking it under one-fifty," Jerry suggested. "The police don't put up with this."

"I have a police radar and police radio detector in here. I turned it to go off if they're close. We're safe."

"This is some new idea of safe," Jerry said, hanging onto the door handgrip.

It was more than a house, it was a mansion. I guessed being DNC Chair paid well. Stacey's housekeeper was out in front with a dog and a basket of puppies.

"I didn't know Stacey was into dogs," I said.

"You didn't hear?" the housekeeper asked.

"Hear what?"

"They found her under the rubble. Crushed."

"Quake," Jerry said, clearly thinking about the list.

"That's terrible. I'm so sorry. I saw her just a week ago. It's something I'll never forget," I said.

"She was a pig," the housekeeper said.

"I didn't like her, either," Valiant threw in.

"So are you giving the dogs some fresh air?"

"No, they're out here for a PESA pickup."

"You do know that PESA was prosecuted for killing puppies and dumping them in shopping mall dumpsters in multiple states, don't you?"

"It wasn't my idea. Stacey arranged it before she left this morning. I helped the ones who could get away. But the mother and puppies wouldn't run."

"How old are the puppies?"

"Two days. Stacey had been told the mother was fixed. She was furious when the puppies came out. She talked about giving them to the NRA for target practice."

"I believe it. She hates the NRA—except when it comes to killing puppies," Valiant said.

"Wait. Why would she want to kill puppies?" Jerry asked.

"Our party has been working to exterminate puppies for years. California has taken the lead with its dog-extinction legislation," Valiant informed him.

"And PESA?" Jerry asked.

"It actually stands for People for the Extermination and Slaughter of Animals," I said. "You need to stop reading Establishment propaganda."

"I guess so. My bad."

"It just so happens that my life has been very lonely without puppies and dogs. I've always wanted a set," Valiant said.

"Me too," I added.

At that moment, the PESA truck pulled up. Puppies and kittens could be heard whining in the back.

"I'm here for some more of the trash, I mean puppies," the driver said, getting out of the truck.

"Oh, this is just a sample," I said. "There's a whole room of them inside."

"Inside?" the housekeeper asked.

"Well we have to save them all, right?" I said to her.

"Yes. I'll show you," she said to the driver. Another PESA man got out of the truck.

As the housekeeper showed the men inside, Jerry ran around to the driver's side of the truck. "See you in Virginia."

It took me a minute to realize that this mild-mannered Press Secretary was about to commit grand theft PESA truck.

Valiant and I grabbed the mother and basket of puppies, raced to Valiant's car and very quickly sped out of view.

CHAPTER 22

"What shall we do with the truck after we free all the other puppies?"

"The Potomac is a good place, assuming Jerry gets back."

I looked back at the puppies. "They look like a mixture of Papillons and toy sized Eskies."

"There's a lot of food at my uncle's place."

"But who will take care of them?"

"I guess I'll be working from there a lot."

"On the robot?"

"We'll figure something out."

"How long do you think it will take them to report the theft?"

"Hopefully, it won't make the police reports until we're out of state."

I got a call on my burner phone. It was Paris. "We're trying to locate Jerry. Have you seen him?"

"Not recently. What's up?"

"We need him to do a press conference tonight. We also need you and Valiant back here. He's not picking up his phone either."

"A lot of the cell towers are down. It might take me a few hours to be back. That's kind of late for a press conference."

"I'll tell Gene I'm going to cover for him. I hope you are safe."

"Yes. I decided to get out of D.C. Too hectic."

"Did you hear about Stacey Duncekins?"

"I heard she was crushed."

"In the Truman building. The only building where any of the walls came down."

"Wasn't it built to withstand something like this?"

"It shouldn't have collapsed. Gene is planning an investigation."

"Hopefully it's better than the one the 9/11 Commission did."

"I doubt it."

Back at the ranch house, Valiant and I started to prepare rooms for the dogs. "At least, they'll be getting organic food and filtered water for the time being," Valiant said.

I noticed one of the puppies was bleeding from a scratch on the nose.

"Do you have a first aid kit in there?"

"My uncle has some supplies and there's a first aid kit in the trunk." He went into a storage cabinet in the basement and got out some supplies. "It's a tiny scratch, maybe from a toenail." He used a Q-tip to place some of the blood onto a piece of plastic. Silver nitrate stopped the blood flow. He took a picture of the spot of blood he had collected, put the memory card into the computer, and magnified the picture.

"One thing this proves."

"What's that?" I asked.

"Stacey got the saline—if she was injected at all."

"How do you know?"

"She didn't transmit sterilizing mRNA to the puppy's mother."

"She might have kept the dog a hundred feet away from her. She was willing to have the mother and the puppies killed. But the housekeeper probably was unvaxxed. I bet the housekeeper took care of the litter and mother."

"You could be right," he said.

We put down cushions and paper in one bedroom for Stacey's litter. We had no idea how many additional puppies would be joining us. I was getting nervous about Jerry. I hoped he hadn't gotten stopped on the way back. I started pacing around outside.

"He hasn't been answering his cell."

"Is he really carrying his smartphone around?"

"He got a burner. His smartphone is at the White House. Do you think the North Carolina Highway Patrol stopped him?"

"No," Valiant said, pointing to the truck moving down the street in our direction.

When we got the new additions settled, I counted twenty-one plus the five puppies and the dam we had brought with us. "Are we actually going to keep twenty-seven dogs?" I asked.

"We should be able to find people who need them. Dogs increase the lifespan of older people," Jerry said.

"The government's been killing off as many older people as possible as fast as it can," Valiant responded. "Not many of them left."

"They wanted a press conference tonight."

"I left my cell at the White House. I also forgot my burner there," Jerry said.

"Well, you won't be tracked that way," I told him.

"Am I in trouble?"

"Paris is handling it."

"Now that the puppies are settled, do you want to check out Blackmoriuntur?" Jerry asked.

"I want to get rid of that truck," Valiant said.

Jerry and I followed Valiant towards a park along the Potomac and poof, suddenly the truck was underwater. Valiant ran down the road a little way and we picked him up. "Better let me drive," Valiant said. "Otherwise, it will take us days to get there."

"Hey, I was fast getting back. I didn't drive at one-fifty MPH but I did well."

"After the call from Paris, I think we should all show up for work in the morning," I said.

"We can at least scout out Blackmoriuntur tonight. It's just in Maryland," Valiant said.

When we got there, we found a darkened shop. Behind it was a vacant lot. Valiant went across the street to a tree and climbed.

"Our top techie just climbed up a tree," Jerry said.

"Maybe to get a better view."

In the car on the way back, Valiant explained. "I put up a camera that will be sending a video to the cloud for the next 36 hours. I'd like to get a look at who shows up."

When we got back to the ranch house, we tried to get a little sleep. There were multiple rooms with beds and dogs. I slept with the litter Stacey wanted to have exterminated.

The mother was really loving towards the puppies. "When I was younger, I knew a mother who was like this with her children. Her name was Esther. That's what I'm going to call you." I picked up the most peaceful pup in the litter. I named him Kal, short for Kal-El. It wasn't long before I had all of them named. The girls were Venus, Cynthia and Magic. The other boy was Kucinich. He had been one of the last of the heroes in Congress and so why not? Kucinich and Cynthia were the tiniest ones. Both of them loved being held. I wasn't sure I was going to be able to let go of any of them. When things settled down, I'd have a whole family.

"Will they be alright until we get back?" I asked.

"I'm going to drop the mother and puppies off with my brother on the way to work," Jerry said. "The others should be old enough to handle being left with food and water."

I gave him a hug. "Thank you." I noticed Valiant was looking down as I turned back to him. "These puppies are like family. They are really important to me. On second thought, how about if I drop them off at my parent's place? I should be seeing them more often."

"You're a natural mother," Jerry said.

I gently punched him in the shoulder. "Not for some time."

———

Paris's parents lived in Maryland. Valiant took the outer freeway loop around D.C. to get to their place. As long as I was masquerading as their daughter, I thought it would be wise if I showed up to see them once in a while.

Paris's mom gave me a hug as she whispered, "I don't know what you and Paris are up to, but please be careful."

"I will."

"And who is your young man?"

"He works with me."

"I'm so pleased to meet you. I am Karissa's mom. You can call me Alice."

"Hi, Alice. Karissa is doing a great job at the White House."

"I'll keep good care of your new puppies while you're at work. Dave will be here later to help."

"That's wonderful. Thank you so much."

———

On the way to driving me back to the Capitol, Valiant turned on the car radio. He noted that, "The power in the Capitol Mall is up. The rest of the town is dark."

"I'll be throwing out a lot of food," I said. "It will allow me to get better food."

"Channeling a little of Terry Cole-Whitaker?"

"Long ago, I saw her speak. Very impressive. Did you notice that all the religions, that used to believe in the terrain theory or that had refused prior vaxxes and transfusions, gave up their religious beliefs the moment the government said there was a virus?"

"The difference between true believers and cultists."

"I guess so."

"The cultists just found another guru, that Doctor Fraud guy, to worship."

We heard on the radio that a different PESA truck was found at the bottom of a lake. This time the carcasses of the puppies and kittens were on board.

"I guess they're throwing away the trucks, along with the puppies and kittens these days," I said. "Good thing we rescued the one truckload." I felt sad about the ones we hadn't rescued.

"They get enough in donations to buy a hundred fleets of trucks."

"And all their donors think they're treating the animals ethically."

"I've sure you've noticed how stupid the public becomes when the networks push agendas. Remember how they freaked out about the non-insurrection on January Sixth? Usually, someone revolted against is harmed. The only one killed was one of those 'insurrectionists' let into the Capitol by the Capitol police before one of the Capitol police took selfies with the crowd and then shot her," Valiant said.

"And the whole pandemic narrative. The people who died, virtually all died of medical malpractice."

"I have a confession and I hope you'll be speaking to me later."

"What?" I started to hold my breath. Had I made a mistake in trusting him?

"I helped Lee put together that file on Eve Gordon. I didn't know it was you."

"You?"

"He had me pull school files, a birth certificate and some other documents. I didn't run the DNA."

I froze. He knew. My carefully guarded secret wasn't a secret. What would he do with the information? The killer also knew. I looked at the door handle and thought about jumping, but part of me felt certain I could trust him. Could I?

"Someone else knows. The documents were brought to my apartment later the night Lee was killed. Someone took the file contents from his hand after he was killed."

"It was me. I did that."

CHAPTER 23

"You took my documents from him after—"

"After he died. I knew he had the documents and I was responsible. I had already made sure there was no official record but he had the hard copies. I came up through the secret passage to steal them, but he was already dead. Someone must have used a silencer. I replaced the contents of the file and snuck the real documents out past security later that night."

It took me a minute to process it.

"I swear I didn't kill Lee."

"I didn't think you did. It's just that you know." I felt awkward like I had been caught in public in my underwear.

"For what It's worth, I'm, well, I've really liked you ever since you took over the sub-department. I'd never do anything to hurt you. I didn't realize until Lee was comparing it with your records earlier that day that he was targeting you."

"That answers some questions. Who do you think ran the DNA?"

"Remember a couple of weeks ago, Lee said he had to leave early for the afternoon?"

"I remember Gene was looking for Lee one afternoon and not happy he had left without telling him."

"I was going to Lee's office and overheard him say he would be at the lab in about an hour. I thought it was interesting he wasn't using the official lab, which wouldn't have taken an hour to get to—unless it was something he didn't want Gene to find out about. I thought he might be having health problems."

"Did you hear the name of the lab?"

"I only heard a few seconds of the conversation."

"Someone had to get my father's DNA."

"I don't have those answers, either. Are you mad?"

"Actually, I'm—" I thought about my feelings. I should have been unnerved that he knew but I wasn't. Just the opposite. It was better someone on my side knew than someone who would spring it on me later. "I'm relieved, grateful. Thank you for having my back."

"If it were me, I'd be freaking mad about it all."

"I don't even know if my dad is alive. Though quite frankly, I'd rather have a robot for a father than the real one."

"If you want to talk any time, I'll listen. I can only guess what you are going through."

"First, let's figure out who is behind all these killings. Then, I'll have time to focus on me."

"You matter. You don't need to put yourself last."'

"Six, or rather nine, nine-and-a-half people have been killed."

"You realize that, if we tell anyone someone high up is killing people, they'll call us crazy."

"Which is why we need evidence in case we are on the upcoming death list."

Inside the White House, there seemed to be utter chaos. "How soon can the President make a statement about the earthquake?" Paris asked.

"I'll have the team prep him as soon as we get the narrative."

Gene came up and handed me a script. "See that it's as close as possible. Have him cut the Shakespeare."

"Yes, sir."

"I looked at it. You want him to say this?"

"It's not what I want. It's required."

"Yes, sir. Who wrote it?"

"The new acting chairman of the DNC."

"Of course."

As I handed the paper to Valiant in the lab, he said, "You're kidding."

"He wants the President to follow the script as closely as possible."

"I thought Stacey was dead. Who took over for her?"

"I didn't ask. Maybe the head of the School of the Americas."

I went up to my office. Duane was there. "I want to apologize, again, for last week. Would you like to do dinner tonight?"

"I'd love to but maybe another night."

"Sure."

"'I'm not too familiar with Hushpuppies. I hope everything is going well in your sub-department."

"Quite."

"Is there anything you need? I may not be in charge of your section, but I've got Lee's office."

"Lee was always able to keep everyone in line. Now workers are sluffing off."

"I'm sorry to hear that. Would you like me to speak with them?"

"No. Even their identities are confidential."

"I see."

"I suppose your sub-department is slacking off too."

"Actually, I've got a good team. They've been working overtime."

"Lucky."

Next, Jerry dropped by. "You wouldn't believe what I'm to say in this press conference."

"Oh, I just might."

"It's insane."

"And someone will probably follow through. I keep looking for the telescreens and the swastikas."

"The telescreens are installed through most of the city. I guess you don't have yours yet."

"That's why I don't carry my smartphone anywhere."

"Looks like trackers are in the vaxxes too."

"Great world we're living in."

I watched from the side as Jerry went to the podium. This was one press conference I wanted to see. "I'm going to make a quick announcement, but I won't have time for questions."

Smart, I thought.

"We have discovered that the Republican National Committee working with the Government of Kiribati orchestrated the earthquake that has taken down our city. An alert has been put out for all terrorists within the Republican Party to be picked up in connection with the terrorism, which killed the former head of the Democratic National Committee. Remember, they may be armed and dangerous. If any member of the public sees a Republican, we have set up a hotline for tips. Thank you."

He walked off the press room stage quickly. "How did I do?"

"Aside from your having sounded insane to a sane person, the reporters look as if they are taking it in stride."

"I should have known this was coming since that claim of an insurrection at the Capitol. A lot of innocent people could get killed, not just the nine we know of." He muttered to me.

"Nine-and-a-half," I whispered.

"Can you signal a spaceship to take me out of here?"

"I've been waiting for that for years."

I went down to the basement. "Who is he today?"

"He just processed through Charles de Gaulle. I guess we'll find out when he gets up there."

I followed the President up to the Oval Office as cameras rolled in. I stood between Jerry and Paris against the wall. Much of the White House staff lined the walls and the areas behind the cameras. Gene told the camera crew when to start rolling. The feeds were to go to all televisions across the country. Smart TVs would be turned on. Every station was carrying the speech.

"Ladies and gentlemen, tonight is an historic night."

"It's late morning," Paris whispered.

The President continued. "'The reason why we find ourselves in a position of impotency is not only because our only powerful potential enemy has sent men to invade our shores, but rather because of the traitorous actions of those who have been treated so well by this Nation. It has not been the less fortunate, or members of minority groups who have been traitorous to this nation, but rather those who have had all the benefits the wealthiest Nation on Earth has had to offer, the finest homes, the finest college education and the finest jobs in government we can give.

"'This is glaringly true in the State Department. There the bright young men who are born with silver spoons in their mouths are the ones who have been most traitorous.'"

"He's going off script," Paris whispered.

"Well he was supposed to talk about enemies within," I whispered back.

The President pulled a page out of his desk.

"That's the in-house phone list of the current staff of the White House," I whispered.

"Not good," Paris responded.

"'I have here in my hand a list of two hundred and five... a list of names that were made known to the Secretary of State as being members of the' combined Republicans-Kiribati forces 'And who nevertheless are still working and shaping policy in the State Department...

"'As you know, very recently the Secretary of State proclaimed his loyalty to a man guilty of what has always been considered as the most abominable of crimes—being a traitor to the people who gave him a position of great trust.' This is 'high treason.'"

"I guess we're going to have to arrest Ross in his hospital room and whisk him off to Gitmo," Paris whispered.

"'He has lighted the spark, which is resulting in a moral uprising that will end only when the whole sorry mess of twisted, warped thinkers are swept from the national scene so that we may have a new birth of honesty and decency in government.'"

With that, the staff applauded and cheered the President's speech. Paris, Jerry and I lightly clapped. Jerry and Paris both had worried looks on their faces, and I'm sure I did too.

Back in the lab, Valiant said, "How was I to know he would channel Joe McCarthy?"

"We had his feed tapping into encyclopedias but there are thousands of people he could have emulated," Brandon said.

"So what happens to Ross?" Jack asked.

"I don't know. The President just called him a traitor. It's going to be hard for him to continue."

"That was a stroke of genius!" Gene exclaimed when he entered the lab. "The new chairman wanted to be rid of Ross, but we didn't know how—other than killing him off."

"Killing?" I asked. "Is anyone in this Administration into killing?"

"Did you see the body count in Sri Lanka? Total success."

"Except for the blue diamonds."

"We're sending in ground troops to Kiribati. Nobody's about to make that mistake, again."

"At least, they won't have to worry about any opposition, no offensive fire, since Kiribati has no military force."

"Walk in the park."

I thought about all the civilians who would likely be killed during that walk in the park and I wished I could do something to save them.

I went up to my office. I had photographed virtually all the papers in Lee's office, already. Maybe the financial information would help. Who was I kidding? The IRS only went after selected people. They certainly wouldn't go after the current Administration.

My door opened. No knocking.

"May I come in?"

I recognized the incomer from his TV appearances. Adam Shytface, one of the last people I wanted to see.

"If you are looking for Gene, his office is—",

"Karissa, you are the one I'm here to see."

"Me?"

"I understand you are doing research to assist the President with his current positions."

"I'm just a researcher."

"Well, these are the positions we need him to take."

I looked at the list. It included door-to-door seizures of all registered Republicans and a search of social media to determine Republican sympathizers and their contacts.

"I'm a lifelong Democrat, but is there a chance we are going too far? Couldn't this be election-fixing?"

"We're only picking up Republicans."

"But the entire opposing party."

"There are numerous other parties."

"All getting under ten percent of the vote. When will they be on the terrorist list?"

"Not today." In other words in the future.

"And you think the President will simply follow these demands?"

"I've been told that you're the one who can get him to do so. I was told to count on it. I'll be replacing Stacey, in addition to continuing my duties in the House."

"Stacey hasn't even had her funeral yet. Aren't you moving a little fast?"

"Her funeral is on Wednesday. Make this happen before then."

I took the list to Gene. "This isn't something he can do in a speech. I think this list is for you and whoever is in charge of National Security, maybe one of his Special Assistants."

"I don't like it any more than you." He paused. "Give me the list."

"Do we really have to follow the wishes of the party? I mean they only matter during election season."

"We need for them to feel listened to. But apparently, we are to eliminate any chance of losing the next election to keep in good standing with certain other powerful people."

"I have a question for you."

"Yes?"

"This may seem silly, but do all the deaths seem a coincidence?"

"I prefer not to ask questions that could irritate the wrong people."

"Does that mean the wrong people may be involved?"

"Every one of the deaths is explainable."

"The President's speech indicated that certain people were responsible for Stacey's death, though I've never heard of someone killing another person by earthquake. How was that done?"

"I only get the scripts—same as you do. I don't have to figure out what they mean."

"Did the FBI look into it?"

"They just get starry-eyed every time I talk to them," he said.

"I notice a lot of people do. This may seem out of place for me, given my position, but if someone hassles you, maybe I can help."

"Help? How? I can't even discuss national security issues with you," he replied, seeming surprised by my statement.

"And yet, I'm the one who briefs the President. Speaking of the President, is he alive and well?"

"I can't discuss that with you."

"I just wanted to know that we are still legitimately in power."

"We are."

"That answers my question."

"Now get out of here before I make any more slips."

As I walked back to my office, it hit me, my father was alive, somewhere.

CHAPTER 24

He could be in a coma like in the movie Dave. Or he could just be financially benefiting from the schemes. The latter thought made me mad. I had such mixed feelings about my father. I wanted revenge but felt I had missed my chance when I found out I was working with a robot and not the real President. Now, maybe I could expose the real him. But I had to find a way to find him, first. What if he were a prisoner? I could just leave him, suffering. The thought gave me pleasure. I know most would consider it wrong. But he had insulted my mother after he raped her and never cared enough to find out if there was a baby.

Valiant came up to my office. I closed the door. "Any bugs?"

He pulled out his detector for an extra check. "None detected."

"He's alive. Any ideas how to find him?"

"We could search all the wings."

"I don't have access to all the rooms."

"The Secret Service does."

"You have a friend in the Secret Service?"

"Nope, but John seems pretty careless."

"I'll say. He's been selling access passes to the White House."

"Maybe I could buy one."

'"I think he's getting heroin in exchange."

"Happy Days."

"Yeh. There was a video."

"How many sets of initials did you see on the list?"

"About twenty."

"One of those people could have killed Lee."

"I suspect that's the case. But some of the initials could fit multiple people. It's the videos that matter."

"I will resurrect it. My fix may have resurrected it already."

On my way out of the office for lunch, Felicity whisked past me, like a star making a quick entrance. She turned and stopped. "I'm off to a high-power lunch."

No surprise.

"I love your research. And the President's speeches have really improved since you've been in charge."

"Doing my best."

"I may recommend you for a special honor."

"Thank you."

At lunch, I met with Valiant who brought along Brandon.

"I've seen him in the lab. How much does he know?" Brandon asked as Jerry approached.

"The night the President was sabotaged, he found out a lot. Better to have him on our side than talking," I said.

"Can we trust him?"

"If he gets out of line, I know Krav Maga," Valiant said.

"Do you really know Krav Maga?" I asked.

"I studied it," Valiant replied.

"Brandon, you seem somewhat fearless," I said, hoping my estimate was correct.

"Is that a job requirement?"

"What was your relationship with Lee?"

"He interviewed me when I took the job. He would come down to the lab to tell us what he wanted."

"How would he get there?"

"Generally through the door. There were times when he just seemed to appear."

"You think he knew an alternate route?"

"Is there one?" Brandon asked.

"Brandon and I have been friends for a long time. I can't count the number of times he's covered for me," Valiant said.

"Covered?"

"Told Lee I was working on the project when I was doing other things on the computer."

"Should we be saying this?" he asked Valiant.

"She knows."

"About the Pentagon?"

"Did you hack into it too?" Jerry asked, hearing the end as he sat down.

"No!" Brandon exclaimed. "Not me. He knows about that?"

"I know everything. Ask me how the world was formed," Jerry joked.

"Brandon, do you have an opinion about the deaths?" I asked.

"It's an unbelievable amount of bad luck."

"You think it's luck?" I asked.

"You don't?"

"I mean six people and a robot have died in a little over a week. Have you ever seen that many for one Administration before?"

"The team before us. You didn't know them, but they're all dead too," Valiant said.

Brandon straightened up.

"We think they may have stumbled on something," I said.

"How can someone cause a cardiac arrest?"

"That started with a bullet to the head," I said, worried about going out on a limb.

"I didn't know."

"If this discussion is repeated, there will likely be more bodies," I said.

"I'm not telling anyone. I don't want to be next if you're right. I need to get back to the lab."

"Sure," I said. "Lunch is on me."

After Brandon left, I asked Valiant, "Do you think he will talk?"

"No. He has to process this. He's the best when it comes to hardware. We could use that."

"It would have been nice to have a fourth team member. We could do double time if we could go out two and two."

"Cenk and Sam were together. We were together on that bridge."

"Having you with me saved my life. Cenk and Sam probably didn't know they were killing people," I said.

"If it hadn't been for that tip about the dinner with Monica, I wouldn't be here," Jerry said. "Most people want to stay away from danger unless it knocks on their door."

"You do that a lot," Valiant said.

"Do what?"

"Use phrases like knocks on their door."

"I think we'll have to forget about Brandon. If we talked him into it and he got hurt, we'd feel guilty," I said.

"At least some of the local restaurants are up," Jerry noted, watching the waiter as he walked by to another table. "This earthquake was very selective. Georgetown University across the street from the Truman Building wasn't damaged at all. It's as if the quake had a targeting control on it."

"Why didn't I think of that!" Valiant exclaimed.

"Of what?" Jerry inquired.

"Have you seen the patent for HAARP?"

"Go on," I urged.

"According to the patent, it can have the impact of a nuclear weapon."

"It wasn't a nuclear blast," I said.

"It can cause earthquakes. Remember Fukushima?"

"The nuclear disaster that was caused by a Tsunami that was caused by an earthquake," I remarked.

"It was caused because they were dumb enough to let Honeywell put dangerous fission plants by the ocean," Jerry chimed in.

"That set the stage. That wasn't the final cause," Valiant said.

"Let's say Monday's quake was HAARP. That would mean the perpetrator is not a low-level employee," Jerry said.

"A low-level employee couldn't get a signature soldier to impersonate you."

"That lets out John," Jerry lamented.

"Monica has horrible taste," I commented.

"My taste has improved."

"Look elsewhere," Valiant said.

I thought back to the other night. *I wasn't that close to the table. Could a simple disguise have done the trick?*

"Maybe it wasn't a signature soldier. Just someone who looked like you," I said. "And perhaps the earthquake was a real one."

"The list," Jerry recalled.

"What if someone at Georgetown created an underground explosion?" Valiant inquired.

"That didn't rock the campus?" Jerry asked.

"There are tunnels everywhere under D.C.," Valiant said.

"Good point. It didn't even have to be a student. Just someone who knew about explosives and the tunnels," I said.

'There should be some evidence in the tunnel system," Jerry noted.

"There is a tunnel system under the Capitol that connects with the Library of Congress and Congressional office buildings," Valiant said. "Not to mention the White House tunnels, the aqueduct tunnel, the steam tunnels, the electrical power tunnels and pedestrian tunnels, among others. Under D.C., there's a whole network of tunnels. Some are closed and sealed."

"There are also subway tunnels," Jerry commented.

"And the old tunnel under the capitol is still there—even though a new one was created. I understand it was repurposed for mechanical work and for the Congressmen to relax in, but has more recently been closed and sealed off, or, at least, it was supposed to be. There have been complaints about the security failures at that tunnel. We've all seen that someone is good at taking down cameras. There are a lot of possibilities. Let's say they just wanted a series of small explosions near the Capitol while wiping out some of the cable and power lines. And then they had a bigger explosion under the Truman building," Valiant noted.

"Hence, the shaking we experienced while watching the President speak," I said to Jerry.

"Valiant, you know all about these tunnels. You had access to Lee. You are high-tech. How do we know you didn't arrange this?" Jerry asked.

"You don't." Valiant smiled. "And you better watch your step in case you're right." I knew he was teasing Jerry, but his tone made him sound very convincing.

"Some of the old tunnels are supposed to have been filled as new ones were built," Jerry said.

"Maybe the old ones weren't properly filled. Nobody would have been watching them," I said.

"Maybe the person has been planning this for some time," Valiant remarked. "Explosives could have been set up long in advance."

"But how would he know who would get nailed by the earthquake? Maybe the President was right about the Secretary of State," Jerry said.

"He was channeling McCarthy in the speech. The President doesn't know anything, himself—though he seems to be an expert on literature, music and dance," I said.

I reflected on the fact that my initials weren't in the Happy Days file. Why wasn't I there? Did Lee die before he put me on the list or did he elect not to have me on it? What if there were others who were left off the list? Valiant knew my secret. I wasn't worried about him.

I thought about all the leads we could follow. Three of us weren't enough to follow all of them—particularly if we stuck together to avoid being killed. The thought of either Jerry or Valiant getting hurt terrified me—even more than the thought of anything happening to me. I had been relying on Valiant so much in connection with work. He'd always had my back. But I hadn't realized to what extent. And

Jerry was very sweet. He had this helpless quality about him—sort of like a puppy. And yet he had courage. Both men made me feel safe. But it was more than that. I really liked them both.

I went back to my office, opened the door and walked in. That's when the lights went out and my head felt as if it were exploding.

CHAPTER 25

Part of me sensed I was on the floor unconscious. A near-death experience? Images went through my mind: Lee, Lara, Seth, Greg. I dreamed I was sliding across a floor and was hearing sounds of shuffles, like things were being moved within my office. I heard beeps as if my monitor had been turned on and the sound of a flash as if a picture had been taken. "Strangulation." That wasn't yet unless I was dead and missed it. I tried to open my eyes but was too out of it. I felt a hand reach into my pocket and pull something out. My phone? I felt it go back into my pocket. My dream shifted to puppies. *My head.* It felt as if it had been hit with a sledgehammer. I pictured Kal-El being a healing dog, coming over and licking my head to make the pain subside.

"Karissa. Karissa." It was Paris's voice. The headache was back.

"Where is Kal-El?"

"Karissa."

"Kal-El?"

"In the movies. *Superman.*" It was Paris's voice. I tried to open my eyes, but the pain was too strong. "I'm calling an ambulance."

"No hospital. I can't go to the hospital."

"Please get to Karissa's office."

"Please. No hospital. They kill people in the hospitals."

Paris helped me sit up on the floor with my back against a wall, I thought. It was too hard to open my eyes. "What hit me?"

He made another phone call. "Bring some ice to Karissa's office and see if you can check her over. It looks like she was hit on the head."

"No hospital."

"No hospital," Paris agreed.

I managed to partially open my eyes. The first thing I saw was a vacuum cleaner with legs sticking out from the side.

"A vacuum cleaner with legs?" I inquired but wanted to take it back when I saw a more complete picture.

Juan was next to me, the hose wrapped around his neck and the cord wrapped around his leg.

"Juan!" I tried to see if I could rouse him. He wasn't moving. His eyes were open and the pupils were fixed.

"He's gone," Paris said.

"Who? What?"

"It looks like he was strangled by the vacuum hose."

"By the person who knocked me out?"

"From your positioning, it looks as if he may have hit you with his head as he fell."

"Was the door opened or closed?"

"What?"

"When you arrived. Was the door open or closed?"

"Closed."

I looked at the door. "I should have fallen on the floor over by the door. I opened it and boom."

"You have a head injury. Are you sure you trust your memory?"

"Someone was in here. My phone."

I pulled out my phone. There were no obvious signs of tampering, but I knew what I had felt and heard. "Help me up."

"I think you should stay down until the doctor checks you out."

"Please."

Paris helped me to my feet. I could barely stand and almost fell over. He helped to steady me as I went to the desk. I pulled out a metal box from the bottom drawer, put my phone in it, put it back in the drawer and closed it.

"They messed with my phone," I told him. I pushed myself away from the desk, and he helped me to a chair. "Maybe they knocked out Juan and then strangled him."

Frank, the in-house doctor, rushed in. He put a medical bag and an ice pack he was carrying onto my desk.

"She has a head injury," Paris told him.

He examined the back of my head. "You've got a big knot there." He shined a flashlight in my eyes. "Your pupils are normal. You need to have someone check your eyes every four hours for the next twenty-four hours. If you feel any nausea, you need to get to the hospital right away."

He checked over my neck and took my blood pressure. Jerry rushed in through the door. "Karissa, are you—" He turned and saw the body.

"Strangled," I said. "Someone knocked me out. Video. We need to check the security cameras."

A horrible thought occurred to me. "Magnet. Does anyone have a magnet?"

"I have this little one in my bag," Frank said.

I wondered if I looked insane as I ran it over my body. It didn't stick anywhere.

"You should take the rest of the day off," Frank said.

The EMTs arrived.

The lead EMT checked Juan's vitals and shook his head.

"I'll take her home," Jerry said.

"You have a press release to work on today," Paris told him.

"She can't drive herself. I can have the assistant press secretary write it."

"Gene won't go for that. I can have the Secret Service take her home."

The EMTs put Juan onto a stretcher and covered him with a sheet.

"Karissa!" Valiant exclaimed, rushing into the room. "What happened?"

"I was hit over the head. Juan was strangled."

"It might be ruled an accident," Paris said. I hoped he was just saying that over the expectation that they'd cover it up that way.

"I'll take her home," Valiant said.

Jerry didn't look happy.

"Do you want your phone?" Paris asked.

"No. No thank you," I said.

"You might want to take tomorrow off too," Frank recommended.

"Brandon and I can handle things," Valiant told me.

The EMTs were about to leave with Juan. "Please check his head."

"Go ahead," Paris said.

Frank went over to the body and lifted the sheet. He had the EMTs help him move the body over and pushed the hair aside. I could see the blood. Then, Frank looked at me. "That's a bigger bump than yours. It could have happened when he fell. Does he have a history of epilepsy?"

I shrugged.

"We'll have to check his personnel file," Paris said.

The EMTs wheeled Juan out, followed by Frank.

"Someone is going to have to talk to the family," Paris said.

"I'm taking the afternoon off. I can do it."

"You aren't in any shape."

"I'm feeling better now. I'll go home right after."

"I'll take her. If there are any problems, I'll be there," Valiant said.

Paris called personnel, asked for Juan's address and wrote it down on a sheet of paper. As he handed it to me, he said, "Don't tell his wife your theories about malfeasance."

I nodded.

Valiant and I went to the lab. "My phone may have been tampered with. While I was out, it felt as if my phone was removed from my pocket and put back in and it sounded as if something was being shuffled or moved in the office. Also, I was knocked out when I entered the door and Paris found me across the room. Someone moved me. And who dies from being strangled with a vacuum hose?"

"None of the murders are what they seem. I've got another burner, here, in the lab," Valiant said.

'Good. I have the most critical numbers memorized."

On the way to Juan's house, we drove by Oliver North Elementary School. Sections had collapsed. "I guess the Truman building didn't get the worst of the damage," I said.

"They don't care about protecting children—especially uncontrollable children," Valiant commented.

"At least, the kids were avoiding school when it hit."

"I didn't hear about any of the staff being hurt. So maybe they got out in time."

"Georgetown with the ten or twenty students enrolled this year is fine," I said as we drove by the campus.

"It used to be one of the most applied for schools in the country. After schools started mandating vaccines, the most popular schools were in Texas, Iowa, Arizona and Florida."

"Georgia Tech had to turn away ninety percent of the students."

"We're avoiding the elephant. If Paris hadn't found you unconscious, you would be a suspect in Juan's murder," Valiant pointed out.

"They are trying awfully hard to classify it as an accident. Even Paris was willing to go along with that."

"Nice and tidy, as Jerry would say, just like all the others."

"The next three are drowning, explosion, crush, which has already happened, and fall."

"Remind me to stay off the tops of tall buildings."

At Juan's house, his wife opened the door. "Hello, Mrs. Martinez, I'm Karissa and this is Valiant from the White House."

"Karissa, Juan has said so many nice things about you."

"Really? That was so kind of him. He's been one of the best employees, dedicated, thoughtful, honest." Now wasn't the time to remember the video and Happy Days notes. It was time to make Mrs. Martinez feel as comfortable as possible under these horrible circumstances.

"He has always been such a good provider. Our son has leukemia and it's been a hard road."

No wonder he had developed a five-finger habit. "Is the insurance covering the problem?"

"It was vaccine-related and when it was reported, all the medical help from normal providers was cut off."

"Isn't anyone helping him?"

"We found a doctor, but he doesn't take insurance. It's taken all we have to cover the bills. All we have left is the house."

There had to be a way I could help. I wondered if Lee had any stashes of cash somewhere around the office I could turn over to Mrs. Martinez. The heck with the consequences. But in the last week, I hadn't found any cash lying around. Lee must have taken all the payments with him before he was killed.

"Mrs. Martinez, we have some bad news," Valiant said.

"He wasn't fired, was he?" She looked really concerned.

"No," I said. I started choking up. "There was an incident with a vacuum cleaner."

"Vacuum cleaner?"

"We don't know what happened, but the hose wound up around his neck. When he was found, it was too late," Valiant finished for me.

"No. My Juan is not gone. It can't be." She looked as if she might collapse. Valiant and I rushed over to steady her.

"I know this must be hard. We'll do anything we can to try to help you and your son. The White House is bound to have some kind of benefit for situations like this," I said.

"Benefit?"

"Some kind of policy that can help you financially," I suggested.

"But who is going to help me take care of my son?"

"Maybe we can find someone. I know this is a terrible loss. I don't really know what to say," I continued.

"Can we help you while we're here?" Valiant said.

"I'd rather be alone."

As we started to leave, she said, "Wait."

She went into another room. When she came back, she had an envelope in her hand. "He said that, if something happened to him, to give this to you."

"Me?" I asked.

"He trusted you."

"Thank you, Mrs. Martinez. He was a good person. He put you and your son above everything else and that's a real hero."

"Thank you," she said. As we turned to leave, I heard her starting to cry. The shock must have worn off. I turned to see if I could help, but she waved us on.

When we got to the car, I opened up the envelope. There was a key inside.

"Another clue, but what is this to?" I asked.

"It wouldn't be a safe deposit box as those require ID. If it were to his work locker, security has the master key. It looks like a key to some kind of locker at a bus or train station."

"But which one?"

"Or maybe it's a gym locker."

"Tomorrow, maybe we can speak with Mrs. Martinez again. We have to find a way to help her son."

"How thoroughly have you explored Lee's office?" Valiant asked.

"I've been all through it."

"Has anyone looked into his condo?"

"It's in Alexandria, not far from the ranch house."

"You have the address?"

"I was there once. He hosted a little gathering there."

"Let's go."

"Are we going to break in?" I asked.

"I imagine he has top security. I might be able to black out the security."

"If you get tired of your job, a life of crimes awaits for you."

"Care to be Bonnie to my Clyde?"

"If they fire me, I'll consider it."

***

We pulled up in front of Lee's building.

"I have a different solution. Follow me," I said.

I knocked on the manager's door. I flashed my White House ID. "The White House sent me here to pick up Lee Carpenter's files.

It's a national security matter. This is my assistant." I pointed to Valiant.

"They sent someone to pick them up, last week."

"They missed a few."

"She said she had everything."

"She thought she did—until we were trying to find the three-two-five file."

"Three-two-five?"

"I shouldn't have mentioned it, but you seem to understand the critical nature of Lee's work. Please don't repeat that. National security, you know."

"Your pass looks in order." He led me to the elevator and put a card up against it. "Penthouse. Top floor," he told me.

"He must be making big bucks to afford this," Valiant said as the elevator door closed.

"I don't think the White House salaries go up that high," I said.

The elevator opened directly into the entrance to Lee's condo. The whole floor appeared to be his. The place was decorated with statues, a fountain, and vintage furniture. The ceiling was a glass skylight.

"If she, whoever she was, got the files, we're too late," I said.

"Did Lee seem like the type of person who would keep his confidential stuff in the open where any burglar could grab it?"

"Who do you think she was?"

"Maybe Lara? Maybe that's why she's dead."

"They'll try to get it from her daughter. I should contact her and warn her," I said.

"How, without telling her your suspicions about her mother?"

"She suspects it was the jab. I just left out the fact that someone faked what happened at the musical Cabinet meeting. If it were you, where would you hide something?" I asked.

"Not in a place someone might loot."

He pulled some thin plastic gloves out of his pants pocket. "For gasoline and unauthorized searching."

"Do you do this often?"

He smiled. "Not until now, but if we lose our jobs, I may have to take up a new profession."

We looked around. Among other things, there were classic tables, statues of Venus and Minerva and wall paintings. "Those can't be originals?"

"Either that or very good copies."

"That original of Pinkie is supposed to be in the Huntington Library."

"You've been there?" he asked.

"Once. It was my mom's favorite painting. It's by Thomas Lawrence. And look, across from it is a copy of Gainsborough's Blue Boy."

"If those are copies, the artist was very talented."

"Lee's side business? Stealing paintings?" I questioned.

The elevator opened. We ducked behind a couch.

I looked around the side. It was two men delivering a box. "Is anyone here?" one man asked.

"They must have left," the other one answered.

"I don't know. She said it wasn't here. It must have been in his office."

"It wasn't. He checked it thoroughly last week."

"Let's look for a wall safe."

"Or a floor safe."

They started looking around the room. In a minute, they'd find us. I heard the elevator open. "You were just delivering." It was the manager's voice. "This is a secure apartment." I heard a cry from the manager and then a thump. I looked. The manager had fallen to the floor with a knife sticking out of his chest.

CHAPTER 26

I was wishing I had Jerry's gun.

A minute later, I heard the sound of glass shattering. Valiant had moved. I looked over the couch. A lamp had knocked out one of the men. The other man had a rug over his head and Valiant was holding and kicking him. Valiant knocked the man into the fountain.

"Don't let him drown," I said.

Valiant realized what I meant. He lifted and then smashed the wet goon into the Minerva statue, which fell back and broke in half.

"Minerva, a good choice," he said.

I leaned down and checked the manager.

"I'm pretty sure he's gone," Valiant said.

I nodded as I looked at his open eyes and his motionless body. The intruders looked unconscious but alive.

I picked up a key card that had fallen to the ground from the broken statue. "What do you think this is to?"

"It has an inscription on it. 'To Be or Not to Be?'" Valiant pointed out.

"Maybe the President can help us break the code. He's Shakespeare literate."

In addition to the key card, several fat envelopes had fallen out of

Minerva. Valiant opened up one of the envelopes. "Vegas jackpot," he said, looking over the hundred-dollar bills inside. He opened up a couple more. More money.

I started picking up envelopes.

Valiant helped me, reaching into the remains of the statue and finding a host of additional envelopes. "Well, Lee's not going to be using this."

"Let's get out of here."

Valiant knelt down and reached into the manager's pocket.

"You aren't going to rob a dead man."

"Just in case, we need to come back." He took the elevator key card. "I've got an idea."

He tied up the two men and used a sharpie to write on their foreheads, "We did it." Then he dragged them into the elevator and sent it down. "Let's take the staircase," he said, ushering me over to a door next to the elevator.

———

"So now we have a mystery key and two mystery key cards and we're no closer to finding out what happened than before," I said after we were on our way back to the ranch house. "And the security camera probably saw us going up to the apartment. We're likely to be suspects, gloves or no gloves."

"While you were talking to the manager, I disabled the cameras and set them to erase."

"That was fast."

"It was right on the side of the desk. You had his full attention. I thought about punching him for the way he was looking at you."

"What about Lara or whoever came here last week?" I asked.

"That would be in the old recordings. Maybe the police will look into that."

"But they aren't going to tell us."

"You want to get back in there and get the recordings from last week?"

"Not until the police have cleared the place. And the recordings of the men who killed the manager are gone too," I lamented.

"These days, police and officials seem to be looking for the easy way to close a case."

"True."

"They might not look further than those men."

We took a roundabout route to the ranch house. Very roundabout, by way of D.C. First we made a stop by the Martinez's home and dropped an anonymous present in the mail slot. Next, we stopped outside my uncle's house to pick up the Papkimos.

"Your uncle is a retired chemist, isn't he?"

"Did you run a full background on everyone in my family?"

"Paris mentioned it. That's probably why you refused the vaccine."

"Paris got cards for the whole family, but he also found a sympathetic doctor that he and I went to. He figured the White House would be more thorough in checking his credentials for Deputy Chief of Staff. The Doctor had seen me as Eve and so I just used the fake card as Karissa."

My aunt Alice greeted us at the door and directed us to Uncle Dave's study, where the puppies were nestled up next to their mother. Dave told me they had barely eaten. "This type of dog is not much of an eater but I made the puppies nurse some. The mother still had some milk. I ran a test. None of them have been exposed to the mRNA." Apparently, Valiant's observations were correct.

Back at the ranch house, I checked on the rest of the dogs. I had some messes to clean up. They still had water left. Most of the dogs had eaten their food. I tried feeding the Papkimos but they were more interested in cuddling.

"Well, Kal-El," I said, picking up one of the little boys. "I had a dream that you were a natural healer." I put him back with his mother and carried Cynthia down to the basement.

"We've got a big family. Maybe we should get married. Good for the kids," Valiant said.

I laughed. "I love your sense of humor. Though I'm not sure how I feel about the first proposal of my life being a joke."

"Who said, it's a joke?"

I heard the door upstairs open. I carefully went up to see Jerry. "How did things turn out after we left?"

"The death was an accident and so was your injury."

"Like, I believe that. Someone played with my phone and was shuffling around papers."

"I believe her," Valiant said, coming up behind me.

"I believe you too. I tried to call you," Jerry said.

"I left my phone at the office." I handed him my new burner phone. "Call your number on it and you'll have my new number."

"You think they tapped your other one?"

"Not taking any chances. I'm thinking they looked at my calls, texts and pictures."

"You should let your brother know you're okay before he goes looking for you."

"I'll call him."

"Who is this?" Jerry asked, looking at my Papkimo.

"Cynthia."

"Hi, Cynthia."

"I named her after my hero Cynthia McKinney."

"Are the other dogs also former members of Congress?"

"I named one of the boys Kucinich."

"Good choice. He's my hero too. So how did it go with Juan's widow?"

"They've got a son with leukemia. She gave us a key Juan thought was important. We went to Lee's place, found a key card. And we found close to five hundred thousand dollars."

"Are you going to turn it in?"

"We already did, sort of. We dropped it off through Juan's mail slot. Let's hope that helps with the son's treatment. I've got to call my brother. The family's uninsured and so I don't know how far it will go."

"Maybe, my brother can refer her to some trustworthy specialists."

I started to go upstairs to put Cynthia back with her mother and siblings.

I heard Jerry practically yelling at Valiant. "After she was injured, you put her in that kind of danger?"

I went back down. "I'm okay, guys. I'm not a piece of China."

"Jerry's right," Valiant said. "I was out of line in taking that risk with you."

"Jerry, neither of us expected a couple of killers to come up to Lee's condo. And if we hadn't been there, Mrs. Martinez might not be able to afford her son's medical care."

"So you got a new phone," Paris said when I called him.

"I know someone pulled out my phone, messed with it and put it back in my pocket."

"They think you saw the body and fainted, hitting your head."

"I don't faint, and nobody accidentally strangles himself with a vacuum hose."

"It's a nice way to wrap things up without an FBI investigation."

"Didn't they used to investigate all unusual deaths?"

"This Administration has the FBI by the balls. Sorry."

"No problem—except that will make it harder to figure out who is doing what to whom and why."

"It's not your job to investigate. You are not 007."

"What if I'm next? Will they rule it an accident or a suicide?"

"I'm not going to let that happen. I think your main purpose in getting into this is moot. There's mine, but you don't have to risk for that."

"You're wrong."

"What?"

"He's alive. I got that from Gene. Somewhere, he's alive."

"Is it worth risking your life?"

"I don't want anyone else I care about to be hurt."

"I've noticed that you and Jerry are getting close."

"We're friends."

"He seemed really worried about you."

"He's a great guy."

I finally took Cynthia back to her room and gave her to Esther for nursing.

Jerry came into the room. "You could have been killed today. Twice."

"I'm alive."

Valiant came to the room.

"You both need to see what we got on the video of Blackmoriuntur."

"You're watching it remotely?"

"It's in the cloud."

"So what did you see?"

"It's not so much what as who."

"Who?"

We followed Valiant downstairs. "You might want to sit down."

"I'm fine," I said.

"Not you. But you can. It would be a good idea. I want you to relax."

I sat down.

"Jerry, sit down," he said.

Valiant flipped on the video.

Monica went to the front door of the building and someone let her in.

Valiant scanned through to where Monica left Blackmoriuntur with a box and someone I didn't recognize met her outside and took the box.

"Who is that guy?" I asked.

Valiant zoomed in on the picture. The face was a partial. I looked at Jerry and back at the picture. A perfect match.

CHAPTER 27

"It's not me," he said.

"Unless you've split into two, you were here at seven A.M. this morning," Valiant said.

"Signature Soldier?" I suggested.

"Maybe."

"What do you think is in that box?" Jerry asked.

"No idea. The camera didn't have x-ray technology," Valiant replied.

"Why don't I go see Monica and confront her? She may not know what she's gotten herself into."

"You plan to explain how you know about the pickup?" Valiant asked.

"Is the Happy Days drive available, yet?" I asked Valiant.

"Let's see," Valiant said, putting it into his computer.

"Let's go to JC," he commented as he searched for the video.

"Why didn't you tell me this before?" Jerry asked as the video played.

"John's a jerk but after the way Monica treated you, I felt they deserved each other," I said.

He didn't look happy.

"I'm sorry. I guess I was wrong," I apologized.

"We need to tell her."

"And let her know what we're investigating?" I asked.

"She may think that guy she handed the box to is me. It doesn't matter that she broke up with me. She deserves to know."

"Unless she is in on the whole thing. I'd like to think that, if I was dating a guy, I'd know the difference between him and a double," Valiant said.

I looked at him.

"I don't date guys, but if I did."

"I know. It's hard to let go of someone you care about," I told Jerry.

"That's not it. I just don't want to see her hurt."

"If we tip off Monica, we'll be tipping off those she's working with," Valiant pointed out.

"You want to just let her get herself killed?"

"We could make a copy of John's video and have it delivered to her."

"And what about the guy she thinks is me?"

"If she doesn't know the difference, why would she believe you when you tell her the truth?" Valiant asked. "She'll assume you're the fraud."

Jerry shrugged his shoulders.

"If I were going to replace someone, I'd take baby steps. See if I could fool a few people, then maybe a former girlfriend and then I'd feel more certain I'm succeeding," Valiant added. "After that, I'd make my big move."

"If it is a Signature Soldier and their disguises are that good, they could replace any of us," Jerry pointed out.

"We may be stretching our imagination on this one," I interjected.

"All the same, let's develop passcodes," Valiant suggested.

"I'm not going to be fooled," I said. "Not about either of you."

"All the same. We work it into a sentence so it doesn't appear it's a code," Jerry said.

"Maybe you have some clandestine underpinnings," I told him.

"Ice cream," Valiant said.

"The vegans won't like that one," I commented.

"Puppies," Jerry responded.

"Felix," I said.

"The cat?" Jerry asked.

"No. Leiter from the *James Bond* movies."

"The sharks ate off his legs in *License to Kill*," Valiant remarked.

"In that case, 'legs.' I want to keep mine."

"Very innocuous," Valiant said. "I don't think they'll pick up on them. 'I'm hungry but I don't feel like ice cream or my legs are tired or I saw some cute puppies today.'"

"If one person says their word, the person speaking with them has to say theirs."

"Agreed."

Jerry got a beep on his phone.

"You still carry that phone?"

"I switched to a new burner, and I texted my number to a few people. I guess it's on your old phone," he told me.

He pulled out his new burner phone. "Ray has some information."

"Let's go," I said.

"Jerry is right. You've been in too much danger. I'll go along with him."

"You're my date?" Jerry asked Valiant.

"Ray's seen me. He might not trust you," I told Valiant.

"I'll stay in the back corner."

"Ray's got eyes."

"I'll stay out of sight in the car then."

"But I'm coming too," I insisted.

We took off to the bar. At ten o'clock, Jerry said, "He should have been here by now."

We went outside to look around. Nothing. Jerry saw some movement in an alley near the bar and moved in that direction. "You stay back," he urged, but I ignored him and followed. Suddenly he was running. As I got to the alley, I could see why. There was someone lying face down on the ground. Jerry turned him over. Liquid was coming out of his mouth. It was Ray.

CHAPTER 28

Jerry started doing CPR. More liquid came out of Ray's mouth.

Valiant came up behind us. "Not another one."

While Valiant helped Jerry with Ray, I called 911 and then Trey. I thought he should hear from me that I had been at a death scene—once again. The EMTs who arrived pronounced Ray dead.

"What happened to him?" I asked.

"Drowned."

"In the alley?"

"You can drown on a cup of water. In this case, it was a large glass of gin, I'd say, having sniffed his breath," Valiant advised me. "I'm sorry, Jerry."

"Ray didn't drink gin," Jerry said. "He was my roommate. We were meeting next door, not in the alley."

"At the bar. Maybe he changed his drinking habits."

"And you?" a policeman who had arrived, asked Valiant.

"Just a bystander. If this is what happens at this bar, I don't think I'm going inside."

"Officer," I said. "He was going to meet us inside. He wouldn't be drinking out here." While I distracted the officer, Valiant backed out of the alley. He would be difficult to explain when Trey arrived.

"Not drinking. Aspirating," one of the EMTs said as they wheeled him away.

***

Trey called back and suggested letting the police handle this one. As Jerry and I left the scene, I had an eerie feeling. Valiant's car was gone. We walked to where it had been and looked around. No car. A minute later, Valiant's car pulled up with the passenger-side windows down. "Get in."

We did so.

"I'm sorry about your roommate," I told Jerry.

"Yeh. He was a good guy."

"I'm sorry too," Valiant said.

"Well, we might as well go back to the ranch house and sort things out."

"First, I'd like to visit Ray's apartment," Jerry said.

"You know where it is?"

"He didn't want to meet there as he's careful about his residence. I got these things from him before the EMTs arrived."

He held out a set of keys and a wallet.

"And where did you drive off to?" I asked Valiant.

"Looking for anyone who might have left the scene."

***

Ray's apartment was very homey. In the living room, was a desk filled with coloring books, a comfy sofa and a big-screen television that sat on one of the walls. We looked around the apartment. There were no obvious clues that Ray had ever been NSA.

"Well, I guess there's nothing here," I said.

"Not a dead end. Watch." Jerry went to the big screen TV set and pulled on the edges. He pushed part of the bottom right corner and the TV came forward revealing a switch on a wall. "He never trusted Smart TVs. So he wouldn't have one."

Flipping the switch opened a door-sized panel in the wall,

revealing another room. We walked in. There we saw a variety of guns, electronic equipment, and lists of names on top of a desk. Among them were Seth Rich, Gary Webb, Michael Ruppert, the names of about 50 deceased doctors and Jeffrey Epstein.

"You think he was investigating these?" I asked. "Some of the names on this list were also on the list in Lee's computer."

"Or maybe his team killed them," Valiant said.

Valiant started hacking into a computer in the room.

"For a spy, his password wasn't Valiant-proof," I said. "Careless."

"No. I'm just that good. This file has the schematics of Michael Hasting's car."

"He wasn't old enough for that," Jerry said.

"Maybe he was investigating it," I replied.

"Or it was a training film," Valiant suggested.

"I don't think he was a good guy," I said, looking into a file cabinet. I pulled out a thin face covering and put it on.

"Jerry, you've changed," Valiant said.

"And who could better impersonate you than your old roommate," I told Jerry.

Jerry sat down in a chair, seemingly stunned.

"He was probably going to send us on a wild goose chase," Jerry remarked.

"But if they knew about us, why didn't they just off us?"

"Maybe we were useful," Valiant said. "Maybe whatever we are doing is leading them to what they want to know. The murders seem to follow us around. Then, when they're tired of us, they may off you and me and frame Jerry."

"And I went to him for help."

"You didn't know," I said.

"Well, it looks like Monica's accomplice has lost his face," Valiant said. "You no longer need to warn her about the other Jerry."

"I wonder if that box is here," I said.

"I don't know but look at this," Valiant replied. He had pulled out a map of D.C. tunnels with "X's. "I bet this is where they set the bombs to resemble an earthquake."

CHAPTER 29

"Not HAARP?" I probably sounded disappointed. "What is the NSA up to?" I asked.

"Or is it just rogue elements of the NSA?" Valiant asked.

I pulled a camera out of my pocket. "I'm preserving this in case they come knocking at our door."

"Make it apparent on a video that this is Ray's place," Valiant said.

Jerry had been mostly quiet. "I sure know how to pick them. Monica. Ray."

"The school picked Ray for your roommate," I said. "Now he's gone."

Here's something else. "The Vice President. Look at this file. Here is a list of her planned appointments for after she gains the Presidency."

"Well, we have our antagonist," I said. "Maybe."

"The country wouldn't have her except through succession. She couldn't even get one delegate in the primaries," Valiant pointed out.

"She might simply be planning to have the President declared incompetent. All she needs is to record his speeches. No need for her to kill him," Jerry said.

"True. Maybe it's time to call in Trey."

"You sure you can trust him?" Valiant asked me.

"He is the top guy protecting the President. Or the robot."

"You may be right. It might be good if we let someone know."

"How about Gene?" Jerry suggested. "That way, if Trey turns out to be a problem, which I don't expect, someone else will see what is going on."

"Jerry stand by the cabinet. I want to get a photo and video of your face by the fake one."

"Don't the Signature Soldiers fake identifications and backgrounds? Theoretically, anyone could be a phony. The real Jerry could be hiding in the closet and the one standing here could be the phony."

Jerry start laughing as did I. Valiant wasn't laughing. He kept his straight face for a minute and then smiled. "Nah, a fake one wouldn't have stolen a PESA truck."

I picked up my burner phone again and started to dial.

"Wait. I want to copy these files before anyone busts in," Valiant said. He had me wait half an hour before calling Gene.

"Well, I guess that should end your concerns," Gene said after arriving with Trey.

"Concerns?"

"I could tell you had doubts about the deaths. If there was a killer, this is evidence." Looking over the mask, he said, "And Jerry, you must feel relieved. This should set to rest any questions anyone might have regarding your activities. Guilt must have overcome Ray causing him to drink himself to death."

"But he inhaled the drink."

"He must have been pretty drunk to do that," Trey said. "Look here." Trey opened a drawer in Ray's desk, "He has passes to the White House. That explains how he got in to cause all that havoc over the last eight days. You were correct to raise your concerns about the access, Karissa."

"It's best if we don't go public with all this. You three are heroes," Gene added. "So, I assume you'll let this go. If a Signature Soldier went rogue, we don't want to call attention to issues with the program. National security."

"I'll let it go," I said. "But there is something I want first. May I speak with you, privately?"

I pulled Gene into the hall. "If this is a raise," he reacted.

"I'm not interested in money. I want to see the real President. We need to reprogram the robot and it will simplify Valiant's job if we could see the real President."

Gene thought for a minute. "Is there any hope for resurrecting the first robot?"

"Valiant says it would take too long." I paused. "Seriously, Gene, there is no telling whether he will do a musical or a tragedy next or simply play Dr. Strangelove."

"Dynozap wouldn't have a problem with Dr. Strangelove."

"I noticed."

"We have the funeral for Stacey tomorrow. You should probably rest after what you've been through. On Thursday I might be able to arrange something."

"Thursday."

"We owe you a debt of gratitude. These deaths have been creating havoc."

Gene and I went back to the others. "So for now," he told Trey and the rest of us, "We collect the evidence and call this closed."

The others nodded.

On the way back, we dropped off the drug video of John in an envelope with the gate guard at Monica's condoplex. He said he'd get it to her right away.

"Maybe you and Monica will get back together," Valiant suggested to Jerry.

"That's over. I want a different kind of girl."

"The power is back on in D.C. I guess we can all go home now," I said.

"What about the rest of the investigation?" Valiant asked. "Happy Days."

"Happy Days is blackmail information," I noted.

"What about John?"

"I'll handle him," I said.

"Tough lady," Valiant responded, smiling.

"No more chances," Jerry said. "I want you to stick around for a while."

"If Ray is the killer, John's only a pathetic crook. The White House has cameras," I said.

"Ray would have known how to cut the cameras and lights," Jerry said. "I still can't believe it about him."

"You saw the Jerry disguise. He was about your size."

"He was my roommate in college."

"Allowing him to know enough to fake being you," Valiant said.

Back at the ranch house, Valiant put the video and file copies away in a space his uncle had created under the floorboards.

"I can take you home," Valiant told me.

"I'm going to have Jerry do that," I said. I was worried about Jerry in view of the revelations. Valiant looked crestfallen. Jerry looked very happy. "Are the two of you up to dividing up the puppies? I'll take the Papkimos back to my place."

"I'll take the collies and pit bulls back to mine," Jerry said. "I've always wanted a collie."

"I'll take the mutts and the Belgian shepherds," Valiant said.

"Will your manager mind?" I asked Valiant.

"I'll tell them it's for a White House fundraiser."

"My brother has a large place. He can take some of the dogs off our hands," Jerry said.

"I'm not letting go of my Papkimos."

Valiant went upstairs with me to collect the Papkimos. "You sure Jerry's car is big enough for all those puppies?"

"These will sit on my lap. They're small." I picked up Kal-El. "Besides we have Superman to make everything okay."

"Yeh."

"Valiant, Jerry is still in shock. This isn't personal." He perked up a little. I touched his shoulders. "You've kept me sane at work for a long time. We all need help once in a while."

I leaned up and kissed his cheek. As I moved back, he reached around me, pulled me to him and kissed me on the lips.

CHAPTER 30

I tried to push him away, but part of me didn't want to. His kiss was sweet, and I liked it way too much. I couldn't let this happen. I fought the feeling and found the strength to push him back. Maybe I shoved a little too hard as he fell back over a Belgian shepherd that had followed him into the room. "Valiant, let's not go there."

"Right. Sorry."

"No. It was sweet. I'm just not ready for that kind of thing."

"Sure." His heart didn't seem to be into the "Sure." "I'll carry Esther, Kucinich and Cynthia."

"She's Ms. McKinney to you." He smiled. He looked at the shepherd. "Traitor," he said.

On the way to my place, we stopped by a grocery store to pick up new food and bottled water. I couldn't be sure my supplies weren't poisoned while everything was going on. Jerry carried the food and water up. Esther and the puppies were small enough that I was able to sneak them up to my place under a coat. The puppies were going to be tiny adults, probably about three to four pounds each. I put the

Papkimos in my room. I had it easy with only six small ones. Jerry had fourteen and Valiant had seven much larger puppies.

"Would you like some help?"

"I'm fine. I'll see you at work tomorrow."

As I restocked my cupboards and refrigerator, I removed the old food and water bottles and threw them into the trash chute.

A few minutes later, there was a knock at the door. It was Valiant. I backed up, hoping there wasn't a repeat of our last time alone.

He could obviously see that I was uncomfortable as he said, "I'm just here to check for bugs, bombs, and so forth." He apparently meant what he said as he was solely focused on checking my apartment. He even checked for boogeymen under the bed.

"Thank you," I said. He held out his hand to shake mine, almost formally. Maybe I had been too cold before.

"Let's not let that interfere with our friendship. Please," I said.

He smiled. "Do I seem that shallow? Good night."

I was a bit concerned about having a crook like John in the White House, but his crimes were minor compared to the murders that had happened or the crimes involving the President. I could now no longer claim plausible deniability. Thinking of the list, the letters "GH" had murder and prison by them. Why hadn't I looked yet at the video? I had found time for other things. *Was I afraid*? Maybe Gene had served time. Or maybe it was a video of someone else with his initials. If prison had been involved, he had paid for his crime.

On Tuesday, John hadn't shown up for work. I didn't see him when I arrived on Wednesday. Maybe Monica had threatened to expose him and he'd hit the road.

The President now thought he was Tootsie and kept demanding skirts, instead of slacks. He kept asking where Julie was. Before I had left the lab, he turned into John Wayne, better for perceptions. I was glad he didn't have a gun. A couple of times, he said he had to take out Liberty Valence. I wasn't a John Wayne fan. I kept remembering what Wayne had to say about African-Americans. But that was minor compared to what the real President had done to my mom.

A teacher had brought a classroom of children to the White House.

Jerry walked in with a bundle of puppies. I thought of my Papkimos. I hoped they were alright.

He showed the puppies to the teacher and students. "A recent study has shown that having a pet helps children become better learners and more compassionate. Do any of your students who do not already have a pet, have families who would be accepting of one of these?" It was a good sales pitch.

The teacher looked perplexed. "Have they been fixed: spayed and neutered?"

"Spaying and neutering puppies doesn't fix them. It breaks them and causes cancer and early death. We don't want these kids depressed."

"I don't want my puppy to get cancer," one boy said.

"Me neither," a girl agreed. "I want an intact dog."

"Their parents would need to give permission."

"Do you have a cell phone or would you like to call the parents on an outside line?" Jerry asked. "These are official White House exhibits and I'd need the information on anyone taking a puppy."

Kids started rattling off their names and information.

"Wait, children. We don't even know if your parents will agree," the teacher said. "Let's see if you even like the puppies."

The kids started playing with the collie and pit bull puppies. I saw a little girl who was shy. I picked up one of the boy collie pups and handed it to her. "For me? Nobody ever gives me anything." The puppy was licking her face.

"Would your parents let you keep it?"

"I don't have a daddy. My mommy said she'd get me a dog if she could afford one."

"I'll tell you what. I'll see to it you get a canine health insurance policy to take care of any medical emergencies. Dogs like human food and so you can feed it scraps from your table."

"That's not what I hear," the teacher said.

"That's because the dog food companies are good at publicizing false claims that their food is better. 250,000 dogs died in a short period of time a while back in this country from eating premium dog food. Even the most popular brands are mostly just feathers and bones and other garbage humans don't want. Dogs will even become vegetarians if you let them."

"He looks like Lassie," the little girl said.

"He's a boy. How about Laddie?"

"Laddie, do you want to go home with me?"

"What's this?" Paris asked coming into the hallway, watching press photographers snapping pictures of the puppies and children.

"Public relations. Animal awareness month," I whispered to him.

"I bet the President's popularity will double after this. Great idea," he whispered back.

"Not my idea. Jerry's."

Jerry seemed to be beaming.

I went over to him. "What about your brother?"

"He agreed to one of the pit bulls. I've always wanted a collie and took one of the boys."

"I knew you couldn't let them all go. What did you name him?"

"Mr. President."

"Perfect. He'll get my vote in the next election."

Down in the lab, Valiant said, "I wish I had thought of that idea. I've still got seven. You realize if we got married, we'll already have thirteen children."

"Ha!"

"But think of the children."

"Tomorrow, I get to see my father," I whispered almost under my breath.

"I'm not going to ask for his approval. If I got it, you'd probably never speak to me again."

"Would you stop joking? I'm nervous."

"About seeing someone who would do that to your mother?"

"I've hated him for so long. Make sure I don't kill him."

"Is that why you're here?"

"I wanted to expose what he was like. The robot would be a better father."

"Maybe I could program him to go to father/daughter dances. He'd be the life of the party."

"That's for sure. Except, you and Paris know he's not real."

He made zipping motions in front of his mouth.

"I've been programming Spanish into him for the trip to Mexico," he said.

"Castilian or Latin American?

"Shoot."

"Well, you have two days to fix it."

I went upstairs to my office.

"Would you like to go to lunch?" Duane said, coming into my office.

"It would be nice, but they're watching me closely. Hit my head yesterday."

"Maybe Thursday?"

"If they don't make me work through lunch. Today, we have the funeral for Stacey and Friday I have to go to Mexico."

"You? Rising up in the West Wing."

"They might need additional research material while we're there. The President keeps confusing the President of Mexico with the President of Zimbabwe. "

He laughed. "Babysitter to a demented leader. I understand Alzheimer's only gets worse. Soon you'll be changing his diapers."

"I'll let you do that. I'm sure diapers are minor compared to the rest of your work. Hushpuppies is a pretty powerful sub-department."

"Isn't it!"

I dropped by Paris's office. "I'm hearing the FBI is thinking of hiring you to find all the missing bodies from the last fifty years."

"Ha! I've had my fill of bodies."

"Gene and Felicity are touting your praises."

"Felicity? What business of hers was it?"

"She's a Special Assistant to the President."

"The real one or the robot?"

"Good question."

"I'm going to see him on Thursday," I murmured, lowering the volume of the conversation.

"Don't fall in love with your dad."

"They'll have to hold me back to keep me from killing him."

"Get lots of pictures. Of course, if you kill him, make sure the cameras are off."

I nodded.

The funeral was an ostentatious event. Stacey would have loved it. There were violins and harps. The President came out to speak, accompanied by Gene. "She was a great teacher."

"I didn't know that," I whispered to Valiant.

"Learn something new every day."

"She knew the risks and yet she courageously decided to go to her next adventure so that she could advance womankind. The world watched as she was blown apart. Seven lives lost. Seven of the greatest Americans. We will never forget her. And though she is in pieces, her pieces will forever live in infamy."

"Is he confusing Stacey with Christa McAuliffe? Stacey may have been crushed but she is not in pieces," I whispered to Valiant.

"Who were the other six?" Dippy, who was sitting on the other side of me, asked.

"I guess they're still digging out the bodies." If she didn't know the President had left reality, I wasn't going to tell her.

"It's amazing how they put the pieces together so she could have an open-casket funeral. Reconstructive science has advanced a long way, partly thanks to me."

"Of course. Really amazing," I replied back to Dippy, hoping she'd be quiet and let me hear the President's speech.

"Her children, Scott and Caroline, can know that the world celebrates the life and courage of their mother. When Steven said goodbye to her that morning, he had no idea that he would never see her again."

"Who is Steven?" Dippy asked. "Her husband was Philip."

"I guess he was her boyfriend."

"Really? Are Scott and Caroline his children? She and Philip had Susie and Wendy."

I turned to look at the two children in black. Gene rushed up to the President's side. "Isn't that beautiful? The President just compared Stacey's life and sacrifice to that of Christa McAuliffe. He's right. She was a great woman, just like Christa, and will forever be missed."

"I was about to add," the President continued.

"I'm sorry, sir, but we have to evacuate the building. There has been a breach in security."

The rest of the President's words were lost in the rush to exit.

"I wonder why powerful people have no qualms pushing, shoving and trampling each other," Valiant whispered as he and I avoided getting knocked over as we moved toward the President.

"Beats me. But that breach was a save."

"Who knew he was going to follow the wrong script."

"Script?"

"We were programming in NASA history for his meeting with General Colton."

"I hope the security breach postpones that meeting," I said.

On the way out, Gene grabbed my arm. "If meeting with the real one helps, I'll make sure it happens tomorrow."

"Thank you."

Later as I was leaving the West Wing, I saw Felicity staring. I had undoubtedly fallen from grace. "Karissa darling, you look so tired. Rough day?"

"No. Nothing out of the ordinary. I cried during the service. I didn't know that Stacey was a teacher. I'm sure Scott and Caroline will be so proud of their late mother. Though, not half as proud as Steven."

She looked odd at first. "Of course. Steven. I've been calling him the wrong name all these years. I hope he didn't notice."

"I'm sure he didn't."

That evening, I was supplementing the puppies' feeding with organic formula. For either a Papillion or a toy Eskie, five was a large litter. Things seemed a bit dull, compared to the events of the last nine days.

Answering a knock at my door produced Jerry with Mr. President. He was a mahogany sable collie and very much into licking. He and the other puppies Jerry had rescued were several weeks older than mine.

"Just so long as he doesn't eat my puppies."

"Mr. President? That would be high crimes and misdemeanors. My brother checked. His blood is clean too."

Another knock at the door produced Valiant.

"Is this the one you kept?"

"He's cute," I said. "And he's the leader of the free world."

"Meet Mr. President," Jerry told him.

"Well, my Mr. Putin can outeat your Mr. President."

"I knew you were a Russiabot," I said.

"Not a Russiabot. I'm all of the bots: Iranian, Syrian, Kiribatian, Nicaraguan."

I laughed. "So where is Mr. Putin?"

"Hanging out with President Maduro and Che Guevara and their canine troops."

"So the two of you are going to Mexico on Friday?" Jerry asked.

"We want to make sure the other Mr. President," I said, looking at the little collie. "Doesn't turn into Nero and fiddle while Mexico City burns."

"I'm going to ask to go too. After all, the President, the one from the White House, might need some water for the fiddle or to do a press release after the meeting. Besides, it would be a shame to break up the team."

A thought occurred to me. "We're going to need a dog sitter. I can't expect your brother to take them all in."

"I already thought of that. Jack and Brandon have agreed to help out if it's too much for him," Valiant assured me.

"Confusing Stacey with Christa McAuliffe was really sick," Jerry said.

"It could have been worse. He could have confused her with Lady Macbeth," Valiant responded.

"Lady Macbeth would have been more appropriate," I said.

"Or Lucrezia Borgia," Jerry threw in.

"I'd suggest finding a way to disconnect the AI, but I'm starting to like the new President," I said.

"Believe me, we've tried to disconnect the AI. But we have to avoid the President exploding."

"Exploding? I didn't know about that part."

"It's a fail-safe in case anyone tries to look at his memory card. Remember. He was supposed to go to China."

"Look where the AI President, along with his masters, have already gotten us," Jerry said flatly.

"The destruction of Sri Lanka. War with Kiribati. I understand the Secretary of State has already been placed in indefinite detention as an enemy combatant. The NDAA applies to him too."

"Good old Obama," Jerry said.

"I remember my mom was furious when he signed the first NDAA authorizing indefinite detention of American citizens," Valiant chimed in.

"How did she feel about his executive order to assassinate American citizens?" I asked.

"She didn't like that one either."

"I wonder how she'll feel about the new orders to round up Republicans," I said. "They'll probably do a mass execution."

"She was a Democrat, last I knew, but we need to stop that."

"The roundups have already started," Jerry said.

"Great," I responded, facetiously.

"What if the President changes parties?"

"That would be interesting," I said. "Maybe he'll have the whole White House staff arrested as the new terrorists."

That night, I was more excited than ever. I was going to meet my father. I was not excited like a daughter but like a victim who was about to meet the criminal who had assaulted her. When I found where he was, when I saw him, I'd be able to figure out the best plan for revenge.

In the morning, I arrived early. John was not there, again. Maybe he showed up late or maybe he had run after Monica got the video. Gene was busy. "I'll see you in an hour to check out that matter," he said.

I went to the lab. "I've been working on the old robot. The parts came in. So old fake Pres will sort of be up by the end of next week," Brandon said.

"What about the face?"

"That's the hard part. I'm not a plastic surgeon and we can't let one in. But I found a site explaining the techniques for creating the Signature Soldiers' fake face masks. The NSA has devices that can whip them up quickly. I'm also not an artist and, even at full speed, I'll be doing it by hand. It will take me to the end of next week at the earliest to get it done and that's pushing it from the two weeks I really need."

"If you succeed, I'll talk to Gene about giving you a bonus."

"Good boss."

I turned to Jack and Valiant. "You too."

"She's the best," Valiant said.

"Now, we need to just survive the week and next with this guy," I said, looking at the current President. I turned to Valiant. "Gene said an hour and that was half an hour ago."

Valiant took my hand. "I'll be there for you. If you want to kill him, I'll find a knife. If you want to rescue him, we can figure that out too."

"The former is more likely. I'll be fine."

"Who do you want to kill?" Brandon asked.

"My sixth-grade teacher. She pulled a nasty prank on me when I was in grammar school that I never forgot."

"Hopefully, she got twelve of the vaccines," Brandon said. "I gather she had a sex change operation since she's now a 'him.'"

I smiled. A realization hit me. "You're one of us." I was thinking about the jab. He was too awake to have been jabbed.

"I just want to keep my head. I told you I supported you." He was probably thinking about our prior conversation, I guessed.

"I told you we could trust him," Valiant said.

* * *

Half an hour later, we were in Gene's office. He called in Jeb Hunter, a guy I had seen around. "He's the only one in the Secret Service detail who knows the truth," Gene explained.

"What about Trey?"

"As the head, he'd have to take action if he found out. He draws more attention too. If we tried to convince him to help, that might lead to exposure."

"Hi, Jeb," I said.

He shook both my hand and Valiant's and then looked back at Gene for instructions.

"Who else on the staff knows?"

"You, Valiant, me, Jeb, your brother, your staff, and the Special Assistant know about your sub-department."

"How about the Vice President?"

"We can't even keep track of who she sleeps with or what country or century she claims to have grown up in. Now, she was raised on a plantation during slavery."

"How about the First Lady?"

"If she never sees him again she'll be happy. When Stacey Duncekins and Rusty Rigger informed her they could arrange to make him President, she made certain demands, and we've followed through. One of them was she would only assist him with public appearances and she had the right to kill him if he came to see her privately."

"I can understand," I said so quietly that only Valiant could hear.

"What was that?"

"I said, 'that's convenient.'"

"As soon as you use the information you need for your work, you have to forget everything you see."

"I haven't seen John, lately."

"He took an emergency leave."

Wise choice, I thought.

As Gene walked us out, he acted as if he were giving us a tour for research purposes. "You are familiar with all the offices and workings of the West Wing. I want to make sure you can provide a profile of the remainder of the White House to be kept in the archives for posterity."

As we started to walk between the buildings he said, "I know you are familiar with the promenade. Many TV shows have depicted presidents walking along this path."

"We'll see if we can find some pictures of Presidents walking along this to include in the report. This really is a magnificent building," I remarked.

I was wondering if this was too elementary, given that I had been at the White House for quite some time and Valiant, even longer. But the staff seemed to be ignoring us, anyway, as we passed, apparently bored by our conversation.

Gene continued the tour through the East Wing, pointing out where parties were thrown.

"We're not planning another event are we?" Lill interrupted us as we passed her.

"Next week," Gene said.

"Darn. Couldn't he stay out of town? See a few museums and do some fishing?"

"We'd like to have you accompany us to Mexico."

"On your death bed. I've got the flu," she rattled off, clearly not sick.

"Very nice seeing you," I said.

"It's an honor," Valiant told her.

"Whatever."

We left her stewing in the dining room as Gene took the elevator to the top floor. "The regular bomb shelter is under the first floor but that is too obvious. Everyone knows about it."

He pressed a spot in the elevator control panel and it opened to reveal a secondary control panel. "It took months to create this new facility." On the new panel, I could see buttons for lower levels that were apparently hidden, much like those to our lab. "This will take us way below the bomb shelter and the subterranean tunnels."

"What about the architects and builders?"

"There was a serious accident at the next site they were renovating."

"Any survivors?" Valiant asked, getting the drift.

"Unfortunately, no."

"Could it not have been an accident?"

"Is that an accusation?"

"No. I'm just noting that there have been accidents in the last week and maybe Ray or someone was behind that too."

"Ray is dead. I checked his file today. He was a particularly nasty hitman. You're lucky you're alive."

The elevator opened up onto a luscious playroom. "Are there children down here?"

"Just the President and the robotic crew that the first tech crew from your department created." The first tech crew was all dead, but I figured Gene might not have known we knew that.

"Why were they let go if they had so much information?"

"They all signed non-disclosure agreements."

"Have you kept track of them?"

"They had full clearance. If they had talked, it would have been made public by now."

"Could that have been what Marissa Tracy was researching?"

"I guess we'll never know."

I looked around the room. There was a swing set, a slide and a Disney video playing on a wall. We went out of that room to another room with a giant sandbox. There, someone resembling the robot was sitting in the sand playing with a toy shovel.

CHAPTER 31

The real President kept picking up sand with the shovel and letting it drop back into the box. I heard a cry from under the sand. He picked up an anatomically correct baby girl doll. Apparently, she had taken the swimsuit optional approach to artificial sunbathing. He brushed the sand off her hair. "Flowers," he said, checking out the scent.

Valiant put some earphones attached to a mini-computer over the President's head, while I spoke to Gene. There had been no security check on us and so Gene didn't know that I had a video camera with the lens sewn as a button on my jacket. "So this is the real President, mentally down to the level of a child. Can he speak? I mean other than 'flowers?'"

The President grabbed my pant leg. I tried to pull it free. Gene helped to pull my father's hand off. The President started to cry. "Mommy, this man is mean to me. Will you help me?"

"I'm not mean. You've got to stop grabbing girls."

"She's my mommy. Can I have some ice cream?"

A robot, this one looking like a robot, came into the room.

"Get him some ice cream," Gene said.

"Can we have an ice cream party?" the President asked.

"Remember Mommy, you promised me an ice cream party if I was good."

"An ice cream party sounds great," I said.

"Ice cream for all," Gene told the robot.

"I've been really good. I haven't spilled any sand out of the sandbox."

"That's very good," I said.

"Mommy, I drew a picture for you."

He reached outside the box and handed me a paper with stick figures drawn on it. "That's me and that's you and we're a family."

"How long has he been like this?"

"Since before he was elected. We knew a year in advance he was declining and put together the original tech team. Initially, it wasn't easy hiding him between drugged performances where he repeated what came across on his earpieces. I constantly had to supervise him and my wife thought I was cheating on her."

"So he was mentally a child prior to the election?"

"Not quite at this stage, but yes."

"You did a good job of concealing that from the voters. If they had known—"

"It wouldn't have made any difference. We stuffed enough ballots to win if he didn't get any votes at all."

"Thank goodness for the mail-in ballots and the drop boxes."

"Only the ones with the correct political affiliation were counted."

"Of course," I said. "If the other side didn't vote in person, theirs weren't counted at all."

"Naturally, the other party had to get some token votes that were allowed."

"Naturally."

"What was the real vote count?"

"Best estimate. He lost by ninety percent."

"Thank goodness, the news media called anyone who questioned the election a Russian, a terrorist, or a conspiracy theorist."

"We've owned the news media for a long time."

The robot brought in the ice cream.

"Mommy, will you feed me?"

Gene nodded at me.

I sat down and started feeding him his ice cream.

"Mommy, eat yours."

I took a spoonful from a different bowl.

After I finished feeding him he asked, "Can I eat yours too?"

"Of course, darling," I said.

"Can we play with the trains later?"

"That would be fun. Do you like trains?"

"I love trains. I push a button and the train blows up," he said, throwing his arms up and looking in the direction of a train set that appeared to have been reconstructed recently.

"It's a little like the one Gomez Adams used to have. It's his favorite toy but expensive to replace the trains," Gene said.

"That's what the White House budget is for," I responded.

"Are we in the White House? The President lives there. Can I see him?"

I looked at Gene. "He doesn't know?"

"He keeps forgetting."

"Darling, you're the President."

"I am? Can we start a war?"

"You already have. You've started more wars than any other President."

"Yay for me."

Valiant removed the headset.

"Have you got what you need?" Gene asked.

Valiant nodded. I got up.

"Mommy don't leave me. Please don't leave me," the President whined.

There was something tugging at my resolve. I wasn't dealing with a monster who had raped my mother. Well, I was, but the rapist had died with his brain. This was a child and he thought I was his mommy. I found I had conflicting feelings. I still hated him, but I also pitied him.

Back in my office, Valiant said, "He may be mentally gone, but never forget what he did. He is largely responsible for the mass incarceration of Blacks. He wanted to execute Julian Assange."

"I know. It's just, today was the first time I really met him, and he's a child. But you are right. Child or not, he shouldn't get away with his crimes. I just need some time to process it."

"That will give us a little more time on the job before we're looking for new ones."

I handed my jacket with the button camera to Valiant. "Make a hundred copies for my mother. She deserves for the truth to be exposed."

Valiant put an arm around my shoulder. "I know this is hard."

Jerry walked in. "What's up?"

"He's a child."

"Who?"

"The President."

"He's alive?"

I nodded.

"Well, I'm not surprised. If the robot was done a couple of years ago, he's bound to have declined more."

"He thought I was his mother."

"Mommy, your son did not turn out well."

I smiled a little.

"If we expose this right now, the Vice President takes over," Valiant said.

"She's a piece of work," Jerry said.

"I'll have to think about it."

"You aren't thinking of exposing the whole thing," Jerry reacted.

"Mr. Straight and Narrow, I wouldn't have expected you to demand keeping this quiet."

"I was hoping the robot could teach me to dance."

I almost laughed. "Thanks."

I had been through all the files again and again. The computer that was now sitting in my office had an almost bare hard drive. I didn't want to lose anything if it was confiscated, again. I thought of Duane. Maybe I could get him talking.

I called down to Duane's non-existent lab or whatever it was and asked him to come to my office. He seemed suspicious. "Sit down, it's a peace offering. I was going to suggest lunch, but let's go Dutch."

He seemed a little relieved. I got the impression Dutch was his style. He didn't seem the gentlemanly type.

Jerry came in. "Lunch?"

"Sorry. I have a prior date. I'm sure there are lots of other people you could take to lunch." He looked at Duane and I hoped he was picking up on what was going on.

Duane looked at the menu and was deciding between the eagle and rhinoceros. I wondered if he knew they were endangered species, two of many served at this exclusive restaurant that catered to D.C. officials. Coming to this restaurant was Duane's idea.

"Lee and I used to eat here regularly," he said. "The old House Speaker comes here almost every day for humpback whale burgers and double gin martinis."

I ordered a salad without any meat. Duane ordered fried gorilla fingers, real ones.

"I was just thinking that we should work together to get funding for both sub-departments," I said. "The first day, I learned that some of the contractors are very grateful, if you know what I mean."

"I figured Lee was taking a little extra home. How much have you taken in so far?"

"Nothing. Paris was there when they tried to bribe me and I thought it was a test."

"Maybe we could split the profits."

"That's what I was thinking. But it would help if I had a sense of what your sub-department did. I mean. I can't promise anything if I don't know what I can follow through on."

He leaned in and started whispering. "At Hushpuppies, we eliminate obstacles."

"Obstacles? Like red tape?"

"Like whatever gets in the way of our benefactors. Who do you think created the plandemic to scare people off from the polls?"

"You did that?"

"The scare provided more than an opportunity for election rigging. That was an important side effect. If it hadn't worked, I might not be in the White House."

"So you're saying the President's Party would have lost but for the, um, scary cold? Brilliant. But they still counted absentees, didn't they?"

"Did they? We round up the legitimate ones and replace them with millions of our own in every state," he said with a proud smile on his face.

"Double brilliant. So your sub-department does paperwork."

"That's just the fun stuff. That's not all we take care of. Have you noticed how many natural health doctors aren't speaking?"

"Censorship?"

"And."

"Floating in the river? Oh my, wow, that's exciting."

"You can't imagine."

"My department is really boring by comparison."

"What kind of research are you doing?"

"Well, there is a desire to destabilize opponents and we're supposed to find the Achilles heel of, say, foreign countries or the other party." I had to make up something.

"I guess we're the action department and you're the data department. I think we really could work together."

"Definitely."

I wondered if some of the recent corpses had been treated to Hush-puppies's efficient operations.

Jerry asked to take me out to dinner. He wouldn't be going on the trip and he gave me the sweetest invitation. That and his puppy dog eyes convinced me. Jerry reminded me of little Kal-El, who had really taken to me.

He took me to a vegan restaurant. "The food, here, is organic. I thought you would like it."

"It's great," I said, noticing inside waterfalls and flower gardens. "This isn't even on the tourist lists. How did you find it?"

"I'm the Press Secretary. People are always offering to take me out to lunch or dinner. They think that's the way to get secrets."

"And of course, that's not who you are."

"Did Duane tell you anything?"

"I think his department is creating fake pandemics, election fraud and all the natural doctors dropping dead. Don't know about the rest of the accidents, natural deaths and so forth."

"Sort of carrying out the NDAA." Jerry was referring to the National Defense Authorization Act, initially signed into law in 2011 by Barack Obama and repeatedly signed into law every year thereafter. It included things like the indefinite detention of American citizens without rights or due process.

"Except, I gather they were working on it before they were working for the government. Duane seemed very enthusiastic about his work. Watch your back around him."

"Did you record it?" Jerry asked me.

"Of course. That's not all. I got video on the President. I hate him, but mentally, he's a baby. If I destroyed him, he wouldn't even know it."

"Why would you want to destroy him?"

"I'm not saying I would, but I was saying that, if I did, he wouldn't know it. Have you spoken to Monica?"

"She hasn't called me. I started to call her, but I think it's better for her to call me first."

"You're probably right. At least, she's warned about John."

"Just because we're not investigating the murders anymore isn't any reason we can't keep going out. We could go out on dates."

"Sure. We've become friends and it's nice going out with friends."

'Friends," he repeated.

"Good friends."

As Jerry escorted me to my door, I told him I needed to get some rest for the trip. I opened it and the Papkimos rushed over to me. Esther jumped into my arms. "My brother and I are going to have our hands full with your Papkimos, Valiant's dogs and Mr. President."

"I'm sure you can handle it. I still can't believe you drove off with the PESA truck. Very impressive."

"When you get to know me better, I'll do my best to be more impressive."

"You're fine, just the way you are."

He smiled and then looked more serious. "Be careful. I guess you and Valiant will be doing a lot of work on the trip."

"Trying to keep the President from accidentally starting a war."

He laughed. "Well, maybe I should hang out in a bomb shelter until you get back."

I hadn't been inside more than two minutes before there was a knock at my door. It was Valiant. I let him in and went over to the couch. "Any complications I should know of?"

"He thinks he's a telenovela star right now."

"Maybe you could educate him on Mexican history."

"I'll try. I'm going back for a few hours tonight. Then, I'll try to get some rest for tomorrow."

"We're only going to be there for the afternoon. The shorter the better."

"Did you tell Jerry about your dad?"

"It was just dinner. He's a good friend. And no, I haven't filled him in on my history."

"Because part of you doesn't trust him?"

"No. Because I don't want anyone to know about it. For all intents and purposes, Eve is dead and buried and my life would be too complicated if she were resurrected." Something about my response seemed to perk him up.

"I'll keep your secret to the grave."

"Please don't mention yourself and grave in the same sentence. I need you alive."

"You need me?" He perked up more.

"I couldn't do my work without you."

"Oh. At least, until you bring down the Administration."

"Is that what you want?"

"It's what you want. Or is it?"

"It's hard to hate a baby. But I just needed to look at his face to know how evil he was."

"Was."

"Was."

<hr>

That night, I kept turning over and over, seeing my baby father, hating him one minute and feeling sorry for him when he called me "Mommy" the next. He wasn't a baby. He had just reverted to a baby. Maybe that was punishment enough for him. He had been replaced and all he had were toys and ice cream.

<hr>

The next morning, I was still exhausted when I went to work. I had taken a dozen Vitamin B12s and hoped their energy boost would kick in soon. Jerry had picked up all the puppies bright and early to take them to his brother's place.

I went into Paris's office. He closed the door and put his arms around me.

"Karissa was so lucky to have you for a brother."

"I was lucky to have you for a cousin. My mom was overwhelmed when you agreed to help out."

"It wasn't just for you. It was also for my mother. I'm so sorry though that your sister couldn't have her own name on the grave."

"She would have wanted this. If the Administration hadn't lied and forced a poison injection on her, she'd be alive."

"She was so sweet. I miss her. You were just the big brother of my best friend."

"And now I'm your big brother."

———

As Valiant and I followed Gene, the President, Felicity, and the Secret Service detail onto Airforce One, a chill went through me. I didn't believe in premonitions, but if I did, I might have been nervous.

When we arrived at a private runway in Mexico City, we were greeted by Mexican military officers, several dignitaries and a couple of lower-level employees named Maria and Carlos, who were among the official greeters.

"The President will meet with you this afternoon," our President was told. The Mexicans were speaking in English to our President, probably as a courtesy or probably because they didn't think the President was smart enough to understand Spanish.

There were a number of limousines. The President, Gene, Felicity and Trey were in the second one. Valiant and I were in the third with Maria and Carlos. "I hope you enjoy your brief stay here," Maria told us.

"You don't have to speak English. I understand Spanish."

"I'm trying to perfect my English. It is the international language. If you don't mind, I'd like to continue the English."

"That's easier for me."

"It must be such an honor to work with the President."

"I could say the same to you," I said. "Your President is my hero."

"Really? A lot of your countrymen don't feel the same."

"A lot of our countrymen are brainwashed by the mainstream media," Valiant said, joining the conversation.

"Is he as good in person as his policies are?" I asked.

"Oh yes. He's wonderful. The people love him."

"Your country is a lot freer than ours."

"We've had an influx of Americans sneaking into Mexico for the freedom," Maria commented.

"They were masking kids until the President said it wasn't necessary. Now, he's thinking of masking them again," I told them. Felicity had informed me about that on the plane.

I looked at Valiant and he smiled sheepishly and then followed up. "The loss of freedom and masking was part of his push for the jab. If he had gone against the agenda, certain people would have been upset. Of course, now they have new jabs and he needs to push those by making things even more unpleasant for those not getting them."

"I'm sure he has good reasons for what he is doing," Maria said.

"The initial masking was before I came there," I said.

I thought about how, if my father had been sane and honorable, he would have blown apart the whole masking and injection nonsense. Unlike my dad, Valiant had been a good guy all along. In fact, he had risked a lot to be heroic whenever he could be. I smiled at him.

"Are you two in love?" Maria asked.

"What? Where did that come from?" I asked.

"The way you look at each other. Carlos and I are dating too."

"That's great. Valiant and I are just co-workers," I replied.

"I think not," Carlos said.

"I wish we could stay here longer. Everyone seems so nice," I said, changing the subject.

It wasn't long before we were in the Plaza de la Constitutión, or El Zócalo, in Mexico City's main square. The Palacio Nacional was magnificent and bold in appearance. I was surprised to see it was unprotected by Mexico's version of the National Guard troops and fencing that now protected all the government buildings in D.C. Apparently, Mexico's President was not paranoid. Well, ours wasn't frightened unless someone took away his ice cream, but the party that was in charge of our country was terrified of the voters.

"Isn't it beautiful?" I asked Valiant.

"Very beautiful." I turned, noticing him looking at me.

"I meant the Palace."

"I saw it. It is beautiful."

As we entered I was surprised by all the cats. I thought of my Papkimos and hoped they would be safe until I got home.

Visitors seemed to be moving freely around the Palace. Of course, their photo IDs had to be checked at the door. I got the impression that Trey had demanded that. It wouldn't have been that simple in the U.S. where fear ruled the day and people were kept out of government buildings without special approval. The Mexican President had lived elsewhere, at Los Pinos, until 2018, when the President insisted on moving back into the National Palace. Diego Rivera Murals were everywhere. The meeting was to take place in the courtyard. As we walked towards the courtyard, the Secret Service demanded that the Mexican military remove all onlookers. except for authorized press and personnel, from the area.

"International delegations are always welcome," Auturo, the new chief of staff for the Mexican President said. "But we will not allow the Presidents to enter without the proper precautions. If anything goes wrong, it would be counterproductive to diplomacy."

Our Presidential robot was taken to a room near the courtyard as we were escorted upstairs to watch from the second floor. After all, we were just research assistants.

"They've separated us from the President," Valiant said worriedly.

"Well, Gene will have to make sure all goes well. And there is Felicity."

"I'd feel safer if they had allowed us to bring more of our control equipment," Valiant said. "We could remotely fix problems from the second floor if we had it. All I have is this small remote to close his mouth if he starts declaring war."

"They seemed concerned about surveillance. I guess their President doesn't need a remote control."

"Well, he's on his own now. Look, it's happening."

We watched as the two leaders met in front of the courtyard fountain. Gene stood back behind the fountain with other dignitaries. I could see Felicity smiling and waving at people from one of the other observation areas.

Our President began speaking in Spanish. Translated, our President said, "It is gracious of you to meet with us on this historic occasion.

Our countries have been at war and we suffered great losses when you overtook one of our forts in Texas, killing Jim Bowie and Davey Crockett. But we are here to accept your apologies for the act. In return, we are asking that you turn Tecate over to us. It's a pleasant little town."

Translated, the Mexican President responded, "I did not realize you had such a great sense of humor."

The viewers laughed and applauded.

Suddenly, the Mexican military came rushing in, as they escorted both Presidents back. A wand-type device an officer had was aimed at our President and the two leaders were separated.

"What? What's going on?" I asked Maria, who had come up to us, along with Carlos.

"They've detected a bomb. We'll go find out more and let you know."

The Secret Service were arguing with the Mexican soldiers as our President noticed he was no longer the center of attention.

The President changed that by moonwalking towards the fighting officials, jumping backward over a chain, continuing his moonwalking, leaping onto the edge of the fountain, spinning, slipping, falling into the fountain while hitting his head on the edge and disappearing in a blinding explosion.

CHAPTER 32

The explosion threw us down to the floor. I managed to get up. A thick cloud of steam, accompanied by dust and smoke filled the air. I tried to look into the courtyard as I got up. The explosion was echoing in my ears and everything I was hearing was like in a tunnel. As far as I could tell, there was no sign of either President or the fountain, but even if they had still been there, the air, everywhere, was so thick, I wouldn't have been able to see them.

"Is the Mexican President okay?" I asked, finding myself choking on the smoke and dust.

"I can't see too much," Valiant said.

"There," I heard a voice say. It was a soldier, pointing some kind of wand at us.

Someone grabbed Valiant and pulled the mini remote from his pocket. Valiant went into action and quickly had the soldiers disarmed while I was still trying to see through all the smoke and particles that were almost blinding me. A hand grabbed me and I was pulled out of the area. I felt something going over my head. It was some kind of head covering. My jacket was pulled off and something else was put over me. I heard screaming but the hand kept pulling me. I was having trouble breathing but the crowd around us was rushing down the staircase and pushing its way out of the building while officers outside were calling, "Halt."

The crowd wasn't listening as smoke and fires were expanding out from behind and over us. I hoped the damage would be minimal. The building looked fireproof.

Someone said, "Explosion. Somebody killed the President." The chaos continued, while Valiant, whom I could now see, was pulling me down the street.

"I thought the fail-safe was only to go off if someone messed with the program."

"The smack to the head on the edge of the fountain must have damaged the card and set it off."

We went into some kind of marketplace. There were stalls with people selling goods. Valiant purchased some new clothes for us, that we insisted on putting over us in the stall. I saw soldiers entering the marketplace. Valiant pulled me under a table until they passed. Everyone seemed distracted by the soldiers and nobody was paying attention to us.

One person did notice. It was a man in, maybe, his twenties. "What's wrong?" he asked in Spanish.

"We're undocumented," I replied in Spanish. "From Peru."

"My sister is in Peru trying to get out. Maybe you know someone who can help her?"

"Maybe," I told him. "Give me your information. We have some connections, but we need to get to them."

We were given the details on the man's sister. "Here, I'll get you out," he assured us.

He gave me bundles of items while he told his wife to watch the shop. Then, he had us carry them to his truck. He drove us north to Ecatepec de Morelos and dropped us off by a bus stop as he encouraged us to go north towards Pachuca.

"You have to be losing money helping us," Valiant said. He handed a fifty-dollar American bill to the man.

"American dollars?"

"That's what we used to get out of Peru."

The man drove off. Valiant pulled me away from the bus stop. We walked south for several miles and stepped into a little shop and picked up a couple of pairs of sunglasses and a dark wig for me and a blonde one for him. From there, we walked to a bus going south on 85 and took it to Sahagun City. From there, we planned to get on another bus, headed for Veracruz. It was handy that we knew Spanish. Much of Mexico was light-skinned and light-haired, contrary to what many movies show. In or out of our disguises, we didn't look out of the ordinary. Also, many Americans traveled through Mexico on a regular basis. Still, we didn't want to look like us.

"Let's hope they don't put up our pictures," Valiant whispered to me.

"That's all we need." We had changed our hair and appearance, but most people in Mexico, unlike most in the USA, were not wearing masks. So our faces were potentially recognizable. I hoped the polarized sunglasses would help defeat photo ID or that it was not as prevalent in Mexico as in the U.S.

"Don't worry," Valiant said. "Aside from the money, we're faking it fine."

"But the store owner who helped us may see images of us and talk."

"Good point. That's why I chose the bus coming here as opposed to the one going north. But they may learn from him, we got out of Mexico City."

We walked around, looking for alternate transportation. We passed a gas station with a motorcycle for sale. "Can you drive one of those?" I asked Valiant.

"That's my plan." He purchased it and we continued on toward Route 150 D until we saw a military presence ahead on the highway. "I think we're going another way." He pulled onto the dirt and started driving west. He took 117 towards Tlaxcala and then 119 north. We took 146 through Villa de al Carmen Tequexquitla and then 140 to Veracruz.

It was late. "We're going to need a place to stay," he said.

"Handled."

"What?"

"Go north. My mom has a place just outside Playa Linda."

"She's alive?"

"You did the research."

"She seemed to just drop off the map about the time of Eve's supposed death."

"I moved her down to Mexico. It's freer here, and I figured there would be less backlash if I were caught. I didn't even tell Paris where I located her, but he helped out sort of blindly."

I knocked on the door. Nobody answered. "I hope she's okay. What if they found her?"

"Let's stay positive."

I went over to the pine tree in the front yard. When I moved her in, my mom had shown me where, under the tree, she planned to put the spare key. It was gone. "Somebody has the spare key. My mom would have put it back if she had needed to use it."

"Let's go around back."

"There's an alarm system."

"Do you know the code?"

"Unless it's changed."

With a bit of relief, I found that the code to the back gate was the same. I was able to use another code I remembered for the back door.

"Why isn't there an electronic lock for the front?" Valiant asked.

"There is. But you have to go through the outer door to get to it."

I looked around. There was blood all over the kitchen floor.

CHAPTER 33

"Oh no."

"Let's check out the house," Valiant said.

I started to grab a knife from the kitchen counter, but noticed it was covered with blood. I reached in the drawer and grabbed another knife. We started with the basement. It was locked. I used the code to unlock it. Unlike my father's, my memory seemed to be working fine. Nobody appeared to be inside. I went to the safe room and used that room's code. It was empty. We ran upstairs and checked room by room. When we got to the master bedroom, there was somebody lying on the bed.

"Mom."

"Eve?"

"Thank God. What happened?"

She sat up, and I noticed her hand was wrapped in bandages.

"Stupid me. You'd think I'd know how to cut up onions without cutting myself."

"Should I get a doctor?"

"I used silver nitrate. The bleeding has stopped, but it bled a lot and I really messed up the kitchen. If I had known, you were coming, I would have cleaned it up by now."

I ran over and hugged her. "I'm so glad you're okay and I'll clean it. The key was missing from the tree."

"It's in the living room. I was going to put it back, later tonight."

"You should probably get some stitches for that hand, Mrs. Gordon," Valiant advised.

"It's fine. I used some super glue after the silver nitrate and then covered it after it dried."

"You remembered." Years ago, I had cut my hand and an emergency room physician had used super glue instead of stitches. He said it would scar less.

I removed the bandages. "It looks like you sealed it tightly. Mom, I was so worried about you."

"I've been worried about you. I didn't want you to take that job." She touched my face with her uninjured hand.

"Dad's alive!"

"Of course." She didn't look surprised.

"I mean they replaced him with a robot, but he's alive and his mind is completely gone."

"A robot?" That seemed to surprise her.

"That's who won, or didn't win, the election and who has been pretending to be President. I'm in charge of the robot. But now, it's probably been blown to pieces."

"What?"

"We were in Mexico City with the President or rather the robot there and something exploded. I think it was him. It looked like it was the robot or something right by it. It could have been the failsafe but I've been thinking. It shouldn't have been activated by that fall."

"Slow down. Did you get hurt?"

"No. We were in an observation area."

"Who is this?" She looked at Valiant.

"Valiant. He works with me. He's a really great guy who is always there for me."

"I'm glad my daughter has you. Be good to her."

"I'll try. I am very pleased to meet you, Mrs. Gordon and I'm glad you're okay. Your daughter really cares about you." He paused. "Is your Internet up? I don't mean to sound cold. We need to find out the status of everything."

"No problem. It was working, but I don't use it really."

"Mom isn't much into the Net," I told Valiant. "I assume you can make it look like we're not here."

"I'll reroute the connection when I get a computer."

"Maybe Jack or Brandon can help with our situation. Or Paris."

"I'll contact Brandon."

"You really trust him."

"I do."

"In the books, it's the person the main character trusts the most that usually turns out to be the villain," I said, half teasing him.

"I think we discussed that. I do think we can trust him not to be a storybook villain. We need some new passports and a way back to the States."

"Will they be looking for us up there?"

"I'll find out from him."

"Are you two in trouble?" My mom looked worried.

"I don't know. Valiant had a remote device to shut off the President if he did something crazy like singing 'Hello Dolly,' and they found it on Valiant before we ran. They may have thought it activated the bomb. I don't even know if any real people were hurt in the explosion. I'm hoping the Mexican President is okay."

"Nobody here knows I'm related to you or Paris," my mom said.

"That could keep us safe for a few days. Lee found out who I was, but even the Secret Service doesn't know."

"Lee?"

"My former boss. He's dead."

"Dead? That job sounds too dangerous."

"We found the guy we think killed him, but we don't know what caused the explosion if it wasn't the fail-safe?"

"Would you like me to make dinner? I mean, if you injured yourself starting dinner, you are probably hungry," Valiant told Mom.

"It's late."

"We haven't eaten either," I told her. "Valiant, could you put the motorcycle away and reset the alarm?" I told him the codes.

"I know. I watched. No problem."

I sat down on the bed as Valiant went out.

"It looks like you've found yourself a nice guy."

"Oh, we're not. I mean, he works for me."

"He doesn't look at you like an employee. And he's very handsome."

"I know. I just can't get involved with anyone, right now."

"You've told him your secret?"

"He actually discovered it himself. He's saved my life a number of times."

"That's the kind of guy I want for you."

"Well, a guy for me is a long way off."

"Is there anyone else?"

"Well, there's Jerry. He's a friend too. He's the Press Secretary."

"The guy who lies for the President? I think Valiant's the one."

"The one?"

"The way your voice goes up when you mention his name. It doesn't when you say 'Jerry.'"

"Jerry is really sweet. And he really, really likes me. Also, he doesn't work for me. But, no, I'm not picking him, either."

"I need to get up."

"No. You need to stay here. You've injured yourself. Besides, you took care of me all my life, and now it's time for me to take care of you."

"You're a victim of what happened to me too. You need to be pampered."

"I'm not one of those girls who blames her mother for who her father is. You loved me all my life and that made up for everything. I wouldn't be who I am if not for you."

"But you've given up your whole identity."

"It's okay. I've gotten a lot of respect and it would be too complicated to change things now. Besides, you are safer if they think Eve's gone. No liabilities for the President."

"You say he's like a baby?"

"Yeh. I still plan to bring him and the Administration down."

"Honey, it was long ago. Let it go."

"I can't. Not after what he did to you."

"What he did was awful, but I've got a consolation that's so much better than anything I lost." She put a finger from her non-injured hand on my nose. "I've got you and that makes it all okay."

"You're the best mom ever."

I gave her another hug.

"I think you'd like my mother, Mrs. Gordon," Valiant told her as he re-entered the room. "She's really nice too."

"Call me Terry. That's the name I'm using down here."

"Terry, what would you like me to cook?"

"I was going to make some veggie loaf, but there is some lasagna in the refrig that you can warm up."

"I can handle it," I said.

We decided to make the veggie loaf. My mom had a special recipe that was always delicious. "My mom likes you," I told Valiant.

"I like her, but I hope she doesn't accidentally injure herself, again."

"Accidents happen. I've done that to myself while cooking. She's not the type to get help when she needs it, and that's my major concern."

"Now I know where you get that from."

"If only, we could always protect those we love."

"I'm sorry I didn't see that fiasco coming. I knew they had put a fail-safe on the robot. I had tried to disable it before the trip and discovered it had a fail-safe for disabling the fail-safe. We figured if we just let it alone, it would be okay."

"Do you think someone else tried to electronically disable the robot but not in keeping with its coding?"

"There are hackers everywhere. I should have turned off the robot's remote signal access. I just didn't know what he would do or say."

"Could it have been an accident, like a kid playing with a remote control car that was on the same frequency?" I inquired.

"I don't think so."

"'Explosion' was the next thing on the list. 'Crushed' was supposed to be after the explosion, but that's already happened."

"You think that the murders are still continuing?" he asked.

"It fits."

"It doesn't make sense. Why would Ray cause his own drowning if he was behind it?"

"And leave all the evidence in his apartment. And how could he do the explosion if he were dead?"

"The real killer could have set him up."

"Which means the real killer is still out there," I noted.

"As far as the Mexican authorities are concerned, we're the real killers. We better stay out of sight until we can get new passports."

"Under other names."

"Or find an alternate way back up to the States," he said.

Mom loved the veggie loaf—or so she said. She insisted on coming downstairs and having us all sit at the table. "My daughter is a really smart girl."

"I know. Smart and beautiful and courageous too."

"She has too much courage, sometimes."

"I've seen that. I won't let anything happen to her. I promise to protect her with my life if necessary."

My mom smiled. I shook my head. I wasn't getting matched up. Now was not the right time.

"Do you have a computer I can use until I pick up a laptop?"

"In the basement."

"I need to make sure my actions are anonymous. I may have to do some fixes on the computer to arrange that."

"Be my guest."

"He cooks too," my mom pointed out after Valiant left.

"Mom, you aren't getting me married off."

"Not married, but I do want to know that someone is watching out for you."

"Paris is too."

"I know. But he hasn't kept you out of danger, apparently."

"He's got a job. The Administration was responsible for the death of his sister."

"A terrible loss. She was such a sweet girl."

"She had a fake card and Jerry's brother would have faked her booster affidavit, but dad came to her school and he, or someone who was with him, convinced her or rather pressured her into getting the shot. Her death was within twenty-four hours. All her organs shut down."

"My sister-in-law Alice must have been destroyed by that. Before you brought me down here, she was trying to keep from falling apart —especially since you, Paris and Dave decided that you, instead of Karissa, were to have the funeral."

"Yeh. She was more than devastated. She wished her daughter had listened to her about the dangers of the vax and she felt guilty on top of the loss. At first, she believed that her daughter went along with it because she wanted to be part of the in-crowd with her friends and graduate with them. Neither Paris nor I think Karissa would have done that."

"Peer pressure is very strong. I'm glad you didn't succumb to that."

"I had a good teacher. And Paris is a lot like the brother I never had. At times, it's like he almost sees me as the sister he lost."

"He's always been a good boy. I am usually a good judge of character."

"Except—" I stopped.

"My one mistake. I wasn't romantically interested in him. I was so excited about being hired by a Senator. I saw him as a father figure until then. He—"

"I know. He was awful. He is awful and I don't care that he called me 'Mommy.'"

"He called you 'Mommy?'"

"And he plays in sandboxes in a bunker and blows up trains, Gomez Addams style."

"The trains sound like something I would expect from him."

"I could expose him, destroy him and his Presidency. Hmm. There was an explosion today. I assume Gene got what was left of him out of there. Actually, the explosion is SOP for our government. It's always trying to blow up foreign leaders or their countries. Our foreign policy is—well, you know."

"I do. I saw it when I was working for him, but he wasn't President and he wasn't in charge back then. I was going to quit when he. Well, I knew he did some bad stuff, but I let it slide when I shouldn't have. I guess it was because he was kind of like a father figure to me."

"The lesson seems to be no second chances."

"I said he was one mistake. I made others. There was that guy that the neighbors brought in to help organize the house."

"I remember that. Well, that was their mistake too," I laughed. "Or rather, a disaster. He was supposed to help, but he turned out to be a hoarder and trashed up your house and wrecked your car."

"And then of course he convinced me it was my fault. That was easy to do."

"Because you accept responsibility for everything—even when it's not your fault. Please don't accept responsibility for anything I'm doing. I did it over your objections. It really bothers me to have a father who is so evil. But never think I blame you for him. I'd never be that self-absorbed and delusional."

"Are you hurting? After growing up without a father and then seeing him?"

"No. I realize that I was lucky. You took all the negativity. Thank you." I hugged her, again. "I owe you big time."

"No. I owe you for being the most understanding, loving daughter in the world."

I noticed we were both tearing up. "Mom, I know you want me to be safe, but I want you to start putting yourself first."

"I knew your heart was in the right place, back during COVID, when you continued to give me five hugs a day, and refused to mask up or get that terrible poison. You also brought me down here to protect me from any repercussions of your new job."

"That was the hardest part. I told you to pretend I was hugging you until I could see you again."

"And now?"

"It's almost over. I don't think I can go back to being Eve, but I'm going to get out. I'm going to expose these creeps and get out. Then I'll come down here and join you. Maybe I can change my name again."

"And Valiant. Would he join you down here?"

"I don't know. He has his job. I couldn't ask that of him. Besides, we're not dating or anything."

"Keep telling yourself that." She started to get up. "I need to make up the other two bedrooms for you and Valiant."

"I'll take care of it. Sheets in the upstairs cupboard?"

"Yes, But."

"I'll handle it."

Tonight, I took my mom upstairs and tucked her in. "I love you, Mom."

"I love you too."

I had missed her so much. I kissed her forehead and went to put fresh sheets on the beds. Valiant came upstairs. I had finished making up the rooms and was debating about whether to lie down or go downstairs.

"I couldn't reach Brandon. Working hours are over and he's not doing his email. He's probably sleeping. But I managed to check out the news. The Mexican President is alive and unharmed, but they couldn't find the remains of our President. The bomb was plastique with a timer."

"That doesn't sound like a fail-safe."

"It wasn't. It was an actual bomb. We're wanted in connection with the bombing."

"I figured," I said.

"But our names are misspelled and our pictures are off. They're close but not quite right."

"Well, someone must have made a mistake and the services ran with it. That's good news as we are hiding out. Is the picture of a blonde?"

"Yes, but not quite your shade."

"I'll become a redhead, next. If they get the correct picture, I'll still look a little different."

"It wasn't a mistake. It's a picture of us entering the Palace with Maria and Carlos. The features are just a little off. Our noses are different shapes, and our eyes, foreheads and hair are off a little."

"Blurry shot or altered?"

"Altered."

"How close are the names?"

"We'll need new passports. They are close enough that we could be nailed. The news is a powerful brainwasher. By now, Maria and Carlos could actually believe that's what we look like."

"Our government will know better," I said.

"If the American people think we tried to blow up the President, we could both be in trouble."

"Maybe we should hang out in Mexico for a while."

"I could go for that. I'm sure there are people who would pay me to do tech work, and you could be my business manager."

"I bet Paris and Jerry are trying to figure things out. Do you think it might be safe to contact either of them?"

"Paris is your brother. Jerry is a safer bet. Let's do it first thing in the morning."

"I don't know if I can sleep tonight."

He walked over to me and put his arms around me. "I told your mom I wasn't going to let anything happen to you and I meant it."

"If we could get around the agenda, imagine what we could have done with the President."

"World peace, an end to all emergency orders, revocation of the NDAA and the PATRIOT Act."

"Of course, we never would have gotten away with that," I commented.

"They are searching for the President. When they don't find him, they'll either assume our government whisked him away or presume he's dead."

"Was anyone killed?"

"Two of our Secret Service detail. The Mexican officials and forces were further away."

"And you say it wasn't the fail-safe?"

"No. An actual bomb."

"Trey? Is he alright?"

"He was lucky. He was off to the side. Broke his arm in several places and he got a concussion."

"Good. That he's alive, not that he was injured. How about Gene?"

"Essentially undamaged. Minor cuts and bruises. "

"Brandon said it would take a week to fix up the old President when we last saw him," I recalled.

"Let's hope the search drags on until then. The world will believe whatever the President says about the circumstances. Maybe, they'll decide some international terrorist tried to blow him up and got away."

"Just so long as they don't presume the President dead in the meantime."

"We should try to hang out here, at least, until then."

"Or go back to help supervise the project. On second thought, we're compromised, and we have to wait for new passports."

"I might be able to buy some on the black market."

"Your talents always amaze me," I said.

"We might find some tourists who look like us and pay them to wait to report the loss."

"That's a possibility."

'Your mom keeps a clean house."

"Oh gosh, you should have seen what happened to our house back in the States. Some friends got this jerk to help with fixing up my mother's house. He destroyed her car, picked up trash from the street and stuffed it in her house, such that you couldn't even walk in the door."

"Sounds like he had a real problem. What happened?"

"I called the police. My mom didn't want him arrested and so they let him go. One of the officers took pity on her and had a brother who was in the junk business. It took a day to restore the house."

"The police can sometimes be of use."

"Not usually though. They are working with the feds to round up Republicans, right now."

"That's one of the things we can fix if we go back."

"Gene would have replaced us if we had tried before. And he might, if we do it when we get back."

"As Jerry would say, a last hurrah for us."

"A great way to go."

"I bet you were popular in high school," he said.

"I stayed mostly to myself. I was the studious kind."

"Boyfriends?"

"Nosy."

"Sorry."

"No boyfriends. Yours was the first kiss."

"Me?"

"Yeh. Don't let it go to your head. I have nothing to compare it to."

"Was it good or bad?"

"It was acceptable." It was a lot more than that, but I wasn't going to tell him.

"Jerry never kissed you?"

"No. And don't look so happy. That doesn't mean I'm interested in you."

"I didn't say it did." He started to walk towards the door. "You love me."

"That's a ridiculous leap of logic."

"She loves me," he said to himself, loud enough for me to hear him as he walked out and went to the room that I had made up for him. He called back. "Is this my room?"

"Yes. It's all ready."

"See you in the morning, girlfriend."

I hoped my mom didn't hear that. I knew he was half-teasing me. Or maybe he wasn't. Maybe he thought if he said it enough, it would be true.

"I'm not your girlfriend."

The next morning, I was awakened by a knock at my bedroom door. It was Valiant with a tray of food.

"If we lose our jobs, you could get a position as a chef."

"I can't take credit for this. Your mom put it together. She said you like fresh fruit in the morning."

The tray included watermelon, strawberries and black grapes. "All my favorites."

"She says it's all organic too."

"Of course. My mom taught me to avoid pesticides."

"She was telling me about all your accomplishments. Are you performing in the talent show?"

"Nope. You performing?"

"Vicariously through the President."

"Does the robot you're fixing sing and dance?"

"He mostly falls down."

"If we can get him together."

"There won't be a human body for them to declare dead, at least. With all that smoke, they can't know for sure what happened to the President."

"If he had continued his speech, he could have been exposed then and there. The whole government could have been brought down."

"Except they think we were the ones who blew up the President and maybe stopped another war. When they think about it longer, we could be declared heroes," he mused. "Do you still have your burner phone?"

"Yeh. It doesn't work here."

"It's just as well. I'm going to fix it to get a voice connection. Jerry has access to the State Department."

"Not anymore. Ross got carted away. He might even be in Guantanamo."

"It will be crowded when all the Republicans arrive. I bet, despite political differences, they'd fight alongside any Cubans who rescued them. Maybe, in exchange for getting them out and bringing down the government, they could donate that part of the island to Cuba. Or they might declare it 'America in exile.'"

"You aren't a Republican," I pointed out.

"And I don't agree with them on most issues, but I do support rights and freedom.

"How far the Democratic Party has fallen. The Republicans are now closer to Democratic values than the Democrats."

"Fallen? Crashed and burned," he noted.

"And the remains are nowhere to be found."

"FDR would have declared the DNC a terrorist group and he wasn't into declaring political parties terrorist groups."

"JFK was going to get rid of the CIA and end the war in Vietnam.

We know what happened to him and his brother. After that, the party started selling out."

"But not fully until the 'New Democrats,'" Valiant said.

"The Deep State, Wall Street Democrats, you mean."

"Have you thought about changing your political affiliation?"

"To what? Show me a third party that is serious and I'll jump."

"Politics," my mom said coming into my room. "My daughter always had a head for that."

"I learned my morality from you."

"You've barely eaten."

"I talk too much."

Valiant forewent the chance to turn that into a joke. "Eat. I'm going to see if I can reach Brandon."

After he left, my mom said, "He really cares about you."

"You said that last night."

"I think you care about him too. And you seem to agree on politics."

"Right now, I could be on the most wanted list. They have my name spelled wrong, but they could correct it any minute."

"I have your passport."

"My passport?"

"Your original one."

"But she's or I've been recorded as dead."

"Did you notify the State Department?"

"No. But the death records and the passport records may have been coordinated."

"You're alive and you're Eve. Take it back." She seemed excited about the possibility of helping me find a solution.

"Maybe Valiant can check whether the passport number is still valid. But that doesn't let Valiant off the hook."

As I joined Valiant downstairs, he had Brandon on the computer in a video chat.

"As soon as word came down, I altered the picture and names in the press offices."

"You hack too?" I asked.

"I learned from the best." Watching Valiant beam, I knew what Brandon meant.

"But won't they change it back?"

"It's already been released around Mexico. Did you notice they said that you had black eyes, instead of hazel?"

"That will help," I said. "What are they saying at the White House?"

"They are claiming the Mexicans tried to kill the President. There is talk of an invasion. The Vice President has taken over until the President is found."

"Wonderful," I said sarcastically.

"She wants to have the President declared dead so that she can make it permanent."

"We can't let that happen. We need time for the President to resurface," Valiant said.

"How could the bomb have gotten in?" I asked.

"They don't check world leaders for explosives. Somebody had to have planted the explosive on the President before he entered the plaza."

"Would that be somebody in the President's detail?"

"Very likely. Think of who had access to him who might know he might not notice."

"Well everyone thinks he's demented. Gene knew he was a robot. Remember the list. Murder, prison, bribes?"

"List?" Brandon asked. That's right. Brandon was on the Net during our side discussion.

"Lee had a list. I don't know specifically who but somebody with Gene's initials had that description in a possible blackmail file Lee had on Whitehouse personnel."

"Thanks for the tip."

"Talk to Jerry," I said quickly. "Let him know we're okay for the moment."

"You trust him? I've got to go. I think Gene's in the outer lab."

Brandon disconnected.

"Anyone on the Secret Service detail could have planted it on him," Valiant said.

"Probably not the two who died," I responded. "How about the Mexican team that met him at the airport? Maybe they didn't like his positions on the issues."

"The Secret Service should have caught that. But they could have been distracted."

"With the two countries accusing each other, this could become a war zone. Their President survived and if ours is declared dead—"

"That will seal the deal. And the VP would just be the girl to set off the nukes."

"Maybe we should tell her the President of Mexico is hot in bed."

"But sleeping with him won't elevate her politically."

I sat down next to Valiant and we searched for information on the Internet about our President. At least, he hadn't been declared dead yet, but it was considered an attempted assassination or a possible actual assassination. Apparently, the Mexicans were more thorough in their investigations before jumping to conclusions.

"Care to go for a swim?" I asked. "We're going to have to wait to hear more. The pool has a covering."

"A glass covering."

"This isn't the United States where there are drones everywhere."

"Our government has eyes everywhere. Gene or one of the others may be behind what happened."

"On second thought, I don't have a bathing suit."

"Yes, you do," my mom said, coming into the basement. "I just picked up some clothes for you. I guessed at your size, Valiant. I also got this." It was a red short-hair wig. She handed me a bottle of temporary red hair dye. I hadn't noticed her going out. I needed to be more observant.

"How much do I owe you?" Valiant asked my mom.

"It's on me."

Valiant was working downstairs when I finished with my hair.

"And I thought you looked phenomenal as a blonde."

"Don't get used to it. When this is all over, I'm going to be a blonde again."

That's when I saw Jerry appear next to Brandon in the chat. "You sure they can't trace this?" he asked.

"I'm securing it on this end too."

"Thank goodness you're okay. Paris and I were so worried," Jerry said.

"Someone planted a bomb on the President and we need to know who."

"You think it's more of what was going on here?"

"Explosion," I said.

"That means Ray wasn't our man. He's dead."

"We're thinking he was set up," Valiant said.

"Next is 'crush.'"

"'Pit and the Pendulum,'" I commented.

"We need a strategy. The Vice President is using the *Twenty-Fifth* to claim she's permanent," Jerry informed us.

"They need a declaration of death. No body," I said.

"She's trying to go around that as there is no evidence he's alive."

"Can Gene and Paris fight that?"

"Gene says the President was rushed off. He credited the two of you with saving him?"

"How is that possible when they removed the remote from Valiant and declared us the perps?"

"Our government is claiming they made a mistake before the air cleared."

"Then, we better be able to produce the President."

"First, you have to get out of there," Brandon said. "The Mexican Government still wants you and there's a reward for your capture. Apparently, they aren't buying Gene's claim."

"We need passports and a way out."

"I'm working on that," Brandon said. "Are you in a safe location?"

"Yes," I said.

"Contact me at home tonight."

They ended the video chat.

"The afternoon's ours," Valiant said.

"I haven't spent much time with my mom since I've been working at the White House. How about if we do lunch with her?"

We went for a quick swim and then we went to the Playa Linda resort. I had warned Valiant that my mom didn't drink alcohol, and so we ordered some virgin piña coladas and sandwiches.

"I could totally live down here," I said. A voice inside my head said, *With the law breathing down your neck.* We would have to clear our names before that happened.

My mom went back to her house, while we walked along the beach. "I think your mom is trying to match us up," Valiant said.

"It's not fair. I have my resolve."

"To live your life as a single lady."

"To not get involved with anyone while I'm working for the White House."

He put his arm around me. I didn't remove it. I actually liked it.

"I am not getting involved with you."

"Okay, but for anyone looking at us, we could pretend to be young honeymooners."

"You think that's a good cover?"

"Better than the D.C. assassins."

I put my arm around him too. "This is just for curious eyes."

"Of course." He turned towards me. He was looking into my eyes and it was freaking me out. Not because I didn't like it, but because I did. I didn't move back as his lips came closer and closer and then touched mine. The kiss deepened and I felt like I was going to collapse. *What is going on with me?* I realized that both of my arms were around him and his were around me and I couldn't stop kissing him. I had to regain control of myself. I pulled back and he released me.

"That should have been convincing," I told him as unemotionally as I could.

He smiled. "It convinced me."

I smacked him on the arm. "That's not going to work."

"What?"

"Getting me to fall for you."

"Okay," he said. He still had an arm around me and we continued walking on the beach. My head was a little dizzy, but I was going to ignore anything that didn't feel normal, intellectual. I didn't have time for emotions.

Next, we walked along the docks and I looked at a schooner. "Would that get us home?" I asked.

"Until the Coast Guard demanded our passports."

"We need to get into the country unnoticed and then surface with the President."

"Who isn't, yet, ready. Brandon and Jack are working hard to get him into shape but it will be days," Valiant pointed out.

"I'm glad that Brandon changed the images and altered the spelling of our names."

"They are still too close to ours for comfort."

"The red hair helps a little. But you're right. Not enough."

"If we were with the President, we wouldn't need passports to get back in."

"I suppose getting the original robot into Mexico would be harder than getting fake passports," I said.

"Much. The green in your eyes sparkles in the sun. They shift between green and golden."

"It's called hazel. I wonder how your eyes would look in brown. Now that's a guy I might fall for."

"I'll get contacts."

"I was joking."

"I'm liking it here too. I could settle down in Playa Linda."

"With your skills?"

"Maybe we could set up a robotics operation. Nah, I prefer people to transhumans."

"I don't know. I think I prefer Fred Astaire to Mr. Sandbox."

"They have the best deserts here," he said, looking at a shop with strawberry crepes.

"Those are French." We picked up half a dozen to take home after we were assured they were organic. "A lot of the organic farms are in Mexico," I told him.

"It's better than California fruit," he said.

"You know about the California Governor forcing them to irrigate the California fruit with oil fracking wastewater, I take it."

"As a kid, I couldn't get enough of it. After my mom found out, she forbade me to eat California-grown anything."

"Well, my favorite wine is from Denmark."

"When we get back, I'll get a bottle to celebrate."

"As long as there are no more murders. What if Paris or Jerry or even Gene is crushed before we get back?"

"Who benefitted most from the President blowing up?" Valiant asked.

"One person," I said. "And she's trying to have him declared dead."

"We never suspected her. Were her initials on the list?"

"We never went through the rest of the names. And we never investigated the keys or the other clues."

"I don't think her brains put her second in line. Wrong part of her anatomy," he said.

"Ray's demise ended our search. Someone is killing people." I thought about the various clues. "The keys?"

"I put them in my wallet before we packed up everything at the ranch house. Not that they're going to do us any good down here."

As we walked back to Mom's place, I saw it. "Look. That truck."

"Northgrail."

CHAPTER 34

"It's doing business in Mexico?"

"It's stopping for gas." It looked as if it was headed for Veracruz.

We went over to the truck. "Northgrail, what's that?" I asked the driver as we acted like we were walking into the station for a soda.

"It's a small contractor."

"In Veracruz?"

"No. Out of Boca Inglesia."

"What does it make or do?"

"Movie explosives."

"Movie?"

"We have to create explosions that appear real."

"Can people be hurt in those movie explosions?"

"If they're too close but usually they have on protective clothing, and filming is cut before the explosions."

"Do they just work for the movie industry?"

"They have some other customers, but I'm just a driver. I pick up and deliver."

"Did you deliver anything to the National Palace recently?"

"That was for Sam. It was for some kind of evening celebration."

"Yesterday?"

"I guess the celebration got called off. Hey, you look like—"

"Constance, stop boring this man. My wife has been asking questions of everyone she meets down here. She's a reporter for AP."

"A reporter? Please don't print our conversation."

"There's nothing to print. I mean, just some movie contractor. There are hundreds of them."

"Right. Hundreds."

"Well, honey, enough trying to get a story. Let's get back to the honeymoon suite." With that, he started nibbling on my ear. I smiled and tried to pretend that this was normal for us—even though, inside, I was feeling like I was going totally crazy. I wished he weren't so attractive. We continued walking into the station for a soda as if that was our destination and grabbed a couple of cokes that we would never drink—though I knew Mexican cokes were safer than those in our country. As we paid for them and left, we noticed the driver looking at us. We pretended to be ignoring him. Valiant kissed my neck and I turned giving him a hug before we walked off towards the resort, not planning to go home until we were in the clear.

When we got back, we told my mom that we'd be taking off the next day for the Yucatan Peninsula. I could see there was a sadness in her eyes. I suspected she had hoped we'd stay longer. "That's wonderful, honey. I hope you have a great time."

"We will do our best to come back and stay longer next time." *I said "we." What was I thinking of?* This last day had refreshed me, giving me the energy to continue, but it hadn't cleared my head where Valiant was concerned.

"I've even suggested to Eve that we come back here and start up a computer business. Of course, she has so many capabilities, she could do anything," Valiant told my mom.

Oh boy. My mom's going to think we're together, which we're not.

"That would be wonderful," my mom said.

"Well, it certainly is a lot freer here than in the United States. We've got to clear up what happened yesterday in Mexico City first, but I don't think that will be difficult." I had lied about the lack of difficulty, but I wanted her reassured.

When we contacted Brandon, Jerry was there. "I'm coming down to get you," Jerry said.

"What do you mean, 'You're coming down?'" I asked. "You've got a job."

"I'm taking a leave."

"We're on the run and we don't want anyone accused of being an accomplice. You're known and they'll be watching you."

"She's right," Brandon said to him. "You'll put them in more danger."

"Paris is arranging for new passports to be delivered to Juarez."

"We're not going that way. Remember Northgrail? It's in Boca Inglesia."

"Maybe, we can find some answers," Valiant said.

"What do they do?" Jerry asked.

"Explosives—like maybe, what blew up the President. And the driver made a delivery to the National Palace yesterday," I said. "He claimed they do movie explosives, but I bet that's just a cover."

"You going to be in Boca tomorrow?"

"That's the plan," Valiant said.

"Haven't you put Karissa in enough danger?" Jerry looked unhappy.

"It was my idea," I said.

"You can't drive there."

"I can do a lot of things that might surprise you," Valiant said.

"We saw a Northgrail truck. There has to be a road," I noted.

"They probably picked them up from a nearby port, maybe Cancun or Río Lagartos."

"That makes sense. The driver didn't act as if he were guarding any top-secret information," I said, turning to Valiant. "He probably didn't know what he was delivering."

Valiant looked up a map on part of the screen and pointed to the area we were planning to go. "I can cut through here on my bike."

"It's much more roundabout to go there from Veracruz by motorcycle than by boat. Part of your trip will be off-road through a swampy jungle. Your motorcycle could get stuck, leaving you in the middle of nowhere," Brandon said.

That was a big clue he had guessed where we were. Maybe he had watched parts of our journey on a satellite feed. Brandon seemed to be looking at something. "I can arrange two boat tickets from Veracruz for the day after tomorrow if you can make it there."

"What about ID? Using our names could be dangerous." I could see Jerry and Brandon talking.

Jerry chimed in. "Can you go to the Casa Morales in Veracruz tomorrow after midnight? Ask for Jeffrey. He can arrange everything you need."

When we got off the computer, I said, "Mom will be happy."

"I'm not happy he mentioned Veracruz over the Net," Valiant said.

"You think he's tapped?"

"No. But codes are better than exact information when you're hiding out."

"He spoke as if we were going through Veracruz. He didn't say we were there. Besides, if someone picked up the discussion, they'll be waiting in Boca Inglesia."

"True. I must have messed up more than he did. The transmission was encoded. So I'm just being overly cautious. Still—"

"Mom will be happy about the slight delay in our plans."

I was right about Mom being delighted. The next day, she gave us a tour of Veracruz. I was worried about her being seen with us, but she insisted and I had a feeling that Valiant would make sure she stayed safe. I had seen some of the city when I arranged for mom's house, here. But she knew all the good spots. We were in a hotel bar having lunch when a news bulletin was blasted out. We saw our pictures and I feared they had tracked down our location. Instead, it said in Spanish that the couple had been arrested.

"They've arrested someone? But this is bogus. We need to clear them."

"Not until we were in the States," Valiant said. "Mexican jails are not nice."

"But they are innocent."

"Maybe they were the ones who ordered the explosives."

"Look at the background and Maria and Carlos next to them."

"But we were with—"

He touched my hand. He didn't want me to say more. Of course, he was right. There was very little we could do for them while being suspects ourselves. "Let's hope, we find something in the Yucatan."

***

Later that afternoon, Valiant continued working on something electronic he had started the night before. "What is that?"

"An EMF reader. If there is a facility in Boca Inglesia, it's likely to have high EMF readings, compared to the surrounding area, given that we're mostly dealing with jungle and water."

That night, we went to the Casa Morales Bar and looked around. We did look a bit different. My hair was up under a hat and very red. Valiant's red wig poked out from under his sombrero. "You know your hat looks out of place here," I said. All but a couple of other people had removed theirs or didn't have one.

"Does anyone look like a fed?"

"Do you have your bug detector?" I asked.

"I wish. If anything goes down, I'll distract while you run."

"No deal. Where you go, I go and where you stay, I stay," I told him firmly.

"That's from the Bible, almost."

"We're in this together."

"I promised your mother I'd keep you safe."

"So I stay with you, and you'll have an opportunity to keep protecting me."

"He looks familiar," Valiant said, looking at a man, entering the bar.

It took me several double takes to recognize our contact. I got up and started to go over to him. He gave a cutting motion at his throat.

"You know him?"

"Yes."

The man went outside.

"Let's go."

Valiant got up and we went outside. Out front, I didn't see anyone. "We lost him. I thought I recognized him, but maybe I was wrong."

A car drove up and the passenger door opened. A man's voice said, "Get in."

Valiant tried to hold me back, but I got in, followed by Valiant. "Ben Stafford."

"Jeffrey to you. I'm doing this incognito."

"Stafford." Valiant was starting to put things together. "Any relation to—"

"My brother."

"He's the doctor who didn't give me the injection."

"I told you I'd deny."

"It's okay. Valiant's one of us. And he already found out about you on his own."

"Jerry called in a big favor. I was about an hour north of here, enjoying life when I was told I had to get down here and get you a boat."

"You're getting us a boat?"

"Tomorrow morning, we set sail for Boca Inglesia."

"How long have you been here?" I asked.

"I just arrived yesterday morning."

"What about the Papkimos?"

"They're safe with my housekeeper. Don't worry. She's unjabbed."

———

The next morning, we said our temporary goodbyes to my mom, promising to return after things got cleared up. I knew there was a possibility we might meet our doom in trying, but I needed to be optimistic. We went to the dock. Ben or Jeffrey had rented a yacht, complete with a skipper.

"Meet Marcus Wricher," Ben said as we boarded it. "He's an American who has settled down in Veracruz."

We said our "Hellos" to Marcus.

"What made you decide to move down here?" Valiant asked.

"Too many hassles up north. An ex-wife."

We set off for Boca Inglesia.

"We'd be there by now if I had taken the bike," Valiant told me.

"The boat's a better idea. And if we had gone to Cancun without Ben, it would have been a lot harder to rent the boat there for the rest of the journey."

"Plus, we get to rest," he acknowledged, as we relaxed on the boat. "I wonder why he is taking it so slowly."

"Maybe to make it look like a pleasure cruise," I said.

I got the impression that Ben was watching us. I had a feeling that it had something to do with his brother. It made me a little uncomfortable.

I was up on the deck when Ben approached me. "My brother really likes you."

"He's really nice. We're really good friends."

"He didn't tell me what was going on with you; just that you were in danger and had to be incognito. But you've been incognito all along."

"That's a long story."

"My brother has no idea who you are, does he?"

"I would appreciate if you kept my secret. The fewer people who know, the safer everyone will be."

"Why would a beautiful young lady have to fake her death?"

"Certain good people helped me out so that I could have a fresh start. I don't want anyone hurt."

"I don't want my brother hurt."

"I don't want that, either. When we get there, if there is any danger, you are free to go as well."

"You think there might be danger?"

"I don't have any reason to expect danger but it seems to follow me around."

Ben went inside. Valiant came up to me. "What did he want?"

"He doesn't want me to hurt his brother. Jerry doesn't know who I am, and I asked Ben to keep it confidential."

"Do you think he will?"

"I don't know. He's a doctor. But I'm pretty sure he thought I was dead until he saw me last night."

"Have you seen the skipper's cabin?"

"No. Should I have?"

"This yacht is well protected. The skipper must have twenty rifles on his wall, along with some pistols."

"I guess I should feel safe."

"He seems personable."

"Something about Skipper Wricher gives me the creeps. I guess it was the way he mentioned his ex-wife. I wonder if he screwed over his kids the way—never mind."

"The way your father screwed over your mother and you?"

"Look," I said. "Sharks."

"Just don't go swimming there. I wonder. Why did Brandon and Jack want us to go this way?"

"I guess that motorcycles don't do well in that particular jungle," I surmised.

"At least, we're off the grid. That is if Ben doesn't sell us out."

"He faked my jab. I trust him."

"How did you get your new ID, complete with a different jab?"

"Paris knows someone who fakes the IDs for the Signature Soldiers. He faked mine as a favor to Paris."

"Nice. Maybe he can fake whole new backgrounds for us."

"I simply traded places with Karissa when she died."

"She had a heart attack at a very young age."

"It was from the jab. Paris blames the Administration's policy to push jabs. Her college class was convinced to get the jab. She already had a QR code and knew better too."

"I remember you told me about that."

"Her education was finished remotely by me."

"In record time I gather."

"I was homeschooled. I was very advanced. And with COVID, they let us test out of most everything."

"You're more than two years younger. You finished college remotely before you were eighteen. You earned those credits."

"I didn't earn someone else's life. I still feel guilty about it, but I had the approval of her brother and parents. So I keep telling myself I'm partially doing it for Karissa."

That night, the stars were more beautiful than I had previously seen them.

"They look a lot different outside the city, don't they?" Valiant asked, though the answer was an obvious "yes."

"Maybe it's right that the VP takes over. After all, the current P is incompetent."

"She's awful."

"But that's not for us to judge," I said.

"She didn't even get one delegate in her primaries, and she never would have been VP but for the rigged election."

"And anyone questioning the rigging is considered a terrorist, along with the Republicans."

"We can get the President to reverse that."

"If they let us. I'm wavering between thinking my mission is complete versus wanting to help people. Technically we're high-tech criminals. Even though we're taking orders from Gene, that's no excuse under the Nuremberg principles."

"They threw out Nuremberg before you arrived. COVID," Valiant noted.

"I think they've totally ignored it for decades, dropping anthrax on North Korea, Tuskegee, the radiation experiments and so many of the things they did through the COVID vaxxes and boosters."

"The people who have had the boosters on top of the original injections are mostly metallic or dead by now."

"Lara. Who could be the control putting thoughts into their heads?"

"Supposedly the jab has a tie-in with 5G. There are no secrets between our government and the elite private sectors."

"I remember when people who had been jabbed went by 5G towers and found their personal data reading out on their cell phones," I noted.

"Remember when the government started reading text messages?"

"Text. Ray sent Jerry a text the night he died. He should have known better than that. What do we do when we find Northgrail?"

"I was going to use a pretext to check it out."

"You mean 'we,'" I said firmly.

"It could be dangerous. I'd feel much better if—"

I was not about to be protected with his life. "We're in this together, remember. What was it Tobias said to Tris after she had been captured? 'You die, I die.'"

"I'd rather not think of that outcome. Also, the third *Divergent* book was terrible," he noted.

"I know. I returned the whole series after I read it. The movie series ended well, though."

"I want you to know, I would do anything to protect you."

"But I've still got free will, and this is my investigation."

"Only because Jerry asked you for help."

"I was in the hospital morgue when they faked Lee's murder as a heart attack."

The next morning, we approached the Boca Inglesia mangroves, where vegetation and trees filled the areas between the natural channels. The boat started going up and down the channels. The water was beautiful. We passed the ruins of the first Latin American church as I mostly focused on Valiant and his EMF detector.

"Do you want to stop here?" Ben asked. He really didn't know what we wanted.

"Not here. Keep going." Suddenly, Valiant exclaimed, "Stop!"

"Here? There's nothing here but trees," Ben said.

"We like trees," I said. They anchored the yacht close to shore and Valiant and I took a raft to the shore. The area was very swampy and we had to push our way through the trees. It was hot and there were insects, but we were wearing full-length protective clothing and a little mosquito netting over our faces. "I never liked masks and it almost feels like I'm wearing one," I said. "The truck definitely couldn't pick up supplies here unless they were carried in on a boat?"

"Northgrail has to have an outlet onto the ocean or a river," he said. "But the readings are very high here. The facility has to be below sea level. I figure they need escape hatches in case there is a breach."

We looked around. "Right here, the readings are extremely high, but I don't see any entrances."

"Look," I said. It was two people standing about 50 feet away from us, smoking cigarettes. "Maybe this will teach employers at secret facilities to ban smokers." We hid behind some brush as we watched them.

After they finished, they went to a place near where we had found the high readings and waved a card over the ground. The card looked familiar but we were a ways away.

The ground opened up and they went down inside. The ground closed with the dirt and moss covering over the entrance making it blend in, naturally. "Handy," Valiant said.

"They had a card."

He pulled a card out of his boot, where he had stuck most of the contents of his wallet. "Remember this?"

"Minerva's gift."

We walked to the same location and he waved it and the ground opened. We looked down. There was a ladder which led into a closed room, not a room, an elevator.

"Your pleasure."

"Down James," I said with a British accent, feeling like I was in a *007* movie.

The elevator descended. When it opened up, we were greeted by men with guns, big guns, pointed straight at us.

CHAPTER 35

"And you are?" one of the men asked in English. I guess we looked American. Frankly, he did too.

"We were sent by Lee."

"Lee Carpenter?"

"Right." I relaxed. My hunch may have paid off.

"There are reports of his death."

"Greatly exaggerated," I said. I figured it might throw them off. They didn't show any reaction.

"Come with us," one of the men said.

He showed us into an office.

A man in a suit who looked like a Wall Street type walked in. "Lee sent you, huh?" Definitely a New York accent.

"Correct," Valiant said.

"And why did he send you?"

"He couldn't come for obvious reasons." Valiant was cool, calm, matter-of-fact in his speech. I was thinking he really would make a great James Bond or maybe John Drake, as in *Secret Agent*, given that he didn't carry a gun.

"If you're with Lee, what was his favorite fairy tale?"

"Rumpelstiltskin," I said.

"Very good."

"And you are?"

"Mike Johnson and Sandra Monroe," I made up. "I need to make sure you are the correct contact."

He didn't take the bait to tell us his name. "Why didn't you contact us by the normal channels?"

"We wanted to make sure there were no leaks. It seemed safer to come here in person. It looks like someone tipped off the Mexicans. Their President was unharmed by the explosion. Lee wants you to make sure all your employees are discreet and more successful in the future if you know what I mean."

"And what are you here for?"

"Parts and extras."

"We sent the fake skin and materials out to D.C. last week. They should have arrived." My guess was someone was still making the orders from the White House. I wondered who ordered the materials and who was to be replaced.

"We need backup materials—in case of problems."

"In case the new fail-safe goes off. Lee complained about the second model not having a fail-safe and insisted one be added. Maybe, you could tell us who the parts you sent were to create? I want to make sure it was the correct official."

"The FBI chief."

I shook my head. "Lee told me it was to be the head of the NSA. You sure you got the order correct?"

"It was your mistake. You'll have to pay extra for both the change and the backup parts you just requested. You have the green?"

"You'll get it upon delivery. You know we're good for it. We'd like a rush on the backup parts."

"The cost is going up. It will be double."

"I'll have to speak with Lee, but I assume he'll be willing to pay the price."

"That's what I like to hear. I'm Jason Hicks. Is that who you were supposed to meet?"

"Testing me? Naughty, naughty."

"Okay. I'm Mark Edwards."

The man who had earlier spoken to us with a gun in his hand came into the office. "JB, we've got another digital order from HC." Wrong initials for Mark Edwards. I wondered if he was using a pseudonym as well.

"Another suicide? Who this time?"

"An informant. Infiltrated the Haitian sex ring."

"How many does that make for her?"

"You'd think she would be more careful not to have so many people ready to testify against her, wouldn't you?" If he was talking about the person I thought he was, she wasn't in the White House, but she was still a key player. She could have her own account.

"I would," I said. I thought about Lara and then about the list of names we had found at Rays, which included some supposed suicides.

"Those nanoparticles really make it easy," Valiant added.

"The new nanochips in the boosters work even better than the originals. It's a nice improvement over having to set up suicides directly."

"Much better," I said. "Took out a secretary who was fighting the agenda."

"We have to get creative with the unvaxxed. We're looking at putting chips into their tap water."

"Of course," I said.

"The lunch should be ready and I'm starving. Would you like to come join me in my residence?"

"Sure," I said.

His residence was like a large apartment. Instead of windows, pictures of windows lined the walls. His cook had set up plates of grapes, lobster, potatoes, rice and a spinach salad with something resembling French dressing at the dining room table. We sat down and ate buffet style. The lobster looked as if it had been unhappy to have been cooked and so I skipped it.

"A vegetarian," JB remarked.

"Healthier that way."

"Not with most vegetables. BG has been buying up all the farmland and is dumping all kinds of toxins in the food."

"Says a lot for organic."

"Glyphosate's in much of the U.S.'s organic food. Makes people more susceptible to programming. Russia, Mexico and some other countries caught on and banned it."

I looked at the potatoes on my plate.

"I get mine from selected dealers. If any glyphosate is found, there's always the suicide switch." He laughed and we laughed along with him. "I may be the last man standing in a few years."

"Of course, the meat may also be tainted."

"You do your homework. Most people have no idea what they inject into the cows and other animals."

JB or Edwards, or whoever he was, opened a bottle of French wine. "I'm sure you know that all California wines have glyphosate. I only get mine from top European distributors." I took a sip and poured the rest into a plant by the table. I wanted to keep my wits about me, and I didn't really like grape wine.

"California wines also have oil fracking waste in them, even the organic ones," Valiant noted.

"Yes, leave it to the California Governors to poison the farming water while using the bulk of the clean water on fracking and water companies. It's almost funny."

"Then they pretend there's a water shortage when they're the ones who have wasted all the water," Valiant added.

"I don't mind. I take my lead from them in investments. They make a bundle and I make a bundle."

"Smart," I said.

"Would you like to see how we work the cooperative deaths of Americans?"

"Love to," I said.

"I'm in," Valiant said.

Our host took us into a room with computers and circuits. "Each person vaxxed or boosted has a digital ID implanted."

"Kind of like the vaccine passports," I said.

"Better. The particles implanted in them react to our signals. We type in the ID and hit the sayonara switch if they are to have a heart attack, the suicide switch if they are to you know, and the kill switch if they are to kill someone."

"We've had you very busy in D.C. over the last couple of weeks," I noted. Valiant was carefully watching the programmers as I spoke with JB.

"No more than usual. However, the list was a bit of a surprise."

"The voices."

"That's easy. We type in the words and they translate into the person's voice. We don't need to do it ourselves. Our clients are sometimes given the code and they design the voices."

"Such as Lara."

"Lara Leonard.? Your people have had her code for some time."

"I know. That's why I brought her up."

"Do you worry that your truck drivers will get caught?" Valiant asked.

"They haven't yet. Most of your supplies start out by submarine. You've noticed we don't have a road in here."

JB took us to the underground port. "They dock here. We have to be very careful to create a perfect seal and then suction out the water. Otherwise, there will be flooding." There was a switch assembly on the wall. I noticed a few diving suits.

The gun guy came back into where we were standing. "JB, we have a problem." He looked at us and I had an uneasy feeling. He whispered something to JB. Our host laughed, which made me more uneasy.

"I need to show you one of our more interesting operations."

"Actually, we need to be going. We've got to get back before we're missed by the wrong people."

"This will just take a minute."

He guided us to a room. The walls were barren, made of metal.

"This is interesting, but," Valiant started to say as the guy with the gun pointed it at us. A second later Ben was marched into the room by Skipper Wricher at gunpoint.

"Ah, one of my top assassins. He killed his own mother-in-law."

"Great guy," I said sarcastically.

JB turned to the first guy with the gun. "Tabor, we're in elite company. This is Valiant Rimmel and the beautiful young lady is Karissa James. So nice of you to come visit us. We were expecting to have someone else to test out our special chamber, but you'll do nicely."

Valiant started forward but stopped as the gun was pointed at my head.

"One move and she dies quickly."

Valiant stayed back. JB and Tabor backed out and closed the door with us inside. I heard a key turn in the lock.

"Was this your plan? Did Jerry know you were going to get a gang of criminals to throw us into a locked room?" Ben asked.

"It's not just a locked room," Valiant said, looking around the place. "It's much more than that."

As if on cue, the walls started coming together.

"'Crush,'" I said.

CHAPTER 36

"I wonder who he was expecting," I said.

"We're going to die here," Ben lamented.

"Not if I can help it," Valiant responded.

"Do you have a bar to stop the walls from crushing us? Like they tried to do in *Star Wars*?" I asked.

Valiant reached into his boot and pulled out the keys we had collected. "Well, it's worth a try?"

"Which one?"

"From Mrs. Kinsky? Maybe Kyle was onto this."

"Seriously?" I asked. It was a million to one chance.

The million to one came through. The door unlocked. But the walls continued to close in.

"Why would he have a key to the crusher room?" I asked.

"Maybe he helped design it. He was away a lot working on special assignments."

We carefully opened the unlocked door for a view. Tabor was standing with his back to us. Valiant tripped him from behind, as he twisted Tabor's arm, taking the gun from Tabor's hands and then knocked him almost unconscious. As JB, apparently hearing the sound, came rushing up, Valiant tossed me the gun as he tackled JB and another approaching gunman. Then Valiant and Ben took the key cards from the three men and threw them into the room and locked the door.

"That was against my professional ethics," Ben said.

"If you want, we'll let you go back in there," Valiant responded.

The room was almost soundproof, but I heard a faint set of cries. Part of me cringed, as I didn't believe in win-lose scenarios. In the moment, I couldn't think of an alternative, though.

"I guess the crusher worked. I would have expected them to know where an off switch was located," Valiant said. "Are you okay?"

"I'm okay with escaping. We have to flood the complex." I figured the workers would be out through the hatch as soon as the flood started.

"There's something we have to do first." We followed Valiant to the digital ID room. The Minerva key card gained him access to the room. The men inside were surprised when we came in with guns aimed at them. Valiant took control of the main computer and I saw that files were being deleted. "Now, if you try to warn anyone, you won't be working anywhere. We'll be outside with guns pointed this way. Wait for the signal and then we'll let you leave through the above-ground exit."

"We don't like it any more than you," one of them said.

From there, we ran to the underwater port. Valiant waved Minerva's key card for admission to the area and started pressing buttons.

"Are you crazy? If this floods, it will kill us too," Ben said.

I assumed Valiant had an idea what the buttons did. Or, at least, I hoped he did.

"It needs an additional key," Valiant said as the control panel displayed a demand for another key. Waving Minerva's and Kinsky's keys didn't work. "No, it couldn't be." He pulled out the key Martinez had left for me and inserted it into a keyhole.

"Well, he was a thief. Maybe he took it from Lee, thinking it was important." Valiant turned the key and the controls were operational. Then, he tossed a wetsuit and an air tank to Ben and another set to me. Valiant started dressing in a third as he continued pressing buttons, more effectively this time. "One of them should work," he said, trying the different cards. And it did. I saw an onscreen image of a door between an outer chamber and the sea slide open and the water starting to rush in. The door behind us started to slide closed. I put one of the extra air tanks in the opening to keep it open to the rest of the underground. Valiant put the contents of his boots into a small plastic bag he had in his pocket. "Wait," he said. He pulled out the key card he had used for the crusher and tried it on a reader next to the inner sliding door. It didn't work. He tried the other cards. JB's card opened the door wide and locked it into the open position. Ben pointed the gun at the door to the compound in case anyone tried to enter.

Next, Valiant opened the door to the outer chamber and then, quickly, returned the key and key cards to the plastic bag and slipped it into one of his boots. As the water started rushing in, I saw armed men start to come our way through the compound door. Seeing the wall of water, they turned and ran back. Valiant grabbed my hand and pulled me down to the floor as the water rushed over us. I felt Ben's hand next to me on my other side. As the rush of water calmed down and filled the area, we started swimming through the airlock. Valiant guided us out into the Gulf. Somewhere I lost Ben's hand.

Valiant and I wound up on a beach with trees nearby. I pulled off my oxygen mask. I was feeling dizzy, nauseous and very weak.

Valiant pulled me into his arms and held me. Somehow that helped. "It's a touch of the bends or maybe the mixture in the tanks was off. You'll be okay."

"You?" I managed to get out, still feeling sick.

"I've got it too. But you make me stronger."

"My head."

"It will go away," he said, reassuringly.

I felt better. "Ben! We've got to find Ben."

We ran along the shore. We saw him lying under a tree. Valiant pulled off Ben's facemask and started doing CPR, similar to what Jerry had done with Greg, but with less grace and certainty. Valiant started blowing into Ben's mouth. I noticed that Ben's tank was empty and I wondered how long he had been he had been oxygen deprived. Valiant kept up the CPR for what seemed forever before Ben started to move a little. Valiant continued to blow air into Ben's lungs until Ben pushed him away.

"Yuck," Ben uttered.

"Thank goodness," I said. I looked around. "Where are we?" I asked.

"I don't know," Valiant said.

"Look, it's the yacht we came on," I said, seeing it go from a nearby channel into the ocean.

"Let's get out of sight," Valiant insisted.

Ben could barely move and we pulled him behind a tree.

"Do you think Wricher saw us?" I asked.

"If he did, he'll be turning this way. He had guns on that yacht."

"I don't see anyone else on deck," I said.

"It looks like he's alone, but we can't count on it," Valiant noted.

"Where did you find him?" I asked Ben.

"Jerry said to find someone who would give us a ride to Boca and agree to follow our guidance. He didn't say to watch out for someone who might kill us."

"But you were careful in the bar."

"That place was known for some shady criminals. Sportsmen aren't supposed to be New World Order criminals."

"Why not? Doctors and nurses are killing their patients with those vaccines," Valiant said.

"I take it you are clean too."

"Yeh. I do hacking. I faked my results."

"I'd suggest we work together to help purebloods, but you're too crazy."

"We're alive, aren't we? And maybe millions of others have been spared too, with the destruction of that place," I said.

"They might have more facilities," Valiant said.

"That's what I was afraid of," I remarked. "Did you have to say what I was trying not to think?"

"Sorry."

"He's gone on. Maybe he thinks we're dead."

"I wonder who they planned to crush. That was next on the list."

"Jerry? He was the one Marissa contacted," I said.

"My brother?"

"They've been setting him up for the last two weeks. You heard about those two reporters? The murder-suicide?"

"I heard."

"Someone wore a disguise to frame Jerry. Your brother and I were at the scene of the deaths of Seth Moore and Gene Hemmings trying to find out what Marissa was going to tell Jerry."

"Are you saying you were helping my brother?"

"A lot of people are dying and we were trying to find out who and why."

"I may have misjudged you. I thought you were getting Jerry into trouble."

"Maybe we are all getting each other into trouble, but there is safety in numbers. People keep dying and none of us wants to be next."

"So you weren't dating my brother?"

"That was Monica. She's a real slut, if I may say so." I didn't have any problem calling other girls sluts if they were.

"We're in agreement there. He brought her to dinner one night and that was obvious."

"Both Valiant and I really care about your brother. I never want to see him hurt and neither does Valiant."

Valiant didn't say anything, but he nodded.

"We need to find a way off Boca Inglesia," Valiant said.

"Walking and swimming," I suggested.

"We could make a raft. It might take a little time," Valiant said.

"Cancun is to the south. I think there is a hotel off the coast, somewhere,"

"If you want to swim," Valiant said. "Chiquila is to the east."

"Forty miles."

"Making a boat is sounding better," Ben said. "I was with the Girl Scouts. I know how."

"Girl Scouts?" Valiant and I asked in unison. "I didn't know you were. I meant were you?"

"No," he answered me. "The Boy Scouts were an exclusive club and my parents wouldn't let me join. The Girl Scouts accepted boys."

"Let's hear it for the Girl Scouts," I said. "I was a Camp Fire Girl. I don't have the foggiest notion of how to make a boat."

While the guys used the long twining reeds to help secure branches they pulled off from the trees, I waded in the water. I was enjoying the water when suddenly Valiant dragged me away. "Didn't you see the shark?"

"Thank you."

I spent the rest of the day, sitting under a tree. As night came, the raft was near completion. A boat was visible on the horizon.

'Someone else coming to shoot or crush us?" I asked.

"No missiles are firing yet," Valiant said.

"That's because our cell phones are dead and they've nothing to locate us with," I remarked.

"Mine's waterlogged too. Maybe, they'll give us a ride," Ben said. He started towards the water.

"Ben, it could be a clean-up crew. As in bang, bang," I said.

He came back to the bushes.

"The raft is almost done. It might get us over to a hotel on Isla Blanca," Valiant told us.

"Do we need to worry about the sharks?" I asked.

"As long as we stay on the raft, we'll be okay," Valiant said. "I've made a spear in case it gets close."

"It's too bad we don't still have those guns," Ben said.

"It was difficult enough escaping," I added. "You think we should have brought out guns?"

"I don't know how well they'll work after being water-logged," Valiant said. I looked at him. "I'm a hacker, not a marksman."

"I like to be prepared," Ben said.

I thought about Ray's list. "Seth Rich, JFK Jr., and the other names. Nobody ever questioned the apparent murders."

"We know who Seth Rich and JFK Jr., were a threat to," Valiant said.

"All that would have been before Duane's time. It wasn't his Hushpuppies that did it," I said, ignoring the obvious.

"Hushpuppies could be the continuation of another program. Kind of like the OSS turning into the CIA. If Hushpuppies was into eliminating obstacles, we could fall on that list."

"Well, crushed was on Lee's list and he was over Duane," I said. "Maybe Marissa had evidence of what really happened to someone on that list."

"Everyone suspected Seth Rich was murdered. The supposed killers were blind thieves who didn't bother to take any of the valuables. Then members of the DNC ordered the police to call off the investigation," Valiant recalled.

"The one officer who exposed the odd conduct of the investigation is dead," I said. "Wricher knows who we are. We could be added to the list if we're not on it already."

'What, these people killed JFK Jr.?" Ben asked.

"We can't be sure of anything—except there were a lot of names on a list."

"You don't trust Duane. Do you think Duane might be behind the latest killings?" Valiant asked.

"My intuition says 'no,' but his sub-department certainly has ties. Whoever contacted JB, did so on behalf of Lee—unless Lee has another Department."

"Ever hear of Killenpro?"

"That name appeared on something I saw, but as far as I know Lee was only operating the two sub-departments: ours and Hushpuppies."

"And the two sub-departments were separate sections of the same department before I got there," Valiant said.

"I guess they had split up the functions to avoid the wrong person talking. But Kyle's team apparently worked on both," I said. "That's probably why they were killed after they were let go. Maybe," I surmised.

"And it was all under Lee."

"Neither of us came in until well after the fake election and the start of the current Administration and had no knowledge of the stuff Hushpuppies was doing. After the dead trio, apparently, nobody from our section had any connection to Hushpuppies," I continued to speculate.

"Plausible deniability."

"How is what we are doing plausible deniability? We could wind up in prison, just like Duane," I pointed out.

"We aren't killing anyone and the real President is alive and President—even if he got virtually no votes."

"The election was faked?" Ben asked.

"You don't really believe the American people elected a brain-dead President, do you? And if they had, why would the party be working so hard to stop recounts or to classify the opposition party and anyone calling for election verification 'terrorists?'"

"I'm feeling like I'm having one of those 'Aha' moments."

"And this may just be the tip of the iceberg. Wait until we find out what else is going on under our noses," Valiant said.

"I'm not sure I want to," I said.

"You are going to fill Jerry in on this."

"I hope you'll keep this confidential from anyone outside me, Valiant and Jerry."

"He knows this stuff?"

"Much of it," I replied.

The boat, which had gone by, swung back. It seemed to be searching for something. It went inland along a channel and then back out. Finally, it appeared to give up on whatever it was searching for.

"I guess someone was concerned we had survived," I said. "And wanted to make sure that didn't happen."

After dark, we set off for Isla Blanca. We used branches for oars. The ride went well. But then, I noticed sharks in the water following us. Valiant kept a spear he had made near him, ready to defend us from anything that came too close.

Something was coming up fast. "It's the Seniorita Linda," Valiant said. That was the boat we came on. Shots were fired as we tried to lay down flat. "I'll take my chances with the sharks."

"Me too," I replied as we both dropped off together. Ben followed our lead. The shots continued. It was too dark to see what Wricher's shots were hitting, but I suspected he had a night scope.

A shark approached me. In the moonlight, I saw its teeth as it opened its mouth.

CHAPTER 37

There was another spray of shots as Valiant and I ducked under water and under the raft. I was starting to run out of breath and then his lips were on mine, breathing air in. We came up together.

I didn't see Ben. "Ben!" I called. Something was floating right by us. It was the shark. "Ben!" He surfaced right before another round of bullets hit nearby, causing us to dive back under.

When we resurfaced for air, the boat was about to ram into our raft and we were looking up the barrel of a rifle. There wasn't enough time to dive as everything seemed to slow down. Wricher was pressing the trigger as his boat jolted. Something had crashed into it. He turned, misfiring. It was the other boat we had seen. On the deck of the other boat, Jerry was holding a gun aimed at Wricher's head. Wricher turned to point his rifle at Jerry. Jerry fired and the skipper fell.

"Nice shooting," Valiant said as the three of us got aboard the boat Jerry had rented.

"You're paying for the damages," a man was saying to Jerry.

"It's worth it," Jerry replied. He gave me a hug. "Never frighten me like that, again."

"Oh you don't know the half of it," I said.

He released me and looked at Valiant. "You almost got her killed."

"He saved all our lives. Earlier. At Northgrail."

"What is that?"

"What isn't it? It was an assassination bureau and they were using the boosters to program people to kill themselves or others."

"The vaxxes?" the man with Jerry asked.

"This is Max. I hired him and his boat to rescue you."

"Hi Max," I said.

"Hi. I'm glad I didn't get one, then."

"You're definitely safer without one," Valiant said, shaking Max's hand.

"These two are like super spies," Ben said. "You should see them in action."

"Guess we have a backup profession if we get fired," I joked. "We might have perished if you hadn't rescued us," I told Jerry. "Superhero Jerry."

Jerry smiled.

"I have some rooms for us over at the Real Hotel Isla Blanca. We can go back home tomorrow."

<hr>

Jerry had room service bring us up some food. It turned out that we weren't the only ones with exciting news. The Vice President had arranged for the President to be declared dead.

"He's been declared dead?" I asked.

"Not yet. It seems that everyone else is dragging their feet to her chagrin," Jerry responded.

"Has she been moved into the White House?"

"Not until he's declared dead. But she's acting President. She already has an office there and is now acting out of the Oval Office."

"Does she know about our work?" I asked, pointing to myself and Valiant.

"She hasn't yet been briefed on the existence of the sub-departments or the sub-basements. Paris said that Gene called him and the staff from your sub-department and Duane's into his office and informed them that they could all be arrested if the truth came out. So they've created an alternate set of duties and work agenda. Brandon has been cooking the books for your department, and Duane has done the dirty for his department."

"Wait. The President's dead?" Ben asked.

"They don't have a body," I said.

"Presumed," Jerry clarified for him.

"How are Brandon and Jack doing on finishing that project?"

"Days, away. The supplies arrived. They came from Northgrail, I gather."

"They won't be getting any more supplies from there," Valiant said.

"Let's hope they have all they need," I added. "We still don't know who contacted them after Lee's demise."

"What are these projects?" Ben asked.

"Haven't you been exposed to enough insanity today?" I asked.

"Keep it to yourselves."

"Paris has been really worried about you. So have Gene and Felicity. Felicity seems to be your biggest fan," Jerry said.

"Really? She's everyone's best friend."

"In your case, it might be good. She says she wants to give you a promotion when you return—if you return."

"How nice. But she won't be Special Assistant to the President anymore."

"No. More like Vice President."

"What?"

"The former VP, now the acting P, has nominated her."

"What are her qualifications?" I asked.

"Special Assistant to the President."

"Have you noticed the current Vice President doesn't know the first thing about world policy or domestic policy or much of anything else? She'll need someone from the Administration to fill her in on just about everything. Her number one project has been to increase the prison population with little kids and their parents," Valiant pointed out.

"I'm sure she'll create new laws to do just that," I said.

"So who is Felicity loyal to?"

"She has been advising the VP to slow down and wait for proof of death."

"Do you think Felicity will switch her allegiance?"

"She can't. All anyone needs to do is trot out the real President and Ferris's Administration will be brought down," Valiant pointed out.

Valiant used Jerry's laptop to check out the Net. "You know, that Wricher guy not only killed his mother-in-law but he almost killed his wife. His daughter had him removed from her FAFSA because of the domestic violence and she defeated him in a lawsuit. Then some church in Southern California made him their CEO."

"Was that a branch of the Covidians?" I inquired.

"No. It was a Unitme Church."

"I know about them. They differ from Religious Science in that they think all acts of violence are perfect acts of God. No wonder they chose him as their CEO," Jerry said.

"So what was he doing running cruses?" I asked.

"Apparently in his spare time, he was Northgrail's top hitman and also a lookout for anyone approaching their Mexican headquarters, according to a blog. The blogger died of natural causes. Secret defense contractors make big bucks."

"I don't think I'm joining his church," Jerry remarked.

"If you're into New Thought, Religious Science is a bit more accountable," I said.

"I prefer traditional churches," Jerry said.

"Those are cool too," I responded.

"I've treated some patients who had near-death experiences," Ben commented. "That nonsense about the brain activity after death being just electrical impulses doesn't meet with medical science."

"So you believe the NDEs are real?" I asked.

"If it was just brain activity, which it couldn't be, then their stories wouldn't match and they do. After I treated an NDE patient I had known since high school, I did some checking."

"How long was the person dead?"

"Ten hours. We had called it hours before, but she hadn't been taken to the morgue. Suddenly she was awake, remembering people who were in the room that she couldn't have known were there unless part of her was conscious."

"I hope there is life after death. I hope Lara and—" I looked at Jerry. He still didn't know the truth. "Others have a better life. And Ray too."

"Ray?"

"I think he was set up. He wasn't the bad guy. He was investigating them. Northgrail was carrying out at least some of the list. They tried to crush us and were responsible for Lara. Even before the vaccines, they were in the assassination business."

Jerry looked thoughtful. "I'm glad. Ray and I were really close in college. After he went into the NSA, I didn't see much of him, but I couldn't believe he had turned evil until that night."

"I'm pretty sure he didn't," I said.

"Lee was tied to Northgrail," Valiant said.

"That—" Jerry started to say but didn't finish. I got that he was going to slur Lee.

"Until Wricher brought in Ben at gunpoint, we had gotten a free lunch by pretending to be sent by Lee," Valiant told Jerry.

"Hey, I worked for the guy and I got his job, just not the oversight on what he was doing with Northgrail."

"Just starting wars and bombing unarmed countries," Jerry said.

"How is Kiribati?" I asked.

"All the leaders there just got assassinated. Our government claimed it was a rogue hit, but Paris told me the insurgents had all worked for the WHO, the NIH and the CIA and were trained at Fort Benning, Georgia. Of course, they are claiming it's a people's uprising, an orange revolution."

"They always do. I guess the best approach is for a foreign country to have nukes. Have things cooled down with North Korea?" I asked.

"The leader made a speech about how the world might have lost its greatest comedian."

"Glad they're continuing to take it in good spirits. Did our military get that it was a joke?"

"They haven't acted, but you can be sure they will if the VP moves up."

The next morning, our plan was to take a boat to Coatzacoalcos. From there we were going to travel by a four-wheel-drive vehicle to Salina Cruz. "A valuable crew will be meeting us there with a boat," Jerry said.

As we were preparing to leave, I asked Jerry, "Why the complicated route?"

"According to our release, you came back on Air Force One with the Pres and aren't really here."

"Passports? My mom has one I can use."

"You're covered. Brandon had special ones made up that will pass a quick inspection."

"About the couple that was arrested, we will help them, won't we?"

"They were there. For all we know they accepted the explosives. They just weren't in the picture that Brandon altered to make you disappear."

"On the news today, they looked beaten," Valiant said.

"Mexican prisons aren't as bad as America's, contrary to reports. I bet some of the prisoners are angry about the assassination attempt on their President. I expect they'll be put into solitary pending trial. If they can't link the explosives to them, they could be let off."

"Do you think they are Americans?"

"They are, and they've been at the scenes of other bombings."

"But I don't want them convicted on false evidence."

"Let's see what happens."

I would have liked to have gone by Veracruz again to see my mom, but nobody but Valiant knew her location. So it was better this way.

After Wricher, I wasn't sure I could trust anyone commanding a boat, but Jerry assured me he had checked this captain out thoroughly. He used to be with the Mexican Navy and had a clean record.

The sun was hot but the sea breeze cooled us down. The ride to Coatzacoalcos went smoothly. So I started to relax. There, we said our goodbyes to Ben. "I hope the rest of your vacation is quieter and friendlier," I told him.

"I owe you an apology, not just for renting a mobster's boat, but for questioning your intentions with respect to my brother and the Administration."

"No worries. What I am doing is not technically legal."

"I have experience with the not technically legal. I've given a lot of saline doses to people who insisted on the jab and shot up quite a number of oranges so I could give out vax cards to those who didn't trust any injection. I couldn't bring myself to be part of ending their lives."

"Now that the mind control has been confirmed—"

"I'm going to stock up on saline."

I gave him a hug. "I owe you an apology for putting you in so much danger."

"My brother was the one who commandeered me. It's on him."

"But you love him, anyway," I told Ben.

"I'm glad we were able to do some good. It just didn't feel good at the time."

Jerry came up and gave his brother a hug.

"Next time, tell me when I need to have an Uzi up my sleeve."

"Sorry about that, bro."

"Keep safe. It looks like you've got yourself into a dangerous situation."

"I've got a gun and my friend has the chops and kicks."

"I saw. He could be in Kung Fu movies."

They hugged again.

"Don't get killed. Mom wouldn't like it," Ben advised him.

"I won't."

The four-wheel drive, we picked up for next to nothing from a junk dealer, looked like it had seen significantly better days. "Consider it a challenge," Jerry said. "I didn't want to go to a major dealer or rental agency." On the road, we found it had a broken air conditioner. So we were rather hot and sweating on the way toward Salina Cruz.

Jerry was following a map for the best off-road routes and a couple of times I wasn't sure we were going to make it over the dips and rocks. But the vehicle seemed to be holding up. That is until we got to a dry riverbed. As we started across, it got stuck in the sand. The four of us pushed and pulled to get it out. The vehicle didn't have a jack, but that wouldn't have helped much with the unstable sand underneath. When we finally got it free, we found that a tire was flat. That's when Jerry noticed the spare was also flat. We looked for a tire repair kit and air pump and there were none.

"I'll never criticize my brother for being unprepared again," Jerry said.

"It's on me too," Valiant responded. "I should have checked over the vehicle."

"You wanted a new 4Runner. I should have listened."

"If you two are through with the one-downs-man-ship, do you think we can ride on the rims?"

"For a ways. Maybe the whole way," Jerry said. But at the next ditch, we couldn't get the jeep out. Two of the rims were bent from a fall against rocks in the ditch.

I looked around. We were in the middle of nowhere. "Not good. No towns within walking distance and we don't have supplies for a cross-country hike," Jerry said.

We were stranded with the hot sun blazing away.

CHAPTER 38

Jerry pulled out his case, and we pulled out a couple of backpacks with spare clothes and food that we had picked up in Coatzacoalcos before starting on this part of the journey. Jerry had brought some clothes for us with him, but we figured we might need a couple of changes, given that our suitcases we packed at Mom's place had been lost at sea.

It was hot and I stripped down to a bathing suit I had picked up that morning in the hotel gift shop. Valiant removed everything to reveal his swimming trunks.

"In the Sahara, they put on more clothing to protect themselves from the heat," Jerry said.

"We didn't bother to buy any white robes," Valiant responded to him.

"You might wind up badly sunburned."

Valiant turned his shirt into a hat to shade himself and then helped me do likewise.

"I didn't bring my swimsuit. Here goes." Jerry pulled off his slacks and shirt. His underpants looked like they could double for a swimsuit. So I figured, he wouldn't get arrested for indecent exposure if they did that here. Valiant had his wallet contents once again tucked into his new boots, along with our new passports. If we went to an airport, they'd make him take the boots off, but Jerry had a different plan that didn't involve flying. Jerry tucked his passport and wallet into his socks.

The guys took turns carrying Jerry's suitcase, which included his computer among other things. We took breaks when we could under trees. After about ten miles, we were getting overheated and tired as we came across a farmhouse.

Sadia and Juaquin, the couple who owned the farm, were a little leery about strangers at first. "Our car broke down. It's really hot. Is there a chance we could come inside to cool down and maybe get something cold to drink?"

The couple seemed a little flustered and then finally Sadia said, "Sure." She reached out a hand to me. "You poor little thing, having to traipse across the countryside like this." She glared at the guys.

Inside, they gave us some lemonade and we talked about the best route to Salina Cruz. We had circled too far to the east. We were in the vicinity of Tuxtla Gutiérrez. Juaquin offered to drive us to Arriaga, where we could catch a bus to take us up Highway 190 toward our destination.

We caught a bus that would be going up highways 200, 190 and 185. We were told it would be a few hours before the bus reached Salina Cruz. As we sat there, Jerry pretended to read a newspaper. Valiant and I asked him for a couple of pages. Jerry had done more TV time than us, but we were the initial suspects, though the pictures were off. We sat in the seat one up from the back, squeezing all three of us into one seat.

From the paper, I could see that the Mexican President and his staff were fine. They were still looking for our President and wondering if our President paid the assassins to set off the bomb while the President was whisked away. Of course, they couldn't find any real DNA for other than the known victims at the scene. The explosion was large enough that nothing but mechanical pieces were found. They had found pieces of a secondary bomb at the scene. "The fail-safe," Valiant whispered. "The primary bomb must have set that off too."

There had been protests outside the jail where the suspects were being held. Mexico did not have the death penalty, but people wanted to make sure they were prosecuted to the fullest extent possible.

There was a picture of our Vice President who was on the verge of being President if the other robot wasn't repaired in time. She was mourning the loss of a President, whose demise she couldn't be certain of. She was starting to name her Cabinet from a list of her past guy friends. The HUD secretary was going to be a former mayor of a northern California city. Her Secretary of State was going to be Adam Shytface. Her Attorney General was going to be her almost former husband. They were getting divorced so she could appoint him.

The heat was finally getting to me. I dosed off. When I came to, I noticed that my head was on Jerry's shoulder and Valiant was sleeping with his head on mine. "Sorry," I said.

"Any time."

As the bus was pulling into a stop outside Juchitán de Zaragoza, Valiant started to stir as well. "Let's switch buses," he said.

"Why?" Jerry asked.

"The farmer may have recognized us and told someone our route."

Jerry suggested we switch to a bus that was taking a more scenic route, reconnecting with 190 and then going down 185D to 200 into Salina Cruz.

185D bypassed towns and seemingly was an express route to Salina Cruz and Jerry thought that was a better route.

Outside of Santo Domingo Tehuantepec, Jerry said, "Look at the scenery. Mexico wouldn't be a bad place to live."

"Look," I said. The bus stopped and took on a couple of new passengers I recognized. "They were there at the Palace," I told Jerry.

"Maria and Carlos," Valiant said quietly. "What are they doing on a bus, instead of an official limousine?"

They sat down in seats toward the front. We went back to pretending to look at the newspaper. "We need to get off at the next stop," Jerry said.

I didn't see any stops coming up, but as we passed a river on 185D, the bus got a flat tire. As the driver and his assistant went out to change it, Valiant and I rushed out a rear side door and cut under the bridge to the river. There were some trees alongside the bank and we hid among them. Several other passengers got out as we watched the bus. "I don't see Jerry," I said.

"There." He had gotten out the front door and was moving quickly to get under the bridge, holding his suitcase. Maria and Carlos appeared to be looking for something, maybe us, among the other passengers. Jerry wasn't at the National Palace and so they may not have realized he was with us— if they noticed him. Still, they were heading in our direction when the driver's assistant personally ushered them to join the other passengers going back onto the bus. They continued looking around in our direction but didn't appear to see us.

As the bus took off, we started walking a ways from the side of the road. "A checkpoint or toll station," I commented, pointing at the highway.

"Good, we got off," Jerry said. We kept walking and got to a motel, located next to a gas station.

"Let's get some rest here," Jerry said. "I've got this." He went into the office and came out with a room key. The door opened to the outside and was on the backside of the motel.

I was pretty tired. "This is Wednesday. It's been five days. If we're not back soon, we could be in trouble."

"Let's cool down here for a couple of hours and then get going. Our boat doesn't get here until midnight."

"Another boat?" I asked Jerry.

"Did we have any problems on the way to Coatzacoalcos? We just don't go on any private excursions with assassins."

"Good point."

Valiant went out and got us a couple of mushroom pizzas.

"Nice," I said. We ate in the cool room.

Jerry did not look well. "What is it?" I asked.

"Nothing."

"Seriously. You look sick."

"It might be food poisoning."

"We've been eating the same food you have since we met you."

"Yesterday for lunch, I had some fish."

"If it was from the Gulf, you're looking at heavy oil," Valiant said.

"It may have been undercooked. Excuse me." Jerry ran to the bathroom and threw up.

"They have corn-syrup free coke here. Coca-Cola Syrup was used for generations to calm upset stomachs," I said.

"With who knows what's in it. Our government was going to spray coca crops with glyphosate," Valiant said.

Jerry looked like he was going to collapse.

I went to the gas station and got him a Mexican Seven-Up in the hopes it would help. It seemed to relax him a little until he threw up again.

"It could also be a little heat stroke," I said.

We decided to wait a few more hours to let Jerry rest and try to recover. It only took an hour before he said, "We should get going. Let's have the manager call us a taxi."

The taxi driver picked us up and we requested a ride to downtown Salina Cruz. Jerry figured that was close enough to our destination that we could walk the rest of the way.

"You can drop us off here," Jerry said as we got downtown.

"Here? No, no. This is the bad part of the city. I'll take you to the good part and you'll see."

"That's not necessary," Jerry said.

"But it is. I'd never forgive myself if you did not reach your destination."

"Our destination is downtown," I said.

"No, no. It's right here." A garage door opened and in he drove. We were in some warehouse district and this was one of the warehouses.

Jerry pulled out his gun. "I suggest you take us out of here."

"I don't think so."

The driver ran out and the car door closed and locked before we could get out. We tried to open it but the inner locks wouldn't work. Then suddenly a sizzling noise started up. "Something is coming in through the vents," Valiant said.

CHAPTER 39

Jerry tried to smash the window with his gun and it didn't break. So he blasted the window with bullets as we all started pulling our tops up to cover our mouths and noses. They weren't all that effective at keeping out the fumes. Jerry got out of the car through his window as Valiant assisted me out behind Jerry and then followed. Jerry reached back in for his suitcase. The main garage door we had gone through was closed. We ran in the direction where we had seen a side door on the way in. It was locked. Jerry fired at the lock and it opened. Jerry and I started through.

But Valiant had gone unconscious. *No, he has to be alright*, was all I could think. I tried to lift him, but Jerry was better at hoisting him over his shoulder. The door opened to the outside. We rushed through it and, once we were half a block from our prison warehouse, Jerry put Valiant down against the wall of a different warehouse.

Jerry started breathing air into Valiant's mouth as I continued panicking. "Please be alright. Please be alright," I was begging Valiant. It took a minute before he stirred. He was groggy. "We need some oxygen and a doctor for him!" I practically screamed.

"No," he said sleepily, "I'll be okay. Give me a minute."

"You better be alright," I said, terrified that some damage had been done.

"I think we all need oxygen," Jerry said. He was right. My lungs were burning. "We've got to get out of here."

Jerry helped Valiant up. Valiant was wobbly. We both assisted Valiant as we continued back towards downtown.

"We passed a hospital on the way here," Jerry said. A couple of blocks later, he pointed at it. "There." We went inside.

"Hospitals have been killing patients, rather than helping them since 2020."

"We'll ask for supplies," Jerry said.

Inside, one of the nurses tried to put Valiant in a wheelchair. "It's not necessary. He was exposed to gas as were we. We need oxygen. I'm Doctor Ben Stafford and they are my responsibility."

He showed the nurse his passport, which was apparently his brother's. "I can cover the expense."

They attached us to some small tanks of oxygen with breathing apparatuses and we sat there until our lungs felt more normal. I was glad this wasn't an American hospital, where doctors were not allowed to use their best judgment in treating patients.

"Someone knew we were at the motel," I said after Jerry paid for the oxygen and we left.

"Maria and Carlos may have surmised we'd stop there. There weren't that many motels close to the checkpoint," Valiant said.

"But why try to kill us rather than turn us in? And they were so nice to us in Mexico City."

"Maybe, the motel clerk recognized you," Jerry said.

"We didn't go inside the office. Just you."

"Maybe the pizza place I went to," Valiant said.

"They're bound to figure out we escaped. If we run into more danger, do you have more bullets?" I asked.

"I have several clips in my case," Jerry said. He opened it up and put in a fresh one. "We've got several hours to hang out before our boat is here."

We walked along to a shopping mall not far from the Pacific. The town was beautiful with older houses, parks and hills. There were too many warehouses. I'd had my fill of them. We went into the shopping mall to hang out like tourists until closing.

"Dinner?" Valiant asked.

"How do you stay in shape with all the food you're eating?" Jerry asked him.

"How is your stomach?" I asked Jerry.

"Much better," Jerry said.

"As little as you held down earlier, it wouldn't hurt to get some food and a drink into you."

"Want more pizza?" Valiant asked.

"Let's see what else they have," I said.

To our surprise, there was a Chipotle in town.

"I didn't think there were any operating in Mexico," Valiant said. "Maybe this is a similar chain or an independent restaurant. There's a sign in the window, saying, 'No GMOs.'"

I had a guacamole burrito.

"You don't want anything else?" Jerry asked.

"Nope. This is perfect."

Valiant had two. "She's got good taste."

Jerry had chicken, cheese, beans, and rice in his. "Now this is a burrito."

"Your stomach must really be doing better," I said.

The restaurant had some bottles of fruit juice and we downed several of them. Unlike the Chipotles we were used to, this Chipotle had a TV on the wall. There was a picture of the President with a copy of today's newspaper.

The image flashed to Gene.

"The President is alive and well, but because of the attempt on his life, he is in a secure location. It's time that the over-eagerness to install a new President was curbed until the culprits can be caught. Two of our Secret Service detail are dead. How many more have to die before the reckless push for a new President is halted?"

The TV was subtitling Spanish. Gene showed a picture of the President in a chair. I suspected this was the real President.

"The VP must be fuming over his statement," Jerry said.

"Do you think that will settle it?" I asked.

"Watch," Jerry said.

"The reaction of the Vice President Pamela Ferris was to demand proof that the picture was not altered. In a press conference, she said, 'We want the President at a live public event. If he's alive, he can do that.'"

"That's not even sane if his life is in danger," Jerry said.

"I bet Monica's father is hoping they'll both be thrown out," Valiant commented. "Hey Jerry, maybe you and Monica should get back together— in case her dad becomes the next President."

Jerry glared at him.

"The President's going to have to be up and running ASAP," I said.

After the restaurant closed, I walked out first. The moon was bright, up above. "It's beautiful."

"Yes, it is," a familiar voice said as the barrel of a firearm touched my head.

Another familiar voice said, "One false move and the girl dies." Maria was holding my friends at gunpoint as I looked to see Carlos attached to the rifle pointed at me.

CHAPTER 40

"And you were so sweet in the limo."

"We were eager for the day's events." Her accent had changed a little.

"We saw the delivery list from Northgrail," I lied. "Sam delivered the explosives to you." The driver had said he made the delivery to Sam.

"Right before we met you at the airport. We were worried we wouldn't be able to pull it off when they put us in the limo with you. But while you were looking around, I gave a medal to your President in honor of my country," Maria said.

"How sweet. But of course, it was an assignment. Did it occur to you your overlord might talk? It might be safer to say you were tricked."

"That wouldn't work if we wanted it to. We don't know who hired us or who had Northgrail do the delivery."

"You're just hired hit-persons?" Jerry asked. "How much was the assassination of two Presidents worth?"

"Five million before your arrival and twenty million after we completed our assignment. Unfortunately our President got away."

Maria was doing the talking and I figured that she was the one in charge.

"Sad," I said.

"I can't believe they didn't find the remains of your President. He was wearing the bomb."

"One of the Secret Service persons grabbed it off him before it killed him and died in the process."

"We weren't counting on that. And our fee has been cut in half and will be zero if you turn up alive."

"So what are your plans for us?"

"You have to know that. If you are familiar with the kind of people who would contract the hit. As a consolation, we have been offered an additional five million to get rid of loose ends. And you are definitely a loose end."

"Are we? We could just forget this discussion and call it even," Jerry said. "After all, Northgrail just delivered the bomb. They didn't hire you."

She smiled. "No. This is neater."

A couple passed us by. The two people both turned away, apparently not wanting to get involved. I guessed people in Mexico were like in the U.S.

"Americans. Notice, even tourists aren't going to help you," Maria said.

"So, how do you want them to go?" Carlos asked.

"Well, shooting would raise a few questions. I think they are going to die of a heroin overdose," Maria said.

"All of us?"

"Jet setters from D.C. You shouldn't do drugs."

We were moving towards the docks and we were being led onto a boat. I thought of the President's lack of dexterity, before he became Fred Astaire, and tripped over the side of the boat as I stepped off the gangway. As Carlos turned the rifle to the side and reached down to pull me up, Valiant had a foot to his head. Maria turn to aim her gun at Valiant while Jerry slammed her hand with his case, knocking the gun onto the deck. She reached for it, but another swing of Jerry's case, this time to her head, knocked her to the deck, unconscious.

I looked at the two unconscious assailants and then at the boat we were on. "A yacht. How nice," I said. Valiant used a rope to tie them up. Jerry checked to make sure the ropes were tight. "Get the guns. Who knows who we'll meet up with next," I said.

I took a cell phone off Maria and made an anonymous call to the authorities. "The real palace bombers are tied up on a boat at birth 9B." I got off the phone fast and tossed it in the water.

"It won't be long until our own boat leaves," Jerry said.

"Near here?"

"North of the pier. He's not pulling up to a regular dock"

We started walking north. "That's him," Jerry said, pointing to a yacht that was anchored about 200 feet out from the pier. Someone was coming for us in a raft or dingy. Jerry waved.

"So this is the valuable crew."

"Correct," Jerry told the guy who picked us up.

We were taken back to the boat. "This is Chris. He has won several boat races to Encinitas."

"Hi. I'm—"

This time, Jerry interrupted. "This is Violet and this is Chad."

"Hi, Violet and Chad and it's good to see you, Ben." He winked at Jerry.

He obviously knew Jerry's real identity—even if he didn't know ours.

"We appreciate the ride," I said.

"Ben and his brother Jerry used to babysit me when I was a kid."

"And Chris was the one who grew up to be a multi-millionaire."

"I'm in the yacht and sailboat business."

"It must be lucrative," I said.

"Nobody can get us to Solana Beach as quickly as Chris."

"Lucky for us," I said. "Thank you."

"My pleasure," Chris said smiling at us.

He turned the yacht and started moving it in a northern direction past the town. That's when the shots started from an approaching boat.

"Maria and Carlos must have gotten free."

"Who are Maria and Carlos?"

"They tried to assassinate the two Presidents."

"Oh."

"We caught them and called the police."

So far, none of the shots had touched us. Jerry pulled Carlos's rifle from his case.

"And you have a gun too," Chris observed.

"We got it from them," I said. "When we captured them."

"Well, I always thought you needed protection," he said to Jerry.

Jerry fired at Maria's boat, missing wildly. Another boat started up towards us with guns blazing.

"Well, time to get out of here," Chris said, speeding up the boat.

Chris took off with the two boats following. He zig-zagged somewhat, avoiding the bullets.

"No," Jerry said.

"What?" I turned to see what he was looking at. It was an approaching storm in the direction we were headed. The boat continued forward.

"This is going to be a rough ride," Chris yelled back from the helm as he swiftly moved towards the storm.

Jerry kept trying to hit the boats with the rifle. "Let me," Valiant suggested.

Jerry made one more miss and handed the rifle to Valiant. Valiant hit something that slowed one of the boats while the other continued moving fast and firing shots at us. I could feel water falling down on us as Chris took us right into the storm. It was not long before we couldn't see. The boat was rocking and water was splashing up along the side.

The boat stayed afloat as rain poured down on us. Chris had us put on life jackets. Lightning struck part of the boat as we tied ourselves down to the deck. "Shouldn't we go below?" I asked.

"If it capsizes, we want to be able to get off," Valiant said.

"If it capsizes, we'll probably be killed."

"My job is to protect you," Valiant said.

"You'll guide me safely to my final destination." There was nothing to do but lighten the mood.

Jerry was throwing up again. I crawled across the deck to Jerry. "Sea sickness?"

"Hurricane sickness."

"I don't think the West Coast gets hurricanes."

"What do you call this?"

"It certainly looks like one," Valiant yelled.

"Like the D.C. Earthquake? Arranged? HAARP?"

"Who knows," Jerry said. The boat was rocking worse than ever as sheets of rain pelted down on us. It felt as if the yacht really was about to capsize.

Then as suddenly as we entered the storm, we were out.

Chris came back. "I've been through these before and I've never lost a boat."

"No sign of our assailants," Valiant said.

"If they were foolish enough to follow us, they probably perished," Chris responded.

"I thought we were going to perish," Jerry said. "I'm glad you were at the helm."

"You look like you got a little sick. I have some dry clothes down below."

I noticed the outside of the suitcase, though still tied down was soaking wet. The only major casualty was likely to be the computer

I figured we could relax.

And we did for most of the ride. The morning was beautiful. "We're traveling a lot faster than on the way to Boca Inglesia."

'That's because you had a hitman, rather than a real boatman," Jerry said.

"Is this a Yacht or a schooner?" I asked.

"It's a Gulley-style sportfish yacht," Chris said coming up. "It's got more stability than most of the yachts but also two fast motors and a sail."

"Twin motors?"

"Most sportfish yachts don't, but his one is built to be fast, and stable, but cable of being used as a sailboat."

"Nice," I said.

"Do you have any rice on board?" Valiant asked. "I want to pack the computer with it to absorb any water that got in."

"Rice is something I have a lot of. You ought to take that suitcase down below, rather than tying it down up here."

"Expecting more storms?"

"The weather report is clear, but that last one was not on the charts."

After Chris went below for the rice, I turned back to Valiant. "We're back to ground zero. We've got an enemy who has access to big bucks and the capability to infiltrate the intelligence agencies and possibly even control HAARP."

"Unless that earthquake involved explosions created by North-grail," Valiant said.

'We're not through the list. We just got through 'crushed.'"

Chris handed us a bag of rice and went up to the helm and then returned to us. "Guys, I need you down below."

"What?" I asked.

"Cartel."

"On the sea?" Jerry asked.

"Don't look," Chris said as I started to turn my head. "I don't want them finding the girl if they board."

"Can you outrace them?" Valiant asked.

"They're coming from all directions. Jerry, you stay up here. They may have noticed you wandering above the deck."

"Us?"

"It's hard to tell what they saw but between Jerry and me, we can cover."

"Don't let anything happen to Jerry. He is very important to us."

"To me too. Don't worry."

Chris guided us down to one of the cabins below. He pressed a button that was well hidden. The floor opened up. "Take the suitcase and computer with you."

Valiant and I went down. "You promise Jerry will be OK?'

"That's the plan."

It was dark where we were, but we were surprisingly able to hear as if there was some kind of darkened opening or chamber leading up to the deck.

I could hear a lot of movement up above.

"Chris Everly," a man's voice said.

"Poco, you know I don't carry much on my yacht."

"But now you have guests."

"Guest. Just for the day."

"Then you won't mind us looking around. Any drugs or pretty ladies on board?"

"I wish," Jerry said.

"No drugs?"

"I'm allergic."

"And ladies or young girls?"

"Sorry."

"Ah, a man like you. I would expect at least one pretty lady on board."

"You're the closest," Jerry's voice said as I heard what sounded like a punch, a clunk and a something smacking the deck.

"Forget him."

"If my guest is injured, it will destroy my reputation."

"Your guest has a big mouth. Take me below."

"He's injured."

"Then, I'll eliminate the problem."

I heard a shot. Then more shots.

CHAPTER 41

I tried to push up the floorboards, but I didn't know how.

"Don't," Valiant warned.

"Jerry. He's injured. He's got to be okay."

This was too much. I had to get to Jerry. Valiant pulled me back and held me tight. I could have killed him. I needed to know Jerry was alive.

The boat was moving fast. In fact so fast, we were almost thrown around under the floorboards. Then I felt a hefty thump and more movement and then more speed.

"I got him into this. If he dies, it's my fault. He was only trying to help me." I was crying, this time for Jerry. First, I almost lost Valiant and now Jerry. If Jerry died, I'd feel guilty for the rest of my life. There was more movement. I heard what sounded like more gunfire.

I wanted to scream out, but Valiant put his lips over mine to stop me. I kept pushing. I hated him at this moment. I had to know I hadn't gotten Jerry killed. If only his lips didn't feel so soft.

He pulled away. "They may have taken the boat. If they did, we'll have to sneak off, later."

"Jerry. If he's dead, I'll never forgive you. No, I'll never forgive me. It's my fault. It's all my fault."

I started crying again. "And Chris. He was just trying to help. I got them all killed. Ben told me not to hurt Jerry and I've killed him."

"I think he's smart enough to stay alive, but if he isn't, he wouldn't hold you responsible and he wouldn't want anything to happen to you. These men, they take women and they sell them. Do you want that to be Jerry's legacy, what he risked his life to prevent?"

The boat was moving very fast. I didn't know where we were going. *Was it to a port where they would capture the boat as a prize? What about Jerry and Chris? Would their bodies be thrown overboard? And Valiant.* As much as I hated him right now, if they took Valiant, it would kill me. I had almost lost him in at the warehouse. I couldn't handle losing Valiant on top of Jerry. That was why I wasn't doing what it took to get out, though part of me believed I could fight my way out of this hole.

I started hyperventilating. Valiant cupped his hands over my mouth and had me breathe into them. My breathing slowed down. At least for now, I was with Valiant and this might be the last time I would see him if they discovered us here. Before I could say anything, I felt dampness. That's when I noticed the bottom of the boat filling up with water. We were going to drown.

I had a choice between drowning and being sold into slavery. Not good choices. The water was crawling up my back. Valiant was looking for something to release the floorboards above us. At the same time, he used one of his arms to push me up as close as possible to the floor above.

"I love you, Eve. If we get out of here, we'll I was hoping that one day, we'd—" He paused.

"We'd what?" *Was he trying to propose to me?* A few minutes before I hated him and now all I could think about was that, more than anything else, I wanted him to survive.

"Well, if you felt the same way, I, but maybe you don't."

"Valiant," I started to say. That's when I heard someone above the boards. It sounded as if our intruders were coming for us. The floorboards went up.

"Jerry!" I practically screamed, jumping up into his arms for a hug. "I thought they had—I heard them hurt you and shots."

"Chris and I shot the two men who boarded and then rammed through the blockade."

"The boat is leaking," Valiant said. There was a sadness in his voice, but he was focused on the water filling up where we'd just hidden.

Jerry looked down below.

Valiant was pulling the computer up. "I hope the rice is protecting it. If not, I'll buy you a new one in wherever we are next."

"Chris is going to stop in Encinitas to assess the damage."

"Will the boat last that long?" I asked.

"Let's hope so." Jerry closed up the floorboards.

Valiant was looking at me funny. I didn't know what that meant. I reached a hand out to him. "We're all safe. That's all that matters." I turned to Jerry. "You were hurt. I heard it."

"I have a bit of a glass stomach. When he punched me, I went down. I looked worse than I was, and that gave Chris the opportunity to grab a gun. After he fired, I pulled one out from behind my back and finished the other guy. We gave them a burial at sea."

"Heroes. Both of you." I gave Jerry another hug.

Valiant seemed glad, but I could tell something was bothering him. "I'm happy you're safe, man. Karissa never would have forgiven me or herself if you hadn't been."

"You? You had nothing to do with it," he told me.

"I'm the reason you're in Mexico."

"The murders are the reason I'm in Mexico, but it's great seeing you."

I knew he was just trying to put me at ease. "You're always the diplomat and way too sweet for your own good."

After Chris docked in Encinitas, he looked over the damage. Somehow the boat had held together. The floor had formed a substantial seal over the leak. I suspected he'd made sure it was prepared for a leak. "We have three choices," Chris said. "We can continue with a different boat, you can go overland, or we can wait until some repairs are made."

"How long will the repairs take?" Valiant asked.

"Repairs that will hold will take at least a day. We can do temporary repairs in about four hours. However, if we hit another storm or another boat, we could lose the yacht."

"It's your boat," I said. "I wouldn't want you to risk it."

"I'll find a way to cover the loss if that happens," Jerry said. "It's important that we get back as quickly as possible and as unnoticed as possible."

It was already Thursday. I hoped the other original primary Presidential robot would be ready when we arrived. A genuine investigation into the attempted assassination could reveal what we had been doing at work, and we could all wind up in prison. I should have thought about that long ago, but I thought I'd find a way to expose my dad quickly and then get out of there.

Valiant was a little more solemn.

"What's wrong?"

"I guess Jerry is a really good guy."

"Yes, he is. I hope we will all stay friends after this is all over."

"Of course."

"Next are fall, microwave, collapse and fire. But with Northgrail gone, is the list over?"

"Not for the person who orchestrated everything. The jabs were an international directive issued by the WHO and the NIAID. According to many whistleblowers, there was no actual data to back up even that a pandemic existed in 2020."

"You think there might be another facility in Switzerland, which has no extradition treaty?"

"Maybe, or elsewhere. We can't count on Northgrail being the only contractor involved. Someone was using them. There is always Blackmoriuntur and who knows what?"

"Maybe, we'll have a new purpose when we get back. We take down all the players who are behind the insanity."

"We'll have to get Gene to go along with it," Valiant said.

"And Felicity. She'll go along with whatever Gene wants," I said.

"Unless the thought of becoming Vice President has put stars in her eyes. I don't trust her," Valiant remarked.

"She's a bit of an airhead. But she doesn't like bad publicity," I noted.

Jerry joined us for lunch at another Chipotle. "Chris is overseeing the repairs. We've got a crew of several guys working on it to speed things up. What do you say we check out Ensenada while we're waiting?"

"That would be fun," I said. "I do like Mexico. People are less paranoid than in the U.S."

"I don't like the cartels," Valiant said.

"Do you prefer the one run by the Administration back home?" I asked.

"Not to mention, the Cartels work for our country's CIA," Valiant noted.

"Good point," Jerry said. "Maybe I'll move down here too."

"With your brother in Mexico, how are the dogs?" Valiant asked.

"Ben's housekeeper really likes dogs, but I don't think she's ever taken care of that many at once."

"Ben really cares about you," I told Jerry.

"Sometimes I think he cares because he's supposed to care."

"He really does. We had a conversation about you on the boat to Boca."

"You were talking about me?"

"Yes."

"He wanted to make sure I didn't get you into any trouble."

"I think it was the other way around. If I hadn't come to you about Marissa, you'd—"

"Have been a sitting duck when the explosion took place."

"I guess we've managed to keep each other safe."

"How about we check out the Zipline," Valiant suggested.

It was a ride nearby where people traveled over a valley, a lake and trees on equipment hanging from a zip line.

"That would be fun," I said.

"I'm afraid of heights," Jerry told us.

"We can do something else then," I responded.

"It's fine. I'll watch the two of you."

"That doesn't sound like fun."

"Not to you. You two are adventure freaks," he responded.

There was a pair of side by side zip lines. Valiant took one and I took the other. We were pretty secure and it felt safe. "Look. Paddle boats down there, ahead," I called to him. "Jerry might like those."

"Jump," he yelled.

I looked at him.

"Now! Unhook and jump to me."

Maybe it was instinctive, but I did as he said. As I jumped to Valiant who grabbed me in his arms, I saw why. My line fell. I was safe but other tourists on the line were dropping. They were people I didn't know. I hoped they would survive. I looked back. Carlos was at the starting point and was going from my line to Valiant's. I saw two of the attendants struggling with him. Shots were fired and the attendants fell. Carlos went to Valiant's wire with some kind of cutter. We were going to fall.

CHAPTER 42

"Drop," Valiant said. "Water."

I held onto him as he dropped. I heard more shots. As I came up, I noticed that Valiant's line was still intact. Carlos was hanging off the boarding area. It wasn't that much of a drop, but Jerry was reaching for him. It was a bit of a distance, but it looked as if Jerry had clasped Carlos's hand and was trying to help him as Carlos brought up the other hand with something, I assumed a gun, in it. Jerry let go as the gun fired.

"Fall," I said.

We both looked at the start of the ride as we treaded water.

"It wasn't that bad of a fall. Look Carlos is running," I said.

"But they couldn't have planned for one of their own to fall," Valiant commented, treading water.

"It was meant for us."

"How did they know we'd go here?"

"It could have been anywhere. Remember JB said we weren't who he was expecting. Apparently we replaced the target."

"Plans readjusted to eliminate complications? Adds up."

Mexican police were rushing to the area. I knew that Jerry wouldn't want to be seen in Mexico in an incident that might wind up publicized. I saw him moving quickly through the crowd. He grabbed a hat from someone in it and was climbing down into the canyon.

"We've got to get to him. Wait!" my conscience set in. "People fell. We need to help them."

"I don't hold out much hope for anyone who fell in the canyon," Valiant said.

"It's awful. Maybe we weren't the target."

"They went for both lines, yours first. I'd say you were the target. If you weren't here, they might have thrown you off your apartment balcony."

"I wonder if they'll do it again."

"If they get the wrong target."

"I mean, have they yet crushed the person they were expecting at Northgrail, and will they try to get us to fall again?"

"I'm not going to let them hurt you."

Police were also climbing down below, possibly looking for Jerry or to help the people who fell. Jerry was rushing away as quickly as possible. Then, he seemed to disappear. "Maybe he's hiding until he can get away."

"We need to get out of here before we have to answer questions," Valiant said.

We started swimming. A couple of people helped us onto their paddle boat and took us to the start of the paddle boat ride. As we got off and disappeared into the crowd, I said, "I hope Jerry's okay."

"You really care about him."

"Of course. He's our friend who risked his life to save us."

"If Jerry is coming for us, we should go where he can find us."

We had agreed that if we got separated, we'd meet at the boat. "Carlos is running around with a gun, I think. He wasn't there after the fall," I said.

"Let's hope he broke something or accidentally shot himself. If Jerry was smart, he's already doubled back towards the yacht."

As we left the area, I saw helicopters arriving and ambulances. "Let's hope nobody was seriously hurt," I said.

"You were over the deepest drop when he cut it and nobody was near you."

When we got back to the boat, Chris let us know the work was done but Jerry wasn't back. "Did you hear about the shooting?"

"At the Zipline? We were there. It was Carlos, the guy who tried to ram the boat last night. I'm worried about Jerry. He stopped Carlos and took off."

"They said there were two shooters."

"Jerry had a gun, but he was trying to stop Carlos. Did they arrest anyone?"

"They said they found one and shot him."

"Let's just hope it was Carlos. Jerry would have surrendered," Valiant said.

"This is Mexico. You can't trust the police," Chris said.

"Should we go back?" I asked.

"You two should stay here. I'm going to listen for bulletins. Jerry had Ben's ID on him. If they name the person they shot, we'll know." Chris went below deck.

My stomach was almost dropping out of me. Waiting was killing me.

I ran onto the dock. "I can't wait any longer."

"Neither can—" Valiant stated to say but was interrupted. Carlos popped up from the where he was hiding on the yacht berthed next to ours as we were rushing past it on our way back to the scene. His gun was pointed at us.

Panic went through me.

"Any last words?" he asked.

CHAPTER 43

"Duck," Valiant said.

"What?" Carlos replied as Chris hit him with the boat's anchor.

"Nice hit. Got him," Valiant said.

"That means it was Jerry?" I asked, looking at Carlos and starting to cry.

Valiant held me. "I don't think so."

"What's wrong?" Recognizing the voice, I turned to see Jerry rushing towards us down the dock.

"They said they shot a suspect," I said.

"Him," Jerry said. He pulled off Carlos's shirt from his unconscious body. Our assailant had a bandage underneath.

"What's going on?" another yachtsman asked.

"The guy who did the shooting. He tried to get a ride on that yacht." Valiant pointed to the one next to ours. "And he collapsed. I understand there's a reward. It's yours."

"Thank you."

"We better be off," Chris said.

"Don't you want to wait?" the other yachtsman asked.

"The doctor has a baby to deliver," I said.

We hopped on Chris's yacht and took off.

"Hopefully he's in jail for a long time."

"You three do lead exciting lives."

"Did anyone get killed?"

"One of the attendants he shot."

"The attendants were so nice. That's sad."

I gave Jerry a hug. "I thought you had died saving us again. Don't you dare let anyone harm you while you're rescuing me! Do you know the guilt I'd have to live with the rest of my life?"

"You were the primary target. You're also the one Carlos took first at gunpoint back at Salina Cruz."

"I noticed that too," Valiant said. "From now until this is over, we need to step up our protection of Karissa."

"I'm fine, and I don't want to be treated like a baby."

"I promised your—" Valiant stopped. I knew he was going to mention my mother. Jerry didn't know about my alternate identity.

I watched Valiant as he and Jerry started talking about the travel plans as the boat left the docks. I had to pull myself together. If I kept worrying about my two accomplices, I would be useless. I had always liked Valiant, but it was more than that. I felt safe with him. He was fun and exciting and he cared about me. While I had been working in the lab, he had always had my back, worked extra hours at the last minute, and made me feel like I was competent and capable when I felt neither. The thought of him protecting me against these killers or of anything happening to Valiant made it hard to breathe. There was something really innocent and kind about Jerry. I couldn't handle anything bad happening to him either. I went below deck and laid down in the cabin. When we got back to Washington, I had to find a way to take them both out of the loop.

Things went smoothly traveling north to Solana Beach. Well not quite. The U.S. Coast Guard caught up to the boat after we were passing North Island. This time, Jerry waited below the floorboards in case he was wanted in Mexico. The Coast Guard came below and our fake passports passed the test.

"What were you doing in Mexico?"

"Just went down for some sport-fishing."

"Where's your catch?"

"We ate what we caught. The Pacific fish are mostly gone, courtesy of Fukushima."

"We hear that a lot. Have a nice evening."

———

From Solana Beach, Chris gave us a ride south to UCSD.

"Thank you," Jerry said, giving him a hug.

"You sure your ride is going to be here?"

"We're meeting him at Glider's Point in an hour," Jerry said. "Your timing was perfect."

"The Point is closed at this time of night."

"He said he'll be there."

Chris stopped in the UCSD student parking lot.

"Are you okay, Eve?" Valiant whispered.

"Yeh. I'm just tired."

"Would you like to go for a walk?"

"I'd like to be by myself for a while." I turned and, pointing towards the ocean, spoke louder to Chris. "The Point's over there, right?"

"Across Torrey Pines Drive and down that side road, past Scripts."

"I'll see you guys in an hour. I just need some alone time."

I started walking around the campus and then decided to venture over toward the Point. Several people passed me, walking toward a drum circle at Black's Beach at the bottom of the cliff. It was a nice drop from the Point to the beach and the path looked like a healthy climb.

"You do drumming?" It was Maria's voice.

Before I could turn, I felt the barrel of another gun at the back of my skull. This time I was alone with no backup. *Not again*, I thought.

CHAPTER 44

"Don't you get tired of this?"

"I'm supposed to make sure you don't make it back."

"Why me?"

"You're an obstacle."

"You work for Duane?"

"Who do I work for? That's a mystery isn't it?"

"Care to solve it?"

"I've seen those movies where the bad guy tells the good guy everything before the good guy is supposed to die and then the good guy manages to survive. I'm not going to do that. For starters, I'm the good guy just doing my job. For seconds, I think it's better for people to die, wondering."

"Do you kill many people?"

"I'm very good at what I do. And the pay is spectacular."

Maria grabbed my arm and pulled me away from the path and towards the point with her free hand as she continued to hold the gun at the back of my head.

"Is Carlos with you?"

"He was a liability. I can't do liabilities?"

"You killed him? I thought you were in love."

"Parting was such sweet sorrow."

"Do you remember what happened to Juliet?"

"I'm not into poison. Carlos will have to explore the afterlife, alone. Well, not quite alone. He'll have you."

"Glad you aren't the jealous type."

"We're here. Now jump."

"Sorry. My mother told me never to jump off cliffs."

"The bullet or the cliff."

"I guess you'll have to shoot me," I said. I glanced down, again. The cliff was pretty steep and it was a long way down. The survival chances seemed zero.

"Goodbye," she said as she pushed. As she did, I reached around and grabbed onto her.

In the background, I heard a yell, "No!" We struggled and both started to go forward as we lost our balance. I let go of her as we started falling. Just as I prepared to meet my maker, a hand reached down and grabbed my wrist. And then another hand grabbed my other wrist and I was pulled up to the top of the cliff. I lay there, barely believing I had survived. Maybe I hadn't. My arms and my legs were still there. I felt my head. But the biggest clue was the guy looking into my eyes.

"I couldn't let you go on an adventure without me," Valiant said.

"It wasn't a fun adventure. I didn't think you'd like it."

Jerry and Chris were rushing over to us. Jerry looked over the cliff. "It looks like she hit bottom. People are starting to rush to her."

"I'm not sure, but she might work for Duane."

"Duane?" Chris asked.

"Duane. She said I was an obstacle she had to kill. Duane said his job was to get rid of obstacles."

"From now on, I'm not letting you out of my sight," Valiant said.

"Me neither," Jerry chimed in.

"Not even to use the ladies' room?"

"I'll come in if you're in there over five minutes," Valiant said.

"I definitely feel protected. But what about the two of you? I've almost lost each of you in the last couple of days."

"I think as long as you three have each other, you'll be alright," Chris told us.

"Oh, here's Tristan," Jerry said.

Jerry and Chris went over to greet the man walking over to us.

"Enjoying the stars?" Tristan asked me and Valiant as we joined them.

"Lovely," I said.

"Tristan drives very fast," Jerry assured us.

"Now, that Tristan's here, I'm going home to get some sleep," Chris told us.

"Goodnight, Chris, and thank you." I gave him a hug.

"I don't get many of those in California."

Valiant shook Chris's hand. Tristan and Jerry said their goodbyes as well.

"I understand you're to take us to an airfield, somewhere?" I asked.

"It's north of Bakersfield. We should be in D.C. by morning."

On the way, he turned on the radio in the minivan. Jerry and Tristan were upfront. Valiant and I were in the back.

"Today, the Chief Justice swore in President—"

"What!" I over-shouted the radio. "They can't do that. The real President hasn't been declared dead."

"They rushed it," Tristan said, turning off the radio. "It happened at 7 P.M. this evening and she was sworn in at 7:05."

"How did she get him declared dead when there was no body?"

"It was determined by the Intelligence community that he couldn't have survived the explosion and it must have blown him to dust."

"The dust would have DNA."

"Probably bribed a coroner's jury," Valiant commented.

"The first coroner's jury was killed by an exploding gas leak. A building collapsed on them," Tristan informed us.

"That was supposed to happen after the microwave," I said

"Microwave?" Tristan asked.

"Washington plays hard and fast with the rules," Jerry said. "When the rules don't fit them, they cheat." He paused. "Deep state is pro-war and the President's meeting with the Mexican President is considered a threat to our war agenda. Remember, they wanted to get Mexico's anti-war President with the explosion."

"But the President did threaten Mexico, sort of, over the Alamo."

"They didn't show that in the videos, but the Alamo was before Mexico went anti-war. Nobody could take that seriously."

"But the photograph?"

"The press agreed with Ferris that it must have been faked. That and the later broadcast—" Tristan said.

"Later broadcast?" I asked.

"The Chief of Staff had the President go on live TV and say, 'I'm alive. Have some ice cream.'"

"If it was a live broadcast, that's what she asked for."

"It wasn't in front of an audience."

"They can't declare him dead when he's not finished," Jerry stated.

"Finished?" Tristan asked.

"With hiding, I mean."

I kept reflecting on the list. "Maybe the fall was postponed because we survived earlier in the day. Or maybe the fall was thwarted by Valiant. And microwave was supposed to be after the fall."

"Fall? Microwave?" Tristan inquired.

"How fast were we going up the coast?" I asked. "I mean, the normal speed for a yacht is about twenty-five miles per hour."

"Not for Chris," Jerry said. "His boats are the fastest on the continent."

"How do you guys all know each other?"

"We grew up together," Tristan said. "Chris may be fast on the sea, but I'm much faster by car."

"And at flying," Jerry said. "He's our pilot."

"Nice," I said.

"Has the VP had the movers come into the White House?"

"She's started. She is throwing a large party tomorrow night to celebrate her new home. She's already designated two million for the move. Lots of pink hearts and pictures of incarcerated parents in chains in every office."

"I wonder if we still have jobs."

"Technically, we don't exist," Valiant said.

"We're researchers. But yeh. She might ask us to do some real research."

"There's always the Net. I could look up the mating habits of flounders or one of the other useless things our government likes wasting money on."

"My goodness. What will happen if she discovers—" I didn't finish with the word "father," but Valiant caught my drift.

"They'll probably kill him," Jerry said, picking up that I was talking about the President.

"She's officially moving in tomorrow?" I asked.

"That's what the news said. Of course, it lies a lot," Tristan pointed out.

"We're not the only ones who know that," Jerry said.

"Happy Days," I said to Valiant. "We need to see the list and whether the VP, Pam, I mean, is also on it. Then we need to get to Him. No. I need to get to Him."

"I need to be there too. Someone is out to kill you and I'm not going to let that happen," Valiant said.

I didn't say anything.

"I can record him live, saying more than 'I'm alive,' and sounding like an ice cream salesman. You need me there," Jerry said. "After all, I am the Press Secretary."

"Probably a good idea. Even if the truth wipes us out," I said, looking at Valiant.

"You talking about the ro-thing or the real President?" Jerry asked.

"The real one. Both of you, stay away from Duane. He might be the one. Valiant, you see if you can help Jack and Brandon finish the project—if there is still a place to do it."

"Do you know if the Chief of Staff and the Cabinet have resigned?" Jerry asked.

"The staff is balking, claiming that the transition wasn't legal. Hemmings and the Attorney General have filed an injunction to return to the pre-succession status quo, claiming the succession was based on fraud," Tristan informed us.

"Will it work?"

"A decision is expected tomorrow. "

I had Tristan turn on the radio.

"The Supreme Court has granted a temporary injunction to prevent the transition until after the court makes a full decision," the radio news blared out. The commentator added, *"The Chief Justice, who has already sworn in Pamela Ferris, was among four dissenters from the decision."*

"Like any President really has real power," I said.

Tristan changed the station.

"This injunction is dangerous. It leaves us without a clear commander in charge of the country. Republican Justices are trying to bring down our country."

He switched stations again several times with different commentators uttering the same line about the decision being dangerous.

"The Chief Justice is a Republican," I commented. "That blows away that argument."

"He didn't want to be rounded up," Jerry surmised.

"He changed his voter registration this morning," Tristan said.

The next station, after saying those lines, announced, *"The Dean of Harvard says the injunction is likely to be terminated when the court reaches its final decision. On the bright side, Ferris has ordered new drapes to cheer up the Oval Office."*

"I wonder if those drapes will also include pink hearts," Jerry said.

"I was thinking something more obscene," Valiant reacted. "Involving whips."

"I didn't want to mention that," Jerry said.

"That gives us until the decision to fix things," I said.

"One week to declare him dead without a body or any evidence of a body."

"We'll have to act fast," Jerry said.

"We should have gotten back earlier," I lamented.

"They were expecting the project done when we got back," Valiant informed me. "Last time, I spoke with Jack, he said there were a lot of problems. He could cut down on the original estimate of two weeks, but not by much."

"Let's hope it's in some kind of shape to at least fake it."

"I'm the one who should have been there."

"Right. The miracle worker. You were too busy saving my neck over and over again. I guess I'm to blame for everything."

"What is it with you two and guilt?" Jerry asked.

"My father was a minister," Valiant told Jerry.

"That explains it. I didn't know you had a father," Jerry said.

'Ha! I did."

"What happened to him?" I asked.

"A flu vax."

"Then you knew," Jerry said.

He nodded.

"I knew and so did my mom. She'd like you, by the way," he said looking at me.

"Vaccine side effects were supposed to be rare, but these new ones are nothing like that. In the first six months, more died from the COVID jabs than from all the other vaxxes combined over the last fifty years," I noted.

"You three haven't been vaxxed?" Tristan asked.

I worried he might stop the car and dump us by the side of the road. A lot of pro-vaxxers were wishing death on the unjabbed.

"Have you?" Jerry asked him.

"No way. I'm not stupid."

"Then we're all clear," Valiant said.

"Is that what this is all about?" Tristan asked.

"Those nanoparticles—they were controllers," I let out.

"What?"

"They had the stats on all the vaxxes and were controlling some of the recipients into dying. At least, the ones that weren't already killed by the vaxxes."

"That has to be stopped."

"We stopped one controller facility."

"These people are evil. The Mark of the Beast," Tristan said.

"I don't know about the Mark of the Beast," Jerry said. "But I was there when they got a woman to stab herself."

"I wonder if Greg hadn't been vaxxed. That's why they needed to fix the computer. They couldn't control him."

"It sounds like you are into some pretty dangerous stuff."

"You're just giving us a lift and then you're out of it. It would be best if you didn't say anything until it's all exposed."

"I haven't heard a thing."

"Oceanside," I said as we drove through the city.

"Bye, bye Marcus Wricher," Valiant remarked.

"May he rest in hell," Jerry said

"If there is one," I commented.

"Who is Marcus Wricher?"

"The CEO of the Unitme Church here. He's a hitman who has apparently killed a lot of people."

"It sounds like he blew a hit."

"I hit him first," Jerry said.

"He was about to kill Ben, Valiant and me."

"Good work. I didn't know you were capable of that."

"When your family and friends are about to die, you discover how far you are willing to go to save them."

"Thank you, again," Valiant said.

"I'm sorry I brought you both into this," I said.

"Please cut the guilt," Jerry said, sounding irritated. "I don't need your pity."

"Pity? Until a couple of weeks ago, I never realized that you had so much courage. Pity didn't enter my mind."

I thought about it. I was overcome with guilt when I thought I had lost Jerry, twice. Maybe I was too controlled by guilt. I wondered how far I would go to avoid feeling guilty.

When we pulled into the airport, I was expecting a little plane that might have to make a couple of stops. It was a large private jet that almost gave Air Force One a run for its impressiveness.

"You can make a lot more money in the private sector," Tristan said.

"Apparently," Jerry observed.

"People will pay a lot to ride without jabs or jabbed pilots."

As we settled into our seats, Tristan offered us a drink.

"I could use one," Jerry said. He handed Jerry a bottle of champagne and a glass.

"You?" he asked me.

"I need to be as alert as possible."

"I'll pass too," Valiant said. "Have any bottled water?"

"Sure. And the refrigerator is well stocked," Tristan said, handing Valiant and me each a bottle of water. "It's about a four to five hour flight to D.C., depending on whether we can pick up a tailwind."

"Will we be landing at Dulles?"

"Virginia, near Alexandria."

"That's perfect," Valiant said as Tristan walked to the cockpit.

"Maybe leaving the White House will be good. Who am I kidding? Press secretaries don't make that much in the private sector."

"I'm sure you can find something in public relations," Valiant said.

"What do they pay for non-existent projects?" Jerry asked.

Our salaries would normally be a taboo subject, but Valiant answered, "Seven-fifty K."

Jerry almost choked. "750K?"

Valiant nodded.

"You're making more than me too. I never thought of it but you are definitely worth more," I said.

"You're priceless and they should appreciate you more," Valiant told me.

"I need more appreciation too," Jerry said.

"How much are you getting?" Valiant asked me.

"Only 500K."

"I'm quitting and getting a non-existent job tomorrow. This is crazy," Jerry said.

"I guess they felt that, with extra bucks, we'd keep our mouths shut about our work. I can only imagine what Duane makes—especially if he's killing people," Valiant said.

"At least, you two are doing something good," I said.

"Good? Lying for a kakistocracy is good? Imagine what would happen if one of us exposed it," Jerry responded.

"Might as well at this point. The world needs to know what a sham everything's been," I said. "I'll still probably go to Gitmo."

"If the VP is responsible for the deaths, she'll walk free while you two pay the price," Jerry said.

"That's something to think about Karissa," Valiant said. "I'm OK with paying for my part, but you don't deserve this."

"The VP doesn't even know how to read a map. We're up against someone with brains. The truth is I came in here to destroy the Administration, and that's what I plan to do."

"Wait. You wanted to destroy the Administration this whole time?" Jerry asked.

"I knew it was up to no good and my plan, all along, was to expose it. Does this change that nice impression you had of me?"

"No. I'm just surprised. You seemed to fit in well."

"I did my job, but I was working to collect evidence. And I still don't have what I want."

"I've got a video that day we went with Gene," Valiant said.

"We need to nail those responsible for all the murders, make sure they can't do it again, and we also need to find a way to stop the wars." I had said this before, but it needed saying again.

"So you're like a corporate spy?" Jerry asked.

"No. I'm doing it for personal reasons. There's no money in it other than my salary, and I would have done it for free."

"You must really care about the state of the government."

"I care about a kakistocracy that makes murder and rape A-okay. I bet Monica is looking better and better."

"Actually, no. I admire what you are doing."

Jerry poured himself a couple more glasses.

"I hope he'll be okay when we land," I whispered to Valiant.

"I'm worried about you. You need to lighten up on yourself."

After Jerry dosed off, I told Valiant, "They are probably planning to kill my dad, and I don't know if I care."

"Except he's not himself. I saw your reaction when he called you 'Mommy.' It brought out some of the mother in you."

"I still hate him. You'd have to be a woman to understand."

"I understand. If someone had raped or abused my mother, I'd hate him myself."

When the plane landed, we woke up Jerry. "We're back."

Tristan had arranged for a car to be delivered to him at the airport. "Enjoy," he said.

"Is this a Humvee?" Jerry asked.

"Humvees are old hat," Tristan said. "This is designed for today's world."

"Looks like a tank," I commented.

"I've seen the schematics," Valiant said. "This has better pickup than any tank or Humvee, and it can knock down brick walls and climb mountains."

"What about you?" I asked Tristan.

"I've got other plans."

Our first stop was the ranch house. "We need to look at those files," Valiant reminded us.

Arriving to an empty house, I said, "I miss the Papkimos. I hope your brother's housekeeper is taking good care of them and of Mr. President and Mr. Putin."

The first thing we looked at was the Happy Days file. GH was indeed Gene Hemmings but it wasn't what we thought

"Who is that?" I asked.

"I don't know," Valiant replied.

A document flashed of a conviction of Vincent Hemmings for murder. He had denied guilt and claimed that some kind of cabal was behind the killings. He insisted he was set up. He was in prison awaiting execution when a video shows Gene bribing a guard to release his brother. A body from the morgue was put in Vincent's place.

"Do you think he was set up the same way you were?" I asked Jerry.

"Maybe. Gene could be in a lot of trouble helping a convicted murderer escape."

"Was it reason enough to kill Lee?"

"To keep his job and himself out of prison, not to mention the authorities doing a search for his brother. Maybe," Jerry replied.

"But I don't think it's him," Valiant said.

We looked again at Operation Northwoods 7. "There are fall, microwave, collapse, and fire to go. Of course, I've already almost fallen twice."

"We need to get to the White House," Valiant said. He copied all the files and we rushed off.

"We've got a tail," Valiant said. We diverted off 395, taking 110 towards the Francis Scott Key Memorial Bridge.

"Do not—" Jerry started.

"I wasn't planning that, again."

"So far, the tail isn't shooting," I said optimistically.

Valiant took several turns. I noticed we were on Wisconsin Avenue heading towards Observatory Circle and Embassy Row. A tank pulled in behind us. "Now, we've got two vehicles tailing us?" I asked, rhetorically.

"At least, nobody's shooting, yet," Valiant said, echoing my earlier optimism. "Scratch that."

Fire bombs were launched out of the tank and we were the targets.

"We're going to die," Jerry said, matter-of-factly.

CHAPTER 45

"What does he have? A Molotov cocktail thrower in there?" Jerry asked as the fireballs kept coming.

"I think that's Napalm," I said. "Look at the flames behind us."

"A more modern version, but it's apparently encased to explode on impact," Valiant said. "He's taken out half of Wisconsin Avenue," Valiant added, as he zig-zagged to miss the bombs.

"Ouch," I said. A car behind and to the side had been hit, had stopped and people were rushing out of it.

Several firebombs hit buildings off to the side. "He's firing the whole area, just to get us," I said as we moved onto sidewalks, sped through parking lots and across grassy areas.

People rushed out of a flaming grocery store. The area behind was filled with smoke and one of our tails appeared to crash into the burning store. A second later, the building exploded.

"You'd think the D.C. police would be all over this," I said.

"Maybe they think he's a BLM protester," Jerry commented.

"Most of the people who burned down the cities were infiltrators," I pointed out. "Not real BLM."

"I guess they think we and the guy following us are with the D.C. police, then," Valiant said.

"Shit, are those missiles? One took out that whole building. Hope nobody was inside," Jerry said. He normally didn't swear—at least not that I knew—and so he must have been panicking. I was too scared to panic.

"I think that building is condemned," Valiant said.

"What's this?" I asked.

"The Whitehaven Parkway."

"And now?"

"This is or was the Oak Hill Cemetery. At least nobody is being killed, there," Valiant said.

"That one made a crater. I recognize the place. It's the Rock Creek Trail," I noted.

"Now, we're on Massachusetts Avenue," Jerry said. "How can you two be so calm?"

"We're probably going to die, and I don't want to do so in horror." I responded. "Isn't that the Embassy of Haiti that just got blown to pieces?"

"Our government's currently running Haiti anyway," Jerry said. "You wouldn't happen to have any champagne or one-fifty-one in the car, would you?"

"Sorry. I didn't want a ticket for an open container," Valiant responded.

"That's a big deal under the circumstances." I joked, not knowing what else to do.

Valiant drove through the gates of the South Korean Embassy as embassy guards started firing at us.

"Shit," Jerry swore again.

"Jackpot. Now, we've got both Deep State and the South Koreans after us," I said

Valiant turned our vehicle around and fled as an even larger bomb exploded, behind us, hitting the Embassy.

"So much for public relations," Valiant noted.

"We need to get out of here before World War III starts," I remarked.

"Bye-bye Japan," Jerry said as an explosion rocked the Japanese embassy. He looked as if he was bouncing between almost passing out and preparing to jump from our vehicle.

"The embassies aren't completely collapsing. Maybe most people are getting out of the way," I commented as I hoped my words were true.

Valiant cut through Dumbarton Park as firebombs took out a significant number of trees.

"Where are you going?" Jerry asked.

"The Potomac," Valiant said. "This souped-up tank or whatever it is seems to do very well on hills and at knocking down fences, hedges and brick walls. Maybe, it will float."

"I can't swim," Jerry reacted.

"You travel on yachts and don't swim?" I asked.

"There's no need to swim on a yacht."

"There goes Italy. Now, we've got the Pope against us," I said.

"Who is this guy and why hasn't the Air Force been called out?" Jerry asked. "He's blown up more embassies than the CIA."

"He's got to be government with connections," Valiant said.

"Oops. New Zealand. It's a good thing we're way ahead of them and their aim is so bad," Jerry said. "Maybe we'll be the last ones standing in D.C."

"New Zealand's okay," Valiant assured us. "He missed the building."

"Our government never was good at aiming bombs. Ninety percent of those taken out by drone bombs are civilians," I commented.

"At least, there's only one guy behind us at this point," Valiant said.

"Who somehow has the ability to tell the Army and the Air Force to stand down," Jerry noted.

"Maybe it isn't us. Maybe it's a D.C. renovation project," I said.

"Firebombing?" Jerry asked.

"Burning down the old to make way for the new."

"At least, the puppies are on the other side of town," Jerry said.

"You'd think there would be sirens warning the people to get underground or something," I remarked.

"Where are all the law enforcement? The National Guard?" Jerry inquired. "Standing down too?"

After crossing through some parking lots, Valiant cut down 37th, towards Reservoir Road.

"So much for Georgetown Admissions," I said.

Valiant cut through another cemetery on the way to Cooper's field. He zipped around the football field.

"I guess they'll need new artificial grass," I noted.

"They needed the '*Pentalawn 2001*,'" Valiant remarked. Next, he went through the Hayden Memorial Garden.

"I hope that bush you just ran over isn't valuable?" The adrenaline was making Jerry a little loopy, I surmised. "You sure you don't have champagne?" Jerry asked.

"You really want me to get a ticket for open-carry?" Valiant asked.

We were now riding down some trolley tracks.

"Oh good," Jerry said sarcastically.

"Remember the trolley dilemma," Valiant joked.

"I don't think that made Jerry feel better," I said.

"You sure we aren't going to crash going down this steep slope?" Jerry asked.

"We haven't crashed yet," Valiant said.

We had crossed Canal Road and were in the Chesapeake and Ohio Canal.

"I can walk in this," Jerry said. "It's really low, right now."

"And those firebombs will boil it within a fraction of a second," Valiant responded. "We need to get out of here." We were up, cutting through the C & O Canal Towpath and the Capital Crescent Trail as the firebombs continued.

Once again, we were headed for the Potomac.

"Is this air-tight?" I asked.

"I don't know, but I'm not planning to stay in it to find out," Jerry said, reaching for a door.

"If it's watertight, maybe we can get to Virginia."

Jerry cringed, undecided.

As we entered the Potomac, to our surprise the thing floated.

"This is a nice new innovation. It's too bad, we're sitting ducks," I said as firebombs went over our vehicle.

"We're out of here," Valiant said.

"I'm not wearing fireproof clothing. I'm not sure I want to be out there with no protection."

"I can't swim," Jerry said.

"I won't let you drown," I told him.

Valiant pushed the door opener.

"Take a breath and hold it," I told Jerry.

An explosion rocked the vehicle.

"That one missed," Valiant said.

Jerry joined us in jumping. Before hitting the water, I heard an explosion make a direct hit on our vehicle. I felt bad about the vehicle. But more than that, I was terrified people had been hurt during the various other explosions.

"Breathe," I told Jerry. He did, just before Valiant and I pulled him under water.

After a couple of minutes, we needed to breathe. Valiant and I rose to the surface, bringing Jerry up with us for some air. As we did, we saw a helicopter hovering with men holding what looked like Bazooka-type weapons pointed down below at the tank that had followed our car into the water. Unlike our vehicle, it looked like the tank was sinking. The helicopter fired at it and the tank fired back, blowing the helicopter apart. I saw people jumping out of the helicopter. The helicopter crashed into the part of the tank that was not yet submerged. It exploded. We swam back towards the D.C. side and sat down between the Potomac and the Capital Crescent Trail. I saw four people who had jumped from the helicopter coming towards us in the water. At least, they knew how to swim. Valiant and I reached out our hands to help pull them onto shore quicker. Then we all rushed across the Chesapeake and Ohio Canal, which went above our waists. Jerry was correct. It was low.

"You're South Korean?" I asked one of the people we had helped. I had noticed the flag on the side of their helicopter.

"That tank attacked our embassy."

"They should never give a tank to a demented driver," Jerry said.

"What is wrong with him?" the South Korean asked, looking at Jerry, who was standing dazed.

"Nothing."

A man, not one of the helicopter people, came out of the water and was pointing what I guessed was an AR-15 rifle at us.

CHAPTER 46

"Gene?" I asked.

The laugh did not sound like Gene's.

"That rifle's probably water-logged," I said.

The man fired a shot at the ground by my feet and laughed, again, as Valiant threw a mound of dirt at his face. Jerry, Valiant and I took off running across Canal Road. The man who looked like Gene pursued and then shot at us as we weaved around the traffic, almost getting hit by both cars and bullets. As we reached the other side, we heard brakes and a thud. We ran behind a bush and turned. A truck had hit the man with the AR15, and a car had plowed into the truck as both braked to a stop.

The truck driver got out, fuming mad. The gunman was lying in two pieces on the road. The truck had cut him in half.

"You alright?" I asked the truck driver.

"Alright? Look at the blood on the front of my truck."

"Jabbed," Valiant whispered.

I looked at the smart car behind the truck. The front end was smashed and it looked as if the airbags had malfunctioned. Jerry and I ran over to the car. The man inside was unconscious but alive.

I pulled my burner phone out of the waterproof pouch, Valiant had given to me earlier that day as a souvenir of our earlier adventure. *Great timing.* The phone worked. I called 911 and then Trey.

"Are you going into the funeral business?" Trey asked.

"I can't pull him out without injuring him more," Jerry said.

While Jerry stayed with the car and its driver. I went over to Valiant and the gunman's body.

"Meet Sam Seber," he said, pulling off a mask that was, then, only partially on Sam's face.

"I'm sure he's looked better. But I thought he was dead."

"That mask," he observed.

"Gene, or what's left of it, looks like him."

"A Signature Soldier?" He took a wallet from Seber's pocket.

He pulled me behind a bush. "Look at these ID cards. Different names and key cards. He even has one here for Jerry. Definitely Signature Reduction. And—" He handed me Gene's ID card.

"So Ray was probably innocent."

"Clearing his name doesn't help after he's dead."

The police arrived. They got an ear full from the South Koreans, who were calling the bombing of their embassy an act of war.

"We don't have jurisdiction over wars and embassy bombings."

I went over to them. "There's an injured man over there." I pointed to Jerry and the car.

"We're the police."

"He needs paramedics," I responded.

"Did you ask for them when you called?"

"Yes."

"We're only here as a courtesy," the lead officer told the Koreans. "You need to make a report, online. We've got more urgent business."

"Donuts?" I asked.

Valiant's eyes widened at my sarcasm. He started to go for the rifle in the road, apparently expecting the police to attack me.

"You have a problem with donuts?" the other officer asked.

I threw up my hands and went to the side of the road to sit as the officers took off.

"In our country, the police take reports," one of the South Koreans said.

"I'm pretty fed up with this too," Valiant replied. He sat beside me. "You okay?"

"I'm Tan," the South Korean man who had done the speaking said as he joined us.

"Mike and Sandra," Valiant said. We had used those names before.

"Valiant, when are the paramedics getting here?" Jerry asked as he came over.

"I thought you said your name was Mike."

"Charles here always calls me by my nickname."

"Charles looks like the President's Press Secretary."

"I get that all the time," Jerry said, coming closer. "The driver is hurt, but I think he'll be okay if the paramedics ever make it over here. I used my shirt to help stop the bleeding."

I felt more than a little guilty for not having assisted the driver. Jerry seemed to have it handled, but I was wondering if I was growing too used to death and injuries. I needed to get my old more-helpful self back.

A White House helicopter landed. Trey and Alan, another Secret Service Agent, got out.

"We have an injured driver over there," I said, again, pointing to the car. "Could we drop him off at the hospital?"

"This isn't an ambulance," Trey said.

"It seems to be the closest thing D.C. has to one."

"We're going to have to pry him out," Jerry said.

"Trey turned to Alan. "Use the pliers from the toolbox to help get that man out. Quickly! We need to get out of here."

"We should probably take the seat with him in case of a neck injury," Jerry said.

Alan went over to the car and started working on getting the unconscious man out as Jerry and Valiant assisted him. Finally, when they had the seat out, the ambulance arrived. It was two hours after 911 had been called.

The paramedics put the man on a stretcher. He moved and then went still. One of the paramedics felt the man's chest and then they placed a sheet over him.

"Aren't you going to do CPR?" Jerry asked.

"New D.C. rule. DNRs on all cardiac arrests."

"This was caused by a car accident," I pointed out.

"No revival. That's the rule."

"You must be working for a funeral home," I said to them.

Jerry lifted up the sheet and he and Valiant started CPR.

"Do you have a defibrillator?" Valiant called, almost angrily to the paramedics.

"There's this thing," one of the paramedics said, pulling one out of the ambulance. "But we were told not to use it anymore. It might cause cardiac arrests."

"Give it to me," Trey said. He handed it to Valiant.

"Thank you," I told Trey.

I was worried that it was too late, but the man came to. "Stop," he whispered. I could tell he was in pain. I felt relieved, and I was sure Jerry and Valiant felt relieved too.

"You said the tank was one of ours?" Trey asked.

"Yes. And the guy who firebombed Georgetown and Embassy Row was Signature Reduction."

"Those guys are crazy. They pick the most psycho of all the recruits and provide them with everything, new identities and higher salaries than the Secret Service has." He emphasized "higher salaries."

Tan came over to Trey. "You with the government?"

"What do you need?"

"You bombed our embassy. We want repair costs and general damages. Five hundred million will do for starters."

"Send your request to Pamela Ferris. She's in charge of paying for damages now."

I looked back at the river. "Look. What's left of the car kept going. It made it across the Potomac, and somebody is stealing it."

"Good. Tristan can report it stolen." Valiant said.

"It works. The insurance company will go after the thieves for all the damage," Jerry said.

"You're starting to get into the swing of things," Valiant said. "We'll make a dishonest guy of you yet."

"What was that?" Trey asked. I had thought he was out of earshot.

"Just a joke," Valiant said.

As we got into the helicopter, I asked Trey, "Where is everybody? Large sections of D.C. are on fire. No firetrucks. No National Guard, No police, except a couple of guys who wanted donuts."

"Everyone's at the parade."

"Parade?"

"Ferris is having a parade today. She insisted the FBI, the intelligence services and military be there. She even called in the National Guard for the parade."

"And the military is just following her orders?"

"The intelligence services, the National Guard and the Army are. The Navy, Air Force and Marines are supporting the elected President."

"How about the press?"

"They're treating her Presidency like the second coming of Christ."

"I bet she won't get them the ratings our President got them."

"You may have trouble getting into the White House."

"We have our passes on us."

"They've been revoked."

"Why?"

"Orders of the VP."

"SCOTUS hasn't ruled yet, has it?"

"No. But the lead security technician's with her."

"I have no doubts," Jerry commented.

"And who are you with?" I inquired of Trey.

"I'm neutral. I'm waiting for the decision."

From the air, we could see the parade. It looked like there were more participants than spectators. Actually, I didn't see any spectators, except for some people who were trying to cross streets that were blocked. The military was there as well as orchestras and several movie stars.

"How much did this cost?" Jerry asked.

"More than I and the rest of the Secret Service made in the last five years."

The helicopter engine started clanking, humming and making other loud noises.

"What's wrong?" Valiant asked.

"I don't know."

"With all the sabotage, maybe we should walk."

"You can't get in by walking."

"Great." The clacking and humming got worse and then I heard the engine cut out as it went silent. Nothing seemed to be working and we were going down.

CHAPTER 47

The White House was near. The pilot maneuvered to make the helicopter glide forward as we lost altitude.

"Are we going to make it?" I asked.

"Your guess is as good as mine," the pilot said, not reassuringly.

Down it went, right on top of the White House fence. We jumped out on the White House side before it fell, taking the fence with it.

"Do you think that was natural?" I asked as we tromped towards the White House.

"It's not my job to determine what's natural," Trey said.

"You're the head of the Secret Service!" I practically shouted. "If someone is sabotaging things and killing people around here, it is your job to determine if the President could be in danger."

"The Intelligence Services—"

"Haven't done a thing to stop the murders. Why didn't they tell us in advance about the bombing in Mexico?"

"It wasn't planned."

"It was ordered by someone in the White House. We were at the facility that made the bomb and had it delivered. They were deliberately trying to kill both Presidents."

"And you know this because—"

"We found the bomb factory. I told you."

"You need to be debriefed on this. I'll call in the FBI."

"Remember, they're not with the President, anymore. They're at the stupid parade protecting the would-be President."

"You talk as if you know the President is alive."

"The picture and video Gene showed were real. Remember, I'm the researcher for the President. I know him when I see him. And Gene doesn't fake videos like that."

A short time later, we were in the White House. Since our passes had been deactivated, Trey asked John to accompany us.

"You don't trust us?"

"Protocol."

"I'd rather have Jeb."

"He's with Gene."

"Then you can escort us to his office. It looks like John is busy."

At that moment, Monica entered the security area.

"You can't come in. Your card is a fake," John told her. "You will have to wait for the D.C. police to arrive."

"What? You gave me the pass. You gave me a fake pass?"

"I barely know you."

"You slime!"

Jerry leaned in towards Monica. "He's got your number."

With a smile, I gave Jerry a friendly punch on the arm. He really was over her.

Trey took us to Gene's office.

"Jerry, work some of your magic to get us out of this," Gene said.

Trey left and closed the door.

"Why don't we just have the real President walk out onto either the Truman Balcony or the Promenade Balcony in the Residence and wave? The cameras can get a close-up," Jerry suggested.

"There are some problems."

"Jerry knows," I said.

"This was supposed to be—"

"We found the people who made the explosives. It's a contractor working with the White House."

"The White House?"

"Northgrail. The bomb was delivered to Maria and Carlos, who were trying to kill both Presidents. They repeatedly tried to kill us on the way back."

"Actually, they were mostly trying to kill Karissa," Jerry said.

"Why you?" Gene asked.

"I don't know. But they practically burned down D.C. trying to kill us earlier today, and I wouldn't be surprised if they fixed the Secret Service helicopter."

"Signature Reduction is involved," Valiant said. "A gunman was wearing a facemask with your face on it."

"The intelligence services are with the VP. They may think she is more controllable. If the President isn't alive, there might be a war with North Korea or Mexico."

"We were supposed to go to war with Mexico?" I asked.

"Why do you think they have both countries accusing each other of the bombing?" Valiant pointed out.

"Northgrail was also responsible for several deaths, including Lara's, Marissa's, Seth's and Greg's."

"How do you know?"

"They showed me how they did it. It was the magnetic nanoparticles in the jabs. A computer activates them. They were using them to create murders, suicides and heart attacks. Greg got the saline and so they nailed him electronically, using Blackmoriuntur Technologies."

"Who in the White House?"

"Who benefits?" Valiant asked

"That was my question," Jerry said.

"Are you saying Pamela is responsible?"

"She comes out the ultimate winner. But she may not know about the ace we have up our sleeve," Valiant said.

"The real President," Gene muttered.

"You're going to have to produce him. Frank can do a DNA," Jerry said. "That will prove that he's the real deal."

"I can't have Frank examining him," Gene said.

"I don't understand," Jerry said.

"He doesn't know everything," Gene said.

"How did you get him to speak on camera?" Valiant asked.

"I told him the ice cream party would follow."

"Well, tell him we'll have an ice cream party and blow up a few trains if he waves to people first," I suggested.

"Frank will declare him incompetent."

"Tell Frank, his current condition is temporary because of the explosion he survived."

"Frank will want a secondary exam to release him for duty."

"But it will just be a mental exam."

"That would mean the—"

"Project," Valiant said.

"Would have to be more alert and capable."

"We might be able to pull it off," Valiant sort of assured us.

"We'll need protection for the President," Gene said.

"You think the Secret Service will stay quiet about what they see at the balcony wave?" Jerry asked.

"Let's check out their loyalty beforehand, and you'll be the only one near him. Exclude John. We'll bring in the First Lady too," I suggested to Gene.

"She hates him."

"But she's been playing along since before he was elected, right?" Valiant asked.

"It might work."

"Valiant and I need to check on that other matter."

As Valiant and I left Gene's office, John came up. "I have to accompany you through the White House."

"Good, we're going to my office," I said.

When we got there, I informed John, "You can't come in. The contents of my office are above your security clearance." I closed the door in his face and locked it.

Valiant and I went through the secret staircase into the lab.

Brandon and Jack were working furiously. The robot looked like the President. They were close. Levitson, who was generally very quiet, was eagerly joining in. "I can't get the voice right."

"The muscle controller and sound card were destroyed," Jack said. "We've put new ones in, but there are problems."

"Mr. President," I said to him.

"What's up?" He sounded like Donald Duck.

"Raise your hand," Jack said. The President raised a leg and started hopping.

"Keep working, boys. You've come a long way and I'm really proud of you."

"Are we going to go to prison?" Levitson asked.

"I hope not. Can we get it done today?"

"The way things are going, I'd say tomorrow."

"The lab could get raided by the military later today. I don't mean to push, but this is an emergency."

Valiant grabbed some equipment and a laptop. "If we're going live, I'll need to hack into the networks so they can't pre-empt the President."

"You can do that?" Levitson asked. "On second thought, I don't want to know. The more crimes I am part of, the more years I'll get."

"I hope they've been paying you well," I said.

"Very well," Jack said. "Four-hundred thousand."

"Same," Brandon said.

"Three-fifty," Levitson joined in.

"I've got mine in overseas banks," Valiant said.

"Gold," Jack said.

"Why didn't you suggest that to me?" Levitson asked.

"It's never too late," I said. "Even if they do get the White House, they don't necessarily know this lab is here or what it does."

"Karissa, the person who destroyed the robot knows," Valiant pointed out.

"Right. And he or she could send the Secret Service down here to collect evidence."

"Maybe, we should stop and do clean up," Jack suggested.

"I have an idea," Valiant said. "I'll see you later, Karissa."

"Hey. About time you joined in," Brandon said. "We can't do this without you."

"I guess it's time for me to get to work," Valiant said. "Before you go—" He handed me another burner phone and picked up one for himself. He called mine from his new one. "That's my new number."

"How many of those do you have?"

"I've got another ten left."

"Before I go, I want to know how the parts order got to Northgrail?"

"We don't go through Northgrail," Brandon said. "Whatever parts they sent weren't for our project."

I went back up to my office. As I exited, locking the door, and started walking down the hall, John asked, "What are you doing here without an escort?"

"I was just looking for you. I just looked over my office and I have a lot of personal stuff to pack up."

"You can't take files."

"I was talking about nail polish, suits and a hair dryer."

Personally, I hadn't left any of my personal stuff there. Lee had created the paperwork that I had been going through, but I hadn't put my department's information on the new computer. I had been afraid that Duane would raid the office. Gene seemed to trust Duane, but I didn't. Maria's words kept coming back to me. Her words could have been a coincidence but, in my mind, it was Duane speaking.

"I need to go to Gene's office. You can either guard my office where Valiant is or escort me back to Gene's."

He looked at me. "I'll escort you. Valiant better be there when I come back."

I met an unescorted Jerry in the hallway as I went into Gene's office.

"You need an escort," John told him.

"He's hiding from you," Jerry said.

John let out an "Ugg" as Jerry closed Gene's door behind us in John's face.

To Gene, I said, "It's coming, as long as he doesn't need to speak or follow instructions or wave."

"That bad?"

"At least, it looks like him. Duane may be involved too. Hushpuppies is about eliminating obstacles and that's what Maria said she was doing when she tried to kill me."

"He didn't mean by killing."

"Are you sure?"

"I'm not sure of anything. But I've checked out Duane. He's clean."

"I don't mean to question your checking."

"I don't think Duane's a suspect. He discredits obstacles, fixes elections and pushes smear campaigns. That's what his department does. You don't think I would authorize murder, do you?"

"No. Not anymore."

"Anymore?"

"Lee had a file on people called Happy Days. It had videos and evidence against people in the White House. I believe in protecting family and I respect others who go to the max to do so."

Gene's facial expression indicated he got my drift.

"Has anyone eaten anything today? We might think better with food in us," I said.

"The kitchen staff is gone," Jerry told me.

"I can make lunch. There are usually frozen pizzas and sandwich materials. I don't recommend eating anything from an open package these days, though."

I was asked to bring in a plate of cold cuts and three pizzas, including a veggie pizza for me. Jerry and Jeb accompanied me.

As soon as we left Gene's office, John caught up with us. "Lunch," I said. "Geneva Conventions. Or do you want to be prosecuted for war crimes?"

"Is there a war?"

"There will be if you don't let us eat."

"Why is Valiant staying so long in your office?"

"There's a lot of work there."

"I didn't hear any sounds."

"Teach you to eavesdrop. He works quietly. He's a pro."

John escorted us to the kitchen while Jeb went back to Gene's office. I popped a pizza into the microwave.

"Microwave," Jerry said.

My eyes opened wide. Jerry pulled me back out of the kitchen.

"What?" John started to ask as the microwave behind him exploded. John fell to the floor.

CHAPTER 48

"Another explosion," Jerry said.

Jerry shrugged and knelt down next to John as I went to Frank's office. He was still here.

"I'm sorry for what happened," he lamented. "If it's any consolation, we're all leaving."

"We think the VP is behind the murders."

"Well, unless you can prove it, it won't matter."

"I think you better accompany me. There's been another incident."

We got back to the kitchen and Frank leaned down. "You said explosion?"

"Yes. We saw and heard it. Look the glass is shattered."

"It's more than that. He's been microwaved. Look at his complexion tone." Frank opened up John's mouth. "The inside is cooked."

"I'll never eat microwaved food again," I said, trying hard not to react.

"A traitor in the White House, right now?" Jerry asked. "The VP and intelligence services are at the parade."

Jeb, who had joined us and apparently overheard the conversation, said, "I don't think anyone has used the microwave since yesterday."

"Then, it could have been the VP," Jerry noted.

I had lost my appetite but I had promised something to the others.

"Let's see if there are any sealed cold cuts and wraps." Jerry, Jeb and I took several sealed containers for sandwich materials, along with a sealed package of organic wraps back to Gene's office.

"We'll probably be held up here for hours," I said.

"We can go to the American people," Jerry suggested.

"The VP is controlling the news media. Anything that says any of the staff is not one hundred percent behind her is deemed, 'misinformation,'" Gene informed us.

Trey knocked and was invited inside. "John's dead?"

"They killed him," I told him.

"You were operating the microwave," he said to me.

"There was a list. Microwave was on it."

"I'll never eat anything microwaved again, either," Jerry said.

"What list?" Trey asked.

"It was on Lee's computer. It was called Operation Northwoods 7."

"That sounds like a conspiracy theory."

"If so, it was Lee's conspiracy theory," I said.

"I think it was meant for Karissa. They've been trying to kill her since she accompanied the President to Mexico," Jerry told him.

"All we are asking for is time to convince everyone the President is alive," I said. "Do you really want to help a cold-blooded killer sit in the Oval Office?"

"I'll have to think about this." Trey exited Gene's office.

"What do you think?"

"I don't know," Gene said.

"If he joins us, the rest of the Secret Service will follow," Jeb said.

"I often use the microwave. That could have been meant for me," Gene said.

There was a knock at the door.

"I saw John's body carried out." It was Alan, the Secret Service agent who had helped Trey pick us up.

"That's why we need to discover who is behind the killings before we allow a change in government. Someone tried to assassinate the real President and we'll never find out who is killing who if the VP takes over before we uncover the truth," I told him.

"Tried to assassinate the real President?" Alan asked.

"The President is alive," Gene said.

"Then where is he? Why hasn't he said anything other than 'I'm alive' and 'Have some ice cream?' Why hasn't he attended any meetings in the last week?" Alan asked.

"The assassin is still out there. No, not out there. Here. Or maybe, she left to put out a fire at her place," I remarked. "It's in Georgetown."

"The VP?" Alan asked.

"We think so," Paris said, entering the office.

"John and I were like brothers. I'm with you and I know Pete and Beau will be too,'" Alan told us.

"Talk to Trey. He's on the fence."

Alan went out.

"I've heard from an insider in the Supreme Court," Gene said. "They're going to rule for the VP."

"How long do we have before the decision comes through?"

"Two hours."

"She'll get the Capitol Police to join her, along with the National Guard and Army in removing us from the White House," Paris noted.

"And will anyone back our President?" I asked.

"We've got the Navy and the Air Force. General Token stated that the President has met with the Joint Chiefs for three minutes on two occasions since he's been in office. He is certain the video was the President he's been meeting with and nothing is out of the ordinary," Gene replied.

"Great. If we want a sea or air battle, we're covered," I said.

"We also have the Marines," Gene added.

"Well, that's a relief. So we have the Seals, the Marine Raiders and the Force RECON units and they've got the Green Berets, the Night Stalkers and the Rangers."

"Maybe we should just sit back and see which one is stronger," Jerry suggested.

"It would help if all the Secret Service was on our side," I said. "Imagine the damage from a new civil war."

"Don't forget, the VP is also protected by Secret Service," Gene said.

"She's protected by Carney. He's John's cousin," Jeb noted.

"She's still got the Green Berets and the rest of her detail," Paris said.

"Remember January 6, 2021? The Capitol police invited people into the Capitol. They were peaceful and yet the police shot a woman and put others into indefinite detention without rights," I reminded them. "They might call us insurgents."

"Let them try," Jeb said firmly.

I looked at Jerry. "You might want to check out how the housekeeper is taking care of the puppies."

"I thought you got rid of those things," Gene said.

"His brother's housekeeper is watching mine and Valiant's."

"And the one I kept. They should be safe out there as long as we're in here. They were shooting firebombs at us, outside."

"Karissa, you're young. You have the rest of your life ahead of you," Gene said. "You can walk away from this."

"I'm in. I may be crazy, but I'm in." I thought about my team. "I better give the option to my team."

I picked up Gene's phone and called the lab. "Valiant, we are assessing the risks in staying. You and the team are welcome to leave."

I heard a pause on the other end. A second later, Valiant responded. "We're all in. It's too boring outside."

I laughed. Gene gave me a weird look. "Everyone's in," I said.

I turned to Paris. "You?"

"I got you into this. If anything happens to you, your mother will kill me."

"You mean your mother," Gene said to him.

"Correct."

"There's the official bomb shelter. It's got Internet and a command center. We could go there if the going gets rough," Paris suggested.

"In two hours, it could be over," Gene said.

"It's all up to the Supremes and they haven't been popular since the '50s," Jerry joked.

"They still play them on the oldies stations," I said. "What's your reading of the Supreme Court?" I asked Gene.

"There's the inside report plus even the AG thinks it looks bad for us."

"How can it look bad when the President is alive? I say we go ahead with the plan. Take him to the balcony of the Residence and show him off. Have him wave."

Gene looked at Jeb. "We've got nothing to lose. Even if he's later declared incompetent, that will give us time."

"Do we have any bullet-proof transparent shields? We were chased by a tank with a seemingly limitless arsenal of firebombs earlier today," I remarked.

"We can have Secret Service agents on the roof and bullet-proof glass around the balcony," Gene said. "The Truman Balcony would be easier to shield than the Promenade Balcony."

"I'll notify the press and put out a public announcement," Jerry told us.

"Let's see where Trey stands," Gene said.

Gene buzzed Trey, who joined us.

"We want the Truman Balcony bulletproof in the next hour. Can we do it?"

"It's been done before. It won't be perfect, but it can be arranged."

"Karissa check on your team. Jerry, Paris and I will be arranging the press conference. Trey and his team will be securing the area. At the right time, I'll be on the second floor and you and Jeb will be bringing up the President."

"I'd like to be on the balcony," Jerry said. "I'm in this far. I might as well be in all the way."

"Sure. I'll bring the First Lady there," Gene said.

In the lab, Valiant had gotten the President to stop lifting his leg when asked to raise his hand. But his walk was a bounce and his voice now sounded like John Wayne's.

"Did they do that much damage to his sound card?" I asked.

"I might be able to modify a soundboard from the computer but there isn't really room for it with all the other electronics."

"There's more. He keeps spinning his head around, Linda Blair style," Jack said.

"Great. *The Exorcist.* Maybe, we should call in a priest," I said.

"We could use heavenly support if we're going to finish."

"We're less than two hours away from the SCOTUS decision. Any chance you could finish by then? Maybe he could pretend to have laryngitis."

"We still need to work on adjusting the springs and limiting the neck movement."

"It would help if the MSM could be pre-empted. I didn't say hacked, but pre-empted, to mysteriously cover the story," Valiant commented.

"Valiant," I said, softening my voice quite a bit. "Whatever, happens, I know you are doing your best. Without you, I couldn't have survived the last few weeks."

"You are a lot stronger and more capable than you realize," he said softly. "You're the reason we're still here, that we didn't walk long ago."

"Thank you." I gave him a quick hug but he continued holding me. Somehow in his arms, I felt safe, like somehow everything would be alright.

"Now, go save the world. We have your back," he said.

I returned to Gene's office. Paris and Jeb were there.

"The major stations are calling the President's being alive misinformation and are refusing to cover it."

"All they have to do is see him."

"They don't want to. They've been that way since COVID. They are looking at the money they'll get if a new President does more to reward their backers in the pharma-military-industrial complex. As far as they are concerned, the public will believe anything they say, whether true or not."

Jerry walked in. "We have several reporters from the Indymedia and a few hundred people who will be live streaming from their cell phones."

"What if the cell companies cut their service?"

"We're prepared for that," Paris said. "I have an exec from a new phone company prepared to hand out phones that don't rely on the apps that are being used to censor information. They'll be able to live stream to the cloud and directly to multiple sources, including their email lists at once."

"How are the boys coming?" Gene asked.

"I'm sure it's just hours away."

"Good, we'll announce a full press briefing tonight," Gene said. "Jeb, would you take them down by way of the residence and prepare the President? Have him put on a dark blue suit, a light blue shirt and that tie with flags on it. Oh, and pants."

On the way to the residence, I asked Jeb, "He may be out of shape. What if the suit doesn't fit him?"

"My concern is he'll look like he's aged years in one week."

"Make-up," I said. "With the right makeup, we can minimize that."

We went to the press office, where Jerry picked up a makeup kit. "I should probably go with you."

When we arrived in the correct sub-basement, the President was eating ice cream. "You're right, he's aged a bit," I said. The robot hadn't aged since taking office.

"I brought down a movie quality makeup kit. We're going to tape back the sags, fill the lines and then use the final makeup. They do this in the movies all the time," I said.

"Have you ever applied movie makeup?" Jerry asked me.

"No. Have you? Maybe you can do it better," I said to Jerry.

"I've had it applied to me but no. You do it and I'll watch."

We had the President sit in a chair.

"I like the sandbox."

"That's later," I said.

The first thing the President did was to try to eat the foundation. "Yuck. Bad ice cream."

"This isn't ice cream. The ice cream party is after you wave at people. We're all going to have a big ice cream party. But it's a surprise and you can't tell them about the party or the ice cream."

"Surprise? Party? Thank you, Mommy."

I had to keep myself from rolling my eyes.

"Why does he think you're his mother?" Jerry asked.

"Who knows?"

"You look a lot like her," Jeb said. "I've seen pictures of her when she was your age."

That comment made me want to throw up. "She did a lousy job of raising her son," I said coldly. "I mean, he's such a warmonger. But we're all in this too deep to turn back now."

"You really do look like her," Jeb said, continuing to stare at me. "Are you related to the President?"

"You'll have to ask Paris if we're any distant relation. Jeb, you've been with the President a long time. Do you remember when he went to Georgetown University to push the jab?"

"That was the robot. The original team was operating him then. He spoke briefly and left. Then the VP took over. A school employee who wasn't even a nurse supposedly administered the jab."

"Do you remember her name?"

"I wasn't there but I heard the VP recommended her for a job here."

"Why do you ask?" Jeb inquired.

"Just wondering." So it was the VP who had Paris's sister killed, not necessarily intentionally but through the jab.

The President started to go back to the sandbox.

Jeb moved in front. "Your mommy wants you to come with us," he said firmly.

"I don't want to. I want ice cream now!"

"If we get you a bowl of ice cream, will you come?" I asked.

"Yes. Ice cream."

Jeb turned to the robomaid. "Ice cream, please."

"I get ice cream," he said. "Mommy has big cones."

"Excuse me! You don't talk that way about your mommy," I said.

"Even as a kid, he's a pervert," Jerry remarked.

"He's basically the same as ever, only in toddler format," Jeb said.

The President jumped into the sandbox and landed hard on his bottom. "Ow. That hurt."

Good, I thought.

After the President ate the ice cream, we tried to assist him out of the sandbox. "No. I want to stay here."

"You promised."

"I had my fingers crossed."

"If you don't get up and come with us, Daddy is going to give you a spanking." I didn't know if his father spanked him, but I was hoping that would get some action.

"Daddy won't spank me."

Jerry took off his belt. "You want to bet?"

"You're not my daddy."

"Your daddy is busy. He sent me to spank you if you don't come."

"Is Daddy going to be there?"

"Yes. He'll be watching you wave at the crowd," Jerry said.

"I don't like my daddy."

"If you come, I'll tell him to go away," Jerry said, continuing to play along.

"I'll get you some more trains to blow up," I said.

"Okay!"

Jeb and Jerry took the President's arms and lifted him up. "He needs to change," Jerry said. "Remember the suit, shirt and tie?"

"You mean put the clothes over what he has on, right?" The President was in shorts with a diaper sticking out the top, and a shirt that read, "The Mummy." The last thing I wanted was to see my dad naked.

Jeb held the President up while Jerry dressed him. As Jerry put the shirt on, the President bit his ear.

"Ow!"

"I'll take it from here," I said. "Bad boy! If you bite anyone else, no ice cream for a week."

The President started crying.

"More ice cream afterward," I reminded him.

"I'll come if I can feel your cones."

"And if you touch my cones, I'll cut off your hands, and you won't be able to eat any more ice cream ever."

That silenced him.

I let Jerry arrange the President's tie, which he did while standing as far away as he could and still reach the President. "No biting or no ice cream for a week," I advised.

"I don't like him," the President said, looking at Jerry.

"I don't like you either," Jerry told him.

The President started to cry, again.

"He didn't mean that," I said.

"You said it first," Jerry pointed out.

"Now, we are going to take you upstairs to the residence, and you are going to walk outside with a nice lady. Then you are going to wave at the people below and walk back inside. Show me your wave," I instructed him.

He started flapping both arms.

"How about you just hold up your right hand?" Jeb suggested.

He held up his left.

"That will be fine," I said.

Jeb and Jerry assisted him to the Executive Residence of the White House and into the elevator as I followed. The good news was that, since I was just a researcher, I didn't have to go out on the balcony with him. We had sharpshooters on the roof in case anyone fired from the crowd. The Air Force was standing by in case we saw any tanks. What could go wrong?

On the second floor of the Residence—the center section of the White House— we met Gene and the First Lady in the Center Hall.

"This better be quick," she said. "Moe looks ridiculous."

"He just escaped an attempt on his life in Mexico," I said. "He's still shaken up."

"Trey and I will be accompanying you and the First Lady out onto the balcony for protection," Jeb said.

"May I sit down, now?" the President asked.

"No," Jeb, Jerry and I said in unison.

We all walked into the Yellow Oval Room. From there, Trey came in from the Truman Balcony. We have a large crowd of people outside who are eager to see you," he told the President. Trey pulled me aside. "What's wrong with him? He looks unsteady."

"He's scared. They almost killed him in Mexico."

Trey nodded. He went back to the President. "There's nothing to be afraid of. We have you well protected. We have a full detail of Secret Service agents and a plainclothes detail of Naval and Air Force officers below and above. The Seals are around the perimeter. The Air Force is in the air, awaiting any command you have for them."

"Can I be a cowboy?"

"That makes sense," I covered. "I mean all the Forces are taking care of the crowd and we could use a hero from the Old West. Good joke, sir."

The First Lady was rolling her eyes. "Can we get on with this?"

"Not yet," Frank said, rushing into the room. He swabbed the President's mouth and put the swab in a plastic container. "DNA. I'll verify this right away." With that, he left and I breathed a sigh of relief that the President hadn't eaten the swab.

Accompanied by Jerry, Gene went out to announce the President. After doing so, they stood back. The President and his escorts moved forward with Trey taking the lead but standing in front of the First Lady so as to not block the people's view of the President. Jeb followed behind. Both Jeb and Trey wore earphones to monitor information from the others protecting the President.

There were lukewarm cheers from below. Moe had never been able to fill a small room when he ran for President, but now a bunch of gawkers wanted to see the dead man. I saw the President lift both hands to wave. Before I knew what was happening, Jeb pulled the President and First Lady back as Trey shoved them back from in front. There was an explosion and the balcony blew apart.

CHAPTER 49

The President, First Lady and Jeb were on the floor safe as Jerry tried to cover them. I rushed over to them. Gene had been knocked to the floor but managed to get up. But Trey had still been on the balcony at the time it appeared to be blown apart. Jeb, Jerry and Gene helped the President and First Lady get up and move into the Center Hall. The air was thick with debris. We all ran for the ground floor, making sure the President did not trip. As we reached the ground floor of the Executive Residence, there was another explosion from above it.

"We're all going to rush through the press room to the West Wing," Jeb said.

"I want to get my jewelry," the First Lady insisted.

"That isn't safe."

"It's your job to make sure it is. And I don't want to spend a minute I don't have to with this idiot."

With that, she pulled away and rushed back upstairs.

"West Wing," Jeb said. I heard sounds from behind us.

"The West Colonnade is open," Jerry pointed out.

"We're going through the Palm Room, then the Press Offices and finally the briefing room," Jeb said. "It's safer."

There were sounds at the main entrance. Paris rushed to us. "The Army is trying to break in. That was a missile which was intercepted."

"Some interception. Is Trey okay?"

Paris shook his head. "I guess our defenses are lacking."

"I'll say," I said. I hoped the headshake meant that Trey was hurt but alive.

"We have to get the President to safety," Gene said.

"The lab," I suggested.

"The lab?" Jeb asked. "I've never been there."

Gene went to speak with some of the Secret Service agents.

"Sub-basement. It doesn't exist," Paris told him. "But once you enter, you're an accessory if you talk."

Jeb gave him a funny look. "I'm holding up a President, wearing diapers who thinks your sister is his mother. I don't think there is anything that could make me more complicit."

Alan raced over to us.

"The First Lady is in the residence. Get her down to the tunnels," Jeb said.

"Tunnels?"

"What? Were you hired yesterday? Everyone here knows about the tunnels. So does the public because they keep talking about them in movies and TV."

"Oh. Those tunnels."

"Paris, would you handle it? Alan, you get the Secret Service and Air Force to protect all the entrances."

"There's fighting outside between the services."

"Who's winning?" Gene asked.

"It's hard to tell."

"Has anyone been killed?"

"They're mostly beating each other up."

Gene turned to me, Jeb, Jerry and Paris. "You four get the President somewhere safe. I don't want to know where until this is all over. Alan, you get the First Lady and join them. That's a priority."

"Let's go," I said as Paris and I led the way to the lab.

Inside the lab, Valiant greeted us, at first looking a little surprised at Jeb's presence. "I saw it on several streams. It looks like the missile was intercepted, making an even larger explosion."

"That's what Congress funded. Bigger explosions," I said.

"We've got to get him somewhere safe. Gene doesn't want anyone, including himself, to know where we've gone," Jeb told him.

"I know a place in Virginia," Valiant said.

"We need to pick up the puppies on the way," Jerry said. "I think the housekeeper will start shooting them if she has to deal with all those dogs any longer."

Valiant gave me the key to his uncle's place. "I think that's the safest place. I'll meet you there if I can get out."

"You have to get out. That's an order."

He smiled. Then, he sketched out a map of the path through the tunnels to the Jefferson Memorial.

"They might recognize us."

"You can put on some facemasks when you get out and carry some trash bags like homeless people."

"We'll need transportation," Jerry said.

"I can't wear a facemask," I said. I had had nightmares about suffocation.

Valiant handed me a Guy Fawkes mask. I put it on.

"Do any of you know how to hotwire a car?" he asked.

"I think I can," Jerry said.

"You are full of surprises," I responded.

"I've got another idea," Paris said.

He called Gene and spoke to him. "Okay. Let's go."

"Okay."

The lab had its own special exit into the tunnel system. Handy. We weaved our way through the underground and came out at the Memorial.

"Hey, what are you doing here?" It was a D.C. Police officer. He must have thought we were rising from a nap.

"Sorry. We're homeless and we got tired of walking."

"I'll have to take you in. Especially, Guy Fawkes."

"That's the only mask that fits my wife. She's pregnant and I need to get her to the hospital. We'll leave now," Jerry said.

"I don't know," the officer responded.

We rushed to the street before the officer had time to think about it. "This way," Jerry said, taking us further away from the White House. There was a car on the side of the road with emergency flashers on and the engine running. Someone was underneath the front of it with most of his body and legs sticking out from under the front.

"Inside," Jerry said.

"What?" I asked.

"Inside," Jerry said.

We got in the car. Jerry backed up so as to not hit the guy and then took off.

"That poor man."

"That was Pete Rogan. I recognized his shoes. He's Secret Service."

"Ah. It was planned," I said.

"Right," Paris said. "Gene arranged it."

I was sitting in the back with the President between me and Jeb. Jerry and Paris were in front. From there, we drove to Ben's house.

"These puppies keep peeing," Filomena, the housekeeper, yelled at him as she came out. "And Mr. President keeps attacking Mr. Putin."

"We're taking them off your hands," Jerry told her.

He and I went inside and we piled the dogs into an old Mercedes in Ben's garage. Jerry got into the driver's seat. "This car doesn't have tracking on it, but we don't want that other one tracked to my brother's house. We're picking up Paris at Rock Creek Park."

Jeb, the President and I got into the backseat. I put Mr. President on the President's lap. "A doggie. I get a doggie." I put the Papkimo basket on my lap as the others rode on Jeb's lap, the floor and the front passenger seat.

We picked Paris up and then I got a call on my burner phone with instructions. "We have to?"

"What?" Jeb asked.

"We have to pick up the First Lady. Alan's going to meet us a few blocks from the White House. They got out through a different exit."

As we stopped to pick them up, the First Lady was very irritated. "I have to get in the car with those horrible dogs?"

"They're friendly."

"I like them," the President said. "May I keep one, Mommy?"

"We'll see," I said. I watched him carefully, not trusting him with a puppy.

I thought of the stories of college students putting fifteen people into a Volkswagen. This car was larger but, between dogs and humans, we had a larger crew.

We all had to have puppies on our laps, but Lill wasn't having any of it as I handed one to her. "This puppy is ugly." I looked at him. To me, he was one of the prettiest dogs I had ever seen.

"He seems to like you."

"Ever hear of a hot dog? Wait until I get you into the kitchen."

"Look how calm he is," I said as the dog lifted his leg and peed on her.

She screamed.

"You two had kids. Didn't they ever pee on you?" Jerry asked.

"Never. The nanny raised them."

"No wonder your son turned out like that," I commented.

"What?"

"Never mind," I said.

Jerry pulled the car right into Valiant's uncle's garage and we raced into the house. Well, some of us did. Others had to be dragged, which wasn't easy while carrying fourteen dogs.

"Kucinich, you look bigger than you did last time I saw you."

"You named him Kucinich," Lill growled. "I hate that man. Does anyone have a vacuum cleaner to suck in the rat?"

I held the basket of Papkimos close.

"This one is really sweet," Paris said, putting Esther on the floor.

"The Papkimos are Esther's babies."

"Are they all named?" Jeb asked me.

"Actually, yes."

Jeb put the Belgian he was carrying on the floor. "Is he available?"

"That's Patrick Henry. He's one of Valiant's puppies, but I bet if you promise to be nice to him, only feed him organics and not remove his manhood, he'll let you keep him."

"Hey Pat, I've got a son who would like you."

"Unfortunately, you can't call him right now. The call could be monitored," I said.

"My wife probably figured that out when the news showed the balcony exploding."

I turned on the main floor monitor. "It's not a smart TV, and it does not have a backdoor for the networks or government."

It showed Raquel Madcow.

"The people expected to see the President. But instead were almost killed when the balcony collapsed. The Supreme Court has ruled that the Vice President is lawfully the President since he has not been seen or heard from in a week. If you see or hear of any videos of the President on the balcony before the explosion, those are fake news."

"Great. He was visible and held up his arms. Well, hopefully, Frank will prove the President is alive," I said.

All of us but Lill, Moe, Alan and our furry friends went down to the basement. Paris looked around on the net. "He has multiple VPNs, doesn't he?"

"Yes. What are you looking for?"

"I just wanted to see if the videos posted."

"According to this guy in the *TLAV* chat, one video with the President got ten million views, almost instantly, before it was pulled. The word is getting out."

"I thought *TLAV* was censored."

"Pirate streams. It's the most informative show on C-Nineteen, and thousands of people offered their YouTube addresses to keep *TLAV* on *YouTube*."

"I've watched that," Jeb said. "It does have the best information on the plandemic. If it weren't for *TLAV*, I would have gotten the injection. Or I mean--"

"You're in good company. How did you fake it?" I asked.

"I went to Ben Stafford."

"My brother," Jerry said.

"One of us should go upstairs to make sure the First Lady doesn't really cook the dogs," I said, moving in that direction.

"Alan is up there. If anyone tries to harm a dog around him, he'll throw them in the Potomac, regardless of their political status," Jeb said.

"I just can't handle being called Mommy anymore. I'll make some food for the First Couple and everyone else, including the dogs," I said.

"I'll help," Jerry offered.

In the kitchen, when the others were out, Jerry said, "Spill it."

"What?"

"He's the guy who raped your mom."

"How did you know?"

"You and Valiant were talking on the plane."

"When you were asleep and drunk?"

"I was drunk but not asleep. If I were Paris, I'd kill him."

"You might as well know the rest. Paris isn't my brother."

"You mean he's only your half-brother."

"That will work."

After we ate, Jerry, Paris and I went downstairs. I went to the place where the original flash drive from Mrs. Kinsky was and inserted it into the computer.

What could be the password? I asked myself. "Jerry, if you were working on an illegal project, what would you use for the password?"

"Criminal, crook."

"His wife may have been vaxxed and gone crazy."

"Poison."

I tried it. To my surprise, it worked. The data on the file was more than about the Presidential project. It was about the ingredients in the jab, and about the controls that were created over people.

"All the conspiracy theorists were right," Jerry said.

"Yep," I agreed. 'He probably was either vaxxed or saw what happened to his wife before he died."

"This document includes what they were doing at Northgrail. Blackmoriuntur was a local delivery system for them for various items, including bombs! Monica picked up a box there. We saw it on the video."

"And she's been at the White House," Paris said. "You had a video of Blackmoriuntur?"

"Long story," I said. "John was controlled. Maybe she was a patsy and he planted bombs before we took out Northgrail."

"Monica might remember what he did with the bombs if that's the case," Paris said. "She had a fake pass and he threw her out."

I turned to Jerry. "Let's leave Paris, Jeb and Alan to supervise the situation here and to make sure the dogs don't get cooked while we check out Monica."

We took off in an old car Valiant's uncle had in the garage. It was a little clunky, but I wanted to leave Ben's car for the others and didn't want to drive the one we had taken to the former DNC chair's house. I brought some cherry bombs with us that I found in the uncle's garage.

"Valiant's uncle must be a cool person," Jerry said. He had really lightened up.

We parked a ways away from Monica's apartment. We lit and threw a couple of cherry bombs across the driveway while security was talking to a driver. As the gate security ran to check out the noise, we rushed inside. I remembered Apartment 305.

Monica seemed confused when she answered the door. "Security is supposed to—"

"Not for the White House," I said.

"I hear you're out."

"You were thrown out today," I responded.

"That creep."

"John?"

"He made me all kinds of promises, gave me a fake pass and had me running errands for him."

"Like picking up a box at Blackmoriuntur."

"More than one. You were in on it. You took one for John and I gave him others in person"

"That wasn't me. It was a look-alike."

"Sure, like I believe that. I was going to deliver the final one I picked up last week today, and I didn't get in. I'm going to throw it away."

"You have it?"

"Not for long."

"We need to see it," I said

"Why?"

"Do you know what was in it?"

"I don't care."

This is when Jerry chimed in. "Monica, we were friends, aside from just dating."

"Well, now you're with Karissa."

"No, he's not," I said. "He never was. We're just friends."

"Sure."

"She's telling the truth. Monica, how about showing it to me for all the good times we had together? I mean, we went to some pretty nice places on our dates."

"You really aren't dating her?"

"No." I didn't know if he was saying it because it was true or because he was just saying what she wanted to hear. Either way, I didn't have any negative feelings about his words. My reaction surprised me. I had considered the possibility of dating him. I needed to focus.

"We work together. Doesn't your dad work with women in the office?"

"He doesn't go on dates."

"We were on a research assignment as there was a threat to the White House involving the press corp."

"Really?"

"Really," I said.

She went onto the patio and pulled a box out from under a chair.

I handed Jerry plastic gloves I had brought in my pocket and put on some gloves myself. I had picked that up from Valiant.

"Why are you using gloves? My prints are on it."

"It's not about prints. I don't know if there is something toxic inside." I didn't say the word "explosive."

"Remember the anthrax," he said.

"Well, masks don't work," I said. "Hold your breath and stand far back."

She did as we opened it. Inside were explosives with a timer set for today at 5 P.M.

"That's an hour from now," I said.

"Into the Potomac?"

"Sure. But Monica, you said you delivered more than one?"

"This was the fifth box. The other four were much larger. I picked this one up last week and then, on Sunday, couldn't remember why I wanted to take it to the White House. John hadn't called me since then. So I showed up today."

"If the others were set for the same time, the White House could have some explosions set for today at 5 P.M. These are ready to go off. This may be the only unplanted one. The team is there with the President!"

I was a lot more worried about the team than the fake President. My stomach started knotting up, and I controlled the urge to run back to the White House. I pulled out a little camera and took some pictures of the bomb. I called Valiant. "Get out with everything you can. Four big bombs may be going off in an hour at the White House. Notify Gene."

"Let's go!" I said to Jerry.

"What about me?" Monica asked.

"You want to go up with this bomb if we don't get to the Potomac on time? Stay here, safe, while we dispose of it," I advised her.

"I wouldn't want anything to happen to you," Jerry said to her.

"Really?" she responded.

"Let's go," I said to Jerry.

———

In the car, I told him, her whole relationship with John may have been programmed in.

"I don't know if I feel anything about her, anymore."

"That may be you protecting you."

"I think I need to be with someone less self-centered."

"Did you know her before she was vaxxed?"

"No."

"Maybe that was part of the jab. I've noticed that people who have been vaxxed turn much more selfish than those who haven't."

"Maybe. But I want someone more like you."

"That's sweet," I said. "I'm not that great. There's a lot you don't know about me."

"I know that the President is your father. I think he'd be a terrible father-in-law, but I'm okay with it."

"Darn," I said as we got into traffic. "I bet with a possible war waging at 1600, people are deserting the area. Traffic."

"We can't let the bomb go off here."

I pulled onto the sidewalk. "The D.C. police are probably still busy." We were on East Street, heading towards 66. I had been hoping to take 66 north to throw the box off the side of the Francis Scott Key Bridge but even the sidewalk was jammed and I knew we'd never make the Key Bridge. "We'll have to park and run for Teddy Roosevelt," I said.

Jerry grabbed the box and we ran towards the Kennedy Center for the Performing Arts. We planned to rush by it and then throw the box off the Theodore Roosevelt Bridge, which crossed to Theodore Roosevelt Island before crossing the Potomac River for Virginia.

At that point, a helicopter landed right by us. It wasn't the Secret Service. It was the D.C. Police. An officer got out.

"Did you leave your car on the sidewalk?"

"Sir, this box has to be thrown off the bridge in ten minutes," Jerry said.

"Well, this is going to take a little longer." He pulled out a pad. "Give me your license."

"I don't have it with me." It was true. I had left my ID at the ranch house.

"Reckless driving, illegal parking, failing to follow street signs, driving without a license."

"Sir, this is a bomb with a timer set to explode," I said.

"Are you threatening me?"

"No sir. I'm trying to save the city."

"The super-hero excuse."

He went back to his writing. Jerry, somehow quickly pulled the officer's gun from his belt while the officer's attention and hands were on his pen and pad and slugged the officer.

A shot was fired from the helicopter as we ran for the bridge. We knew we were being followed and were dodging bullets. We ran between some cars, figuring they might stop shooting, but they didn't. An officer shot out a tire and the car swerved to the side, hitting another car with several cars piling up behind. We kept running as more shots were fired.

"You'd think they'd care a little about collateral damage," I said.

"You kidding? The D.C. Police?"

"We're on the bridge. Give it to me to throw," I instructed.

'What if it doesn't go far enough? See if we can make it to the island and throw it from there," Jerry said.

"We may not have time."

"We have two more minutes."

"That's cutting it close."

Someone blocked our way. "Are you running from the police?"

"Throw," I said to Jerry, knowing we weren't going to get further. Over the rail and out over the river it went.

The explosion was bigger than I thought. It jolted the bridge. I looked around and we were okay. But it was nothing compared to a much larger explosion coming from D.C., about the location of the White House.

CHAPTER 50

The guy who had blocked our path had fallen down but otherwise seemed unharmed. With everyone else looking in the direction of the explosion, we took off for Virginia. We kept running towards Colonial Village as I pulled my flip phone out of my pocket and tried to call Valiant. No answer.

I tried Valiant again and after a continued lack of responses, I called Paris to pick us up.

Jerry was trying to get in touch with the White House Press Corp. "Nobody, there, is answering. We were seen with a bomb. We could be top suspects in any attack in D.C."

"I don't care if I'm a suspect. I'm worried about my team. They were only staying there for me."

"Especially Valiant."

"He's got to be okay." I was feeling my heart sinking and found myself praying that he was fine. I hadn't been all that religious, but now I hoped for divine help.

When Paris picked us up, he gave us the news. "There's nothing left of the White House. I guess there's nothing to fight with the VP over."

"Monica delivered the explosives to John, who was undoubtedly under Northgrail's control. She didn't know what she was delivering," I said

"You realize people will just see that as a conspiracy theory, don't you?" Paris responded.

"Yep. Who are they suspecting?"

"Everyone on the old team, including you and me. There is an arrest on sight, deadly force permitted."

"It's worse," I said. "Valiant wasn't answering his phones. Do you know if the remaining people got out?"

"They say they are going through the rubble now, looking for bodies. But I don't know how with the fires the explosion caused."

"What about the sub-basements?"

"The bombs created a crater. They suspect even the bomb shelter in the East Wing was taken out."

"Valiant, Jack, Brandon and Levitson," I mouthed. But my mind flashed to Valiant and the kiss he had given me at the ranch house what seemed like a century ago. He had to be okay.

"We'll know more, later."

"What about Frank?"

"He should be at the Medical Center running a rush DNA. I think he'll report the results before going back."

We went back to the Virginia house in silence. Part of me kept praying. But if there was a God up there, why was this happening to my country and to the world?

Back at the ranch house, the First Lady was upset. "They blew up my house."

The President said, "Boom. That was the best, yet."

"At least he's stringing together longer sentences," I said.

I looked at the TV. The crater was so deep, it probably took out the tunnels. I wanted to cry, but part of me wanted to hang onto hope. Valiant had to be alive and I was going to hang onto that hope until they proved otherwise.

"They must have used much bigger bombs on that than those in the box we threw," Jerry said.

"The video Valiant erased from the cloud would have made Monica look guilty but if she was controlled, those who ordered the hit on the

White House are really to blame," I said. The video also would have falsely implicated Jerry.

Jerry filled Jeb and Paris in on what we discovered.

"And I can't get in touch with Valiant," I said. I went into the basement. Part of me felt like I was dying, but not because of my situation. I didn't care if I went to prison. Nothing mattered anymore.

Jerry, followed by Paris, came down to the basement. "They could have found a way out. We did warn them. This ranch house belongs to Valiant's uncle. I wonder how long it will take them to find us."

"I don't know. You might want to get out while you can," Paris said to him.

"Do you think I want to miss the rest of the excitement?"

"This isn't your battle," I said. "That ended when we proved you had nothing to do with Marissa's murder."

"Also, I like the company. Where am I ever going to find another girl or crew that doesn't have poison running through their veins?"

"What about the videos of the appearance of the President on the balcony? Those went viral before they censored them."

"They'll probably confiscate the footage and arrest the journalists for violating the Espionage Act. They routinely do that when they want to hide the truth."

"Enough people saw him who could testify and sign affidavits."

"They are denying that was him. They said it didn't even look like the President."

"He is the President. The DNA will prove that."

"The Senate is holding a special session to approve all of the VP's cabinet officers and her new VP. They also are pushing a new anti-terrorism bill that she has promised to sign saying that anyone ever questioning anything about the government is a terrorist."

"This isn't the first takeover by someone who didn't win an election. Maybe we should all just quit, get new IDs and retire to Mexico," I said.

"I've been thinking about that," Paris said.

"Jerry, we can say you weren't with us. Maybe we can create an alibi for you."

"No. I couldn't pull it off. Besides, as insane as this government was, it was saner than the one that's taking over."

"Karissa, we can tell them you died from the after-effects of the explosion and I can take them to the DNA to prove it," Paris said.

"No. I'm staying." If Valiant was gone, part of me wanted to die and was okay with going to prison. In fact, I thought I deserved it.

"Wait," Jeb said, holding out his phone. "It's Frank. He's called a press conference."

We went upstairs and Jerry turned to a news station.

"And now the plot thickens. The President's physician has run a DNA test on that person who went out on the balcony and in a minute he will reveal who it was," Raquel Madcow announced.

"Do you think it will prove he's a fake?" Joe Interndeadonfloor asked.

"It's academic now. We're hearing that there could not have been any survivors from the explosions. They apparently blew themselves up. Fortunately, President Ferris was in the Capitol. "

"Here it is."

Frank came out of the front doors of Bethesda and stood before the press.

"I personally took DNA from the man who came out on the balcony. Because of recent developments with testing, we were able to get it done the same day and the results are conclusive. The man on the balcony is the President, the real President, not an imposter."

The feed cut to a vaccine commercial. We turned to another station and there was a commercial for a military contractor. Then the TV went black. A minute later, there was an announcement.

"The new President is preparing for an address tomorrow. To stop all fake news, there will be no more telecasts on any stations, tonight, with the exception of the re-swearing-in of President Ferris and the swearing-in of her new Cabinet and the new Vice President. You will find all Russian-backed social media propaganda sites are down as well. If you caught the broadcast from a place that looked like Bethesda, it was a fake broadcast coordinated from Moscow to interrupt the real broadcast."

"This had been coming ever since the Obama Administration went after Julian Assange," I said.

On the computer, I checked out my official email. It was shut down.

"Well, none of us exist."

"They blew up my house. I want them to pay for a new one," the First Lady said.

"If they found out we escaped, they'll have us and you arrested," Paris told her.

"They can't arrest me. I'm the First Lady."

"They'll pretend you're an imposter, just like the President."

"If we're dead, maybe they won't look further," Jerry said.

"I wouldn't count on it," Paris responded. "The Intelligence Community doesn't like loose ends."

"I hope the uncle picked up this place through an LLC. That will make it harder to locate us," Jerry noted.

"They've got facial recognition cameras everywhere. They probably have a good idea where we are," Jeb said.

"They have had a hard time keeping them up. That's part of the reason they feel the Signature Reduction Force is needed," Paris said.

"Meaning?" I asked.

"People keep shooting out the cameras, particularly in Virginia. Signature Reduction soldiers can walk down the street and secretly record everything, including conversations inside houses. I told you that, Karissa."

"Let's hope the shooters have been active here," I said.

I went upstairs and lay down on the bed I had claimed a couple of weeks before. Esther crawled up on the bed, carrying Cal-El. I picked up the other puppies and held them all next to me as I tried to sleep. But all I could think of was Valiant. I thought about my mom and how he had hit it off with her, how we had almost been killed in Boca Inglesia but somehow he pulled us through. I thought about our fall into the water in Ensenada and how he had saved me at Glider's Point.

"You have an out. You're Eve," Paris said, coming into the room. "You took off for a trip and the wrong person was buried. Karissa perished when the White House fell."

"I don't care about me. I'll lose almost everyone I care about if this continues, and I may have lost Valiant already."

"You really care about him," Paris said.

"I'm not supposed to care about—not while all this is going on."

I was out of it until the next morning, switching between trying to sleep, sobbing and wandering around. Jerry tried to bring me some food, but I couldn't eat.

The next morning, Paris told me that the VP's people had all been sworn in the night before. She was about to do an address. We all started watching on the living room non-smart TV.

"The terrorists are dead. Now we must round up everyone who knew the insurgents. We have agents looking throughout the country for anyone who was touched by them, gave them gas, provided food or shelter to them or to any parts of their terrorist cell, or spread misinformation supportive of the terrorists."

"We're a terrorist cell now."

"The real doctor last night confirmed that the DNA did not match the President. If you saw the fake news broadcast, that has been deleted to prevent the public from coming to the wrong conclusion about what is happening. The fake doctor had been arrested, tried and is expected to be executed later today."

CHAPTER 51

"There is no way they had an indictment, trial and sentencing that fast," I said. But nothing was normal now. "We've got to save Frank."

"The *Sixth Amendment* calls for a public trial. Do you believe there was one at all?" Jerry asked.

"Nope. Monica could be in danger too."

"She broke up with me weeks ago. She'll probably talk about how lucky she was to see through me."

"If that was the vax talking, you can't hold that against her."

"Getting the jab in the first place is a choice. Didn't you say there were other centers? Even if the jab files are erased, as soon as new boosters are in operation, people will start acting crazy again, including her, if she's jabbed."

"She says she was. But was she? Any word from anyone who was in the White House?" I asked Paris.

"No. We're on our own."

"Jerry, do you think your friends could smuggle all of you out of the country? I mean, we're all dead, right? Unless we were identified on the bridge yesterday."

"What about you?"

"I've got to go to the White House. I have to see for myself."

"Nothing is alive there," Paris said. "Either they got out or they didn't."

Why won't he contact me? I thought. Out loud I said, "If Valiant got himself killed, I'm going to murder him."

I went back into the basement. Then it hit me. I had left Valiant's uncle's car in D.C. If they traced it to the ranch house, they could be on their way.

"I contacted Tristan. He'll be flying in late this afternoon," Jerry said, coming into the basement.

"I'll be back. I'll leave you the car." I put a scarf around my head.

"Critical race theory," Jerry said. "You'll be better trusted if you aren't white."

"Should I take a bath in black markers?"

"Your hair," Paris said.

"Blueberries."

"I think they'll notice a blue person."

"But not blue hair. Pink and blue hair dye is all the rage these days."

I crushed some blueberries and put them in a shallow tub of water. My skin was a bit purplish but not so extreme as to be non-human. My hair had a definite bluish tinge.

'I'm going with you, sis," Paris said.

"You've gotten too used to that," I whispered to him. "You can stop living the illusion."

He whispered back, "Karissa always thought I was a jerk and I wanted to be closer to her. I wished I had the kind of relationship with her I have with you."

"Lee's drive. There was something about Georgetown on it."

"Let's check it out, first."

The two of us went down to the basement. Jerry and Alan were in the living room with Jeb trying to keep the First Lady from punching out her husband.

The drive showed the Georgetown University assembly where the President was supposed to make an appearance. At the last minute, Gene told the crowd, the President was having an emergency. I could visibly see the problem. The President was starting to spark and Gene got him out of there. The VP, who was excited to replace him, didn't notice. She spoke to the students, telling them they would be heroes and save lives if they were vaccinated. That was when she called Karissa by name to the stage. "I hear you won't get the jab. Your brother will be very proud if you do."

"I'm not getting it," Karissa said.

"Why did she tell them? I got her a card and a QR Code," Paris reacted.

"Integrity," I said.

We continued to watch.

"For our country. Will a couple of students hold her down while the acting nurse gives her the shot?"

I saw a flash of someone come out. She was wearing a hat and her face almost looked familiar."

"Why am I not surprised?" Paris said, disconnecting the drive.

"Who was that? She had dark hair but I don't quite recognize her. I heard it was someone working at the White House and that she wasn't a real nurse."

"Never mind. The less you know when I kill her, the better. Plausible deniability."

"I don't want deniability. I want you safe. Paris, you aren't a killer."

"She murdered my sister. I owe Karissa."

Paris shaved his head and put on a Green Day T-shirt.

"I never liked the shaved head look, but it's okay on you."

<hr>

We took off walking down the road. "We'll need transportation," I said.

"We'd like a ride to the Inauguration," Paris said with an English accent to a man who stopped along the way.

"Ah. Visitors?"

I played along. "We heard these things are exciting."

"I'm afraid, it's already taken place."

"Darn," I said. "We should have come earlier."

"Would you like to see the remains of the old White House? I'm Farley."

"Lucille and Ricky," I said.

"Ah. As in *I Love Lucy*."

"We get that a lot."

"Is anything left to see?" Paris asked.

I pulled a miniature camera out of my pocket. "Is there anything to photograph? Back home, they want pictures of our trip."

"I've been wanting to see it myself. Traffic should be light going in. Most people left the city last night. Fear of more explosions. The outgoing staff was a bunch of terrorists."

"That's what they say. What about the President?"

"The news has been repeating all day that the DNA proved he's a fake and that the real one died in Mexico. The Army is preparing to invade that country as we speak."

I thought about my mom. I really liked Mexico's President. I hoped we could find a way to save Mexico.

As we drove by the Capitol, the VP, or rather new P, was having some kind of ceremony on the steps. Only her new Cabinet and the Supremes were present. Nobody else seemed interested. They apparently didn't like her any more than the old President. Valiant had pointed out that when she ran for President, she didn't even get one delegate.

"I wonder if she will be renting out one of the bedrooms for some fun," I said.

"Her reputation has made it all the way to London. Instead of a First Lady, they'll have a Presidential John," Farley told us.

As we approached the White House, we were stopped. There were barricades all around the area. Paris and I got out and walked until our path was blocked. We could see the crater. The ground had caved in what looked like a mile deep and a red glow from fires that had not fully subsided was visible.

"The subbasements are all gone," I said. I wanted to scream or cry but I felt myself going into shock.

Paris put his arm around me. "They could have gotten away."

"No cell phones?"

"Maybe they wanted to make it look like they were still there. Signals are detectable if someone has a repeater."

"You're trying to give me hope. I don't want false hope. Even the tunnel structure is destroyed. And he had burners."

"I looked across Pennsylvania from the White House. The ground was caved in there too."

"Let's go over to the Washington Monument."

"Look," Paris said. The Monument had dropped. "That tunnel is gone as well."

We went to the Jefferson Memorial. But there was little left as flames were continuing to burn at that location also.

Clearly, the bombs had also been set in the tunnels and they and anyone who had been in them at the time would have been killed.

"Let's go back to the ranch house," Paris said.

"Giving up on revenge?"

"I think there's been enough death for now."

As we started walking back to where the car had stopped, I heard a "Hey, stranger."

I turned. It was Gene, wearing a hat and a fake beard. Suddenly, things looked brighter. I ran over to him and gave him a hug. "Valiant? Is he with you?"

"I haven't seen him since before I left the White House. He called me to tell me about the bombs but said he had to do something before he left."

"The team?"

"Haven't seen them either."

My heart dropped. "Do you think they got out?"

"I don't know. There's nothing left. We should probably get out of here," Gene said.

"I think we have a ride," Paris told him, putting his arm around me and guiding us back to where we had last seen Farley.

"This is amazing," Farley said as we returned to where he was photographing the White House crater.

"Good show," Paris said. "Any chance, you could take us to Virginia? We have tickets to Philly from there."

"Sure. You want to go to the train station in Alexandria?"

"Yes."

<hr>

From the train station, we walked back towards the ranch house. "By the time we get there, everyone will be ready to leave on the plane."

I pulled Paris, aside, out of Gene's earshot.

"I don't want to go," I said.

"Eve, there's nothing else here. If they escaped, do they have a way to contact you?"

"Valiant went with me to visit Mom."

"Then, that's where you'll see him again."

<hr>

As we arrived at the ranch house, everyone was packing up the car. "I am not going to ride with these horrible giant rats," Lill was saying.

"Just to safety. They tried to blow you up. You need to come with us until it's safe," Jerry was saying.

"Ma'am, I suspect my Secret Service agents are mostly gone," Jeb said. "There is nobody to protect you here."

I went over to Jerry and gave him a hug. "I'm not going. Take care of Paris."

"Karissa, there is nothing here for you."

"I know. I just want this to end."

"With you tortured, imprisoned or killed?"

"Whatever. Besides, I've got to find a way to rescue Frank before the execution."

"He's in D.C. Gitmo."

"The place where those incarcerated without charges disappear, where sewage runs over the floors of the cells and the guards beat and rape the prisoners?"

"Maybe, being executed is a step up."

"I can't leave."

"I can carry you."

"You're sweet. Have a good flight. At least, the Mexican President is real. Maybe, I'll see you down there."

"Then, I'm staying too."

"Jerry!"

"You can't talk me out of it."

I wished Paris and the others, goodbye. "Take the puppies. I probably won't be able to take them with me when I finally leave."

As they drove off, another car raced down the street towards the ranch house.

"Who is that?" Jerry asked, as a car pulled into the driveway.

"Felicity?" I figured she would have been with the VP, now P, at a celebration.

"I'm here to rescue my peeps," she said. "You didn't think I'd let you down, did you?"

"And how do you think you can rescue us from what happened?"

"I've got a chopper coming for you. See?"

We stood there as a chopper landed.

"I'm going to go inside and get my phone," Jerry said.

"Why don't we all go inside," Felicity said.

Inside, I asked her if she wanted anything to eat.

"Do you have any dinner rolls?"

"There isn't a lot of bread here."

"How about cookies? I like cookies."

"I think there is a bag of organic cookies. I'll get you some tea to go with them. I know you're a tea drinker."

"Thank you, my friend, as always. Oh, where is the former President?"

"You saw him on the balcony. But nobody believes it."

"Dead? Oh, sad. Well, we've got a new President. And I have plans for you and Jerry. Did any of your team survive?"

"They've been out of contact since the White House blew."

"Sad."

I was in the kitchen, but I heard the door open.

I went out. In the living room was the VP, now P, and to my surprise, Lee. Lee was holding a gun aimed at Jerry.

CHAPTER 52

"I thought you were dead."

"See. I'm good at saving people," Felicity said.

"But why?" I asked Lee.

"There were some things I had to do and my work schedule got in my way. Besides, I knew you didn't like the President any more than I did. And I'll soon be Chief of Staff. Or rather my twin brother will."

I looked at Pamela Ferris, the new P. She gave a cackle. "He comes highly recommended by my new Vice President. She says I owe my new position to him."

I looked back to Lee. "You were behind the attacks on the President?"

"He killed them all, the guy who was shot in his office, Marissa and Seth, Greg, and oh, yes, he ordered the executions of all kinds of other people," Jerry said.

"I wasn't happy that you took out my man Sam," Lee said.

"Was he the Sam who gave the bomb to Maria?" He just smiled and I answered for him. "Of course, he was. But the body in the office looked like you."

"I've been with Signature Reduction for years."

"The corpse they buried didn't have the scar. Do you?"

"You know about that?"

"So you were behind trying to have us killed, behind Northgrail, Maria and Carlos."

"And the bombs. I was surprised you survived. I plan to get megabucks from Dynozap when the war starts. And under our new President, it's just hours away."

"We're cool with all this. If you don't mind, we'll be on our way," Jerry said, sounding nonchalant. "Have a good Presidency and Chief of Staffship."

"Yes, but horizontally. I'm sorry you two will have to die. But, it's no big deal. The world thinks you're already dead. You've already had two lives, Karissa. You don't get a third."

Pamela looked around the main floor as I looked for a way to distract Lee and Felicity long enough to help Jerry get out of the house. "You really think I want to live in this place until the White House is rebuilt? I deserve a mansion with servants," Pamela, angrily, said to Felicity.

"The Army blew up your current residence. This will be safe until the Army and Marines stop fighting it out."

"I picked the wrong Vice President."

"No, actually, you picked the correct one." Following that remark, Lee blew off the new President's head with his gun. Electronic parts in her started sparking.

"She was a robot?"

"She was replaced, long ago."

"But which department was operating her?"

"She was directly run by Dynozap," Lee said.

"Which is why Congress and the News Media immediately went along with the lie about the President being killed in Mexico."

"You got it," Lee said.

"And now, I'll soon be the First Man. Right honey?" he asked Felicity.

She smiled.

"And Dynozap ordered the parts for the new FBI director?"

"Of course, we needed the FBI on our side."

The door started to open again and Lee moved behind me with the gun pointed at my head. I was getting used to being a magnet for guns.

Had Paris and the others come back?

Valiant rushed in. My heart jumped. I didn't care that someone was pointing a gun at me. In my excitement, I exclaimed, "I was so worried about you," as I jumped up while raising my arms up and then around to knock the gun away from the back of my head. "Run," I said as I raced over to Valiant, who didn't move. I threw myself into his arms and he turned to hold me behind him while he stood between me and Lee. "No. Please," I said.

"Well, you're alive," he said to Lee. He whispered, "Stay behind me, Karissa."

Valiant was strong enough to prevent me from pushing myself in front of him and so I tripped him while holding onto him so as to cover him as we fell. As I did so, a shot was fired and I wondered if I had been nailed and was too far gone to feel it. I checked myself. I wasn't hit. *Was Valiant?*

"Valiant," I whispered. "Please be okay." He closed his eyes. "Valiant, please. I need you."

He opened them and smiled. I looked around. Ray was standing across the room with a gun in his hand. Lee was lying stiff on the floor.

"Does anyone stay dead?" Jerry asked.

"You can thank me later. Lee's hitman set me up, and I needed to go undercover. The guy in the alley was pretending to be me to get you to confide in him but was killed by a backup assassin Lee sent after me. So I figured, why not stay dead."

"Well, all is well that ends well," Felicity said. "As President, I'm going to give you three a big raise."

"I have a feeling we're not going to live long in your Administration," Valiant said.

"Valiant and Karissa, you are my special helpers. You went along with some, shall we say, illegal stuff while you were working under Gene. Working for me is better than going to prison."

"You killed my sister." I recognized Paris's voice coming from the back of the house.

"Your sister is here. Tell him, Karissa."

"She killed Karissa," Paris said.

'Wait," Jerry said, looking from Paris to the floor where I was now sitting. "You're." He paused. "Not Karissa?"

"I'm Eve," I said to him and then addressed Felicity. "So you were the nurse?" But I didn't need an answer to know it was Felicity.

"She used to be a brunette before she became a redhead," Paris said.

"Well, let's let bygones be bygones," she said.

I looked around. Ray had lowered his gun. Paris was thinking things over. Felicity leaned down towards Lee. As she lifted his gun, she remarked, "I hate loose ends," Ray's gun was back up, firing at her. She dropped lifelessly on Lee's fallen body.

I turned to Valiant as he helped me up. "What about the others?"

At that point, Brandon came running in.

"Valiant got us all out through the tunnels. He and Alan even rescued the remaining Secret Service agents and a totally operational President."

Jack walked in with the President most of America knew.

"I'm back," the P said as he started doing jumping jacks.

"Well almost," Paris acknowledged.

"Nobody is going to believe any of this. We're wanted," I pointed out.

"I was live streaming, from my cell phone," Jerry said.

"The whole thing?" Valiant asked.

"You brought a smartphone?" I asked.

"It's under a fake name."

"Is it still going?" I inquired.

"It cut out when Felicity tried to shoot Ray."

"Then the world knows I'm not Karissa."

"You were on a secret assignment for the CIA," Ray suggested.

"Nice spin. Will the CIA buy it?"

"They'll wind up being the good guys with an improved image. Besides none of the operatives know more than a tiny percentage of the people working for the Agency. Plausible deniability."

"He's got a point Karissa or rather Eve," Jerry said, shaking his head. "That will be hard to get used to. What are the news services and Dynozap going to do? Make a new VP robot?" Jerry asked.

"If Dynozap was in charge of the old VP, why did she appoint a VP who had been doing vaxxes?" I asked.

"They diversified. The jab is a weapon to annihilate enemies," Ray pointed out.

"Well, we need to fix that."

At that moment I saw Jack pull the RoboP out of the room as Frank walked in.

"I heard you were in D.C. Gitmo," I told him, wondering if he had seen the other P who had been in the car with Paris and the others.

"Somebody or somebodies took out the power and cameras, which is easy to do in a federal prison. Then, a fire alarm went off, and the guards ran, leaving the prisoners to burn to death," Brandon said.

"Then, surprisingly all the prisoners escaped," Valiant added, as he beamed.

"All the innocent people who have held there, since—that's actually great," I commented.

"Not so great. I need to do a full examination of the President. I think the incidents have affected him mentally. He asked me if I was the ice cream man." Apparently, he had seen the other President but not at the same time as ours or he'd be doing more than an examination on the P.

Frank looked at the still-sparking VP on the floor and back at us.

"Lee just told us, Dynozap created and operated her," I informed him.

"And the new Vice President?"

"It's all on the web," Jerry said. "Shootout with the NSA. She was Lee's accomplice in recent murders."

"The Speaker may have to be sworn in on a temporary basis," Frank started rambling. "But given all the damage in D.C. and the fact that I may no longer have a job, I guess, I won't be declaring anyone unfit. So, for now, the original President is still the President."

EPILOGUE

After everyone settled down, Gene escorted the refurbished RoboP to a hotel suite in D.C., along with Paris making sure RoboP was safe.

The real P and the First Lady had an ice cream party in the basement of the ranch house. "You know he's not so bad, anymore," she said. "He sniffed my hair."

"An improvement," I said.

Valiant turned to Frank. "By the time this is all cleared up, he'll have recovered from his shock and be back to normal."

"I can't make any guarantees," Frank said.

I can, I thought.

I went upstairs to the main floor, not wanting to see any more of my real father for a while. Valiant came up and put an arm around me. "Eve, I know you'd like to get back to your mom, but maybe we can stop a few wars first and arrange for the arrests of the Big Pharma execs before we leave."

"That sounds like a good plan," Jerry joined in, apparently hearing the conversation on the way up to the main floor. "I'll do the press releases."

I saw Valiant quickly take his arm off my shoulders. "You two probably need some time to talk, now that the danger is all over."

"Sure," I said.

After Valiant went outside, Jerry said. "I know. I knew when I saw your face in the warehouse garage when Valiant was unconscious. It was like your world ended."

"Well, he could have died. I was also worried on the boat when I thought the cartel had killed you."

"You have a strong guilt complex. When Valiant showed up alive today, your face lit up like I've never seen it. He's your everything, and if you let him go, you'd be crazy."

I didn't know what to say.

"Besides, you really get off on the excitement the two of you generate. I don't think I could keep up with you."

I kissed Jerry on the cheek. "Thank you. I didn't want to hurt you. I've had a hard time admitting it to myself."

"I know. And I just hope I find someone unvaxxed who will love me the way you love him."

I went out to the little lake behind the house. Valiant was sitting there, almost looking depressed.

"Hey, you saved the world. What's to be sad about?"

"I well—I thought you'd still be in there with Jerry."

"We talked."

"Eve, I remember how you cried when we were under the floorboards. He's an upstanding guy. That's what you need."

"What I need is—well, it seems I'm a bit of an excitement freak. There aren't too many guys out there who like to drive off bridges, jump off ziplines and can handle being chased by fireballs, hitmen and police forces. You know where I can find someone who won't let my life turn boring?"

He stood up and looked into my eyes. "You mean that?"

I couldn't deny it any longer. "I'm in love with you. I guess I've always loved you."

He took me in his arms and whispered, "I'm in love with you too, and I always will be."

He released me, looked into my eyes again and then pulled me into an embrace. As our lips and souls met, I knew this would be forever.

Three months later, we were swimming off the coast of Veracruz when we saw a shark start swimming our way. Valiant got between me and the shark as we started swimming as fast as we could. The shark was faster and a second later it crashed into Valiant.

"Hey," he said. "You're not a shark." Inside the shark's mouth was a piece of plastic sticking out.

It was a note. "Urgent business. See you on shore."

We continued on to the shore and were greeted by a couple of waiters bringing chairs and plates of watermelons and glasses with what looked like piña coladas. They sat down an extra chair and Ray joined us. Our twelve dogs finished their digging in the sand and raced over to us.

"We'll have extra watermelon for our little friends, lots of extra watermelon," I told the waiters. One of them nodded and they went to get some.

"Is everything okay in Washington?" I asked Ray.

"It's a little boring now that the wars, regime changes and vaccines have stopped. With the arrests of the leadership of the WHO, the CDC, the FDA, the WEF and half of Congress, the confiscation of funds taken by the MIC, and the disbandment of the Signature Reduction Soldiers, the intelligence agencies are going back to finding cars they've stolen to add to their list of successfully closed cases."

"Poor Ray. What are you doing with your spare time?" I asked.

"I've taken a crash course in robotics."

"Great shark," Valiant said. "Didn't even hurt when he got me. So what brings you here?"

"We're coming up on another election and Paris wants the two of you for his Chief of Staff and his National Security Advisor."

"How about Jerry?" I asked.

"He's Paris's running mate. We're actually going to have fair elections for once. Congress adopted the Venezuelan election system for federal elections."

"That's the one Jimmy Carter said was the best election system in the world."

"That's the one. Your brother or cousin is way ahead in the polls."

"I think Paris and Jerry can handle the job on their own."

I looked at Valiant.

"We're fine. Brandon and Jack might be interested," he said.

"I still don't see why Lee had to fake his own death," I remarked.

"He wanted you and your team to get the blame for anything that happened while he stayed out of the loop with a new ID," Ray said.

"That fits," Valiant noted.

Ray looked thoughtful and then said. "It was really odd how the Governor of California agreed to go along with the election integrity reforms and give the California families back all the money and homes that were stolen from the homeowners under Prop Nineteen."

"Really," Valiant responded. "Maybe he just got some unexpected integrity. It was a wise decision on his part."

Ray half-smiled and nodded as if he had just had an aha. "Can a Robot be operated from 2600 miles away?"

"An interesting question."

ACKNOWLEDGMENTS

This book was written in 2021 when the direction in which our country had been moving and continues to move away from the *Constitution* and a Government of the People had become evident.

I also wish to acknowledge some great individuals who have been inspirations and have kept me grounded in recent years. These have included, among others, America's best-known peace activist Cindy Sheehan, six-term Congresswoman and former Presidential candidate Cynthia McKinney, eight-term Congressman and former Presidential candidate Dennis Kucinich, Jacqueline Hernandez, Malinda Sherwyn, Nancy Howell, James Roguski, Craig "Pasta" Jardula, Fiorella Isabel Mayorca, Ryan Cristian, Jimmy Dore, Stefane Zamarano, Kim Iversen, Lori Price, Max Blumenthal, Peggy Hall, Del Bigtree, Susan Estrella and Judy Young. I also need to acknowledge Jason Bermas for his educational videos regarding the Signature Reduction Soldiers.

NATALIE TRIUMPHS
ABOUT THE AUTHOR

Natalie is an attorney, private investigator, journalist, educator and *Constitutional* and civil rights advocate. She has assisted victims of trafficking, victims of domestic violence, and innocent people who have been unjustly accused in the criminal justice system.

She has been active in the antiwar movement, and the election–integrity movement. Having come from a strong Democratic background she organized and founded the Progressive Caucus of the California Democratic Party, chaired one of the largest Democratic Clubs in her state and worked on over two dozen Democratic campaigns and a couple of Green campaigns. She marched with Black Lives Matter, when the organization was peaceful. She has consistently stood up against attacks on the freedom, rights and privacy of the American people, especially those infringements that have taken place since 2020.

Among her heroes are Dennis Kucinich, Cynthia McKinney, Cindy Sheehan, Ron Paul, Julian Assange, AMLO, the late Paul Wellstone and the late William O. Douglas.